There's one word you don't utter at Prescott High,
not unless you want them to own you.

H.A.V.O.C.

Hael, Aaron, Victor, Oscar, and Callum.

BOOKS BY

C.M. STUNICH

ROMANCE NOVELS

HARD ROCK ROOTS SERIES
Real Ugly
Get Bent
Tough Luck
Bad Day
Born Wrong
Hard Rock Roots Box Set (1-5)
Dead Serious
Doll Face
Heart Broke
Get Hitched
Screw Up

TASTING NEVER SERIES
Tasting Never
Finding Never
Keeping Never
Tasting, Finding, Keeping
Never Can Tell
Never Let Go
Never Did Say
Never Could Stop

ROCK-HARD BEAUTIFUL
Groupie
Roadie
Moxie

TRIPLE M SERIES
Losing Me, Finding You
Loving Me, Trusting You
Needing Me, Wanting You
Craving Me, Desiring You

A DUET
Paint Me Beautiful
Color Me Pretty

THE BAD NANNY TRILOGY
Bad Nanny
Good Boyfriend

FIVE FORGOTTEN SOULS
Beautiful Survivors

MAFIA QUEEN
Lure
Lavish
Luxe

DEATH BY DAYBREAK MC
I Was Born Ruined
I Am Dressed in Sin

STAND-ALONES & BOX SETS
Baby Girl
All for 1
Blizzards and Bastards
Fuck Valentine's Day
Broken Pasts
Crushing Summer
Taboo Unchained
Taming Her Boss
Kicked
Football Dick
Stepbrother Inked
Alpha Wolves Motorcycle Club:The
Complete Collection
Glacier

HERS TO KEEP TRILOGY
Biker Rockstar Billionaire CEO Alpha

RIICH BOYS OF BURBERRY PREP
Filthy Rich Boys
Bad, Bad BlueBloods
The Envy of Idols
In the Arms of the Elite

ADAMSON ALL-BOYA ACADEMY
The Secret Girl
The Ruthless Boys
The Forever Crew

THE HAVOC BOYS
Havoc at Prescott High
Chaos at Prescott High
Mayhem at Prescott High

BOOKS BY
C . M . S T U N I C H

FANTASY NOVELS

THE SEVEN MATES OF ZARA WOLF
Pack Ebon Red
Pack Violet Shadow
Pack Obsidian Gold
Pack Ivory Emerald
Pack Amber Ash
Pack Azure Frost
Pack Crimson Dusk

ACADEMY OF SPIRITS AND SHADOWS
Spirited
Haunted
Shadowed

TEN CATS PARANORMAL SOCIETY
Possessed

TRUST NO EVIL
See No Devils
Hear No Demons
Speak No Curses

THE SEVEN WICKED SERIES
Seven Wicked Creatures
Six Wicked Beasts
Five Wicked Monsters
Four Wicked Fiends

THE WICKED WIZARDS OF OZ
Very Bad Wizards

HOWLING HOLIDAYS
Werewolf Kisses

OTHER FANTASY NOVELS
Gray and Graves
Indigo & Iris
She Lies Twisted
Hell Inc.
DeadBorn
Chryer's Crest
Stiltz

SIRENS OF A SINFUL SEA TRILOGY
Under the Wild Waves

CO-WRITTEN
(With Tate James)

HIJINKS HAREM
Elements of Mischief
Elements of Ruin
Elements of Desire

THE WILD HUNT MOTORCYCLE CLUB
Dark Glitter
Cruel Glamour

FOXFIRE BURNING
The Nine
Tail Game

OTHER
And Today I Die

UNDERCOVER SINNERS
Altered By Fire
Altered By Lead

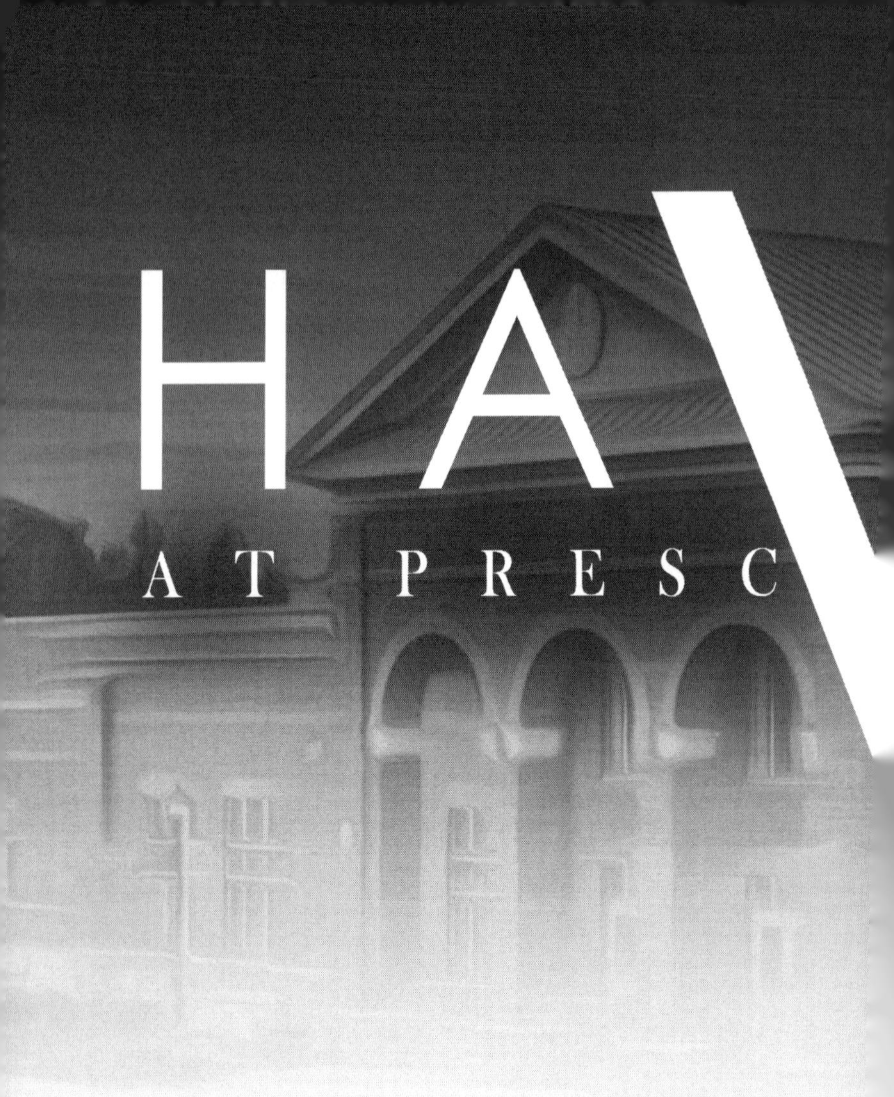
HA
AT PRESC

VOC

OTT HIGH

THE HAVOC BOYS, #1

this book is dedicated to the spirit of creativity and original thinking.
there is nothing more beautiful than a fresh idea.

AUTHOR'S NOTE

Havoc at Prescott High is a reverse harem, high school, enemies-to-lovers/love hate/bully romance. What does that mean exactly? It means our female main character, Bernadette Blackbird, will end up with at least three love interests by the end of the series. It also means that for a portion of this book, the love interests are total assholes; there are also flashbacks of past incidents involving bullying. This book in no way condones bullying, nor does it romanticize it. If the love interests in this story want to win the main character over, they'll have to earn it.

Might be hard though, considering the Havoc Boys are dicks.

If you've read my other two high school romance series— *Rich Boys of Burberry Prep* or *Adamson All-Boys Academy*— then just know this one is a bit more intense, and character growth/redemption are needed more than ever. Stick with us. It's not quite as gritty as *I Was Born Ruined* (the first book in my *Death by Daybreak Motorcycle Club* series).

Any kissing/sexual scenes featuring Bernie are consensual. This book might be about high school students, but it is not what I would consider young adult. The characters are brutal, the emotions real, the f-word in prolific use. There's underage drinking, marijuana use, sexual situations, and other adult scenarios.

None of the main characters is under the age of seventeen. This series will have a happy ending in the third and final book.

Love, C.M. Stunich

CHAPTER
ONE

"Havoc."

The word slips past my lips before I can stop it, before I can question the decision I just spent a whole summer making. It's the first thing I utter when I get past the security guards, drug dogs, and metal detectors that guard the entrance of Prescott High.

The whole hallway goes silent. Everyone in it turns to face me, the girl foolish enough to bring them down on me, those dirty, rotten H.A.V.O.C. Boys.

Hael, Aaron, Victor, Oscar, and Callum.

Each of them is terrifying in their own right, but together? They own this school and everyone in it.

Their leader, Victor, turns around, leaving his open locker behind him, and crosses his inked arms over his equally inked-up chest. He's a fucking monster, this boy, six foot five with eyes like flint, and a mouth that's a hot slash of menace across the bottom of his handsome face.

Like everyone else at Prescott High, he's got a history that's as dark as his violet-tinged black hair.

"Jesus fucking Christ," he says, exhaling laughter along with cigarette smoke. Pretty ballsy to smoke right here in the hallway, but believe it or not, the administration has more important things to worry about. Well, that, and also: everybody knows you don't mess with Havoc unless you're willing to fight dirty and spill blood. "You're one ballsy bitch."

"Don't call me a bitch," I say, my voice cold but firm. I'm not afraid of the Havoc Boys, not anymore, not especially after they tore my life apart sophomore year. I'm over their shit. "And meet me after school in the library."

"The library?" Victor asks, scoffing as he glances over at his right-hand man, the very cocky and (unfortunately) very attractive Hael Harbin. "Are you for real?" I return his dark stare with one of my own. Over the years, my *don't-mess-with-this-chick* look has been honed into an iron point. "Right, okay, whatever, it's your fucking funeral."

Victor takes off, but Hael lingers behind just long enough to look me over. He's maybe an inch shorter than Victor, with a red fauxhawk that should be douche-y, but somehow isn't, and a scar that runs the entire length of his right arm, shoulder to fingertip. Rumor has it that his dad sliced him up with a hunting knife, but nobody knows for sure.

"Request recorded, Blackbird," he says, his voice an easy, overconfident purr, his lips twisted into a shit-eating smirk. When he turns around and heads down the overcrowded halls, I shiver and wrap my arms tightly around myself, leather jacket creaking.

"I hope you know what you're doing," Stacey Langford says, pausing next to me with her posse in tow. She's the closest thing we have to a queen bee here at Prescott, but even she's afraid of the Havoc Boys. Like I said, everyone is. If you're not, you're either new here or not all that smart to begin with. But hey, natural selection eventually kicks in. There's a reason Raven Ashland dropped out and moved away to live with her aunt in Kansas.

"Don't worry about me," I say, watching as people clear out of Victor and Hael's way, moving to either side of the hallway to leave a path. The last thing anyone wants to do is draw those assholes and their attention.

Back in freshman year, the boys made a deal with the rest of the school: call out the word *Havoc,* that dark acronym of their first names, and they'll do anything for you. But only if you're willing to pay their price. And I've just done it. I've taken their word for it and called their gang. Now, I have to see what it is they'll want from me in order to do my bidding.

Most students at Prescott would rather jump off a bridge than risk calling Havoc.

And it's the way I start my first day of senior year.

Stacey is right: I really do hope I know what I'm doing here.

But the phrase *is* fight fire with fire, right?

And I, I need an inferno.

My first day back at Prescott High is tense as hell. I'm witness to three separate fights, and a sophomore getting busted for bringing meth to school. Like, literal methamphetamine. Other schools freak out if a student is caught with a joint. Here, you're just lucky if you don't get hot-boxed while you're taking a piss in the girls' bathroom.

"Bernadette, right?" Callum Park says, taking the seat across from me in the cafeteria. The food here is crap, but at least it's free. It's better than not eating at all, so I choke it down. Callum has a tray, too, but the only thing that's on it is a can of Pepsi, a pack of cigarettes, and a lighter.

"Wow, you remember my name?" I ask, feigning joy as I put my fingers to my chest. "After kicking the shit out of me for nearly an entire year? Good for you." I don't bother mentioning that we've been going to school together since second grade, too. He knows that. All the Havoc Boys know that.

Callum smiles. It's not a nice smile. It's a smile nightmares are made of.

His lips are full and pink, but I'm not fooled by that pretty-boy face of his. Cal's blond hair hides the scars on his forehead, and the lowered hood of his sweatshirt helps shadow the ones on his throat. Blue eyes watch me curiously across the surface of the beat-up cafeteria table as he drums navy-painted fingernails on the edge of his tray.

4

"You know how we work, just like anybody else. You say the word, we name the price, the job gets done. It's not personal, it's business."

It's not personal? I think, staring back at him. Tormenting me wasn't personal? But like me, Callum's an empty shell of a person, so maybe he doesn't lose sleep at night over it. Bad things happened to him, but bad things happened to me, too. And he was one of them. During sophomore year, my ex-best friend hired the Havoc Boys to torment me. I've spent a year and a half wondering what price she paid. Mostly, I've spent a year and a half wondering if the Havoc Boys ever cared about me at all.

"Get the fuck away from me, and I'll meet you after school in the library. Isn't that how this thing is supposed to work?" I narrow my green eyes on him, running my tongue across my lower lip and tasting the waxy texture of my lipstick. I'm wearing a line called *Naked Heat* today, and the color is *Scorched*, this metallic copper shade that tastes even better because I stole it and I didn't get caught. "I call Havoc, I set the terms."

"More or less," Callum purrs in that rough, husky voice of his, reaching up to run his fingers through his golden hair. He flips the hood on his sleeveless navy sweatshirt up. "But don't push it, Bernie."

He stands up and stalks out of the room as my hands shake, and I pick the carton of chocolate milk up. Milk. Like a freaking elementary school student. I drink it anyway and pretend like hearing Cal call me Bernie again doesn't bring back horrible memories.

The Havoc Boys are more than just bullies; they're a full-fledged gang.

Once upon a time, they took me down.

This time, I'm sending them on a mission of my own. I just hope this transaction doesn't leave me broken and bleeding like it did last time.

CHAPTER

TWO

This is such a stupid, fucking idea, I tell myself as I pace out back of the campus' main building, smoking a cigarette and trying to calm myself down. The only way I can face the Havoc Boys by myself is if I steel my nerves first. Otherwise, I might have a full-blown panic attack.

"Run, Bernie, but don't stop. If you do, we'll find you. And you won't like what we do to you if that happens." I choke on the memory, and the cigarette, before ashing it on the side of the broken cement step I'm sitting on and tucking it away again. Can't waste any of it, it's not like I have an endless supply.

"Bernadette Blackbird, were you smoking back here?" Vice Principal Keating asks me, her mouth pursed into a thin line. I give her a smile and a shrug.

"Not me, VP," I say, batting my lashes. "You know me: straight and sober." She sighs, her shoulders drooping, fatigue lining her beautiful face. Ms. Keating is only thirty-two, but she looks fifty. She looked twenty when she started here two years ago. That's what Prescott High does to people: drains the life right out of them.

"You're a good kid, Bernadette," she tells me, pointing in my direction with a freshly painted pink nail. Oh, well, if she's still getting her nails done, then there's hope for her yet. Maybe her soul hasn't been killed by this place? Mine has. "Don't get sucked into this crap." I wonder how many other schools have VPs that say crap? Or worse. I've heard Ms. Keating drop the f-bomb on a bad day. "You're better than this, and you are so close to getting out of here forever."

"With straight Cs, I should be able to get into the community college of my choice!" I cheer, giving her a sarcastic smile and flipping my pink-tipped white-blond hair over my shoulder. "Have a nice day, Ms. Keating." I turn and hike my ratty backpack up my shoulders, marching into the library in my dark jeans, boots, and leather jacket. The whole goal here is to scare people off *before* they get on my ass, not after they've already set their sights on me as a victim.

It's like, to survive at this school, you need a warning system, like a porcupine with spines, or a blowfish with spikes. My piercings, tattoos, and leather outfits help with that. But only a little.

When I head into the library, there's another set of metal detectors, and a campus security guard in the corner. He's not looking at me though, he's looking at the Havoc Boys, his hand hovering over his stun gun. Not that a stun gun has much of an effect on these assholes anyway. Trust me: I tried it once.

"Bernadette Blackbird." Oscar Montauk greets me, standing up from his seat and staring down at me through a pair of rectangular-framed glasses. With his dark hair, aristocrat face, and sharp smile, he should be at Oak Valley Prep with all the rich dickheads. The thing is, Oscar Montauk isn't rich, and even if he is tall, and slender, and wears glasses … I once saw him curb stomp a guy. Plus, he's coated in ink and piercings like all the rest of them. They stop at his neck, fingers of color crawling out from under the collar of his shirt. "You've come a long way, from eating dirt and bleeding out on the gym floor, to hiring us. Something tragic must've happened."

"Seriously fucking tragic," Vic says, kicking his boots up on the table. I glance over my shoulder, and find the librarian looking our way, like she can barely stop herself from saying something. She knows better though, and eventually she turns away and buries herself in a stack of returned books.

I glance back, from Vic to Callum, from Oscar to Hael. Aaron is missing, but that's not a surprise. I'm glad he's not here anyway. The less I see Aaron, the better.

Memories of fingers gliding down my bare belly makes me shiver. Of lips on my collarbone. Of his body moving inside of mine …

No. No, fuck Aaron.

"Alright, Bernie, sit and talk." Vic drops his feet to the floor and then kicks a chair out from under the table. He waves his hand, and I take a seat. I'm not worried about anyone listening or overhearing. Even if they do, they won't be able to use my words against me, not without

9

incurring the wrath of the Havoc Boys. Everybody knows how seriously they take their assignments. "And don't talk in circles around us. We don't like that."

"He should say, we *really* don't like that," Oscar tells me, taking a seat on Hael's other side. Cal is sitting perched on top of another table, eating corn nuts and watching me like he'd very much like to see me run again, so he could hunt me down.

My fingernails dig into my denim-clad thighs.

I look across the table at the four fuck-heads, and I force myself to breathe, closing my eyes for a moment to brace myself. I think of my sister, Heather, and what could happen to her if I don't do this. The thought calms me, and I open my eyes.

"I need my vengeance; I want my revenge."

"And that means what, exactly?" Victor asks, cocking his head to one side, his tongue sliding across his lower lip. He cracks his knuckles as he leans back in his chair, his sweatshirt peeling open at the zipper and flashing all the ink on his neck. "Like I said, be direct."

My eyes flash up to his, those two black pits, endless and full of shadows.

"My life is just a series of failures," I blurt, hating them, hating them the most, those Havoc Boys. If I could, I'd set them on themselves. The best I can do right now is sic their monstrous cruelty on everyone else. "I want them all rectified." Victor scowls at me, and I get the idea that I'm still being too cryptic for his liking. "I need you to … torture some people. I mean, like, the way you tortured me."

I've practiced saying this so many times in the mirror

that I don't even flinch.

The lenses of Oscar's glasses flash as he turns to look at me. The shine fades, and I can see the sharp interest in his gray eyes.

"Who, and how many?" he asks, as he glances down the line of Havoc Boys, like he's checking on their reactions. Victor looks interested, Hael looks bored, and Callum is staring at me with a handful of corn nuts in his palm.

"Seven. If we come to an agreement, I'll tell you their names. Not before."

"Mm." Victor makes a sound and leans forward. "You know we'll take any deal, no matter how savage, but there's always a price. The question is: what are you willing to pay?"

My voice is strong and clear when I reply.

"Anything."

Victor smiles at me, and then pauses, looking up and over my shoulder.

"Sorry, I'm late."

Aw, fuck, it's Aaron. My nostrils flare as he takes a seat across from me, and then freezes, green-gold eyes going wide. He doesn't move, doesn't say anything. We both know what happened between us before.

"Whatever. We know all we need to know anyway." Victor stands up and comes around the table. I stand up, too, and he ends up coming so close to me that I can feel his breath stir my hair. "We'll get back to you on Friday. Remember, though, if you accept our price: you *will* pay up."

Victor takes off, Hael following close behind him.

Oscar and Cal share a look over the top of Aaron's wavy chestnut hair.

He, on the other hand, is still staring at me like he's seen a ghost.

"Of all people, I never expected *you*," he says, almost like he's disgusted. He stands up and storms off, shoving chairs out of his way as he goes. I barely recognize him as he makes his exit, that sweet boy I once knew covered in tattoos, his body hard and taut with muscle. The only parts of him that are the same are the lips that gave me my first kiss, and that loose, mussy hair.

"He's going to have to learn to play nice," Oscar murmurs as he flips open the cover on his iPad. I'm surprised he even has one. Other schools, nice schools, they have iPads and laptops. At Prescott High, we're stuck in the nineties. Or, rather, our funding is. We use lined paper, binders, and pencils. Lucky us. More than likely, Oscar probably stole the one he's got in his inked hands.

"Yeah, we don't treat clients like that." Callum pauses and then smirks at me. "Only marks. You know that, though, don't you, Bernie?"

I stand up and spin away in a whirl of white-blond and pink, storming out the door only to be snatched around the bicep by Victor. He pushes me into the brick wall and then puts a palm next to my face, leaning in.

"Is the first name on your list Principal Vaughn?" he whispers, and when I look away, Vic laughs in my face, his breath hot against my mouth. He pushes up off the wall, stalks toward the edge of the brick patio, and lights up a cigarette.

One of the math teachers—Miss Addie or something—sees us, but then puts her head down and keeps on walking. Pretty sure Hael's fucked her. I walked in on them once. Well, I walked in on him with one of the teachers, her clothes disheveled, her lipstick smeared. I can't remember which of the blond math teachers it was.

"Principal Vaughn." Victor laughs, and the sound is so twisted and full of malice, it makes my ears bleed. "Go home, Bernadette, and we'll see you in the morning. It's still 193 44th Street, isn't it?"

"Don't ever come to my house again," I growl at him, and then I take off for home.

CHAPTER

THREE

My home life is worse than my school life. I've tried to make it better on more than one occasion. I've called social services, but my foster family was even worse. I've tried running away, but then the cops dragged me back and put me on house arrest, and then I was just ... trapped in hell.

Once upon a time, my family was wealthy. But then my father killed himself, and my mother lost the house, and well, I can barely remember what it's like to feel safe and secure, to know there'll be food on the table and a roof over my head.

Pamela, she still lives that old fantasy of having money.

"Bernadette," she calls, trotting down the stairs in pearls and a designer dress. She probably charged them to one of the dozen stolen credit cards she keeps in her purse. My backpack is literally falling apart, and my little sister doesn't have any shoes that don't have holes in them, but sure. Buy yourself a nice dress and some fancy jewelry.

The thing about my mother is, she doesn't do drugs, she only drinks at parties, and she paints a very pretty picture with her blond hair and bright green eyes. I'm almost certain that she's a psychopath. Once, when I spilled a cup of juice on the last of her fancy rugs, she locked me in the bathroom after filling the tub with bleach. The fumes made me so sick that I passed out.

"What?" I stand there in the front entry with my backpack on one shoulder, hating her with every breath and wishing she'd move out of the way, so I could retreat upstairs to my room. Heather will be at the after-school program I signed her up for, so at least for an hour or two, I don't have to worry about my little sister.

Besides, the thing I call my stepfather won't be home for hours yet. He works the swing shift at the police station, an on-duty cop with a taste for depravity. And he has so many friends, so, so many. It's terrifying. I don't feel safe anywhere.

"Can you do that thing with my hair? What's it called? A fish-mouth braid?"

My own mouth tightens, but I don't bother to correct her. If she wants to call a fishtail braid, fish-mouth then who am I to stop her? Maybe she'll look like an idiot in front of all the fancy friends who'd drop her in a hot second if they knew how poor we really were?

"I have homework," I say, refusing to make eye contact with her as I brave the stairs and push past her.

Her freshly manicured nails tighten on the banister, and I do my best to hold back a flinch. I can remember those shiny perfect nails digging into my skin, leaving tiny crescent marks that hurt for hours. The trauma runs so deep, in tracks and canyons across my heart, that I forget that I'm just as tall as she is now, just as capable. The physical violence between us has lessened, but the verbal and emotional abuse remains the same.

"Homework? Since when do you care about homework? That school for delinquents is hardly an academic palace." I ignore her scathing words and head straight for the room I share with Heather. I don't look at Pen's room or think about how I should've made her sleep with me, in a locked bedroom, as far away from the Thing as she could get. I didn't know I had to protect her, my older sister. Maybe in her own way, she was protecting me?

My throat tightens up, and I slam my door as hard as I can, making the walls shake. Mom screams something at me from the hallway, but I flick the extra locks I installed, and then jam my headphones over my ears. When the Thing realized I'd added a chain lock and a deadbolt, he'd looked me right in the face and laughed.

"You think I couldn't get in there if I wanted?" he'd sneered, and then he'd let his fingers dance over the gun on his hip. As if I could ever forget that he's a cop, and I'm just a seventeen-year-old loser who got bullied so bad she was afraid to go to school.

My life is a perfect storm, full of lightning, thunder, and rain clouds, swirling in from all directions. No matter where I go or what I do, I can't escape it. And that's why

I spent all summer thinking, wondering if I should call on them, those Havoc Boys, wondering if their price is worth a pound of flesh.

I finally came to the conclusion after I found one of Pen's journals: it is.

It really, really is.

No matter what it is they did to me.

No matter what it is they *do* to me.

Two years earlier ...

My feet are bare, and the ground hurts. There are sticks, thorns, and stones all over the place, but I can't stop running. If I do, they'll catch me, and I'm afraid to see what those dark grins and awful laughter lead to.

I know what monsters like to do in the dark, and I won't let myself be taken by them, those awful, awful Havoc Boys.

They dragged me out of my bed in the dark, without waking my mother, my stepfather, or either of my sisters.

They told me to run.

So even though it's pouring rain, I do it. I run, and I don't stop until I can't catch a breath, falling to my knees and soaking my pajama pants straight through. I tried to circle around and go back to the house, but two of them were waiting there for me.

I'm just lucky they didn't see me.

Choking on my shuttered breaths, I rise to my feet and keep going, and I don't stop until the rain lets up and the sun kisses the horizon. By then I'm so exhausted, I can barely keep my body upright.

This time, when I go back, they're gone, but I know that's not the end of this.

Not even close.

Somebody called out Havoc, somebody made a deal.

And this time, I'm the mark.

CHAPTER

FOUR

At school on Friday, Victor finally pulls me aside, grabbing me by the elbow and dragging me into the dark theater where Callum is trying on questionable looking masks. The places Vic's fingers touch, they burn. The sensation makes me sick to my stomach.

"We have a price for you," Vic says, circling around me like a shark. I can smell him, too, this pungent mix of bergamot, tobacco, amber, and musk. The stink of it makes me shiver and then bite down on my tongue to hide the reaction. God forbid I give Victor or the other Havoc Boys even an ounce of physical appreciation. They're pretty, I'll admit that. But they don't need to know that *I* know that.

"Finally," I spit, because that caustic, bitter nature of mine was learned, not gifted to me from birth. I never asked to be this way, this ornery, this angry, but I wasn't given many choices. In order to keep myself and my sister safe, I adapted to the harsh world I was thrust into.

19

"Like you said, no talking in circles, be direct and all that."

"What happened to you?" Victor asks, tilting his head slightly to one side, his dark eyes even darker in the mysterious shadows of the theater. Prescott High hasn't received proper funding in years, but Ms. Keating busts ass every fall to raise money for the arts programs. She thinks artistic endeavors can heal damaged souls. It's a lofty ideal, but impractical at best. Nobody can save us, society's throwaways. "You used to be so ..." He reaches out and lifts a lock of my hair, tossing a dark smirk my direction. "Sweet."

"You," I say, without flinching, without hesitating. From a chair in the front row, Hael chuckles, playing with his phone, probably texting some girl. Out of them all, he's the biggest whore, hands down. Oscar sits on the edge of the stage, legs crossed at the knee, working on his iPad again. "Now what's my price?"

"Seven people, identities unknown," Oscar says, his voice mellifluent and mellow, but dangerous as hell, like a fine bottle of brandy one could drown in. It'd be so easy to, with those sweet, smooth sips. Might kill you in the wrong dose, but it goes down easy. "One of whom I'm simply assuming is that cop father of yours."

"He is not my father." The words come out like the first snap of hoarfrost on the branches, unforgiving and merciless, destroying the sweetness of spring and summer in an instant. I've never been more adamant about anything in my life.

Vic watches me, unperturbed, as Callum pauses and slips a *Phantom of the Opera* mask over his face, snapping the elastic in the quiet space. Aaron isn't here, his lack of presence as strong a statement as any words he might say if he were.

"Pardon me, *that cop stepfather of yours,*" Oscar continues as Vic watches me, dark and unyielding, a stone wall that can't be breached. What makes this work, what makes Havoc an option for me, is that they're neither black nor white, just this unrelenting sea of gray. Make a bargain, pay a price, reap the rewards. I know what's expected of them, now I just need to find out what's expected of me.

But I've already had this conversation with myself, and I know how far I'm willing to go: I'll pay anything, do anything, to get what I want. What was left of me, of Bernadette Blackbird, died along with my sister, so my only recourse here is revenge. I'll take it.

"But regardless of parentage, a cop is a cop," Oscar continues, pushing his glasses up his nose with his middle finger. His lenses shimmer in what little light there is. "And that's a big job, dealing with someone like that. I've spent all week calculating the risks, and there are many."

"Too many," Vic scoffs, shaking his head and running his tattooed fingers through his dark hair. He surveys me, a girl he's known since we started attending the same elementary school ten years ago. We were never friends, per se, but I remember when I first transferred from the fancy Montessori school downtown, and the other kids picked on me for being snobby (maybe I was, I don't remember). Victor stood up for me once. He pushed a kid down the slide for pulling my pigtails.

I haven't forgotten.

I also haven't forgotten that when I was fifteen years old, he locked me in a closet for a week with nothing but bottled water, granola bars, and a bucket. All because Kali Rose-Kennedy asked him to. *That bitch.* I've always wondered what I did to make her hate me.

"Why do you do it anyway?" I ask, feeling Vic's hot gaze sweep over me like a summer storm. His attention, it burns as hot as his fingers on my arm. When he looks at me, I can barely breathe. There's a fine line between hate and lust, isn't there? I'm sure I feel equal parts of both when he stares at me with his heavily lidded eyes, long lashes, and hard mouth. This is a man built of sin and heartache. He's as broken as I am. "The whole Havoc thing? I've never understood it. You're not beholden to anyone, so why tell the whole world that you are? That one word can command you?"

"Have you ever been lied to, Bernadette?" Victor asks me, his voice dark and deep and full of shadows. He doesn't move, but there's a charge in the air that says he could destroy my carefully crafted façade before I could even think to try and stop him.

"What do you think?" I snort back, adjusting my leather jacket and noticing that his eyes don't move from mine like most guys. Even with a high neckline, I've noticed that most men only see what they want to see, and oftentimes, it's breasts that they're interested in, covered up or no. Victor keeps his attention on my face, destroying me with that hard gaze of his.

"When you've been lied to by everyone around you, when you have nothing else, you realize the one currency you can carry is truth. So a single word does have meaning. A promise does hold importance. And a pact is worth carrying to the grave." He steps back from me, his boots loud against the polished floors of the stage. "Do you want to hear the price or not? It's not too late for you to back out and run, you know that, right?"

I nod, resolute in my determination. My heart thunders in my chest, waiting, anticipating. Sweat drips down my back. Hael makes a sound, and Callum lifts up the mask, but nobody moves.

Vic maintains that ironclad control over my gaze.

"If we take this job, you become ours." His words hang in the quiet air, almost like a threat, almost like he's warning me away before we even get started. But he underestimates how deep my determination goes. A slight smile works its way across his lips as the door at the end of the room opens and a troupe of theater geeks—or as close to theater geeks as we get at Prescott High goes—steps in. "Get the fuck out," Victor says, not bothering to raise his voice or even glance their way. "We're busy in here."

There's absolutely no hesitation from the group as they scramble to obey Victor's command.

I open my mouth to make some snarky-ass comment, but the words won't come. Instead, I clamp my lips shut and squeeze my hands into fists at my sides. If I make my palms bleed by squeezing too hard, nobody has to know.

"If we take this job," Vic repeats, taking a step closer to me, so close that the toes of his boots kiss mine. He touches a finger to my chin and then trails it along the length of my jaw. I'm trembling now, whether in rage or desperate, needy ardor, I'm not sure. Does it matter? "You become one of us, a Havoc Girl."

I swallow hard.

"Now who's talking in circles?" I manage to get out, wishing he'd stop touching me, knowing that if I take this deal, he never will. Vic's smirk deepens, and he leans in, hovering his mouth over mine.

"You'll do what I say when I say it," he continues, and I feel myself bristling. I hate being told what to do, hate it with a passion. I've been ordered around my whole life, by one person or another, and I haven't exactly ended up on a bed of roses. "In *all* areas." Vic slides his fingers into my hair, and I jerk away. The small act of protest makes him chuckle. "If you want this, you'll be our plaything. You'll be our accomplice. Bernadette, if you want this, it's blood in, and blood out. Do you understand that?"

"I—" I start to answer, but Victor cuts me off with a look, all hard lines and dark shadows.

"No. I don't want an answer yet. Take a few days to think about it, Bernadette. Decide if your life is worth your revenge." He steps back, and I hear Hael make a noise of protest from the front row.

"For fucking real, Vic? Make her answer now." Hael stands up and starts toward the stage, but a slow, menacing look from Victor stops him cold, and he curses, backing up with his palms raised.

"Take the week," Vic repeats, moving away from me and hopping off the edge of the stage, his boots loud on the cement floor. "Because once you give your answer, you can't take it back."

CHAPTER
FIVE

"You'll do what I say when I say it."

I'm not sure Vic could've uttered a single other sentence that would've infuriated me quite so much. The sex angle, I expected. In fact, I was almost hoping for it. Sex is easy if you approach it the right way, just two bodies working off their basic instincts. Never mind that I've only ever been with a few guys, and even then, only a handful of times. Never mind that one of those guys was Aaron Fadler.

"Shit." I grab a book off my nightstand and chuck it at the wall as hard as I can. I'm satisfied when it leaves a dent, but that doesn't push back the anxiety or the worry as I rub my palms over my face. *"You'll be our plaything."* How else am I supposed to interpret that? I'll be at their beck and call for sex, all five of them. What was it that Vic said, a Havoc Girl?

My skin tingles, and I wrap my arms over my chest. When I was in middle school, I watched them from afar with desperation, always wanting to be a part of their little group, knowing that I never would be. And then sophomore year happened, and no amount of pleading could stop that wave of pain.

Biting my lower lip, I stand up and peep in the bathroom door to make sure that Heather's still situated in the tub, playing with her toys and reminding me that I not only have a reason to stay, but a reason to fight.

If I make this deal, Neil Pence will pay. I don't know how, but the Havoc Boys have a certain finesse to their cruelty. It'll be something good, something worthy of my sister, Pen, and of Heather, and of me …

It's Saturday night, and I've already had plenty of time to think.

I'll do it.

It doesn't matter what happens to me, doesn't matter what Vic or his cronies have in store. I'll be their plaything. Who cares? I was in love with Aaron once, I've been lusting after Vic since … forever. They're all undeniably gorgeous, if a little cruel for my tastes.

Fuck.

Am I really going to do this? I've fought my entire life to keep my body to myself. And trust me, men have tried. Men like the Thing. Men like my temporary foster brother. Men like Principal Vaughn.

But then I hear the front door open, and the Thing's voice booms from downstairs, sending a shiver down my spine.

There's nothing worse than him, the ultimate villain in my horror story.

A cop, the son of a well-respected judge, the brother of a prosecutor.

Untouchable, impossible, the epitome of evil.

Whatever it takes to bring him down, I'll do it.

Even if it means getting in bed with Havoc.

I march into Prescott High on Monday ready to make a deal, but I'm already running late, and the school is on lockdown. I have to check in at the office, wait for the gates to be unlocked, and scurry to my first class. I've forgotten that we're having an active shooter drill, so I spend the next few hours learning how to find random objects around the room and use them as weapons.

My first period teacher isn't pleased when I suggest ramming a pencil up the shooter's ass from behind. But at least he doesn't have to hide his disgust with me for long because the lunch bell rings, and I'm off, searching the campus for Havoc.

"They're out back by the dumpsters smoking," Stacey Langford suggests, taking pity on me when she sees me searching the halls. She's barely spoken a dozen words to me since she got shipped here during sophomore year. I figure she's just afraid I'll include her in whatever deal I make with Havoc, and she'll get her ass kicked. As far as queen bees go, she's not so bad. The bullying thing isn't really her angle.

"Thanks."

I head outside and find five boys in black, smoking cigarettes and sitting around some hot rod car that looks far too fancy for the dirty parking lot. Must belong to Hael. He's got a serious hard-on for vintage rides.

"Nice car," I say, and he snorts at me, flicking his cigarette in my direction and standing up with this cocky swagger that makes me grit my teeth. In another school, another life, he'd be the king of the elite, some badass ruling over the high school in preparation for a life of luxury. But that sense of entitlement must've been hard-earned because I know Hael Harbin doesn't have a cent to his name. One time, right after my mother lost the house my dad had bought for her, we spent the night in the same homeless shelter.

"Nice car?" He leans against the roof and taps the cherry red door with his tattooed knuckles, honey-brown eyes glittering. He smells like fresh leather, coconut, and motor oil, a much different scent than Vic. My eyes flick that direction and find him watching me carefully, probably waiting for my answer. He doesn't think I'll accept. Well, fuck him. Him and his idiot friends came up with this whole 'Havoc' thing. Name the job, hear the price, pay up. I'm going to fulfill my end of the bargain, and for three years now, the Havoc Boys have been fulfilling theirs. "This is a '67 Camaro. It's a fucking collectible."

"That's not a '67 grille," I say, gesturing at the front end. "It's too wide. A '68 maybe, but not a '67." Hael gapes at me for a moment, and then smirks. Hopefully he's impressed, but really, I don't know shit about cars. I overheard him talking to a buddy in shop on my way to the bathroom last week.

"Smart chick," he says, and then looks me over, his eyes sweeping me in a calculating sort of way. Unlike Vic, he doesn't get any deeper than my exterior, doesn't delve into my soul with a pair of flint-like eyes. Instead, his gaze takes in my tight leather pants, and black Harley tank with interest. "So, which do you prefer? The Camaro or the bike?" He gestures back at Vic's ride with his thumb, and I give the shiny Harley a cursory glance. For such poor boys, they sure have nice rides.

It's easy to deduce that they either stole them or, more likely, stole the money or parts to make them happen.

Havoc's control isn't limited to Prescott High. I know they have a network of assholes that run the city. It's a little scary, if you think about it, these seventeen and eighteen-year-old boys running their gang. If they're this bad now, what's going to happen in five years? Or ten? *That is, if they even make it that long.* Like me, I assume they all live life under the assumption they've got an expiration date in the not-so-near future.

"I didn't come to talk cars or bikes," I say, glancing over at Vic, Callum, Oscar, and Aaron, all perched on the back steps where the food trucks make the weekly deliveries to the cafeteria. "Actually, I—"

"No," Vic says, that one word spoken so quietly it barely breaks the sudden gust of wind across the lot. But it's powerful enough to halt any further conversation in its tracks. "I said take the week." He looks right at me, and I can see this is yet another test.

"You'll do what I say when I say it."

Fuck.

Aaron glares at me from green-gold eyes, smoking his cigarette and biting back whatever caustic, awful thing it is he wants to say to me. Bet Vic told him to keep his mouth shut.

As I stand there, I feel them looking at me, all five of them with different expectations, different wants. I should be scared to be out here alone with them, but as of right now, I'm a potential client. They won't hurt me, not yet.

"Get lost, Bernadette," Vic says, leaning back on the steps, his expression the most difficult one to read. Hael looks like he wants to bend me over the hood of his car; Oscar looks like he wants to do my fucking taxes; Callum has a much darker, scarier expression on his face. But it's Aaron who looks like he might want to kill me. "Come find me on Friday to let me know your decision. Until then, stay lost, would you?"

Slowly, I back away and head inside, seething with anger.

And even though I try to hide it, a shiver takes over my entire body. As I sweep past, I know that even Stacey and her girls can see it.

Despite my bravado, I really am terrified, aren't I?

But am I scared of Havoc? Or scared of what I might become if I give into them?

CHAPTER

Vic is sitting in his front yard when I bike over on Friday, my boots crunching across the gravel as I climb off and head his direction. He barely glances my way, but I can see the tense set of his shoulders. If I were a threat, he'd neutralize me without a second thought.

"Bernie, what brings you to this side of the city?" he asks, slowly blowing smoke from between his full lips. He's lounging in a plastic chair on the front lawn of his father's run-down little farmhouse. I remember this place well; I spent a whole week in one of its closets.

"I'll do it." The words scrape past my throat, like hot coals burning their way up my esophagus. My hands are shaking, but inside, I'm nothing but white-hot rage. I need this, and I hate Vic for making me crawl all the way over here to tell him that.

"Yeah?" He exhales smoke, his violet hair catching the sunlight. Vic just barely glances over his shoulder at me, the tattoos on his neck crinkling with the motion. "Then get over here and sit on my lap."

My mouth purses. I don't like being told what to do.

"If you want this, you'll be our plaything."

I must be fucking mad. And yet, the only things that motivate me are my sister … and my vengeance. I don't care about anything anymore, not even myself.

Moving forward, I squeeze between two overgrown bushes and toss my ratty backpack on the ground.

Vic's dark eyes follow me as I walk over and straddle his lap. The expression of triumph on his face is like an arrow to the heart, but my heart turned to stone a long time ago. I don't feel it at all.

My body likes his though, so much so that when I adjust myself and feel his hard, muscular form beneath me, I feel my breath catch.

Vic continues to smoke his joint, the sweet skunk-y smell of weed wafting around me. Pot smoke is so much denser that cigarette smoke, and I swear, it rolls off the lips like nothing else. I'm mesmerized, watching him. He puts one, big hand casually on my hip, studying me with a much sharper, much more intelligent gaze than I'd have ever pegged him for.

"Once you say yes to Havoc, that's it. Kiss me and seal the deal. There's no going back after that." Vic spins the joint around and offers it up to me, a bit of ash catching on the breeze that flows between us. Across the street, I can hear two of his neighbors shouting at one another, but over here, in the sun, it's not so bad. When you exist in the ugly, you learn to live in the beautiful.

"But first, smoke with me a little."

"I don't feel like getting high," I say, reaching for his cigarettes. Vic's free hand, the one that was resting on my hip, snaps out and grips my wrist, stopping me.

"Don't you ever have any fun, Bernadette?" he purrs, his voice this viciously beautiful sound, like a predator on the hunt. But a smart predator, one that doesn't expend energy unless absolutely necessary, one that stalks. I shiver, even though I can feel the sun on my back, even with the hot, hot heat of Victor's body between my thighs. I'm not shivering because I'm cold; we both know that.

"No, actually, I don't," I say, but Vic doesn't release my wrist. He stays right where he is, waiting, holding the joint between us. Our eyes are locked, my green ones on his endless black, sharp as obsidian.

"Take the joint, Bern, and chill out a little." His words, they're not a request. Narrowing my eyes, I take the joint and inhale, watching the cherry crackle down the length of the paper. My lips and tongue tingle as I exhale, blowing that thick, hot smoke. There's no helping the coughing, but Vic laughs at me anyway. There's no pleasure in the sound either, just a cold, cruel analysis of the situation.

He has me by the balls, and he knows it.

The weed hits me quick, sweeping over my body and making my hands and feet tingle. I exhale without even realizing it, like I'm taking my first real breath in a long, long time.

"Ahh, there we go," Vic says as I take another drag,

passing the joint back to him. He stabs it out in an ashtray, and then grips my hips with two, big, inked hands and then quirks a cocksure little smile that would have me feeling all kinds of pissed off if I wasn't high. "Now, kiss me and show me you really want this." I lean forward, but Vic stops me, grabbing my chin in tight fingers. His frown is all sorts of cold hell. "Don't half-ass this, Bernadette. A deal's a deal, and we take our shit *very* seriously."

"Don't you think I know that?" I snap back at him, and his fingers tighten on my chin. It hurts, but I don't want Vic to see how much, so I keep my expression stoic.

"You are going to mewl beneath me," he says, his voice neutral but threaded with a darkness that makes my throat feel tight. I'm playing with fire here, but I don't care if I get burned. I want the whole world to turn to ash. "I've been wanting to fuck you since ninth grade."

"Pervert," I grind out, but only because I don't want him to notice how hard my nipples are beneath my tank top. Vic smirks at me and releases my chin, leaning back in the chair.

"It must hurt you, to sit on the lap of the guy that made your life a living hell. It must just tear you up on the inside, a strong girl like you. Submitting isn't exactly your forte, if I remember correctly."

"Why don't you just shut the fuck up, so we can get this over with? I haven't agreed to anything yet. Are you trying to get me to walk away from this deal?"

"I'm preparing you. It's a service I don't offer most of my clients. Be grateful, Bernadette." Victor's face shuts down, and I see the full scope of his brutality. If I push this, if I kiss him and take this deal, I'll end up in his bed. My enemies will end up in the ground; my sister will be safe.

It's all I've ever wanted anyway. Well, the last half of it.

There's no need to drag this out any further: I made my decision this summer, and I'm sticking to it. My own inked fingers curl around his neck, and I try not to think too hard about this. It's just a kiss; I've had other kisses before.

But when I lower my lips to Vic's, and that hot slash of his mouth brushes up against mine, heat slices through me. He puts one of his big hands on the back of my neck and holds me there, his tongue sliding into my mouth and taking over. His kiss is a demand for more, the sealing of a deal, like some kind of fucked-up reverse fairy tale. This time, I'm not kissing the prince to become the princess, I'm tonguing the villain to guarantee the destruction of others.

Watching their downfall should be satisfying, cathartic in a way.

It's hard to think about that though when Vic is holding me so still, kissing me so deep, his cock lengthening beneath me. I can feel it through the black basketball shorts he's got on.

"Fuck me," he commands, pulling back just enough so that his lips brush mine when he talks. My heart is pounding, but I knew this was coming. I said I'd be their plaything, didn't I? I knew what I was agreeing to.

My hands come down and curl under the hem of my shirt, pulling it over my head and tossing it aside. I'm still wearing my bra, but that doesn't stop Victor from sliding his hand up my side and searing me with heat. His tattooed fingers knead the heavy flesh of my breast through the black lace.

We're still sitting in the front yard, but whatever. I'm sure the people in this neighborhood have seen worse.

Vic reaches around behind me to unhook my bra … and then a man comes out of the house, wearing a stained wifebeater and smoking a cigarette.

"Don't fuck your whores in front of my house, you little bastard," the man snarls, stumbling toward us. Vic tenses up, but he doesn't move from where he is. He does, however, let me go so I can stumble up and grab my shirt from the lawn, slipping it back over my head.

"Get your ass back inside, old man, you're an embarrassment." Victor waits while the guy makes his way over, sneering at me in a way that has me bristling. I've been looked at by older men that way for far too long, and I won't put up with it anymore.

If I have to choose between victim and aggressor, I'll pick the latter every time. My life as an innocent has long since slipped from my grasp.

"Get over here girl, and I'll show you how a real man fucks." The old guy with the thinning hair grabs his dick and runs his tongue across his lower lip, making me feel sick to my stomach. My hatred for Victor Channing is only outshone by my lust for him, but this guy … he's repulsive, exactly the sort I've always hated.

Vic moves from his chair in such a fast, fluid motion that he's just a blur. His tattooed hand wraps the other man's throat, and he walks him backward until the creep's being slammed against the trunk of a tree. Victor gets right in the asshole's face, the expression on his one of murder.

"I told you not to touch my girls." *Slam.* He pulls the guy—who I'm assuming must be his father—away from the tree, only to slam his back into it again. "Don't talk to my girls." *Slam, slam, slam.* "Don't even *look* at them."

Victor releases the man, who crumples to the ground right away, choking and grabbing at his throat, before stepping back. Vic glances my way, running his inked fingers over his violet hair, his mouth in such a severe frown that I'd be worried if I were his dad.

"Go home, Bernadette," he says, pulling a pack of cigarettes from his back pocket before removing one and lighting up. "Don't be late to school on Monday."

"I wouldn't dare," I mock dryly, turning and grabbing my backpack and my bike before heading down the street. I can feel Vic's eyes on me all the way to the corner.

CHAPTER

SEVEN

Prescott High is such a dump, this crumbling old stucco-sided building that my grandparents went to school in. It'd be charming and all that if, one: I didn't hate that side of my family, and two: there'd been any maintenance done on the building at all in the last fifty freaking years.

I smoke a whole cigarette in view of the front entrance, knowing the security guards on staff have worse to deal with than some defiant bitch smoking a shorty on school property.

"Good morning, darling," Oscar says, appearing behind me like a specter. I turn slowly, finding his tall form dressed in a white button-down, jacket, and slacks. It all looks very fancy, despite the tattoos on his hands and knuckles. He lives in one of the most dangerous parts of town, too: South Prescott. I'm guessing he bought the suit with blood money. That, or stole it. He wears them a lot. "I hear you're one of us now." The smile that steals across his lips is pure malicious intent. He pauses a moment to glance up at one of the security cameras near the front gate. "Welcome to *Havoc*."

A huge explosion sounds from across the street, and Mr. Vaughn's car—this brand-new, pretentious as fuck Range Rover in a custom shade of *pearl*—goes up in a fireball. I'm all the way across the street, and I can feel the heat on my face.

"Holy shit!" My hands clamp over my mouth as the SUV is engulfed, students screaming, one of the campus cops racing across the road. Mr. Vaughn bolts down the steps in his off-white suit, his jaw slack, eyes reflecting the orange and red of the flames.

The first thing he does is dart his eyes my direction. Our gazes meet, and I smile.

"Don't look at me, although we both know you deserve it." My mouth feels like it's smiling, but all I feel inside is sick, sad satisfaction. The principal rushes forward to grab a fire extinguisher from a passing staff member, and goes to town on the car with it while sirens sound in the distance.

"You can thank me later," Hael says, sliding up on my left side, a cigarette clenched between his teeth. He gives me a hard wink, and then flicks the butt into the nearest trash can. "Set the radiator up with some small explosives on a timer. It'll look like the whole engine just went. Happens you know, on these foreign cars." Hael takes off and clomps his way up the three steps that lead into the front entrance of the school, setting off every metal detector in there, the way he always does.

"How far, exactly, you want this to go …" Oscar runs his finger down the back of my neck, making my muscles tense up. "That's up to you." He moves past me, and I shiver.

We're just getting started here.

Just getting started.

Everything is different today. You'd think that kiss I shared with Victor shattered the world. When I walk on campus, people scurry out of my way, stare at me with wide, wide eyes. They avoid me like the plague while simultaneously letting me know with their body language that if I demand it, they'll succumb to my every whim.

It's surreal as hell.

Victor comes to find me at lunch, waiting just outside the door to the locker room, his big body curled over, hands in his pockets, eyes on the floor. When he lifts them to my face, I feel this strange, tingling sensation take over me, like I did that one time I tried to donate blood. Like I'm fading, like my life force is being drained by his stare.

"Come with me," he says, and I do.

Because with that kiss, I promised I'd do whatever he asked.

Victor leads me back to the area next to the dumpsters where the others are waiting, watching. They're all smoking. Because that's what bad kids like us do, right? *"That stuff'll kill you, you know,"* Ms. Keating likes to say. Once, I heard Hael smirk and shoot back, *"we're counting on it."*

He's right.

Every step closer to the grave is one step further away from this hell we call life.

"Boys," Vic greets, pausing in front of them and then gesturing toward me with his chin. "Glad to see we're out the door and running." He gives Hael a very special sort of look, and I have to wonder if the cocky dickhead thought to get his boss' permission before blowing up the principal's expensive SUV. And before you ask how a principal at a downtrodden public school can afford such a thing, don't bother. I'll explain later. It's one of the reasons he's on my list. "And excellent work in making it look like an accident. They've called off the bomb squad."

"Whoopee, glad to be of service," Hael says, grinning and running his tongue across his lower lip as he surveys me with an appreciative gleam in his eye. First chance he gets, he's going to demand I crawl on his lap, same as Vic. "To be honest, I've been wanting to do that for a long time. We'll consider that one a freebie."

I frown and flip him off, but he just laughs. Aaron scowls, but Callum claps his hands like he's attending a show just for him.

"I hear you're one of us now," he says, pushing his

41

hood back, so I can see his Disney prince blond hair. Only, it's strange because he's not the prince; he's the villain that slaughters the wide-eyed royal and buries his body in the woods. Cal slides a knife from his boot and tosses it to Vic, making me raise my brows. He managed to slip that past security, no problem. It's a little scary.

"Blood in," Vic says, slicing his palm and then handing the knife to me, his eyes deadly serious. "Blood out."

"You're joking, right?" I ask, looking between him and the other Havoc Boys. Aaron is practically seething, a muscle in his jaw ticking. "You want to make a blood pact? Like some middle schoolers on a tree house dare?"

"Take the knife, Bernadette, or I'll do it for you." Vic isn't threatening me with his cool, dark words. No, he's simply telling the truth. I swallow hard and look down at the bloodied bit of blade. He could have a disease. Hell, as far as I know, he could have a dozen of them. But this is what I signed up for, isn't it? *To be their plaything.* I swallow hard and snatch the knife. The last thing I want right now is for Vic or anyone else to see me vulnerable or unsure.

So I slice my palm with the sharp blade, hissing at the pain, and then gasp when Vic clamps his hand to mine, squeezing so hard it hurts and staring so deep into my eyes that I feel like I'm drowning.

It only lasts a couple of seconds, but as our blood mingles, and our gazes lock, I know that I'll never be the same again.

Victor releases me, swipes the blood off on his jeans,

and then tosses the knife back to Callum who catches it effortlessly.

"Just to be clear," he continues, his gaze sweeping across the others before returning to me. "You're on my orders and nobody else's." There's a harsh bite of threat in his words, but I have a feeling it's not exactly meant for me. He flicks his attention to the other Havoc Boys in warning. "And now that we've got our own Havoc Girl, we'll start dealing with one problem at a time, beginning with the issue of my *mother*." This last word comes off his tongue like a curse, like Victor Channing can't think of anything worse than a mom.

"What issue with your mother?" I ask, wondering if I'm overstepping my bounds here. He said I'd belong to them, to Havoc, but what, exactly, that means I'm not sure. Vic told me I'd have to obey his every word, but he didn't say I had to be a meek, kowtowing bitch, right?

Vic laughs, and the sound gives me such chills. He almost sounds like I do when I look in the mirror and wonder what the point of all this is.

"She's gripping my inheritance in her overly manicured claws on some stupid ass technicality." Vic gets out a cigarette as Oscar scribbles something down on his iPad and Hael gets up to molest the shiny surface of his car. Callum just sits there and eats while Aaron glares at the pavement, his shoulders so taut it almost hurts to look at him. "I have to be married before I can collect."

"Married ..." I start, and then the realization hits me like a freight train, and my eyes go wide. "Wait, *what*?"

43

I snap, that last word flinging from the tip of my tongue like a rubber band from a slingshot.

Victor gives me a long, studying sort of look, dressed in a black wifebeater and jeans. He's the picture of delinquency with his violet hair, ebony eyes, and inked body. His muscles are hard, long, and lean, built up from use and not just workouts. He most definitely doesn't look like a high school student. Pretty sure most of us don't, not with the darkness in our pasts or the shadows under our tired eyes. I've lived more nightmares in my seventeen years than most have lived their entire lives.

"You didn't think we wanted you just for sex, did you?" he asks, his bemused tone making me bristle, like I'm an idiot. But of course I did. What else could a bunch of horny teenage assholes want with a girl they don't even like? "If I'd wanted that, I would've asked you to be my whore, not a member of my crew. Now fuck off to class, and let me know if anybody gives you any trouble."

"Stupid, piece of shit, asshole Victor Channing!" I shout, throwing an empty glass beer bottle against the side of an abandoned convenience store. I haven't even made it home yet because one, Heather is still at her after-school thing, and two, I'm too pissed off to go back to that hellhole.

It's the Thing's day off, and if I walk in there in a

blind rage, he'll know it. He'll take advantage of the situation and poke at me until I snap. I've come close to killing him before, and we both know it.

Wouldn't that be ironic justice? The teenage girl sent to prison for life for murdering her cop/pedophile stepfather.

I choke on the feeling of helplessness, as familiar to me as my own breath. It comes in uncontrollable waves, an ebb and flow that I couldn't resist if I tried, just as impossible to resist as holding my own breath until I pass out.

Who cares about a fake marriage? I ask myself. It's a common enough trope, a central focus of dozens of TV shows, movies, books. What's so much worse about pretending to be a bride? Isn't that *better* than finding myself in the beds of all five Havoc Boys?

Hmm.

"You're on my orders and nobody else's."

What the fuck is that supposed to mean anyway?

I slump down the wall and wait there until my anger subsides. I'm committed to this. I spent the *entire* summer hiding out with Heather at the lake and the park, mulling this over.

There are people in my life that have to pay, and I don't have the strength or the resources to make it happen on my own.

So if I have to slip on a ring for Victor's mommy, so be it.

It won't be the worst thing I do this year.

Not by a long shot.

Besides, if I try to leave, I don't know what they'll do. Well ... actually, I guess I do: they'll kill me.

That much, at least, is a definite.

CHAPTER
EIGHT

Sitting with Havoc at lunch every day is disconcerting; I'm pretty damn sure the whole school is staring at us. Other stuff I noticed: Jim Dallon didn't ask to bum a cigarette from me, Mark Charlin didn't hit on me when I was digging through my locker, and my ex-bestie, Kali Rose-Kennedy, saw me coming down the hall this morning and went running.

She's coming down, like all the rest of them. The people who ruined my life. Havoc did a good job. Hell, they really are professionals, but they were the symptoms, not the cause.

I'm taking down the ringleaders of my destruction.

Sometimes, when I feel like this, I'm certain that I'm a ghost, come from the grave for vengeance. There's no way I could be alive, not with the way I feel. Living things shouldn't be so full of misery.

"Where'd you get the sweet bike?" Callum asks, his voice low and dark, rough. Stacey claims a rival gang member once hit him in the throat so hard that he suffered permanent damage. I'm not sure if I believe that, but the guy has this coarse, shadowed sound to his words. "Did you pinch it?"

"I got the parts out of the dumpster behind the cycle shop downtown. Wait around long enough, and they throw out a little of everything. Some elbow grease and YouTube videos was all it took."

I glance over at the shiny red ten-speed on the bike rack and shrug my shoulders.

I'm trying to eat my cafeteria food, this nasty ass greasy pizza plus the bag of chips and soda that come with it. But I can't. I feel like I'll be sick if I do. Tossing the slice of pepperoni down, I sigh and wipe my shiny fingers on a napkin.

"Can I have this?" Cal asks, pointing at my soda, and I nod. Aaron still won't look at me, and I don't care. He doesn't like me in his gang? Too damn bad. He's the idiot who helped create Havoc and their rules: if the client is willing to pay, never turn down a gig.

"Tonight, we'll meet at my place," Vic begins, sitting up straight, and giving a passing boy a look that's all sorts of cold hell. The kid stumbles over his own feet, looking sheepish, and empties his pocket into Victor's hand. It's just a big baggy of weed, but I don't see any money exchange hands. Instead, Vic nods and the student scurries off like a mouse. I hope I don't look like that, like some sort of frightened rodent looking to pay the dog to scare off the cat. "Eight sharp. Bring shit to stay the night. The old man's off to poker night; we'll have the place to ourselves."

"Stay the night?" I ask, feeling my brow go up. Vic frowns and looks at me with that scary ass face of his. My palms go up in a placating gesture. "I'm not complaining, just asking."

"We have my mother's breakfast thing on Saturday, so get ready to gussy yourself up: you're going." Vic rolls toward me, putting his palm on the step on my right side, and sliding his big body between my legs. He smirks and puts his mouth up against mine, brushing across it until his lips are at my ear. "And you *will* impress her. I want her fully convinced we're in love, fucking like rabbits, and destined for forever. You hear me?"

Victor undulates his body, so that his hips rub against my groin, making me groan. It feels so damn good, even with the whole school looking at us the way they are. *What breakfast thing?* I think, but my lips form words without my brain's permission.

"I hear you," I tell him, and he grins, rolling back over and kicking Hael's tray down the steps. Trash goes everywhere, and a girl in a short white dress pauses to pick it all up, her eyes never straying higher than the top of Hael's boot.

Weird.

"We'll need a dress to cover her tattoos," Victor muses as Oscar writes everything down, inked fingers moving quickly as they slide the tip of his stylus against the screen. "My mom hates tattoos. Figure out how to cover up the pink in her hair, too. I don't want it dyed."

"Yes, sir," Oscar purrs, the edge of his lip quirking up in a smirk. He adjusts his glasses, eyes flashing as he glances my way. I pretend not to notice. "Have you thought much about the ring?"

"I have my grandmother's band, that'll do." Victor's eyes scan the crowd before turning back to me. "Make sure everybody knows she's ours. I pity the guy who misses that memo." He rises to his feet and takes off, just before the bell rings.

"See you tonight," Cal whispers, sweeping past me like a shadow. Oscar follows him, still jotting notes, with Hael on his heels. Aaron is the last to go.

"I hope you know what you've gotten yourself into," he says, waiting for me to stand up. He escorts me to class by following three steps behind, and then disappears. I don't know where he goes, but he definitely doesn't go to class.

There's nobody home when I get back from school, letting myself in the back door and packing my sleeping bag, pillow, and some clothes. Mom is gone, and so is the Thing. I'm glad he's not here, and I can't wait for him to see the evil I've unleashed. Fortunately, Heather is off to a sleepover at a well-vetted friend's house, so for tonight at least, I can leave without worrying about her.

I feel much safer biking the sixteen blocks to Victor's house today, like the whole city knows I belong to Havoc. And you don't mess with Havoc, unless you're willing to pay.

I'm going to pay handsomely with my body, but I don't care. There's nothing I want more than vengeance, and nothing that turns me on like danger.

When I arrive, the boys are in the front yard, smoking and drinking. Hael offers me a beer right off the bat, and I take it, finding that my fingers tingle when we touch. He smirks, like he knows exactly what I'm going through, and then gestures at my sleeping bag.

"It's adorable," Vic says, ashing his cigarette, "but you won't need it. You're sleeping in my bed tonight." He leans back in his chair, watching me. I half expect him to order me onto his lap again, but I think this time he's more interested in seeing what I'll do on my own.

I sit down in the center of the group, right on the dead grass, the yellow-brown strands digging into my thighs as I lean back in my red and black plaid jumper, my ratty combat boots crossed at the ankles. They all watch me, like they did the other day when I walked around the back of the school and saw them hanging out next to Hael's car.

Predators.

That's what they look like, like predators.

The thing is, I'm nobody's fucking prey.

Maybe they're more like lions looking for a lioness to mount.

I smile slightly.

I know what I agreed to here. The thing is, I want it. I want them. I always have, ever since we met in elementary school and things were good. Well, maybe neutral. Then bad. And now … they're whatever they are. But I always wanted to belong; I craved it.

"Do you have condoms?" I ask, and Vic snorts.

"You have a one-track mind, Bernadette," he says, sighing and looking up at the sky with those dark eyes of his. I think they're actually brown, but they're so shadowed and full of pain that they look black. The eyes of a bully. I glance away and pick at the grass with one hand, holding my beer in the other.

"Not particularly. I just know what you want from me. And like you said, a deal's a deal."

Victor throws his head back in a roaring laugh, and the other guys chuckle along with him, all of them except for Aaron who glares at me with eyes the color of the sun-dappled oak leaves behind his head.

"Really, Bernadette, it doesn't have to be all bad. I'm a skilled lover. The rest of the guys are ... adequate." Victor flashes a sharp, dangerous sort of grin. He leans forward in his plastic lawn chair, like it's some sort of throne. The way he sits in it, it could be. He exudes confidence, like he owns the damn world. Pretty lofty for a guy who lives in one of the worst parts of town with an unemployed drunk for a father. But Vic Channing, he could have whatever he wants in life— even if he has to take it by force. "And we both know you're not a virgin, so what does it matter?" Vic tilts his head to one side, that shadow-purple hair of his sliding across his forehead. "We have plenty of time for sex, so don't worry about it. When I want it, I'll let you know, and you can service me then." He smiles in a way that gets under my skin, makes my black-painted nails curl into the grass so hard they're filled with dirt.

"Thought you didn't use condoms anyway?" Hael asks, taking two puffs on the blunt and passing it over to Oscar. He waves it away, and Callum takes it instead.

Victor smirks.

"I don't."

My mouth drops open, but he cuts me off with a look. My chest is heaving, but I don't look away. A stare is a challenge I can take on, one that he can't exactly punish me for. I'm not doing anything that goes against the bargain we made.

"So what's the deal with this brunch thing exactly?" I ask, feeling them all start to stare at me again. It's unnerving. Like, maybe I could fight off Oscar or Callum or something, but all five of them? Including Vic and Hael? They could do whatever they wanted to me, and I couldn't stop them.

Hell, they did it before, didn't they? And they were much smaller then, back in tenth grade. They're all huge now, properly filled out. Men instead of boys.

I exhale and release my grip on the clump of grass.

"Some bullshit upper crust, society type garbage," Hael snorts as Vic takes a drag on the joint and passes it over to Aaron. "Doesn't make much sense to me."

"Heh. You are not fucking invited, asshole." Victor turns to look at me, his eyes half-lidded from the weed, his beer half-empty, and a fresh cigarette in his hand. "You'd ruin any chance of me getting ahold of my inheritance." He stares at me some more, and I can feel it, this tension between us, hot and sticky, and desperate to be snapped. At least when he orders me into his bed tonight, I'll want to be there. "It's a luncheon with my egg donor and her bitch friends." Vic reaches into his pocket and pulls out a black velvet box, tossing it onto the grass beside me. My brows go up as I grab it and crack the lid.

"What the fuck is this?" I ask, staring at the diamond engagement ring.

"Your wedding ring," he says, and like, all of that anger comes roaring back again. Sex is one thing, but I did not agree to this shit. My eyes narrow, but Vic just keeps staring at me like he doesn't notice. "You'll come to the luncheon as my fiancée, please my mom, and marry me, so we can collect my inheritance."

"You've got to be freaking kidding me," I snort, but he frowns.

"Not even close. You're not going to pitch a fit about this, are you? Because it's blood in, blood out in Havoc. Do you have a problem being my wife?"

"I …" I start to answer honestly, but I don't want Victor to know how much this bothers me. The sex is one thing, but marriage? I don't want to be legally bound to this prick-hole. "Yeah, whatever. Do I get any of the money?" I look him straight in the face, and he raises a brow, like I've surprised him.

"We'll split the cut, sure, we always do. We're fucking family." Victor throws his feet up onto the small green plastic table in front of his chair and smirks at me. "Welcome to the family, Bernadette."

CHAPTER

The boys order pizza and then gather in the living room to smoke more pot and watch *South Park*. The house is a lot better on the inside than the outside. I expected burn marks on the tables from meth spoons, holes in the walls from angry punches, and the stink of garbage. But it's not like that at all. Instead, there's a candle burning on the table, no sign of trash or dirty clothes on the floor, and humble but serviceable furniture.

Hael pulls me onto his lap, and I find that we have a completely different chemistry than I do with Vic. With Vic, it's like … a hot summer day when you're soaked in sweat and all you want is water and cool, silken sheets. That's Victor. Hael is … like a fireworks explosion waiting to happen. Dangerous, unpredictable, but damn pretty to look at.

He massages my hip with his hand while I try to watch the show. But I can't. I can't think about anything other than that tattooed hand of his smoothing across my flesh.

I'm not sure, exactly, what we're supposed to be doing here, but if smoking weed and watching TV fulfills my Havoc requirements, then fine.

"Maybe I'll take you in the bathroom real quick?" Hael whispers, his mouth teasing the shell of my ear. "See if that sharp mouth of yours is as good at sucking cock as it is at being snarky."

"I get her first," Vic says, with this unshakable calm but overwhelming certainty. He doesn't have to raise his voice or look at Hael to get his point across. He's the goddamn boss.

Hael makes a frustrated sound under his breath and pushes me off his lap onto the couch cushion. I sink into it, the scent of pot and beer permeating the fabric.

"We need to go look at dresses," Oscar reminds the group, pushing his glasses up with a middle finger. He smirks at me, his eyes taking me in in a way that's both appreciative and analytical. "What are you? A size eight?" My brows go up, but I don't answer. It's clear he's not done. "Thirty-eight, G cup."

My smile is wicked sharp.

"Wrong, actually. I'm a thirty-eight triple D."

Oscar lets out a smooth, dark sort of laugh and then shakes his head.

"No, you're not. You're much larger than a triple D. Have you ever had a proper fitting?"

"Do you get custom made leather shoes from a fucking cobbler? Or hand tailored suits from a master craftsman? No, asshole, I've never had a proper fitting.

My bras are from Walmart, and this is the biggest size they have."

I stand up, ready to fight. It's just what I do; it's in my nature.

"Kick his ass, Bernie," Callum murmurs, pushing his hood back and revealing a sea of golden blond hair, streaked with honey and amber. He's honestly way too pretty to be a gangbanger. "He fucking insulted you. Beat him up."

"Yes, by all means, Bernadette, beat me up." Oscar puts his tablet aside and stands up, smirking at me. He clearly doesn't see me as a threat. I glance over at the couch where Vic's sitting, but he's watching impassively, like he doesn't care much either way.

Fine then.

I'd like to punch Oscar anyway, just to prove I can.

I'm not the same girl they picked on all those years ago.

Exhaling, I study Oscar's tall, lithe form. He's got a thin build, but he's bulked it up with serious muscle. I can see that, even through the white button-down he's wearing. He's at least taken his jacket off, and rolled up his sleeves, so I can see some of his tattoos.

"Can you take a punch?" I ask, raising a brow. "Because this is gonna hurt."

"Try me." Oscar just stands there, this infuriating column of grace and poise. I watch him for a moment, scoff, and then start to turn away like I've given up before launching myself at his midsection and knocking him back into the chair. He's so surprised that he lets me get that far, but I don't land the punch. He stops it just a fraction of an inch from his glasses, squeezing my hand in his fist.

"Guys have been going after my glasses since I was eight years old. You should've picked a different place to punch."

"Like your balls?" I ask, and then I slam my knee down and into his crotch. Oscar's face tightens up, but that's the only emotion he shows as the other boys adjust themselves and lean in for the show. Money exchanges hands.

Apparently, this is a bet now.

"Twenty on me!" I shout, and then Oscar is throwing me to the floor and pinning me there. I let him get that far, aiming for his balls again. I'm sorry, but when you're small and vulnerable, you'll hit whatever you can get. I've heard guys mumble dumb shit about how it's dishonorable or uncool or what-the-fuck-ever, but the point is, if someone's hurting me, I figure I have carte blanche to do whatever I need to stop them.

"Deal." Vic's cool calm voice cuts through the rage and goes straight to my brain. But then Oscar blocks my kick with his own leg, putting himself off-balance in the process. We roll, and I end up on top, throwing a hard punch at his throat.

He stops his one, too, but I get a lot closer. Adrenaline surges through me as he tries to buck me off. If he gets me under him again, I'll lose. Hands-down, I will lose. My fight or flight instincts kick in—but it's broken because I only ever fight, never flee—and I wrap my fingers around Oscar's throat. He's able to get a good grip on my wrists, but I have the advantage of gravity. That, and the advantage of being perpetually underestimated.

I push down hard on his throat, and he fights back with everything he has, trying to knock me off his chest. But while I'm strong, I'm also much smaller than him, and fairly light. He's bucking, but I'm not going anywhere. It's easy for me to just ride this out. He can't use my own weight against me.

After about thirty seconds, I feel hands on my arms, and Hael and Callum are hauling me back while Oscar rolls onto his side, coughing and choking and holding his throat. Aaron is looking at me like I'm a crazy person.

"Holy sweet baby Jesus," Hael purrs as I tear from their grips and pace the floor like a caged animal. "That turned me on so hard. You're not like the usual simpering brats we bring back here, are you?"

"You made a deal, and you can't take it back," I snarl, turning and looking at all five guys in return. Oscar is staring at me with this strange mixture of fascination, frustration, and lust. He licks his lips as he forces himself into a sitting position, still coughing. "You thought you caged a kitty cat? You got a fucking cougar. Watch my claws when you take me to bed." I start toward the front door, because if I don't walk or run this anger off, it'll get the best of me, and then I pause, glancing back and meeting Vic's bemused gaze. "And you guys owe me a hundred bucks."

Callum's laughter follows me all the way down the block.

────────────

About an hour later, I head back and find Aaron waiting for me on the front porch. He doesn't look very happy to see me, covered in ink and bullshit. I'm not sure I've ever hated anyone quite the same way I hate him. And trust me: I hate a *lot* of people. I hate more people than I like, that's for damn sure.

"Why are you wasting your time with us?" Aaron asks, sounding bored and tired. He smokes a cigarette with two fingers dipped entirely in ink. There are very few places on his body that are left bare, not even his cock. Trust me: I've seen it all. "You should've taken off when you had the chance, gone to live with that grandmother of yours."

"You'd like that, wouldn't you?" I challenge, clenching my hands into fists at my sides as he turns his green-gold gaze my direction. *Liar. Cheater. Hypocrite.* He's worse than all the others. At least they accept the fact that their feathers are black, that their realm is hell, that they spew fire and shit flames.

Aaron still believes he craps rainbows and wears white wings.

"Like that?" he asks, rising up from the plastic chair on the porch. "Hell no. I've wanted you since we were kids." He takes a drag on his cigarette and offers me the pack with his other hand. I don't take it. I don't want to get closer to him than I have to.

"You're a monster," I tell him, and he shrugs his big shoulders, tucking the pack into the rear pocket of his dirty denim jeans. They cup his ass too tight, emphasize the long beautiful lines of his legs.

"Maybe. But you're an idiot. You had a chance to escape this place, and instead, you chose to dig in deep, just for a little taste of vengeance. It won't be as sweet as you think, cupcake. In fact ..." Aaron saunters over to me and pauses, looking down at me with a dark frown, smelling like tobacco and secrets. "You'll find it leaves the taste of ash in your mouth; it's almost obscene." He cups my jaw, and runs his thumb along my lower lip. "And you won't like it when Victor takes you to bed. He's a rough, angry sort of lover." I turn my face away with a scowl. "I'm trying to convince him to give you to me, but he's determined to have you."

"I'd rather fuck him than you," I say, still staring at the dirt because it's a million times better than looking at Aaron's face. When I turn back, I shoulder him out of the way and head inside.

"You were almost late," Vic says, crossing his huge arms over his chest. He doesn't smile. "You wouldn't have liked to see what would've happened if you were late."

"Let's just get this damn thing over with, shall we?" I quip, and Vic scoffs.

"Suit yourself," he says, and he heads outside. He's got a motorcycle waiting, some badass piece of machinery that's way outside the pay grade of someone who lives in a busted-ass house on the wrong side of town. "You'll ride bitch seat," he tells me, gesturing to the rear seat as Hael squeezes his big body into the driver's side door of his classic car, that cherry red beauty that makes me wet just looking at it.

"Fine."

Vic doesn't have helmets, but I'm beyond caring about little things like my personal safety at this moment. Instead, I hop on and curve my body against the strong, muscular expanse of his back. I'll admit, my head spins a little at his smell, this dark, musky sort of scent that sets all my senses on fire.

But I don't have to let him know that, now do I?

CHAPTER

TEN

The "dress shop" we head to isn't in a good part of town; it's not even in a bad part of town. In fact, it's in the *worst* part of town.

My body is molded to Vic's big, strong back, the sun beating down on me, making me sweat.

I tell myself that the heat in my core has nothing to do with his rock-hard body locked between my thighs, the fresh scent of male sweat and leather teasing my nose. Fuck. *Fuck*, this is torture.

"What the hell is this?" I snap when the motorcycle comes to a skidding stop on the dead front lawn of some trash heap in South Prescott. There's a sea of rusted-out vehicles, a mobile home with rotten siding, and some bitchy dark-haired girl I'm pretty sure I beat the snot out of last year. What's her name, some guy's name turned girlish by adding an *ie* at the end. Billie?

Vic chuckles, and the sound rumbles through me in the best possible way, taking over every part of my body and delving inside. Vic's laugh owns my blood, my bones. What the hell is gonna happen when we fuck for the first time?

"What did you expect? Bloomingdale's?" He snorts as he climbs off the bike, and I follow after him.

I'm not about to dignify that response with an answer, so I stay on his heels as Hael peels into the lot and damn near runs me over with that stupidly beautiful car of his. I go to slam my fist on the hood as we pass, and Vic grabs me by the wrist.

His dark eyes are deadly serious when I look up into them.

"Don't ever touch Hael's ride without his permission," he warns, pulling me along after him as Billie rises to her feet and stretches, popping her ass out like a cat in heat.

"Well, hello there, Victor Channing," she purrs, sauntering over to him and flipping her dark hair, so that I can see the teal color underneath. Her brown eyes slide from him to me, and she frowns. "What can I help you with?"

"We need a dress for my fiancée," he says, just like that, matter-of-fact and without a single shred of emotion. The stare he levels on Billie is intense, so much so that I almost take a step back. Almost. But then, I'm not scared of the Havoc Boys, not anymore.

"Your fiancée?" she asks, blinking stupidly at first me, then him. "Seriously?"

"Did I fucking stutter?" Vic says, his voice sharp enough to cut. Billie takes a step back as the other boys come up the rickety stairs behind us. "Let us in."

Billie turns and scrambles to unlock the door, holding it wide and waiting until all six of us have moved inside before she shuts and locks it. She glares at me as she passes, and I flip her off, tattooed hand held high. Vic stiffens, but I guess he accepts that I can handle my business and doesn't intervene.

"Right this way," she says, leading me through what's actually a surprisingly nice interior and into a side room that's filled with clothing in garment bags, metal racks with hanging poles on all four walls. "What are you looking for, exactly?"

"We'll take a look and let you know," Vic says, moving confidently into the room. Somewhere further back in the house, a baby cries, and Billie hesitates.

"That means *leave*, and we'll pay you on the way out," Callum says, towering over her in his hoodie and shorts. Billie's face registers a true moment of fear before she scampers off. Pretty sure her kid is like, a year and a half old. She had him sophomore year with some guy who's in prison now.

At least I managed to avoid that particular fate.

My eyes slide to Aaron's, and he looks away, green eyes dark, like maybe he had the same thought I did. We were never careful, hardly used birth control. It's a miracle I didn't end up like Billie Charter.

She shuts the door behind us as Oscar starts flipping through dresses.

"Boss," he says, after systematically discarding a good two dozen dresses before he pulls one off the rack.

The other guys make themselves comfortable, like they could care less what I wear, but are determined to be here regardless.

That's Havoc for you, blood in, blood out.

Oscar unzips the plastic, flashing a white dress with long sleeves, but a low-cut back. I've got ink all down my arms, a little on my breasts and neck, but none on my back just yet. He knows my body too well; it's almost scary. That is, if I were capable of being afraid of anything anymore.

"This'll do," Vic confirms, taking the dress from Oscar's inked hand and studying it carefully. "My mother's a sucker for money, and this screams loaded." He tosses it at me and nods with his chin. "Put it on."

There's a challenge in Vic's dark eyes that I meet head-on. He thinks I'm going to shy away from something as stupid as this?

I've been stripped bare in my heart and soul, had my emotions torn off and tossed aside. He thinks I give a shit about being naked?

"This dress is ugly as hell," I say, and several of the boys chuckle.

"Yeah, well, my mother is the queen of the designer label. Never said she had any fashion sense. She buys whatever's the most expensive, doesn't care what it looks like."

"It's your funeral," I mimic, staring at him with a blank expression as I shrug my leather jacket off. It falls to the floor in a heap, and I exhale. Here goes nothing.

My fingers curl under the hem of my shirt, and I tear

it over my head. That dress won't work with a bra, so I reach back and unclasp the hook, letting the cups fall forward and slide to the floor.

"Jesus," Vic grumbles, rubbing his hand over his mouth. Oscar takes notes on his iPad before glancing up at me like he's bored, like he couldn't care less that my bare tits are hanging out.

"Like what you see?" I ask sneakily, but Oscar just gives me this tight, little smile that infuriates me to no end.

"I prefer my women with bigger breasts," he replies smoothly, and I grit my teeth, reaching down to flick open the button on my jeans.

"I prefer my men to be able to hold their own in a fight," I fire back, and Oscar's brows go up as Hael howls with laughter. Vic grins, and I turn away, noticing that Aaron's watching me with a severe frown. Callum, meanwhile, just smiles, almost sweetly.

With a quiet breath, I kick my boots off and shove my jeans down my hips, leaving my panties in place. Nobody complains as I unzip the dress and wiggle into it.

"Allow me," Vic says, moving over and putting his huge, inked hands on my waist. A fire rips through me, and I close my eyes. It feels good when he touches me, too good. I don't like it. Makes me nervous, all that fire and tension.

He zips me up and then steps back as I turn around to face him.

The white dress hugs my curves and reveals just

enough skin to be sexy without showing off too much of my ink.

The expression on Victor's face says it all: he likes this dress. A *lot.*

"Shit, that's hot," he murmurs, rubbing at his chin again. Seems to be a tell of his for when he's deep in thought. In that case, I don't have to worry about seeing too much of it, huh? "But is it too hot? My mom is a serious bitch. She might feel intimidated if you look too pretty."

A frown turns down the corners of my lips.

"You're shitting me, right? Your mom gets jealous of your girlfriends?"

"Never had a girlfriend. And you," he touches his fingers to the side of my face, "you are not my girlfriend: you're my fiancée. Oscar, let's find something more ... matronly."

"What a shame," Hael murmurs, his big body leaned up against the door, like some sort of royal guard. "I like the white one." His brown eyes track over me, making me shiver; I can feel the heat in them from here.

"We'll get two," Vic agrees, jaw working as he watches me. "Billie and her brothers owe me money anyhow."

Oscar selects another dress, something that reminds me of an outfit my great-grandmother might've worn to church on Sunday when the family was still rich. Did I mention she was ninety-nine years old when she passed? And buried in a dress similar to this, kid you not.

As I'm shedding the white dress for the weird

muumuu thing, a man passes by the exterior window and pauses to look in at me as I clamp my arms over my chest in an attempt to cover my breasts.

"Oh, hell no," Hael says as he pushes up off the door and goes for the window with Callum in tow.

Hael shoves the window open and hops out as the man starts to run. The two Havoc boys take off after him as I gape in surprise.

"What the fuck is going on?" I choke out as Aaron steps up to stand beside me.

"That's Kyler Ensbrook. We have unresolved shit with him and his brother." Aaron pauses dramatically and then swings his green-gold eyes down to my face, like there's something here left unsaid but he's not going to be the one to say it.

"That, sure," Vic starts as he glances back at me. "But mostly it's because nobody looks at our fucking girl without consequence." Vic steps over to the window and hops out.

"This is nuts," I grumble as I slip the hideous frock on, and then shove my feet in my boots. Nobody stops me as I go for the window and climb out, following the flattened trail of grass toward the woods. I've just barely crossed into the shadowed darkness when I find Kyler Ensbrook on the ground with blood streaming down the sides of his face.

"I'm going to kill you both!" he screams as Hael and Callum circle him like sharks, and Vic watches, back against the trunk of a tree, tatted arms crossed over his chest. He barely glances my way when I stumble into the clearing.

"Apologize to Bernadette," Vic commands, and I shiver. That's a voice made to control armies, to start riots, to incite violence. Vic could rule the world, if you know, he wasn't just some poor gang-banging asshole from the wrong side of town.

"Eat shit, Vic. Your girl has ugly tits anyway."

Vic's face hardens in a way that's terrifying, this darkness closing in that swallows him whole.

"Break his face and teach him a lesson." Victor pushes up from the tree and turns to head back toward the house.

He's not being hyperbolic here: he's dead serious.

My eyes flick over to the guy on the ground, hands curled over his head, a wet spot forming on his crotch. He's pissed himself. He's quite literally pissed himself.

Fuck.

If I don't do something, Hael and Callum really will —and it's gonna be bad. Trust me: I've seen them at their worst. I know what they can do. I know what they're capable of. It's why I hired them, isn't it?

There's no time to think, so I don't bother standing there and waiting around for the boys to crush Kyler's skull in. Instead, I race forward and kick him as hard as I can in the shoulder. An agonizing scream tears from his throat, but he won't die from a bruise or a dislocated shoulder.

"Screw you, peeping tom piece of shit." I spit on him and swipe my arm across my red-painted lips, smearing color that looks like blood on the ugly frock. Good. Now

I *can't* wear it to the luncheon. "You got what you deserved." I step back and look up to find Callum and Hael watching me.

"Let's get this dress and get out of here. This place is depressing as fuck," Hael says, and then he laughs as I turn and start back the way I came, pausing when Vic grabs my wrist. His grip is firm, but not bruising. I lift my eyes to his.

"Clever little Bernadette," he murmurs before releasing me.

I roll my eyes as we head back to the house and crawl in the window. Billie is banging on the door and shouting something, but the guys ignore her.

"Well, this won't do, will it?" Oscar asks, lifting my dirtied sleeve and giving it a look. He gives me a knowing smile and holds up another garment bag with a single inked finger. "This should do it. No need to try it on: I know your size, remember?"

"Get fucked," I grumble as Aaron gathers up my discarded clothing and tosses me my leather jacket.

"Let's go. We're done here," Vic announces, and Hael moves over to open the door, leaving Billie to stumble in and fall to her knees. "We'll be taking three dresses. Consider your debt paid." He steps past her and continues on. She, apparently, doesn't have a lot going on upstairs because she follows after us.

"Those three dresses are worth double what we owed you," she whines, and Callum pauses, turning and blocking her in the hallway with an arm on either side of the doorjamb.

71

"You're lucky this is the only interest you're paying on that loan. Tell your brothers we said hi." His voice is like a dark dream, this growling, hollow sound that gives me chills. If I had Callum Park leaning over me in his hoodie like that, I'd either make certain I had a knife on me or else I'd back the hell off.

Billie finally seems to realize who she's dealing with and retreats … a little, anyway.

"Oh," Vic says, pausing just before we head out the door. He turns to glance over his shoulder, purple-black hair falling onto his forehead. "We left your boyfriend bleeding out in the woods. You should probably check on him." He starts to turn back and then stops, like he's thought of something else. "And next time he tries to scope out our girl, we'll kill him."

Vic strides across the deck in his boots and clomps down the stairs as I follow after. Without question, I get back on the bike with him.

I pretend not to enjoy it.

But I do.

I seriously fucking do.

CHAPTER
ELEVEN

When we get back to the house, Victor's dad is there.

And he's not supposed to be.

Vic grits his teeth as he climbs off the bike and turns back to give me a look.

"Stay here for a minute."

He takes off for the front door as Hael pulls his hot rod in beside me.

"Fuck, the old man is here?" he asks as he climbs out and uses his red tank top to wipe the sweat from his face. As he does that, I get a nice, long healthy look at his abs. *Damn, he's ripped.* Hael notices me looking and cocks this smirking grin that I meet with dead eyes. I don't care if he sees me checking him out. It's part of the reason I'm here, isn't it? To get the guys that should've always been mine back.

There's some shouting from inside, definitely the result of more than two people.

"Shit." Hael takes off for the front door with Callum

and Aaron behind him, leaving me alone with Oscar in the front yard.

"What's going on?" I ask as he takes a step toward me, his eyes focused above and behind me. When I glance back, I see something I really don't like. That is, a group of men I don't recognize making their way toward us.

My instincts flare, and that fight or flight fever kicks in. Like I said, mine's messed up because it's more like a fight or fight harder instinct, but it works for me.

"Trouble." Oscar sets his iPad on the trunk of Hael's car, and then carefully unbuttons his jacket, tossing it aside. His beautiful tattooed fingers flick open a few buttons, and he reaches inside his shirt, pulling out a gun, a revolver by the looks of it.

Without even blinking, he lifts it up and levels it on the newcomers.

"You should've taken off when you had the chance, gone to live with that grandmother of yours."

Aaron's words make me shiver, and I exhale to calm myself.

This is what buying into Havoc has earned me: violence and turmoil. They are a gang, after all, no matter how beautiful or dark or alluring they might be. No matter what they used to mean to me as a kid.

None of it matters to me now though. As long as I can reap my vengeance and save my sister first, nothing else is important.

"This is Havoc territory," Oscar says, voice smooth and cool, almost businesslike. "What do you want?"

"Who the fuck are you? Some brat with his daddy's firearm?" the man in the front asks, his grizzled gray beard belying the strength in those thick forearms of his. Forearms don't seem important until you realize that the muscles there are what control grip strength.

Oscar smiles.

"Not exactly." He disengages the safety and pulls the hammer back.

"You little punk," the man snarls, and the group makes their way toward us. My heart is thundering like crazy, and sweat is dripping down the sides of my face. Any woman worth her weight in salt knows a group of men equals bad news.

It's just me and Oscar out here. Two against six. And who knows how many more of these guys are in the house?

"Take one more step forward, and I'll shoot you in the thigh as a warning. But only because I'm an understanding sort of fellow."

The men don't slow down, as sure of these odds as I am.

Oscar doesn't seem to give two craps.

He pulls the trigger and hits the leader in the thigh, striding forward as blood and gunpowder color the night air. Within a few seconds, the tide has turned and the leader is in a crumpled heap on the ground, howling in pain. That, and Oscar's gun is pressed firmly against his temple.

"I asked you not to move, and you didn't listen," he says, his voice this dark thread of fire that curls around me, blue flame dancing with menace. Sure, it's all metaphorical, but the fact that the guy's voice is powerful enough to make me see in poetry is pretty impressive. "Do it again, and I'll be forced to make a decision neither of us will enjoy."

"You don't have the balls," one of the other men snarls, and Oscar lifts his gray eyes up to stare at him.

"Don't I?"

A long, silent moment passes, the wind whistling down the dirty street. In this part of the city, nobody calls the cops over a gunshot. Better to let something bad happen to someone else than be labelled a snitch and bring something bad on you and yours.

"These kids are fucking crazy, I told you," one of the other men says, grabbing his groaning, bleeding buddy under the arms. Several of the other men step in to help as Oscar stays where he is, gun held rock steady in one hand. "You tell Vic that his dad owes money to a lot of powerful people."

"My patience is sadly running low," Oscar says, cocking the hammer again for emphasis. "I'm going to count down from ten in my head." He taps his temple with an inked finger. "And if you're not gone by the time I get to one, well …"

The men scramble to drag their friend away while several others come pouring out of the house, booking it down the road with limps and blood and black eyes.

Hael, Aaron, and Callum come out after them with Vic following behind.

He drags his father by the shirt and throws him into

the dead grass, knocking over the plastic lawn chair we sat in together just days ago. My heart begins to beat, and I run my tongue over my lower lip without thinking.

"You piece of shit," Vic snarls, putting his boot on his father's chest, his teeth gritted in anger, a muscle ticking in the side of his neck. "You brought that crap home with you. Are you insane?"

"That's my boy," the man coughs, choking and sputtering under the weight of his son's shoe. "I knew you and your friends would be there for me. That's what family is for, right?"

Vic's entire face shuts down, and he removes his boot, crouching down next to his father with the darkest expression I've ever seen on another human being.

"Havoc does not exist to be your personal police. This is the first and last time we will come to your aid. Do you understand me, old man? The next time those men come looking for you, I'm handing you over with a ribbon tied around your fat neck." He moves to stand up as his father rolls onto his side, face red with liquor, wearing a stained gray wifebeater and holey jeans. It's an outfit virtually identical to what Hael's got on, but where Hael is streaked with grease from being under the hood, Vic's dad is wet with sweat and blood and vomit.

My lip curls.

"Son, you have all that money comin' to you," the old man starts, and Vic laughs. The sound is far from pleasant.

"You listen here." He grabs his father's hair and lifts his head up in a way that makes the old drunk hack unpleasantly. "The only reason I hate Mom more than I hate you is because she ran off and left me here with you. You are scum. Worth less than the dirt beneath my boots. The only reason you're alive right now is because I have a moral code that's so rigid, even my desperate dislike for you can't break it."

"Moral code?" Vic's father laughs, jerking away from his son's grip and scrambling backwards until he finds his feet. The other boys stand in a loose half-circle around him, watching, waiting, while Oscar cleans his gun with a handkerchief from his pocket, and tucks it into his shirt, carefully buttoning it up again. "I know what you and your buddies do. You steal and you fight, you smoke and you fuck. What makes you any different than me?"

"The fact that you don't know the answer to that question is part of the problem." Victor stands back up and swipes some blood from his hands onto his jeans. None of it is his blood. He turns to the side to look at me and frowns, running his fingers through his dark hair. "Hael, Oscar, escort Bernadette home."

My nostrils flare, and I try not to show my disappointment.

If Vic thinks sending me home is a boon, he's wrong.

It's a punishment.

The Thing isn't currently at the house, which is a positive, but if it were, I wouldn't go inside. I'd sleep in the woods out back, in the small pink tent my grandmother gave me when I was six. And I'd sleep there with a knife.

"You don't look so happy to be here," Oscar says, leaning forward between the two seats, his bland, neutral, business-like smile back in place. But tonight, I saw deeper, into what truly makes him a part of Havoc.

"I'm not." I grab my backpack and sleeping bag as Hael gets out of the car and comes around to ... open my door. What the fuck? I give him a skeptical sort of look as I climb out, like one might eye a used car salesman.

He wants something from me.

But, you know, in a way, he's much worse than a used car salesman because I know what a salesman wants. I have no idea what's going through Hael's mind.

"What?" he asks, holding up his hands in a placating gesture. "We take care of our own, Blackbird. Relax. I was just trying to be a gentleman."

"Well, don't," I snap, scooting around him, and giving the big, tattooed car freak a wide berth. "I'm not used to it, and it doesn't suit you."

He laughs at me. Shit, he's always laughing.

"Good point. Catch ya later, Bernie."

Hael climbs back in the car and he and Oscar take off, leaving me alone in my own personal hell. Staring up at the dilapidated duplex in front of me, I sigh and head for the front door.

Hopefully, Pamela is asleep.

But then I walk in and find her sitting on the couch, waiting for me. It's always bad when she's paying attention to me. I prefer the months of severe neglect, hands down.

"Where the hell have you been?" she asks me, standing up and giving my frock a confused look. It's definitely not my usual daywear, that's for sure.

"What do you care?" I ask, and then the hair on the back of my neck stands on end at the sound of a car pulling into the driveway. I'd recognize that car anywhere: it belongs to the Thing. My skin gets tight suddenly, like I'm trapped inside of it with nowhere to go.

Maybe Aaron was right, maybe you should've cut to Nantucket and run? Maybe none of this is worth it? How much more suffering will you have to endure to achieve your ends, Bernadette?

But I'm so damaged, and so broken. I don't even know what happiness looks like anymore. Heather, though, her smile is like a radiant beam of sunshine. She gets it, the meaning of life. I just have to stop the world from snatching it away.

The front door opens and there it is. I refuse to give it any sort of gendered pronoun, or a non-binary pronoun like *they*. It is an it, and it's not even dignified enough for that.

The Thing. The Monster. The Creep. The Devil.

My throat gets tight, and I find it suddenly hard to breathe.

"The hell are you wearing?" he asks, his laughter this slime that coats my skin and poisons me. I want to gouge my ears out with a needle, just to make it stop. Just so I never have to hear that sound again. "You look like one of the old bitches at the bingo hall."

Neil Pence aka the Thing aka my stepfather moves toward me and reaches down to cup my ass. My reflexes are sharp now, honed, not those of the little girl he abused for so many years.

I throw my elbow into his stomach, and he grunts, doubling over in pain as my mother gapes at us.

"Don't you hit your father!" she shouts, taking his side as she clutches at her pearls. Always taking his side.

She didn't believe Pen when my sister asked for help. She's part of the reason Penelope is dead. My eyes narrow to slits, and venom spews from between my lips.

"This freak is not my father," I shout back, hands shaking. The temptation to grab a knife from the kitchen and plunge it through his chest calls to me. I've thought about it before, almost obsessively.

But … I've been trapped all my life, one way or another.

Caged.

The last thing I want is to end up in prison and leave Heather alone with this bitch we call Mom.

Havoc, Havoc, Havoc. I've got Havoc now, and it'll all be worth it: the sex, the fake marriage, the violence. All of it.

"Don't you talk to me like that, you little bitch," the Thing growls, coming for me the way he's done since … well, since before I can even remember. The Thing has been beating me bloody since three months after my father died. Pretty sure he was having an affair with my mother sometime before that.

At least he's never raped me. He's tried, plenty of times. But I wasn't letting that happen to me. No fucking way. We've been battling ever since.

I'm a different person now though. A completely different person.

My right fist flies out and cracks Neil in the face before he can grab me by the hair the way he's always done, throw me against the wall, break my nose.

This time, I'm breaking his, even if I land in juvie for a few days. He might be a cop, but I'm still seventeen, and I know he likes playing with me too much to leave me there for long.

But at the last second, I pull back.

If I hit him, and I end up in juvie, then what happens to Heather? What will Heather do without me to protect her? *The way I should've protected Pen all along. Sure, she was my older sister, but we could've stood together against the Thing, had each other's backs.*

Instead, she suffered in silence, and now she's gone.

Mom didn't believe her when she asked for help, and neither did that cunt from social services. They called her a liar. They said she was making it up to get attention.

My throat closes up, but I pull my fist back. My need for revenge in that moment is superseded by my need to protect my little sister, the Thing's biological daughter, the one person on this earth that he should love unconditionally.

The first person he'll abuse if he gets the chance.

Neil snarls with rage, and keeps coming, like a dump

truck. His massive body slams into mine, but I expect it; I'm used to it. I roll with the momentum, finding my feet near the kitchen entrance. I scrabble up, panting, getting ready for round two when the front door comes flying open and Hael and Oscar appear.

The former moves into the room like a well-oiled machine, grabbing my stepdad by the throat and shoving him up against the wall while my mother screams.

"Bernadette," Oscar greets, picking up my backpack from the floor. He leaves my sleeping bag where it is. "Pardon us, ma'am." He gives my mother a look that's one part polite propriety, two parts cold, unyielding hell, then pushes his black glasses up with an inked middle finger.

"You like beating up girls, huh?" Hael purrs, his face awfully close to Neil's. Pretty sure the Thing has stopped breathing; his face looks purple in the dull yellow light from the living room lamp. "Well, this works out for both of us then because I like beating on guys who beat up girls."

Hael releases the creature to a heap on the floor, and turns back to look at me, his brown eyes scanning my body like he's looking for injuries.

"You okay there, Bernie?" he asks, and I nod, panting still from the adrenaline. Half of me is excited to see the Havoc Boys here, but the other half is wondering why Kyler Ensbrook got the snot beat out of him for looking at my tits when my stepfather has been doing his damnedest to sexually assault me for years, and he gets thrown against a wall? That's it?

He's a cop, Bernie, give it time. Havoc is more subtle than that, and you know it. They can beat up Kyler Ensbrook and walk away, but they can't fuck with the Thing unless they've got a plan in place.

I shake out my hands and stride past him, right out the front door.

"We're pressing charges!" my mother screams, but I ignore her. She just might, has before when I've run away. I don't care.

I climb into Hael's Camaro, shaking, trembling, my fingers curled in the excess fabric of the ugly frock.

"If you didn't want to go home, you should've said something," Oscar tells me as Hael pops his seat forward and lets his friend climb in.

"Havoc keeps no secrets," Hael growls in agreement, and we peel out of the driveway, and down the street.

CHAPTER
TWELVE

The guys take me to, of all places, Aaron's house.

The only place on earth that sounds less appealing than home.

My heart thunders painfully as Hael gets out and comes around to open my door. At the last second, he stops, steps back, and crosses his arms over his chest to wait. The smirk on his face is *infuriating*, but I brush it off. It's hard to stay mad at a guy for doing exactly what you asked him to.

The little suburban house is quiet, almost peaceful in the night. I can hear crickets chirping nearby. Clearly, the guys felt this was the safest place to bring me. Doubt any of them live in much better situations than I do.

Aaron ... is the exception.

I open the door, dragging my backpack with me. I'd have rather slept at Vic's place, in his bed. An all-over shiver takes hold, and I have to bite my lip to keep my hands from shaking.

Aaron is already at the door when we walk up the front path, leaning in the doorjamb with no shirt on, wicked fingers tapping a rhythm on the wood.

He doesn't say anything as Hael hands over my backpack, just turns and pads into the dark house.

"Sleep tight," Hael says, giving me a pat on the back before he disappears around the corner of the garage and climbs back in his Camaro.

Fuck.

With a deep breath, I move in and close the door behind me, making sure it's locked. Aaron is halfway up the stairs, so I follow after him to the second floor.

"The girls are sleeping," he says, tossing my backpack onto his bed. "Try not to wake them up. I'll be on the couch." He starts to leave the room, and I reach out, curling my fingers around his upper arm. Aaron smells amazing, his dark hair wet from a shower. I rest my forehead against his arm, forgetting for the briefest of moments that I'm supposed to hate him.

"Thank you for letting me stay here," I tell him, trying not to think too hard about our sordid past. And yet, there it is, burning like black fire in the recesses of my brain. As soon as I fall asleep, I'll dream about it, I just know I will.

"Havoc sticks together," he says, pulling his arm from my grip and heading down the hallway. I watch after him until he disappears, and then turn back to a bedroom I haven't seen in a long, long time.

It's like a time warp in here.

My breath catches as I sit on the edge of Aaron's bed,

and put my face in my hands.

I don't cry, but I remember.

Oh, I remember well.

Three years earlier ...

I'm standing at Aaron's side in the rain, looking at a single casket, as black and shiny as the hearse that drove it here. My hand reaches down for his, the only other mourner in the cemetery besides myself. Aaron's parents weren't well-liked. Well, his father wasn't well-liked anyway. And his mother was terrified of him.

"She didn't come home last night," he says, glancing my way, pleading with his eyes for a million things I can't give him. Stability. Warmth. Security. "I don't think she's coming back."

"Don't say that," I tell him, but I wonder ... there were clothes missing from his mother's closet, socks and underwear strewn across the floor. And then there was the way she looked at me when I stepped onto the front porch and saw her hastily climbing into a cab.

She isn't coming back.

"What about my sister?" he asks, giving my hand a squeeze. "What about my cousin?"

We both know the story of my brief stint in foster care. Aaron's sweet girls, they wouldn't survive a week. Their spirits would break along with their bodies. My eyes close, and I hang my head, blond hair sticking to the sides of my face. The wetness hides the tears, but I don't know how to help. That happens sometimes, when one broken person tries to lean on another. We're too rickety to keep the other standing. All it would take is a strong wind to blow us both over ...

"I'm afraid, Bernie," he says finally, lifting his chin up and staring across the freshly dug hole in the ground. His father's funeral won't go unnoticed by his creditors. He had a coke and vodka habit to accompany his partying and gambling problems, and shit doesn't come cheap. They'll start looking for his mother, and if they find her ... And on the other side of the coin, if the state finds out a fifteen-year-old is living alone with his five-year-old sister, and two-year-old cousin, they're all screwed six ways to Sunday.

"You'll figure a way out of this," I tell him, glancing over, watching droplets of rain bead on his full lower lip. "You always do." We're both survivors, me and Aaron. We have that in common. I'm pretty sure I'm in love with him, that maybe I have been for years. Young love might be fluffy and fleeting, but at least there's a purity to it that doesn't stain like everything else in my life.

"I wish I could take care of us all," Aaron says, squeezing my hand, his green-gold eyes boring into mine. "I wish I was strong enough."

His expression says that one day, maybe he will be.

No matter what that sort of strength costs.

No matter if he has to sell his soul to get it.

CHAPTER

THIRTEEN

Aaron doesn't bother to wake me up in the morning. Instead, I find myself jolting out of sleep with a gasp, sweat-soaked sheets tangled around my legs, and an unfamiliar room surrounding me.

The sweet scent of maple and bacon fills my nostrils, and I exhale.

He's going to be down there, shirtless, covered in tattoos and cooking breakfast for his little sister and cousin. My heart starts to race at the thought, at just the *idea* of seeing him in low-slung sweats, being all domestic and shit.

Jesus.

I swing my legs over the side of the bed, dress myself in jeans and a white wifebeater, and head downstairs.

"Bernie!" Kara shouts, turning and spotting me from her seat on one of the stools that lines the kitchen peninsula. She hops down and races over to throw her arms around me. Her cousin, Ashley, sticks a bite of pancake in her mouth and watches me warily. We've only met once, maybe twice. And she's younger than Kara by several years. Of course she doesn't remember me.

I return Kara's hug, and then lift my eyes to her brother. He won't look at me, flipping pancakes with one hand and using a spatula on some bacon with the other.

My nostrils flare.

It's like he's angry at me when he's the one that betrayed me, when he pushed me aside and shifted from my most beautiful dream into my worst nightmare. Back in freshman year, I used to fantasize that we'd get married one day, me and Aaron. And then when his dad died and his mom left, I thought maybe we'd raise my sister, his sister, and his cousin together.

What a joke.

I approach the counter and then pause when he plates some food and passes it over to me, finally turning those beautiful eyes to my face. Brown-haired, green-eyed, tattooed Aaron Fadler. My breath catches when he looks at me, but that fairy-tale boy I fantasized about years ago is not the same person looking back at me now.

He's hard, dark, different.

"Breakfast, then I'm taking the girls to a playdate. Vic wants us back at his place after I drop them off."

I nod, but I don't know what to say to this boy. And other than threatening me or trying to get me to run away, I don't think he knows what to say either.

"I missed you, Bernie," Kara says, sitting back down on her stool and smiling up at me with a missing tooth. "Where'd you go?"

I have to think about that question for a long time before I come up with an answer, noticing Aaron's dark gaze swing back to me. Our eyes meet as I stab a piece of pancake with my fork.

My first instinct is to say, *"Aaron didn't want me here anymore, so I went away."* But she won't understand that, and I'm angry with her brother, not with her.

"To tell you the truth, I don't even remember," I say with a smile, turning back to face her. "But don't worry, because this time, I'm here to stay."

If Aaron slams the next pancake down on the plate hard enough to crack it, we all pretend not to notice.

Vic and his boys are sitting in the front yard when we show up, parking next to Hael's muscle car in Aaron's mother's minivan. It looks ridiculous beside the other guys' rides, but it's practical, and it works, and it belonged to his mom, so I know it means a lot to him.

"Everything okay here after we left last night?" Aaron asks as Callum flips his hood back. He nods, so I figure he, at least, must have stayed the night with Vic.

"All fine," Vic says, smoking a cigarette and watching me. I can feel his gaze, this dark, sweet, heat that sweeps over me and makes me want to do bad things. Very bad things. He's clearly studying me and my interactions with Aaron, like he's looking for something in particular. I give him nothing but a dark stare in return, and he grins. "Did you make me a list yet?" he asks, and I nod.

This morning, while Aaron was taking the girls into their playdate—a totally weird thing to see a tattooed teenager doing—I sat in his van and used an old envelope to write down some names.

1. the stepdad
2. the best friend
3. the social worker
4. the ex-boyfriend
5. the principal
6. the foster brother
7. the mom

There are no names there, just titles, because whoever these people used to be to me, they're not people anymore. Just letters on a list.

I hand it over to Vic, and he takes it, reading it carefully before tucking it into his pocket.

"Stepdad spends a lot of time at the morgue, huh?" he asks, which is sort of a creepy, fucked-up question coming from him.

"His name is Neil Pence, and yeah, his best friend works at the morgue, so he's always over there, probably destroying evidence or some shit," I say, feeling my insides twist into a painful knot as my eyes close. That piece of garbage raped my sister, and he never paid for it. She was just an 'accuser', not a victim. Just an attention-hungry little girl who shouldn't have worn that skirt or drank those drinks. My jaw clenches tight, and I have to work hard to control my breathing. "Why?"

Victor lifts his head up to look at me.

"I know why all these names are on here," he says, tilting his head to one side, studying me in that way of his. "Except for this one." He points to the fourth name on the list, and I frown. Hard.

"Is that part of the bargain, what it takes to recruit Havoc? Because as I recall, you don't really care what the reasons behind the request are."

"It's not a part of every bargain," Vic says, rising to his feet and towering over me. Maybe he thinks he's intimidating? He's not. I'm not scared of him. "But it is a part of yours. You're a Havoc Girl now, and we don't keep secrets from each other."

"Why don't we go to this luncheon thing first, and I'll tell you after?" I say, crossing my arms over my chest. I'm not exactly looking forward to either of these events, but honestly, dealing with Victor's psycho mother is the least bad.

I don't want to talk about Don.

Not today anyway.

Victor takes a final drag on his cigarette, chuckles, and then steps past me to put it out in an ashtray on the arm of Hael's chair.

"Come inside and get showered. Ivy will be here in thirty to do your hair and makeup."

"Ivy Hightower?" I ask, wrinkling my nose. That junkie bitch and I used to attend the same free-for-poor-kids summer camp, before we both got kicked out (just after Aaron did, coincidentally). Maybe our blow-out brawl the last day of camp last year was what really did it for both of us? "Why her?"

"Because she works for weed, and she's got a big mouth on her. She'll spread our blessed news all over the school. Hell, all over the city. She gets around, that chick." Vic shakes his head and moves into the house, leaving the door open as he goes.

I wonder if he wants me to shower with him?

My hands curl into fists, and I lick my lips.

"You'll find your clothes waiting for you on the counter," Oscar says, looking up at me through his glasses and smiling—and not very nicely, I might add. His gray eyes sparkle with wicked thoughts behind his glasses, but his voice is calm, almost inflectionless. It must take a lot of effort, to pretend to be so damn disinterested in life. "Underwear included. Vic has very particular tastes."

"Yeah, whatever," I say, moving between Hael and Callum and going inside. Vic is in the bathroom, shirtless, brushing his teeth. He nods his head at the already running shower as I walk in.

"You first," he mumbles, and then goes back to brushing. Frankly, it's hard to find someone terrifying when they've got a mouth full of white, minty foam, but somehow, Victor pulls it off. Wouldn't surprise me if he could pull that toothbrush from his mouth and stab someone with it.

"Fine."

I pause in front of the toilet, and focus on the opaque shower curtain, removing my jacket first, then my top.

Even though I can't see him, I can feel Vic watching me as I strip off my bra, shoes, jeans … and finally, my panties.

It gets hard to swallow, but I pretend like there isn't sweat rolling down my back, like my heart isn't pounding, and I climb into the shower. As soon as the curtain closes, I breathe easy again, washing my body, shampooing my hair, and shaving my legs. Just before I'm about to climb out, Vic gets in with me, completely nude and staring down at me with that dark gaze of his.

My eyes drift down the muscular length of his body and find what they're looking for: the hard, perfect length of his cock. It's big, bigger than I expected, like here's a man who definitely isn't compensating for anything.

I look back up, and he smirks at me.

"I'd fuck you, if we didn't have an appointment," he says, reaching right past me for the shampoo. His wet arm brushes against my shoulder, and I shiver. Victor pauses and withdraws his arm, pushing aside the shower curtain and holding out a hand. "Get out, Bernadette." My gaze flicks down to his inked shaft one more time. "Like what you see?" he purrs, leaning in toward me and putting his forearm on the shower wall above my head.

My eyes lift back up to meet his.

"Aaron said I wouldn't enjoy fucking you," I tell him, and he lifts a single, dark brow, water running down the sides of his face. It's so hot in this bathroom, it's stifling, and it's not just from the steam of the shower.

No, there's a hell of a lot more going on in here than warm water and soap.

"Yeah?" Vic challenges as I struggle to keep my face neutral.

"I think he's wrong," I retort, and then step out of the shower, closing the curtain behind me. Vic's dark chuckle follows me out as I towel-dry and dress in the proffered outfit. After a moment, I hear a very distinct sound coming from behind that curtain.

He's totally jacking-off.

My face heats up, and I snatch the heels off the back of the toilet, opening the door to find Ivy Hightower waiting, Hael standing behind her like an honor guard.

"Bernie," she says, voice saccharine sweet, her dark hair tied up in a high pony, her makeup on point, her brows to die for. I hate the girl, but damn, she has some skills.

"Ivy," I say, stepping out and pointedly closing the door behind me. Not only is the bastard touching himself, knowing that I was listening, but he also got me these awful lacy panties that are going to ride up my ass all day. Maybe that was the point?

There's a chair set up in the dining room area, the table laden with cosmetics. I settle in for the long haul and Ivy gets to work. Not two minutes in, and her obvious fear of Havoc fades away, allowing the gossip to spill from her pretty, painted lips in a wave.

"Billie and Kyler had this big thing at the mall this morning," she starts, going to town cleaning up my brows with this little blue razor. "It was epic. They were screaming, and Billie was throwing things she hadn't even bought yet."

"Fascinating," Oscar murmurs, sighing and excusing himself to the backyard with his iPad in hand. He pauses just before heading out the door and narrows his eyes on Ivy as she picks up a tube of lipstick. "No, not that drugstore garbage. Ophelia will notice. Only quality cosmetics, please. Lord knows you've stolen your fair share of them." He disappears outside as Ivy wrinkles her nose, closing one compartment on her makeup case and opening another.

"As I was saying ..." Ivy continues as I do my best to drown her out, suffering her hands all over my face as she applies my makeup.

Callum manages to endure the girl's presence, sitting on the couch with one foot propped on the arm, his hands wrapped around his bare knee. His legs are crisscrossed with massive scars, the ragged lines shiny and violent, speaking to an unpleasant past. He leans forward, unfolding that lean body of his as he reaches out for his Pepsi.

"Seriously?" he asks, that deep, low voice of his causing both Ivy and me to shiver. "She said that?" It takes me a moment to realize that he's actually engaging in gossip with this idiot. I'd completely tuned her voice out already.

"She did," Ivy gushes, exhaling and making my wet hair flutter around my face. "Like, after you guys kicked the shit out of Kyler last week, she was storming around Prescott talking all this mad crap about how she was gonna leave him." Ivy steps back to examine her work, frowns, and then goes for some boring-as-fuck neutral brown shadow. "Then after their thing at the mall, they met up with her brothers *and* Kyler's brothers. Kali ended up texting to tell me they were talking up a pretty big game about how they could kick some Havoc ass."

Fucking Kali. Just hearing her name pisses me off.

"Is that so?" Callum says, brushing blond hair from his forehead, his blue eyes on mine. He smiles at me, and I frown. It's clear he's doing this on purpose, engaging with Ivy to mine crucial social information about the residents of Prescott High.

"Oh, and it gets better," Ivy says, but then she launches into a completely unrelated story and Cal sits back, flipping his hood up and withdrawing from the conversation again. Neither of us gives a shit about who Stacey Langford is fucking.

A few minutes later, Vic comes out, hair slicked back, dressed like a goddamn yuppie.

My heart pounds hard, and gets lodged in my throat, but I refuse to admit that he cleans up good.

"Khaki shorts, and a short-sleeved button-down? Bro, what the fuck?" Aaron asks, smoking inside with only a small window cracked, acting like he didn't use to dress that way not too long ago.

"We all do what we have to," Victor says, turning to look at me. I'm wearing a white t-shirt with a black suit jacket, three-quarter length sleeves, and a button right in the center. Paired with a khaki skirt, and nude heels, I look like I'm on my way to a board meeting. This new outfit doesn't hide as much of my ink, but it's even less flashy than the white dress I first tried on. "Ivy, you have five minutes."

The girl squeaks and scrambles to her feet, popping a bit of color on my lips before she tackles my hair. She twists it up expertly, hiding the pink tips in a bun, and circling the whole thing with a faux diamond-studded wrap.

"Done," she announces, stepping back and waiting for Vic to examine me. He gives me a once-over, eyes sparkling, and then nods his approval.

"Boys, pay the girl and get her on her way."

Oscar appears as if summoned, like an inked demon in a suit, and leads Ivy Hightower out. Just before he closes the door however, he pauses strategically to look over his shoulder.

"Bernadette Blackbird," Vic begins, kneeling down in front of me. My brows go up as he pulls the velvet box from his pocket, and opens the top, his attention focused solely on my face. "Will you marry me?"

There's this weird disconnect between reality and this moment. My heart thunders, and my palms feel sweaty, even though I know it's all for show, it's all fake.

"Yes," I say, my voice raspy. Aaron turns away like he can't be fucked watching, and I wait as Vic reaches out to take my hand, running his thumb over my knuckles and making me shiver.

Carefully, he slips the ring onto my finger and gives my hand a squeeze, bringing it to his lips for a kiss as Oscar shoos Ivy the rest of the way out the door.

By tomorrow, the whole school will know.
By next weekend, the entire town will know.
Can't wait to see how that turns out.

CHAPTER
FOURTEEN

Oak Park Country Club is full of rich idiots parading around in expensive golf outfits that don't make them look cool—no, instead they just look pretentious and fluffy, like a strong wind could knock them over.

"This place sucks," I whisper as Vic hooks his arm with mine and parades us right up to the front desk. The two bulky security guys working the entrance look at us skeptically.

"We're here as guests of Ophelia Mars," Vic supplies smoothly, and the man at the podium checks his iPad. After a moment, he nods (albeit reluctantly) and gestures for us to go inside.

We're very clearly the only people here with ink, and the stares start within seconds of us entering the building. Without my usual bold cat-eye, racy lipstick, and leather jacket, I feel almost naked, my armor against the bullshit of the world stripped away.

"We stand out like weeds in a daisy patch," I whisper, and Vic smirks.

"They can sense we don't buy into their bullshit. Do you know how scary that is, for people who have no souls? All they have is Prada, Gucci, and BS." Vic pauses, and puts on this smile that's tight enough to form a garrote around my neck. "Mother."

I turn my attention to the right and find a woman dressed not dissimilarly to me, except instead of a skirt, she's got flowing khaki-colored pants on.

Her mouth is like a cut on her face, red and bleeding. Her lipstick is on point, but that angry expression, those dark eyes, she's the yuppie version of Vic.

"Victor," she says, her eyes sliding from him to me. "And who's your friend?" In a split second, I see her scan and dismiss my ink, note the ring on my finger, and decide to hate me for no reason whatsoever.

"Mother, this is my fiancée, Bernadette Blackbird." Vic moves his arm to my waist and pulls me close. "We'll be getting married as soon as we turn eighteen."

"A ploy for you to get your inheritance, no doubt," Ophelia says, nostrils flaring as she turns to me. "I hope you know that you're spreading your legs for a liar. He doesn't love you, and he never will. As soon as he gets the money, he'll dump you on the street and take off to whatever drug den he's currently holed up in."

Vic laughs, the sound much more genuine than his hair or his outfit.

"Oh, Mother," he purrs, turning to look at me. His eyes burn, and I can see he's as interested in fucking me as I am him. "You've got it all wrong." Victor drops his mouth to mine, a burning ember that sears through me, makes me tremble with this desperate, aching need.

It hurts, how much I want it.

It makes me wonder if I'm as much a monster as he is, wanting the man who tortured me for nearly half a year. Once, he and the other Havoc boys set me up, so it would look like I'd screwed Kaydence Mane's boyfriend when all we'd done was study in the library together. She and her friends kicked the shit out of me and left me bleeding on the gym floor.

I must be a masochist.

Or maybe I just hate myself so much, I'll always want what I shouldn't have? My personal poison, delivered in lethal doses by my own hand.

"Please, hold the theatrics," Ophelia says, holding up a hand. "We'll be late to lunch." Vic pauses, pulling away from me just enough that our breath mingles, but there's still room to talk.

"She's jealous."

"Of what? A kiss from her son?" I scoff, and Vic smiles this awful, knowing little smile. "She's a rich, successful heiress. What the hell would she be jealous of?"

"Of passion. She's such a cold bitch, she's never been fucked proper in her life."

"That's a weird thing to say about your mom."

"Yeah, well, what can I say? It's true." He licks my lower lip and flips off some socialites that are gaping at us in the corner. They don't bother me. Honestly, they'd probably give their left nipple to spend a night with someone like Vic.

He backs away from me and takes off down the hall with that confident stride of his, just expecting me to follow. I take a deep breath, shake my hands out, and go after him.

We're having dinner in the Rose Room, this glass atrium situated with views of the sprawling golf course. Inside, there's a huge, round table with an impressive bouquet of flowers in the middle and trays of small, delicate looking appetizers.

"Doubtful anything in this room is edible," Victor murmurs, sauntering in like he owns the place. His presence swallows the whole room.

It's instant, the way he commands that crowd.

"Ladies," Ophelia begins, curling her arm through her son's. She puts on this beautifully executed smile of motherhood and gazes over at him with something that looks like affection. I've been around enough liars in my time to know better. "This is my son, Victor. He considers himself a bit of a rock star." She squeezes his tattooed arm with her fingernails just this side of too hard, but Vic doesn't let on that it bothers him.

The women laugh, and the eyes of some of the younger ones glitter with interest. That is, until they see my ring and their eyes swing up to mine.

"Rock star?" I whisper as Vic turns back to grab my hand. "You can sing?"

"Can't sing for shit, but 'rock star' is the only acceptable term they understand to explain me and my looks."

He pulls me forward and puts his arm around my shoulders.

"And this is my fiancée, Bernadette."

"Fiancée?" a woman with dark hair says, stepping close enough to our little group that her next words are audible only to us. "I didn't know scoundrels like you dated."

"Auntie Cheryl," Vic purrs, flashing a villain's grin. "There are a lot of things about me a crazy old bat like you wouldn't understand." His aunt smiles tightly at him, putting on a show for the rest of the room.

That's when it hits me: what's going on in here is the same as what went on in the street the other day, guns and bloodshed traded out for fake smiles and underhanded insults. It's all a game, a gang war of a different sort.

We take our seats, and polite conversation starts up.

It's pure. fucking. torture.

No wonder Vic was willing to set his gang on my nightmares in exchange for this. What sane woman would subject herself to this hell?

"So, Victor, your mother tells us you're studying overseas, at a boarding school in Paris?"

I almost choke on my bite of watercress sandwich (I had to surreptitiously Google it with my phone hidden under the table before I even knew what it was).

Prescott High, a boarding school in Paris? I'm officially dead. Our piece of shit school is more akin to the catacombs than some fancy academy.

Vic casts me a warning look, and then turns this horrifically blinding smile to the woman in the big white hat. It almost looks like he's gritting his teeth …

"Oh yes, and I'm loving it. It's helping me iron out my hedonistic tendencies."

"Victor," Ophelia snaps, giving her son a warning look not dissimilar to the one he just gave me. "Kids," she says with a laugh, looking back at the women, and they all titter.

The waitstaff appears to take our orders, and I find myself counting the seconds until I can get out of here. Unfortunately, time only seems to slow as conversation turns to me.

"Bernadette, was it? Such a beautiful name," an older woman with gray curls says to me, patting my hand with one of her wrinkled ones. "Tell us, how did you two meet?"

We've known each other since second grade; Vic pushed some kid down a slide for pulling my pigtails. The brat broke his nose when his face met the woodchips.

"We met at an airport," I lie, pulling up some ridiculous fantasy from god only knows where. "I accidentally sat in his seat on the plane." I glance over and see Vic smirking at me. He rubs his hand over his chin in that way he does. The funny thing is, if his mother had been involved in his life whatsoever, she might know that her son and I met over a decade ago. Or maybe even that he tormented me during my sophomore year. Since she doesn't though, I feel free to make up my own story. "It was on a flight from San Francisco to Paris actually, after one of Vic's many visits to his mom." I turn back to the room and smile in the most saccharine, bullshit-filled way that I know, like I'm that bitch Kali Rose-Kennedy. "I had no idea until the flight attendant came to take my breakfast order."

Vic snorts, but several of the ladies smile and nod, like this is actually some sort of believable scenario for them. Actually, I stole it from some crappy rom-com. Since when I have ever sat in first class? Never. Been to Paris? Not once. Been on a plane? Yeah, I never have been.

"That is adorable," one of the women says, putting her hand on Ophelia's. "Your son and his fiancée are so sweet; you must be so happy for them."

"Thrilled," she says, taking a sip of her wine, perfectly shaped brows raised.

An hour and a half later, and I've survived the luncheon on BS and recycled romantic comedy trope nonsense.

"This is pure hell," I say, bumming a cigarette off Vic out back of the country club. We're smoking right next to a *No Smoking On Premises* sign which brings me a small, fucked-up piece of joy. I'm going to make sure to grind my butt out on the head of the founder's statue staring at me from a cluster of shade-loving begonias. "No wonder you figured this a fair price for vengeance. No sane girl would put herself through this."

Victor laughs, that subdued, dark little chuckle that makes my chest feel tight. It's hard to hate someone as much as I hate him, especially when my body's constantly lusting after his.

"Are you kidding me? I could get any girl at Prescott High to do this for me. And I'd only have to pay them in dick."

I wrinkle my nose and glance his way, watching him inhale, little tendrils of smoke escaping his nostrils. He looks like a different person in that outfit, all cleaned-up like one of the yuppie assholes out on the green.

"You're delusional," I murmur, turning away before he catches me studying him. "Everyone in that school hates you and your crew, and you know it."

"They're afraid of me, and that's a whole different sort of animal." Vic flicks his cigarette butt into the fountain, proving he has about as much respect for these rich assholes as I do. "You should know: you're afraid of me, too."

"Like hell I am," I snort, shaking my head and laughing. "I used to be, sure. Not anymore. I've been beaten into a whole different shape." I look up at him and my smile fades away to nothing. "I'm not afraid of anything anymore."

"Can you get your mom to sign off on our marriage?" he asks suddenly, surprising me, his face this dark, impossible mask. "You're still seventeen, right? We'll need her permission."

The color drains from my face at the thought of asking her anything; Vic notices and smirks at me.

"Maybe you're not afraid of me, but you're still afraid of her. Don't worry: we'll get her to sign off." He pushes off the wall, pulls a small bottle of body spray from his pocket, and spritzes both of us. "Let's go say bye to Ophelia."

My mouth tightens, but I follow after him.

I have to, to pay my end of the bargain.

I'll have to do a lot of other things, too. I just haven't been asked to do any of them yet.

Yet.

CHAPTER
FIFTEEN

There seems to be this unspoken thing about me spending the night at Aaron's again. We don't talk much —or at all on Sunday since I just chill in his room and play with my phone—but I know I can't stay here forever. For now, Heather's still staying with a friend. Eventually, I'll have to go home when she does.

Home.

Like that place has ever felt like home ...

On Monday, Aaron wakes me up for school. I help him get the girls together, and he drives us all in the van, dropping them off first, then taking us to Prescott. The sign out front has seen better days. *Prescott Senior High, Home of the Loggers* has been adjusted to have an extra 'F' in front of the school mascot, announcing us as the floggers. Someone's even drawn Ms. Keating with a whip in her hand. Nice touch.

Aaron parks across the street, and we head up the

front walk together, enduring the metal detectors, K9 units, and pat downs before we're released into what's essentially a prison. Bars on the windows? Check. A rigid, airtight schedule? Check. Fellow inmates with grudges and chips on their shoulders? Check, check.

I can see Kali watching me while she pretends to be engrossed in her phone. When she catches me looking, our eyes meet, and she turns away, scurrying down the hall like a rat.

"It's nice to see that your unscrupulous morals allow you to go after a mark that used to be a client," I say when I run into Victor, forcing a tight smile to my lips, my hands curling into fists by my sides. As far as I can tell, Kali sent Havoc after me over a boy, a pageant, and a jealousy so bright it burns.

Pathetic.

"Unscrupulous? No, just business-minded. Kali paid her dues, we delivered her product," Vic replies smoothly, but really he must know I was talking more to Aaron than anyone else. His dark eyes scan the halls, looking for trouble. Nobody meets his gaze; they know better than that. "She's nothing to us." Victor looks right at me, but I can't catch whatever hidden meaning there is in that. *You'll be nothing to us one day, too.* Was that it? "Get to class, and let us know if anyone bugs you."

He takes off down the hall in his boots, holey jeans, and black wifebeater. I'm not sure if I've ever seen a man so confident in himself. It's obvious with each step he takes, the way he slides his palm over his purple-black hair, the way he glances back at me with ebon eyes.

"You can pick your jaw up off the floor," Aaron growls, pushing past me and storming off after his boss as Oscar chuckles and tucks his long fingers into the pockets of his slacks.

"Fancy the boss, do you?" he asks, and I shake my head.

"Not at all."

Lie.

Never in the history of the universe has a lie that great ever crossed the lips of any liar. It was monstrous in its falsehood, the most untrue thing there ever was.

I lick my lips.

"Not at all," I repeat, and then I head straight for my first period English class, the only one of the day I share with Kali. Wish I didn't though. One time she stole my essay, and when I confronted her over it, she lied and spread the rumor that I'd been bullying her. Me. When in reality, it was the other way around. The thieving bitch watches me as I come in and take my usual spot at the back of the room, crossing my boots under the desk.

After a minute, she stands up and makes her way over to me.

"Hey Bernie," she says, tucking green-streaked black hair behind her ear. Ironic, that, isn't it? That her hair is the color of envy ... Kali's dark eyes flick to the door before she returns her attention to me. "Is it true, what everyone's saying?"

"What *is* everyone saying?" I ask, looking up at her. It won't do for her to play dumb here, not after everything she put me through during sophomore year.

Kali called Havoc to make my life a living hell for several reasons, all of them inane, all of them pointless.

One, she came for me over a boy.

Two, she came for me over a stupid pageant.

Three, she came for me because she couldn't handle watching me get the things she felt should've been hers.

So I spent four months afraid to come to school, afraid to stay home. If anything, I can attest to the fact that Havoc is very good at their job. They delivered everything Kali asked for, and more.

And what did she pay them for it?

Even I don't know the answer to that question.

"That you're with Havoc now." She pauses and sniffles. Clearly, she's afraid that I've sicced them on her the way she did me.

I mean, she isn't wrong about that.

My expression is hard when I meet her gaze.

"Not just that you hired them," she continues, and I can tell she isn't the only one in the class that's listening. "But that you're actually *one* of them now, like a member of the gang or something."

I smile as the bell rings, and our teacher—Mr. Darkwood—hustles in at the last second, dumping a stack of books on his desk. He's one of those tragically nice guys who got into teaching to help people. He's always trying to save souls here at Prescott. He's also a literary snob. I kind of hate him.

"Kali, please take your seat," he says, and she frowns hard at me, leaning over to put her palms on the surface of the desk. Our noses are a scant few inches apart, but unlike the last time we faced off, I'm not backing down.

Granted, last time I didn't have much of a choice, now did I? With the full weight of Havoc behind her, Kali was a force to be reckoned with.

"If you send them after me, I'll finish what I started sophomore year," she whispers, and I laugh. I can't help it; the sound just slips past my lips.

"You can sure try," I tell her, lifting a single brow. "But I have a feeling you won't get very far."

Kali slams her palm onto the surface of the desk and sneers.

"Billie and her brothers have teamed up with the Ensbrook boys. They're out for blood after what your pimps did to Kyler the other day. Havoc used to be a powerhouse on campus, but not anymore. Prescott High is a different place today than it was two years ago. Watch your back, Bernadette." Kali shoves back to her feet and moves over to her desk, sitting down just as Mr. Darkwood finishes writing today's itinerary on the board.

I ignore her and focus on my schoolwork about as much as I always do. That is, not at all. Instead, I hold my phone in my hand and debate telling the guys about Kali. If they were willing to beat Kyler to a pulp for looking in a window, what would they do to her?

Eventually, I decide against it and tuck my phone away for the rest of class. We're supposed to be writing poems today, so I put my pencil against the page and let myself bleed across it.

Token friendships between poor girls.

Both of us wanting so desperately for more, our screams drowned out by the wicked silence of the world.

Nobody listens when bad girls cry.

I decide after a good twenty minutes staring at the words in front of me that I hate poetry, that it hurts too much, that I suck at it, and that I'm not writing a damn word more. Mr. Darkwood doesn't stop me when I head into the hall five minutes early and lean against the wall outside my next class.

By lunch, word has already spread about my confrontation with Kali, and I find myself looking up and into the face of a very angry Vic.

"What did she say to you?" he demands, and I know this isn't a request for information. Nah, it's an order.

"She said the Ensbrook boys are teaming up with Billie and her brothers. They're all furious with you, and they're out for blood. She threatened to finish what she started sophomore year."

Vic's jaw tightens, and he rises to his feet, just as Principal Vaughn and a few of his cronies enter the cafeteria and start toward us. Everyone is watching, the whole student body. Not that that's surprising. Vic made me wear my ring to school today; they're all dying to know what's up with that.

"Mr. Channing," Principal Vaughn says to Vic, giving the rest of us a cursory scan. His eyes light on mine, and I glare right back. My only regret in going forward with my deal with Havoc is that my targets might not know why they're being punished or how bad they hurt me with their actions.

My jaw clenches, and I turn away.

"What?" Vic asks, rising to his full height. Even at seventeen and three quarters, he's bigger than Principal Vaughn, made of solid muscle and youthful rage. He could kill the principal with his bare hands, if he wanted to.

"Come with me to my office, please." Vaughn turns like that's that, but Vic doesn't move. Instead, he stays rooted to the spot, mouth turned down in a severe frown.

"What's all this about?" Callum whispers from his end of the table, pushing his hood back and studying the retreating backs of the employees.

"No idea," Vic says, staring after the faculty members before he turns back to us. "Don't care. If I get kicked out of Prescott, it'll just be the inevitable coming to bite me in the ass. Boys, find Kali Rose-Kennedy for me after school. She's been having that rich boyfriend of hers pick her up out front. You'll have to be quick."

"What are you going to do?" I ask, unsure why I care so much about it. This is what I asked for. This is what I'm paying for.

Vic doesn't bother to answer me, and I grit my teeth as he walks off, dismissing my question like it's nothing. Swear to fuck, I'm going to punch him one of these days.

"Don't worry about Kali," Hael says, cracking his knuckles. He's got this shit-eating grin on his face that makes me want to slap him. "We've got it handled. You only have to help if you want to."

"That wasn't what I asked," I start, but then the bell rings again, and the boys rise to their feet. I'm not even sure why they all come to class anymore. They've clearly chosen their path in life, and it's not academics.

"Are you going to help or not?" Aaron asks, looking at me like I'm shit stuck to the bottom of his shoe. I'm not sure what I'm supposed to do after school today, go home with him or head back to my mom's place.

Neither sounds particularly appealing, to be honest.

But either way, I can't leave Heather. Whatever I do, she has to be with me at all times.

"I'll be there," I say, pushing up to my feet and taking my tray with me. Kali is watching us from across the room, like she knows we're discussing her eventual fate. I dump my tray and stack it with the others before I flip her off. As much as she claims not to be afraid of Havoc, she turns away pretty quick and takes off.

If she were smart, she'd run faster. And never look back.

CHAPTER
SIXTEEN

After school, I get a text from Callum that they've cornered Kali on her way back from gym. I run as fast as I can, backpack slapping my shoulder as I jog toward the path that leads to the football field.

That's where the boys are, with Kali held between Callum and Hael. Facing off against them, I find the Charter brothers along with the Ensbrook boys.

Guess Kali was right.

"This is such bullshit," Aaron says, standing at the front of the group, like a vice president while Vic is away. Nobody's seen him since lunch, and it's freaking me out. "What do you care what happens to this bitch?"

Whoa.

Still weirds me out, hearing Aaron talk like a thug.

I pause in the half circle behind Aaron, casting a glance in Oscar's direction. Do these other guys know how fucking crazy Oscar is? I just saw him put a bullet through some random dude's leg. What else is he capable of, I wonder?

Oscar turns his gray eyes over to mine and smiles, an awful sort of smile that promises he's not afraid of violence. He rubs his tattooed fingers over his equally inked-up throat, and I shiver.

"Because we're dating, you piece of shit," Mitch Charter, one of Billie's brothers, says. She's standing not too far behind him, and off to one side, her glare dark and accusatory. Guess she's pissed that we beat the snot out of her new beau.

"Are you also aware that she's dating a boy from Oak Valley Prep?" Oscar interjects, but nobody responds to his accusation.

"Kali knows better than to fuck with Havoc," Aaron says, and then he nods in Hael and Callum's direction. "Besides, we're going to give her a choice here." Aaron turns back around, his face dark and cold and empty. He's had to learn to be that way, to protect his family. The world isn't fair. How fucked is it that such a sweet boy could be turned into this, just for the simple act of keeping those he loves safe? He leans down and looks into Kali's face. "Choice one, we post your porn all over the web, and we send links to your parents, your colleges of choice, and that modeling agency that asked you to do a catalog shoot." He stands back up and frowns. "Or we break your hands. It'll hurt, but the physical pain might be easier to stomach than the emotional."

"If you touch a hair on her head, we will end you, Fadler." Kyler's brother, Danny, takes a step forward, nostrils flared. He's a big guy, too, wider than any of the Havoc Boys, with tree trunks for arms. And he looks pissed.

Heart racing, I run my tongue over my lip and take a second to figure the odds. Five of them, five of us. Not sure if the guys realized it or not after my little tussle with Oscar, but I'm not a throwaway, a tagalong for their little group to fuck and push aside. No, I know how to kick some serious ass, too.

"I can take Kyler," I start, because I think pairing each of us with an opponent of comparable size would be best. Oscar gives me a look and then pushes his glasses up his nose with his middle finger, a signature move of his.

"Does Billie not count?" he asks, and I shrug.

"I beat the crap out of her last year without breaking a sweat; she doesn't even factor into this."

"You go straight to hell, you fucking whore," Billie growls, tossing her teal and black hair over her shoulder. "We all knew you'd be spreading your legs for the Havoc crew sooner or later. But getting them to fight your battles for you in exchange for free pussy? Now *that's* pathetic."

There's a moment there where I don't think. I've trained myself not to. Instead, I just react. I go for Billie without thinking, that pesky fight or fight harder response kicking in. *I'm going to beat her flat face into the fucking pavement,* I tell myself, jerking to a stop as a hard, warm arm wraps my waist and knocks the air out of me.

"No fighting on school grounds," Vic murmurs around a cigarette. It hangs loosely from his full lips, unlit and flopping around as he talks. "We hang our dirty laundry elsewhere." He nods his chin in Hael and Callum's direction. "Let the bitch go."

"Seriously?" Hael snaps, his cheeks coloring with frustration. "This cocksucking idiot had the audacity to threaten our girl, and you're going to let her walk?"

I might be aching for violence, growling low in my throat, but I don't miss the words he says. *Our girl.* It's surreal as hell, but I should've known that the Havoc Boys don't play around. As soon as I said yes, it was on. It's all on.

"Get lost, Kali," Vic says as Hael snarls colorful curses under his breath, obeying his boss whether he likes it or not. "And the rest of you, fuck off."

"Screw you, Channing," Mitch snaps as Kali throws herself into his arms, ever the whimpering, simpering little victim. I should never have trusted her, spilled my dark secrets to her during our sleepovers. All she ever did was turn my own words against me, from my stolen essay to my nightmare with Havoc. Kali Rose-Kennedy is a backstabber, and a nightmare, and I swear if the guys don't take action soon, I will. "Touch my girl again, and we'll find out who's really in charge here."

Vic smiles.

It's not a pretty smile, the way he does it, this ironic, bemused twist of lips.

"Counting on it," he says, and then he scoops me into his arms and takes my breath away.

"Where have you been?" I ask, but his eyes darken, and his face goes cold.

"Later," he murmurs, and then he carries me down the hall for the whole school to see, the engagement ring on my finger sparkling in the sunlight.

It's disgusting, how much I enjoy that.

CHAPTER
SEVENTEEN

On Friday when Victor invites me back to his place, I take my backpack, but I leave my sleeping bag. As usual, when I get there, he's sitting outside in a lawn chair, a cigarette in one hand, watching the sunset.

"Where is everybody else?" I ask, tossing my bag to the ground as I pause near him. He turns those dark eyes over to me, clearly pissed about something.

"Not here yet." Vic ashes his cig out on the metal ashtray and then reaches for my wrist, yanking me onto his lap. A small sound escapes me as I stumble into him, and fire burns through me in a fierce wave, promising that it'll feel oh-so-warm before it hurts, before it burns so bad that I go numb and never feel again.

He stares ahead, at the overgrown foliage that creates a sort of natural fence around his front yard, and glowers. All week, he's been touchy as hell and pissed off about whatever happened on Monday. But when Victor Channing says *later*, apparently he gets to decide when and where he tells us all what happened in Principal Vaughn's office.

"Do you always get together for sleepovers on Fridays?" I ask, and he shrugs, the muscles in his big shoulders moving like well-oiled pistons, taut and ready to fight at the drop of a hat. I recognize that alertness in him, that readiness, even when he's at rest, because I have it, too. Deep down inside of me, a jungle cat paces, waiting to unleash her claws, her fangs, knowing that she has to because it's a wild, wild world out there. One wrong step, one wrong move, and everything comes crashing down.

"Been doing it for years. Keeps us focused. We get most of our work done on the weekends anyway." Victor turns to look at me, the wind ruffling his dark hair and making my heart do strange things inside my chest. "Where's your sister?"

I feel my throat get tight. We haven't talked much about Heather or what she means to me, or what I have to do to keep her safe. But somehow, it feels like Victor already knows. Reaching up, I trace a finger along the hard edge of his stubbled jaw, just to see if he'll let me. I've never actually seen him with a girl, but clearly, he has them. Loads of them, probably. Something dark slithers around inside of me, and I clamp down on the emotion before it can rear its ugly head.

"At a friend's house. But to be honest with you, she's

starting to run out of friends and favors." A dry laugh escapes me as I slide my palm down my face. Tired. So damn tired. That's the story of my life. I feel like I haven't had a proper night's sleep in years. Those two nights at Aaron's were like a dream, an almost painful reminder that I don't often get much rest, not even when I fall into one of my light, fitful little spells of sleep. "And my mom, Pamela, she doesn't like us being gone so much. Eventually, she's going to snap."

Victor chuckles, but it's a dry, dark laugh. Humorless. He lights up another cigarette and holds it between his fingers. Today, some bitch yelled at him for smoking out front of the school. He flashed white teeth at her, told her to shove her anti-smoking propaganda bullshit down her throat, and then flicked the still burning ember of his cig into the backseat of her fancy gas-guzzling SUV, singeing the leather.

She gaped at him, knocking over her diet soda in an attempt to save her precious upholstery.

"The aspartame sweetener in that drink is a known carcinogen. Hell, it'll probably kill you before my cigarettes do me, but you don't see me shoving that shit down your throat. Get fucked and have a nice day."

Clearly, he's in a mood.

I almost … *like it.*

"Let be me real honest with you right now, Bern," he says, making my name into something foreign, hot to the touch. I shiver. "I'm not afraid of *Pamela Pence*." Vic scoffs her name like the sound's dirtied his tongue, dulled some of that hot ember to ash. "She can snap if she wants, I don't give a good goddamn."

"It's not her I'm afraid of," I say. *Lie.* Some dark, little part of me will always be afraid of my mother, will always be that little girl crying because mama's manicured nails dig too deep, pinch too hard. *Go sit on Daddy's lap,* she'd command as I pulled away with what little strength I had. *He's not my daddy,* I'd scream back, and then I'd be forced there anyway, onto the lap of a pervert whose touch lingered too long, whose smile cut too deep ... I choke a little, and Vic notices.

He notices goddamn everything.

"The cop," he says, his voice hollow.

I nod.

We don't talk for a while, and I find myself glancing over his shoulder in the direction of the house, searching for any sign of his father. That guy gives me the serious fucking creeps. Why Vic stays here is beyond me.

I decide to ask.

There are no secrets in Havoc right?

Bunch of bullshit, surely, but if they're willing to play the façade in my favor, I'll take it.

"Why are you still living here?" I ask, and when Vic's gaze passes up to mine, it's like watching the moon eclipse the sun, cutting off all the light but somehow making it more beautiful in the process. "You could have your own place. Shit, you could live with Aaron if you wanted. Really, anywhere away from your father would be an improvement."

"It's all part of the deal," he says, reaching out to

take my hand, fingering that ring on my finger for the first time. He looks at for a while, really looks at it, until I can't take the tautness in the air between us and snatch my hand back. "In order for me to get my inheritance, I have to live with my father until I graduate." His face darkens, storm clouds sliding across an expression that's already too dark, too mysterious, too steeped in shadow. "Get married. Stay married for one year."

That's the part that really surprises me.

I have to resist the urge to hit him.

My teeth grit in frustration.

"You never told me we had to stay married for a year."

Victor's eyes darken and narrow, and he slides that tormenting gaze my direction. Just trying to maintain eye contact with the man exhausts me. He's both a complex storm of emotions, and the complete and utter void of a blue, cloudless sky, all at once. Difficult to read, impossible to predict.

"We'll stay married for *life* if that's what it takes," he snaps out, losing that practiced cool for just a fraction of a section. With a deep inhale, and an emptying exhale, I feel his taut muscles loosen beneath me, the anger in him draining out with a single breath. I can't even imagine, having that sort of control. My heart flutters, and my fingers curl reflexively. I might be sitting on his lap, but Victor Channing and I are both stupidly similar and worlds apart.

Conundrums. Hypocrisies.

That's us.

"Did you think this deal had an expiration date?" he asks finally, and I frown.

"I'm not big on thinking ahead at all," I admit. It's true. My life has never been the sort where I could stop and smell the roses, wonder what might happen tomorrow, or what *could* happen in the future because I'm always worried about now, surviving this exact second and hoping in the darkest recesses of my heart that there might actually be another. Of course, I don't say any of that out loud.

Vic just stares at me for a moment and then runs his huge hand over his face.

"What?" I ask, because all of his non-verbal communication says he's not very happy with me. The way his hand drops from my waist, the way his fingers curl around the end of the chair arm. "You asked me to be Havoc's ... *girl*." I choke on the word a little and feel my body start to shake with that old, familiar anger. "Did you expect me to be happy to be here? Was that part of the deal, too? Because if it was, I didn't hear it."

His face tightens up, but he manages to maintain that ironclad control.

"You're lashing out with anger in an unfamiliar situation, I get it. Been there, done that. Learn to leash it up and set it loose when *you* decide, and you'll find it much more satisfying to control the rage instead of letting it control you."

"What are you, a fucking shrink or something?" I snap, grabbing up the pack of cigarettes and removing one with shaking fingers. Vic holds up a lighter as I slip it between my lips, igniting the tip.

"We didn't ask you to be Havoc's girl, we used to be *a* Havoc Girl. Big difference, Bernadette." Vic pushes me off his lap without warning, and even though he doesn't push hard, I end up stumbling, sprawling into the grass and losing my cigarette in the process. He leans down to look at me, like some sort of king perched up on a throne, and I find myself scowling. "Blood in, blood out."

"You keep saying that!" I shout back, pushing to my feet and wondering if I could take him on, too, beat his ass like I did Oscar, wrap my hands around his throat. It'd probably feel good, wouldn't it? To take revenge on him the way I'm asking him to do to everyone else in my life who fucked up along the way. "I should've added your name to your own list, sicced you on yourself."

He laughs at me then, and I find that I really am a slave to my anger. When Vic stands up, I throw myself forward without thinking, slamming into him. He doesn't budge. It's like ramming my shoulder into a brick wall.

A hot, muscular, *scary* sort of brick wall.

Victor grabs me by the arms and pushes me back, slamming me into the trunk of the tree the way he did his father last week. He doesn't hurt me the way I know he could, but the force is enough to knock the air from my lungs.

So now I'm panting, shaking, standing there and looking into eyes so black they may as well be endless pools to drown myself in.

"Keep a hold of that anger and use it elsewhere. We'll find you an outlet." Victor doesn't release me, his fingers tightening ever so slightly, his ripe mouth turned down in a frown. "When we asked you to be a Havoc Girl, Bernadette, it meant you became one of us. There is no expiration date on this deal."

"And if I try to leave someday?" I hear myself ask, not quite believing there ever *will* be a someday. No matter what Vic says, I feel like my life *does* have an expiration date. I might not like it, but that's just the way this harsh, ugly world works.

"Bernadette, don't try me," Victor says, and then he releases me, stalking over to pick up my still burning cigarette from the dry grass. He swipes out some stray embers with his boot and tucks the smoke between his lips. "How long have you been standing there?" he asks, and I lift my head to find all four remaining Havoc Boys standing near the driveway.

"Long enough," Oscar says, gray eyes sliding over to mine briefly. The way he smiles, that expression could very well haunt my nightmares. Instead, I turn my now burning face down to look at the ring on my finger. I've been taking it off at home because if Mom sees it, she'll have a total meltdown. She never did like the idea of me having a boyfriend. And she *really* wouldn't like the idea of me having a piece of jewelry that's nicer that hers.

I squint at the ring as Hael's irritating, cocky laughter rings out.

"If throwing a girl against a tree is your version of foreplay, no wonder Bernadette isn't interested in you," he says as a shadow passes over me, and I lift my face to find Vic staring at me again.

"It's real," he tells me, reaching out to take my hand and study it for a moment. "All of it." His fingers burn where they touch me, searing straight into my soul. Our eyes meet, and I find it ridiculously hard to breathe. "Worth about … thirty grand, if I remember correctly." My eyes widen, but I don't say anything as he withdraws his hand and turns to face the others.

"We've got a problem," he announces as Aaron glowers and Callum tucks himself into a chair, knees up, dumping an entire bag of snacks on the ground in front of him. He picks up a bag of chips and goes to town, eyes flashing from inside that hood of his. He gives me a wink and a smile, which I ignore. My brain is running on overdrive right now. *Vic has a thirty-thousand-dollar ring that he's never sold?* I stare at it again, and I can't quite make myself believe that there's some sentimental attachment to the damn thing. I mean, he did say it was his grandmother's, but I have a hard time believing that someone like Victor Channing gives a crap about his dead granny.

So what then?

Does he realize that I could run down to any pawn shop in town, sell the stupid thing, and take off with my little sister in tow? Sure, thirty grand wouldn't last forever, but it'd last long enough for me to get us away from here, buy a cheap car and start driving.

We could make a new life in another state, start her at a new school, and the Thing would never find us. Sure, his family has resources, but how hard would they *really* look?

"Yeah, and what's the problem?" Hael asks, slumping into a broken lounger and making its rusted frame creak with his muscular weight. He's every girl's bad boy wet dream, with his mischievous brown eyes, bloodred hair, and tattoos. He's even got the face of a demon on his chest with the words *Hot Rod* on either side. In short, he's the bad boy equivalent of a jock-y douche. And yet … I can almost see the appeal.

"Vaughn pulled me into his office on Monday," Vic begins, and my ears perk up. We all know that part of the story, of course, but the *why* has been saved until later. Until now. I move over next to Callum's chair as he lifts up another snack bag.

"Lap?" he inquires, and then flashes that stupid Disney-prince-hiding-a-villain-grin. "Peanuts?" I narrow my eyes, but I'm not afraid of Callum; I'm not afraid of any of these assholes. I sit down hard on his lap and snatch the food, noticing Vic's eyes skimming over the pair of us. His jaw tightens as he turns away.

Aaron sits in the chair farthest away from me, his gaze on the garage door and most definitely *not* on Vic. Or me. Definitely not on me.

"He said he'd gotten a call from my mother, about the drugs I was hiding in my locker."

"You hide drugs in your locker?" I blurt, and Vic gives me a long, studying sort of look.

In retrospect, it was a stupid question. Of course he doesn't. Only an idiot would hide their drugs in a Prescott High locker, what with the random searches, police presence, and sniffer dogs. And no matter what else they might be, the Havoc Boys are not stupid.

"That was why Ron Cartwright was hovering in the hall then?" Hael guesses, and then he brays another of his stupid laughs. "What a dumb shit. He didn't think we'd notice? Cal and I will pay him a visit next week."

I don't even have to wonder what *pay him a visit* means. Ron Cartwright is going to get his balls shoved up his own ass. Vic nods, acknowledging Hael's words, and then continues.

"I planted the shit back in his locker, and then sent the admins on a wild goose chase." Vic rubs at his chin, a sign that he's thinking. His dark purple tee is stained with sweat on the lower back, even though it's not particularly hot out. That's when I realize that the armpits of my own shirt are wet, and I'm still shaking. What is it that's going on between us?

"You double-double crossed him," I say, and they all turn to look at me like they're surprised to hear me speak. Guess they're not quite used to it, a woman in their midst. Maybe I'm not the only one who's shocked to realize that it's been several weeks of this shit, and I haven't ended up in anyone's bed. Isn't that why I'm here? "Brilliant. So now what? Your mom's trying to sabotage you?"

"She's tried before," he offers, not like it's much of a surprise. But then his dark eyes find mine, and a slight smile—a *very* slight smile—edges his lips. "But I think seeing you frightened her. This is getting real; she might not actually end up with my grandmother's money after all."

"How much is the inheritance anyway?" I ask, not even bothering for nonchalance. I'm interested, especially since Vic mentioned we'd all get a cut. I don't believe it for half a second, but oh well. The fantasy is nice enough.

"Not enough to change the world, but enough to set us up for life." Victor snaps his fingers in Oscar's direction. "Find out where my mother's staying currently."

"What are we going to do?" Aaron asks, speaking up for the first time. I've noticed that Vic relies on the other three more than him, even though it's pretty damn obvious that Aaron is not only desperate for Victor's approval, but also that he hates him.

"I don't know," Vic says, pausing as a car comes crawling down the street. It's hard to see who's in it with the thick wall of foliage, but I notice that Oscar isn't the only one that casually slips a gun from an unseen place on his body. Cal has one, too.

The leader of the Havoc Boys turns to me.

His eyes burn.

As dark as they are, I shouldn't be able to see fire in the shadows. And yet I do.

My teeth clench.

"You know how to multi-task, Bernadette?" he asks me, and I nod, feeling my lips dip into a frown. Multi-task? How about trying to finish homework, shower, and sleep while making sure your little sister doesn't get raped by the man who fucked your older sister into an early grave? How about hating school so much you have tears rolling down your face at the thought of stepping into the hallway, but knowing you have to go because a degree might be your only escape? The bullying, the homework, the shitty home life. Oh, yeah, I know how to multi-task like the best of them.

"Why?"

"We're used to fighting wars on multiple fronts," Vic says, almost absently, his mind already moving onto the next subject. He looks me square in the face. "So, tell me about the fourth name on your list."

My jaw clenches, and I look away.

Vic knows every person on that list because he's been around for so long, because the Havoc Boys have always been invading my life, one way or another. But he doesn't know about Donald Asher.

Nobody but me does.

I glance away, my eyes scanning the wall of foliage near the front of the property and wondering who the hell was in that car. One of the older men from the other night, one of the Ensbrook or Charter brothers, or someone else entirely?

Is that what Vic meant, fighting wars on multiple fronts?

And now, with my list, they'll be starting yet another one.

My eyes flick to the other four boys, wondering how

thin I'm stretching them with my request. They don't seem bothered, and I know they have other accomplices who aren't quite so ... public about their affiliation with Havoc, but still, I wonder.

As I turn my attention back up to Vic's darkened gaze, I can see that he isn't playing around. What he said wasn't a suggestion, it was a command.

"You'll do what I say when I say it."

But in this moment, I can't imagine it, sitting here on the lawn with five men who are worse than strangers. Five men who were the little boys I'd gone to school with, watched from afar, worshipped. And then I'd finally, finally gotten one to myself in the form of Aaron. The perfect boyfriend, the perfect lover ... turned tattooed asshole because life wasn't fair. And I'm supposed to just blurt my secrets out in the open?

"Later," I say, mimicking Vic's reaction from the other day. His eyes narrow slightly, and I can tell I'm seriously getting under his skin.

"No," he says, and my brows go up. Oh really? We're going to test the strength of the leash already? My lips flatten into a line as he stares at me, a brooding thundercloud gathered behind dark irises. On the outside, though, everything is calm, still. "Now."

I rise to my feet and turn, heading for the house and intending to slip into the bathroom for a moment. What happened with Donald ... the thought makes me sick, stirs up a dozen worse memories, two dozen. A lifetime of regret.

I barely register what I'm doing until I've passed the

bathroom and found myself halfway up a small staircase, my palm skimming the rough-worn banister. A few steps later and I'm on the second floor, standing outside a small bedroom.

Vic's room.

My hand tightens on the newel post as his smell wafts over me—that musky mix of tobacco and amber—and the back of my neck prickles with the awareness of someone coming up behind me.

"Get in," he says, and I hear the steps creak as he continues up them, forcing me to move out of the narrow foyer or end up brushing against him.

Besides, my subconscious must've sent me up here for a reason, right?

I step into Victor's room and shiver when the door slams shut behind me. There's a single bed in here, twin-sized, and a desk, a few random rock posters on the wall, and a locked closet.

The one I spent an entire week in.

My breath catches, and I take a step back, accidentally bumping into the man who put me there in that dark square of hell. His warm, hot hands land on my shoulders, and I jump.

"The fourth person on the list ..."

"Donald Asher," I say, letting the name fall fast and hard from my tongue.

Moving forward, I feel one of my Havoc nightmares all over again, the boys' firm grips on my arms and shoulders, the bruises coloring my skin as they dragged me across these very same floors and shoved me in the closet. How loudly I screamed, my nails tearing as I clawed at the door …

I wasn't sure I was ever getting out.

"Don't do that," Vic says on the end of a long sigh, but I'm already moving, grabbing the handle of the door and yanking it open. Inside, there's nothing but a stack of empty shoe boxes and a few hanging shirts.

None of the pain I remember is there, hanging in the air like a poison cloud. None of the fear. I feel like the universe is spitting in my face, leaving such an empty, innocuous spot where I suffered so damn much.

Slowly, carefully, I close the door.

I'm stronger now, but part of being strong means recognizing when you've got a trigger and deciding if facing off against that trigger will truly bring you any peace.

Right now, I don't need the stress.

I turn around and put my back against the door.

"Don is a prep school student," I say, and Vic's eyes narrow, his mouth tightening. He crosses his arms over his chest and watches me with that unyielding expression of his.

I stare right back.

Silence follows, leaving this dark, empty space between us, this gaping void that feels impossible to cross. I'm trapped here, in this impersonal little room forever.

"Get on your knees, Bernadette," Vic says, his voice cold. He reaches down with one hand and flicks the button on his jeans. My own eyes widen, and I feel my pulse begin to race. It's not like I haven't sucked a dick before, but ... "Well?" he continues when I most definitely don't rush to do what he's asked.

My jaw clenches, and I feel that familiar anger rush over me, that need to defy, to fight, to win.

"He goes to Oak Valley Prep. I still know how to find his dorm room. Not an easy task, considering the fact that he roofied me at the restaurant before we got there."

The expression on Victor's face doesn't change.

"Bernadette," he continues, sliding his zipper down. My eyes flick away before he can free himself, and I realize that I'm sweating. "You can't do it, can you?"

I pause and look back, only to find out that Victor's fixed his pants again. His face is a dark shadow, passing over the sun, cutting off all the light. He's terrifying.

"I—" I start, but I'm not about to back down. I knew what I was agreeing to when I made this deal.

"You made a pact with us, and you can't keep your end of the bargain, can you?" Victor's nostrils flare, and he closes his eyes for a brief moment. When he opens them, there's fire burning in his gaze.

"I can keep it," I say, breathing hard and fast. "I've always wanted to fuck you anyway, just to see what it'd be like. It's hardly a punishment."

Tossing white-blond hair tinged with pink over one shoulder, I strut forward confidently and cup the bulge in Vic's jeans. Or ... there should be a bulge, right? Only he's not hard, not at all.

He's testing me, just like with the ring ... My finger passes over the engagement ring without meaning to, and I realize with a sudden burst of clarity that Victor told me about the ring's value to see if I'd do exactly what I thought about doing: sell it and run.

But I'm not going anywhere.

"I want this," I say, looking him in the eyes. He stares right back, and the edge of his mouth twists up in a cruel sort of smirk. Not like Hael's smirks though, something different, something darker, some hidden emotion that plays at amusement, but in reality is on the opposite end of the spectrum.

"Then fucking prove it," Victor says, grabbing my wrist and forcing my hand back. "When I ask you a question, *answer it.*" The threat in his voice is clear, and I find myself shivering, even as his touch on my wrist burns. "Donald Asher, spoiled Oak Valley Prep brat. He roofied you?" I nod, but with Vic touching me, it feels so much harder to admit the truth. I should've just spilled it outside, when all the boys were present. "He raped you?"

"He tried," I say, choking back memories. Rape. It's a miracle I've never actually been raped, but the attempts have been so frequent, so numerous ... I haven't felt safe since I hit puberty, since before. Sometimes I just get so damn tired. "He even invited his friends to join in. I saw his phone just before and locked myself in the downstairs bathroom."

This trailer trash bitch thinks she's too good to put out! Anybody want a taste of a southside whore? Come up to my room and we'll take turns. No condoms required! I'll leave the door unlocked.

A trail of laughing emoji faces followed that group text, sent out to a dozen of Don's closest friends. My hands start to shake, and I think suddenly about Penelope, about her journal, how she felt when Neil was on top of her, and how I couldn't save her, how I could only save myself ...

Closing my eyes, I pull what little self-control I have left around my shoulders, and then open them again to find the leader of the Havoc Boys staring at me with an unreadable gaze.

There's a long pause here where I try to figure out how to keep explaining things to Vic.

Instead, he pushes my wrist aside, turns, and opens the door.

"Out," he says, gesturing with his chin. I slip past him, and he slams the door in my face.

Dark memories crash through me like waves as I stumble down the stairs and shove my shoulder into the bathroom door, locking it and then curling up in the tub to catch my breath. A short time later, I hear the lock click open, and the shower curtain is pulled back. When I look up, I find Callum staring down at me with pale blue eyes and a sad, sad smile.

He puts a bag of snacks and drinks down on the floor outside the tub, tosses me a pillow and blanket, and then crouches down, resting his elbows on his scarred knees.

"Don't worry," he tells me, his dark, rough voice soothing away some of my anxiety, "we'll get him." His smile gets a little sharper, a little scarier. "And he'll wish he'd never been born."

CHAPTER
EIGHTEEN

The following Friday, I find myself at the drive-in near the train tracks, the one that quite literally sits on the wrong side. It's the polar opposite of the one across the street: rundown, cheap, but with stellar food. The other is fancy, upscale, and everything tastes like plastic. There's an ongoing rivalry between the two places, drive-bys and car bombings, wars between the kids from Prescott High and the dickheads from Fuller High.

But at least in my life, things have been peaceful lately—thanks to Havoc, I'm sure.

"Hope you brought some black clothes," Vic teases, tossing me a burger. He sends it my way and leans back on the table, like some model from the fifties, a greaser with a leather jacket and a nice ride, but no real prospects other than a pretty face.

"Are you kidding? All I ever wear is black." I use the bench of the old picnic table to climb up to the top, sitting down between Vic and Aaron, and unwrapping my burger. "Why? Planning on breaking and entering?"

"Here's the thing," Vic says, turning to look my way with dark eyes and a shadowed face. "We have a plan. The question is: do you want in on it?" He pauses, and I look around at the other four boys. All of them are watching me, waiting for an answer that seems inconsequential, but which I'm guessing is either going to win or lose me points in whatever substandard ranking system they've got going on.

Across the street, an orange Mustang pulls into the parking lot and four Fuller High douchebags climb out, dressed in letterman jackets and cheerleading uniforms. Vic flips them off, and their leader returns the favor. Ours smirks, and I just know he's probably daydreaming about all the ways he could hurt them if he wanted to.

"We should kick their asses," Hael mumbles, but Vic, whose gaze is far away and impossible to read, just gives an enigmatic little smirk and shakes his head.

"It's not worth the effort today," he says, and then turns back to me. Waiting. Watching. He's calm now, but I feel like Victor Channing is a cannon, packed tight and ready to explode. All he needs is someone to light his fuse. I imagine, however, that it's a long one. You don't find yourself in control of the most notorious gang to hit Prescott High in years without a long fuse. It's not a job for someone who's liable to fly off the handle.

"Yeah, I'm in," I say, and Aaron's shoulders get tight as he glances our way, mouth set into a deep frown. If he keeps scowling like that, the expression is liable to carve itself into his face.

"Maybe you should actually tell her what she's in for before she accepts, eh Vic?"

But the fearless leader of Havoc simply lights up a cigarette and watches me as I eat, tearing into the burger and swiping a single finger over the front of my leather jacket to clear off a drop of mayo. Some girls I know won't eat in front of guys, like what do they expect the boys to believe? That they never consume more than a light salad? That they don't take shits? I've never been that type of girl.

"We're going to that fancy prep school tonight to find Number Four," Vic tells me as Hael sucks down his milkshake, and Oscar and Callum watch quietly from the next table over. Victor's dark eyes find mine and hold me captive, a prisoner to his gaze. I don't like it, not at all. "If this were regular Havoc business, I wouldn't give you a choice, but this is different. This is the task you set us on, so if you don't want to be around when we take care of it …"

My throat gets tight, and I exhale sharply. There are parts of that list, things that happened, that I can't and won't relive, but what Don did to me, I can handle seeing him pay for that. In fact, I'll probably enjoy it.

"What's the plan?" I ask, and Oscar rises to his feet, handing over the iPad and letting me glance at the image on the screen. It's a picture from the Oak Valley Prep brochure, the one that shows all the dorms. There's a red X drawn on one of them.

"Is this where he sleeps?" Oscar asks, and I nod my head. How could I ever forget? That night is burned into my brain, a red-hot brand of pain that I'm afraid I'll never be able to extricate myself from. See, that's the thing with pain. Once it finds you and grabs hold, it doesn't let go easily. It's always there, a demon with reaching claws.

That's one of the reasons why I stayed, even if I didn't have Heather to care for, why I pushed aside the invitation from my grandmother to go and live with her. How can someone as tainted and filthy as me ever live a normal life? The stink of my memories would be forever present, tainting everything I touched.

It's better this way.

Even if this is all there is for me, at least I'll know that the ones who put me here, they paid. At least I'll know I didn't wait around for karma to take her pound of flesh: the blood and bone of vengeance, it belongs to me.

"They don't have roommates over at that fancy school of theirs," I say dryly, remembering again the text I saw when I picked up Don's phone. *I'll leave the door unlocked.*

A shiver takes over me, and my throat gets tight. Vic frowns heavily and turns to Hael, nodding his chin.

"Get the stuff and meet us at the school at dusk."

Hael nods and Vic rises to his feet, watching as I finish off the last of my burger and lick my fingers clean.

"Come with me," he says.

It's not a request.

With a sigh, I swipe my hands down the front of my

jeans and follow Vic over to his ride.

I have no idea where he's taking me, but if it isn't to collect on his end of the bargain, I'll be shocked.

I'm starting to feel like my payment is past due.

We take all these crazy back roads over to the abandoned jailhouse on Campground Road. It's like way, way out there, and a part of me feels a jolt of fear when we pull into the empty parking lot, dotted with crows and bits of broken cement.

If Vic wanted to kill me out here, he could. Nobody gives a shit about me, so he'd probably get away with it, too. What does it say about me that I'm not sure I care?

He climbs off the bike and stalks across the lot and up the front steps, not bothering to see if I'll follow. He knows I will. With a sigh, I move along after him, my leather jacket just barely enough to ward off the winter chill. Fall is on the way out, winter is incoming, each day one step closer to my eighteenth birthday, to graduation, to a freedom that seems falsified. When I turn eighteen, I'm not suddenly going to have job prospects, and an apartment, and a future to look forward to. I have to make those things happen.

And if I don't neutralize the Thing before my birthday, he could kick me out of the house. He could separate me from Heather. He could hurt her like he did Penelope. And there's not a damn thing I could do about it.

There's a padlock and a heavy chain on the front

door, but it's been snipped, probably by the Havoc Boys. Vic simply waltzes past it and inside.

"Come on," he says, pausing with one boot on the bottom step of the interior staircase before he turns away and starts up it. The steps are covered in leaf litter, but there's at least a skylight above them that gives a little light. The rest of the place is bathed in shadow.

"Gotta be ghosts in here," I murmur, following after him and taking the steps two at a time. Five stories later, I'm panting and sweating while Vic leans casually against an open door and watches me with that dark gaze of his.

He steps outside, and I follow, finding myself on the roof. The sun is setting in the distance, bathing the hills in gold light. Vic moves to the edge and stares out at the tree line, and the sinking ball of sunshine.

"What are we doing here?" I ask, but I think I already know.

He wants to fuck me here, I bet.

"Don't look so resigned," Victor tells me, lighting up a cigarette. "I just like to come here to think. You look like you need a moment." He passes the smoke to me without taking a drag, and I accept it, holding it between two red-nailed fingers. "What ever possessed you to date Donald Asher?" he asks me, and I cringe at the directness of the question. "He doesn't exactly seem like your type."

"He's rich, a ticket out of South Prescott. What is there to figure out?" I ask, and Vic gives me this look that says that even though we're just getting started here, he's done with my bullshit.

"Don't play me like that. You play everyone else in your life. And what do you have to lose with me?" Victor laughs, the sound bitter and broken. "Fucking nothing," he murmurs, watching the sunset.

I turn to follow his gaze as he lights up another cigarette, and we sit there smoking together for a while. All the anti-smoking ads in the world can't change my life or take away the pain. So what if I want to have one, little pleasure in my life? I don't stop anyone else from eating hamburgers that clog their arteries or driving gas-guzzling SUVs that poison the air as much or more than my smokes, so they can all get fucked. Cancer doesn't seem like such a big deal when you don't know if you'll even make it through your twenties.

"You brought me here to think?" I ask, and Victor laughs again, shaking his head like I'm just too much. He rakes his fingers through that purple-dark hair and turns to look at me, his gaze so open and direct that I'm not sure how long I can put up with it. This man, he's buried in secrets, and yet he looks at me like he's an open book. What am I supposed to make of that?

"What else? You think I brought you here to fuck?"

"You read my mind," I quip back, lifting my cigarette in salute.

The look he gives me is pure hell.

"You think if I wanted to fuck you sooner, I couldn't do it?" he asks me, and I stiffen up as he moves closer, tracing the edge of my leather jacket with a finger. "You belong to us now, Bernadette. You're a Havoc girl.

There's no reason for me to drive forty minutes out of the way to have you."

My jaw clenches and I flick my cigarette over the edge, not caring if it starts a forest fire. What does it matter? I want my whole life to burn.

"The anticipation is making me sick; I just want to get it over with."

"No," Vic snaps, his entire mood darkening, violence edging into that one word. "You're not just going to get it over with." I turn to face him and find him watching me with that inexplicable gaze of his, an impossibility, a puzzle without a solution. "No. That's not how it's going to be between us, Bernadette Blackbird." He takes another step toward me, cupping my face in a huge, inked hand. The smell of him poisons me in the best way possible, this smoky amber and musk scent that makes my body feel like a traitor. It's always been that way though, me against my body. This stupid fucking body that's only ever bought me pain. Why does it hurt to hate yourself so much?

"How is it going to be then?" I ask, realizing suddenly that I'm holding back tears. I never wanted to be pretty; it was a curse that was thrust on me. But I've suffered so much because of it, I figure why not? Why not put on mascara and lipstick and leather? Why not, why not, why not?

The monsters come anyway—whether you wear short skirts or sweats. A sob gets caught somewhere in my throat, stifled and drowned out when Vic tilts my chin up to face him, his eyes a dark impossibility, his mouth a slash of definitive heat.

"You're going to love every moment of it, Bernadette. We need each other, you and me."

"How do you figure?" I ask, my voice rough and broken. Just like his. He's broken, too. Maybe that's it, why he thinks we need each other?

The smirk he gives me is cocksure and definite: Victor knows what he's doing to me, how wet I am, how tight my body is clenching in anticipation of his touch.

"I need a way to let my demons out, and you need a way to confront them." He cups the back of my neck with a tattooed hand and tastes me. That's what it is, both more and less than a simple kiss.

My hands fists in the front of Vic's black wifebeater, and all the blood in my body rushes to my head, making me dizzy. Victor's kiss is exquisite torture, a moment torn from the timeline of my life that I can never get back. It both hurts and excites me, all at once.

I offered my body to get my revenge.

I didn't expect to get anything else along with it, but it feels like I'm getting more than I bargained for. Much, much more.

His tongue takes over everything, leaving me aching, reaching, wanting more. Heat sears between our slanted lips as I arch my back and press into him. It only lasts a few seconds, but it could go on for an eternity, and I wouldn't know how to process it.

Vic releases me suddenly, and I stumble back. I don't mean to; it just happens. I can't seem to find my feet or my breath. Lifting my eyes up, I meet his, as dark as obsidian, as endless as the night sky without the stars. He looks at me then with that cold, business-like expression burning away all the passion of the moment before.

"Tonight, we're going to do some bad shit, Bernadette. Do you understand that?"

"I understand," I say, and Vic nods, looking back out across the overgrown parking lot toward the city. He laughs, this dark sort of chuckle that promises bullshit. The thing that makes that sound so scary is that he damn well means to deliver it.

"Let's go fuck up some prep school brats."

He turns and walks away, leaving me to follow along behind him. Guess he's used to that, snapping his fingers and getting people to follow. Even scary motherfuckers like Hael and Oscar do what Vic says.

To me, he seems like the mildest of the Havoc Boys.

But then, like I said, that laugh promises bullshit, doesn't it? And Victor Channing, he's fucking full of it.

CHAPTER

Oak Valley Preparatory Academy is almost two hours outside of town with its own front gate, security force, and cameras. How we're going to get on campus at all is questionable, not to mention exact some sort of revenge on Donald.

Just standing here, I feel a wave of pain hit me, the sight of the school a trigger for what I'm sure must be PTSD or something. What are the key points again? Avoidance of specific triggers? Check. A physical reaction to said triggers? Check. Nightmares? Check.

"How do we get in?" I ask, shoving that pain down with everything I have, and taking a deep breath. Fighting the emotions back like that leaves me empty and numb, but it's better than feeling sick and scared. I'll take it. Licking my lips, I work to channel that numbness into rage. It's the only thing that's kept me safe all these years.

"Simple," Oscar says, tapping something on his iPad. With a whirring death rattle, the generator outside the security office goes quiet, and the lights flick off. With a curse, the night guard comes outside to scan the darkness with his flashlight, not noticing six kids standing in the shadows behind him.

Callum and Vic exchange a look, and the leader of the Havoc Boys gives a curt nod. Like a fucking ninja, Cal flips his hood up, flashes me this cocksure smile, and then moves up behind the guard, hitting him in the back of the head with a goddamn baseball bat.

The man drops to the ground with a groan as my heart begins to pound. *This is for real, isn't it?* There was a reason Vic asked me if I wanted to go, and a reason why Aaron didn't want me here. I glance his way and find him glaring back at me. He's not happy about any of this. Maybe he should've thought about that before betraying me for his fucking gang?

"Is that guy dead?" I ask, feeling this light, panicky feeling take over me. Vic just stares back at me, completely dead in the face.

"What would you do if he was?"

"Vic, come on, knock it off," Aaron growls as Callum comes back over to us, swinging the bat up and onto his shoulder. He reaches up to tug at the tuft of blond hair that sticks out of his hood.

"Nah, he isn't dead. He'll have one hell of a hangover in the morning, but a small price to pay for getting us free entry into this den of assholes." Callum smiles at me and then bends down to snag the guy's keys, unlocking the small gate embedded in the ten-foot fence and letting it swing open with a creak.

"Here," Hael says, passing over a black ski mask and letting his fingers caress mine more than necessary. "Put this on." He yanks one over his red hair as I bite my lip, watching the other guys transform themselves into faceless monsters. My throat tightens up, but I follow along with them, drenching myself in anonymity.

At night, Oak Valley Prep is beyond creepy, a soft white fog drifting across the campus. It looks ominous, towering over us like a brick castle, one complete with torture chamber. Trust me, I know they've got one: I was there. It was called *Donald's Dorm Room* at the time. Still is.

A shiver takes over me that I can't quite suppress, this cold chill that Vic takes note of, flint-like eyes scanning over me. For such a 'bad boy', he doesn't seem interested in fucking girls against their will. Maybe he doesn't get off by shoving his dick in some poor chick's mouth when she doesn't want it? *Maybe Vic is a real man, after all?*

But then I remember the coldness in his gaze when he locked me in that closet, how hoarse my voice was from screaming, how little he cared.

No, he truly is a monster, just of a different breed.

"Show us the way," he says, holding out an inked hand. I nod and turn, knowing the Havoc crew will be close behind me. They're never far apart, these boys. It occurs to me that we're all here because nobody loved us enough, nobody cared. The boys, they created their own family. And me, I just stumbled into it.

"In there," I say, remembering the night Donald brought me back here, how he smirked, and I giggled. How he pushed me up against this wall and kissed me breathless. He was good at that—probably still is—but being a good kisser doesn't make up for the fact that he's a rapist, too. Or at least a wannabe one.

Hael hands Callum a crowbar, but before he can even try to use it, I step forward and grab the handle. It swings open and the boys exchange looks in the dark behind me.

"Posh school, a different sort of hoodlum. They probably think the front gate security is enough." I step inside and find an elaborate hallway with wood floors, brick walls, and stuffy paintings of old white dudes. More than likely, *rich* old, white dudes. My lip wrinkles —because who the fuck actually likes misogynistic, money-hoarding dinosaurs?—and I step aside to let the others in.

We head straight for the curving staircase to our left and up, to the hallway where Don's bedroom is located. I notice that we're all fairly good at keeping quiet, a throwback to dark childhoods and blending into shadows. It's a hard-won skill, but it comes in handy as we slip down the hall and pause in front of room 219. Don's room. The room he invited his friends to, *to have a taste of southside whore.* My mouth fills with bile, and my eyes close. My whole life, I feel like I've been running from men and their greedy hands, their hungry cocks.

And to escape them? To punish the ones that'd already done me wrong? I sprinted into the arms of the enemy. We'll see how this works out, won't we?

Donald Asher, the rich dickhead I dated because, for some stupid, silly reason, I thought he would be better. Hah. Anyway, *his* door is locked. I guess monsters always know where to look for their brethren in the dark.

Kneeling down in front of Don's door, Callum pulls a lock picking kit from his bag, and I get the idea that he's the master of breaking and entering amongst the Havoc Boys.

In two flicks of a fucking lamb's tail, the lock is disengaging with a click, and the door is swinging inward.

My pulse is racing so fast I have to seriously consider if I might pass out.

"We got this," Aaron whispers as he moves around me, that distinctive rose and sandalwood smell of his wafting in the cool air. Like some sort of SWAT unit, all the boys but Oscar move into the room on tiptoes.

"This should be interesting," Oscar murmurs, gray eyes glimmering in a stray shaft of moonlight, his mouth in some semblance of a smile, albeit one that stings like acid. The lenses of his glasses—I notice he's wearing a completely new pair tonight—catch the light as he glances briefly over at me, tucks his iPad against his side, and then holds a single hand out to indicate that I should enter the room.

With a deep breath, I do.

As soon as I enter that room and smell that awful cologne, memories come flooding back, and I have to bite my tongue to keep from screaming.

Donald is lying peacefully in his bed, his snoring eliminated by some special surgery that his father's company funded the research for and now sells to the public for exorbitant prices. Oscar carefully closes and locks the door behind us, giving Victor the nod he's been waiting for.

"Wake him up," Vic commands, and Hael flashes a sharp, cocky grin through the bottom hole of his ski mask.

"My pleasure," he purrs, putting his hands around Don's neck. The asshole's brown eyes fly open, and his lips part to scream. But whatever Hael is doing is keeping him quiet. "Struggle too hard, and I'll snap your neck."

"And keep your mouth shut," Aaron adds, stepping naturally into his own role. Vic remains cold and emotionless, the untouchable leader of the bunch. His ebon eyes slide to mine.

"Let the boy talk, and if he screams, you know what to do."

"Got it." Hael loosens his grip ever so slightly, and Donald begins to choke dramatically, causing Callum to chuckle.

"What the fuck are you doing in my room?" Don demands, the whites of his eyes a dead giveaway to his fear. Honestly, I wouldn't have been surprised to find he'd pissed himself the way Kyler did. When he finishes scanning our group however, something changes. Rage twists his relatively handsome expression into something truly ugly. "What is this, some sort of shakedown? If you all leave my room right now, I'll consider dropping the breaking and entering and assault charges you're facing."

This time, it's Vic who laughs. The sound is low and dark, truly terrifying.

"You think you have room to negotiate here?" he asks, and the sound of his voice strikes fear into my heart. Regardless of that fiery kiss on the rooftop, I'm terrified of Victor Channing. "Truss him up like a pig and take him out to the roof."

"You wouldn't fucking *dare*," Donald snarls, but Oscar is already reaching for the coil of purple rope Cal's got slung over his shoulder. When the rich asshole goes to shout, Aaron clamps a hand over his mouth and leans in.

"Last chance before we choke you to death."

"I'd do it, too," Hael says, all smooth and cocky. He's like … the jock-y football player from a good school, but reversed. Same shit-eating grins, over-confidence, and healthy swagger, but wrapped in tattoos and pain instead of money and a letterman jacket. "And I'd enjoy it. Nothing I love more than showing a rich asshole that he doesn't own the world."

Aaron releases Don's mouth, and Oscar makes quick work of tying him up. Next thing I know, the other guys are dragging Don through the window.

"What the hell?" I murmur, grabbing Oscar's arm. The way he looks down at my hand on the fabric of his suit jacket, I get the idea that I better let go and *quick.* "This is like a fucking repeat of what you did to me."

"No, not even close. Consider it … an ode." Oscar climbs out, and I'm expected to follow behind. Hands shaking, I do, and find myself watching as Oscar ties a rope around Donald's neck.

They're going to hang him?! I wonder, heart racing so fast that I feel dizzy. *Right here, like this?* I mean, I wouldn't put it past them to commit murder, but … this is insane.

"Donald Asher," Vic says, squatting down beside him as the boy who thinks he owns the world gets a nice, sharp taste of brutal reality. "Do you know why you're here?"

"I can pay," Don simpers, his voice a broken, weak thing, so unbelievably pathetic that my lip curls. I can't believe I actually dated this guy. But I was so desperate to escape my life, to get as far away from Aaron as I could, that it seemed like a good idea at the time. "Whatever you want, just name the price."

Victor laughs, and the sound is truly nightmarish, an ephemeral darkness that blots out the brilliant moon. He reaches out and strokes Don's dark hair from his forehead, almost mockingly.

"You think we give a shit about money?" Vic asks, tilting his head to one side, studying his subject. "Do you think that's what motivates us?"

160

"Everyone likes freedom," Don whispers, shaking violently. I smell an acrid scent on the wind that takes me a minute to place: he really has pissed his pants. Not that I blame him. I mean, when the Havoc Boys dragged me from my bed in the middle of the night, I didn't wet myself. But then, I guess I'm made of tougher stuff. "Money can buy you freedom. I've got cash, hidden in the safe. If you let me up, we'll go get it together, and then you can—"

Victor grabs a handful of Don's hair and yanks his head back as Aaron finishes tying off the noose.

"You're insulting my intelligence, Don," he says, looking him dead in the eye. "We're not here for money. Whatever you could give us, it'd be a pittance to you. You wouldn't suffer, and that's the most important thing here." Vic sighs, like he's frustrated at having to explain himself to this pathetic cretin. Meanwhile, I'm fairly certain I'm simultaneously having a PTSD attack and also enjoying the show. A deep, sick sense of satisfaction curls through me, and that's when I know I'm truly evil, as evil as all the rest of them, my perpetrators and the Havoc Boys combined.

They've twisted me, warped me, made me in their likeness.

I swallow hard, but I don't look away or close my eyes.

"And do you really believe that _we_ believe that you'd let us go? No, a monster like you knows that as soon as you have the upper hand, you take it." Vic smiles, but it's not a pretty expression. The way his mouth looks right now, I can hardly believe that just a short while ago, he was burning me with it, searing me with heat. "As soon as we left, you'd have a private army on our asses." Vic pats him on the cheek and stands up. "Besides, you know too much already. Do you really think you're walking away from this?"

"What the hell is this all about? I didn't do anything," Don whispers, wiggling like a caterpillar in his bindings, eyes flicking nervously toward the edge of the roof. At some point, we're going to be heard out here, and the gig will be up. But I stand there, and I make myself trust in Havoc. They weave cruelty, pain, and revenge like fibers in the dark, soothing cloth of reality.

"You've never hurt anyone?" Aaron clarifies, the blind rage in his voice making me do a double take. Whereas Vic sounds calm, cool, collected, my ex is giving off the impression that he actually cares. I mean, if he did, he wouldn't have dumped me and turned on me in an instant, right? "In your short, miserable life, you've been nothing but a goddamn angel? You are a demon, Don, and you'll die like a dog."

"Takes one to know one," Don bites out with one, last burst of sass, and Vic chuckles.

"Undo the ropes," he says, and Oscar nods, moving to untie the silken purple bindings on Don's wrists and ankles. Donald calms down for a moment, but only until he realizes that when Vic said to untie the ropes, he didn't mean *all* of them. "Did you know that our friend here is a master at these silk ropes? He can tie them without leaving a mark. And what's funny is that once the hubbub dies down, nobody will remember the spoiled, rich prep school kid who hung himself from the tree outside his window."

"N—" Don starts to shout, but Hael's already tossed the rope around the limb of the tree and pulled the knot tight. In the span of an instant, before I can even think to protest or wonder if I would at all, Vic is kicking Donald down the sloping roof and … off.

The branch groans, and the rope creaks, but all I can hear is the thumping of my heart as I clamp my hands over my ears.

"Bernadette," Vic says, putting his hands on my wrists and pulling them away from my ears. "Pay attention."

With a sick, lurching sensation in my stomach, I move toward the edge of the roof, guided by his hand, and find that the silk purple rope tying Don's throat has come undone.

He's lying on the ground groaning, unable to get up but most certainly not dead.

My eyes flick up to Oscar's gray ones, so devoid of emotion, so goddamn scary.

"I'm a master of knots," is all he says in that Lucullan smooth voice of his.

I'm at a loss for words, something that doesn't happen to me often anymore. The Havoc Boys have just given Donald Asher the sensation of dying without actually having done anything at all.

The way they locked me in that closet or chased me in the woods.

That's a special sort of cruelty, isn't it?

One that leaves no trace.

"Let's get down there before the little creep wakes up," Hael says with a smirk, not at all disturbed by what he's just done. Is it fucked-up that I'm not either? That I feel like Donald got less than he deserved?

We head inside and down the stairs to find Don struggling to get up, choking and shaking, his pants stained with urine.

"Darling," Vic says to me as he puts his boot on the back of Don's neck and pushes him to the ground. "I want you to go back out the gate and wait for us in the trees. Callum'll go with you."

"Wait, what?" I ask, snapping my face up from Don's sweaty one. "This is my request; I get to watch."

"Not if I say you don't." Vic's face is hard when he lifts his attention up to me, and I feel myself bristling. He's testing me again, giving me another chance to prove myself.

What choice do I have?

So with one, final look at Don, I head back toward the front gates, and the slumped security officer, the mysterious Callum Park on my heels.

"What are they going to do to him?" I ask, feeling my heartrate pick up, my palms sweat. I'm ready for this. Vic knows it. He sent me away on purpose, a punishment for last week.

Callum shrugs, dressed in his sleeveless hoodie and shorts, a pair of boots on his feet. He leans back against the brick half-wall, and the black iron posts that adorn it, curling his fingers around the bars. His blues eyes are bright inside the holes of the ski mask.

"They probably won't kill him," he says, and my brows go up. Probably. Do I want Don dead? What was it that Oscar had said, *"How far, exactly, you want this to go: that's up to you."*

How far *do* I want this to go?

Don is a privileged, spoiled monster. I doubt I'm the only girl he's tried to hurt, and I won't be the last.

I bite my lower lip, shred it with my teeth, but I don't move from that spot. I don't know how to.

After about twenty minutes, the boys come back through the gate, and all of them ... are speckled with red droplets of blood.

"Let's go," Vic says, and as he passes me, he pauses and waits until I meet his eyes. "You can cross that name off your list."

Even though I know I shouldn't, I creep back toward the gate anyway and glance toward the tree where Don was hung.

There's no sign of him, of anything at all amiss.

"Come on," Aaron says, grabbing my arm from behind and tugging me toward him. "Vic wants me to take you home."

"Hael, pinch Don's car; we'll strip it for parts. Cal, crack the safe in his room. Oscar, you deal with the security cameras." Vic barks orders like he was born to it, tearing off his ski mask as Aaron leads me away into the darkness, his fingers smearing blood across the sleeve of my sweatshirt.

CHAPTER
TWENTY

Monday morning gives me a welcome reprieve from the hellhole I call my house. As I take my little sister Heather outside to meet the bus, I can hear my mother and stepfather having one of their infamous screaming matches in the basement.

Eventually, it'll devolve into something worse. They'll start hitting each other and, tit for tat, they'll leave bruises and welts and scratch marks. The atmosphere at home is so toxic that I feel nauseous as I kiss Heather on the forehead and smooth her light brown hair back with my hand.

"Have fun at school, okay, kiddo?" I ask, the only light in my day coming from that little girl's face. There's nothing else for me, no other star to punctuate the velvety blackness of night. When I look at her, I see Pen's face, and my heart breaks and shatters into a million jagged fragments.

167

"I always have fun at school," she says, wrinkling her nose at me, and then waving as she turns and takes off for the bus, ponytail bobbing, the pink charms on her backpack tinkling merrily.

"Forgot how cute she was," a voice says from my right, and I jump, turning to find Aaron waiting next to his minivan, smoking a cigarette. The screams from inside the house echo out the still open front door, and I cringe, gritting my teeth.

"Yeah, well," I say, because all of the mean, horrible things I want to scream at him are stuck inside my throat, choking me to death. I'm not sure if I'll ever be able to get them all out. Or any of them, really. "What are you doing here?"

"Might not be safe for you to bike to school today," Aaron says, waiting at the curb as I head up the walk, grab my backpack, and close the door behind me, silencing the screams.

For a moment, I just stand there with my hand on the knob, breathing in deep.

Then I turn and look at Aaron, really look at him. His chestnut hair is tousled and wavy, his eyes the color of fall, this green-going-gold, just like the leaves on the maple that shadows our ugly street with some much-needed color. He's wearing a red t-shirt, too tight across his broad chest, and a pair of worn jeans with boots.

His body is made up of long, lean muscles, all of them earned on the streets. None of those contrived steroid-and-gym muscles that make up the football team for Fuller High—the prissy upper-middle class school across town.

"Why? What happened?" I ask. *Besides Donald, groaning on the ground, the loose rope still clinging to his thin neck. The blood speckling the boys' clothes. The way Vic looked at me as he swept past.*

Vic.

Fucking Vic.

I feel like he's gotten into my head, like he's invading every pore, climbing down my throat, suffocating me.

"The Ensbrook brothers stopped by the game at Fuller last night and started some shit. Broke the JV quarterback's arm, roughed up some cheerleaders. They did it wearing masks, and everyone's on our asses about it. Like they think we'd waste our time on something as stupid as that." Aaron scoffs and turns away, like he can barely stand to hold my gaze for long. "You should've gone with your grandmother," he says again which just *infuriates* me.

You don't know the whole story! I want to scream.

Grandma isn't related to Heather. Even if she wanted to take her in—I don't think she does—she couldn't. Heather shares DNA with the Thing. If I left, if I went to Nantucket and lounged on the beach in a bikini, dated the cute son of a fisherman, let myself have a normal life … then Pen wouldn't be avenged, and Kali wouldn't pay, and Heather would be alone.

For some reason though, when Aaron looks at me with that stupid handsome face of his, all I feel is anger.

"Let's go," I snap, moving past him, and feeling his fingers grab the edge of my backpack. I glance back at him. He has the letters *H.A.V.O.C.* tattooed on the knuckles of his left hand, just like all the other boys.

Their own not-so-very-subtle gang symbol.

"Eventually, we're going to have to learn to talk to each other," he says, his voice hard, so different from the boy I used to know. There's a fragment of that old Aaron in there somewhere, but that one bright ray of sunshine is swallowed by dark clouds. One day, probably someday soon, it'll cease to exist.

"You think so?" I ask, and he sighs, raking his fingers through his hair. The muscles in his right arm bunch and swell with the movement, causing the sleeve of his shirt to ride up. I can see the names of his sister and cousin tattooed there, right over the generous swell of his bicep.

"You're a part of Havoc now," Aaron says, and I scoff, yanking out of his grip and reaching for the car door. He stops me, pushing in front of me and forcing me back a few steps. Our eyes meet, and I don't care that he smells like bacon and maple syrup, that I know he cooked for the girls this morning, or that everything he does is for them.

Just like how everything I do is for Heather.

"I'm a plaything for Havoc now," I say, and Aaron growls at me, grabbing me by the upper arms and staring into my face, almost pleadingly.

"Were you listening when Vic told you the price? Or are you so intent on your own destruction that you can't see beyond the confines of your hate for yourself?"

Anger and pain flare through me, and I tear myself from Aaron's gaze, leaving scratches on my upper arms.

"You weren't even there," I challenge, meeting his eyes, wishing he'd shove me or slap me, so I had an excuse to lunge at him, take out all the frustrations I've ever felt toward him and his gang on his hard body.

"I was behind the curtain," he spits back, narrowing his eyes dangerously. "Because I couldn't stand to sit there and watch you make the biggest mistake of your life. You would've been lucky if Vic had asked you to be our whore, and nothing else. You're not getting it, Bernadette: you are a part of Havoc now. Forever."

Forever ... Such a foreign concept. Something that exists and can never be broken, something that won't shatter, no matter how many times it's tossed or torn or trampled on.

My mind can't even comprehend it.

"You're a member of the group," Aaron repeats on the end of a long, tired sigh. "Nobody else wanted this but Vic. Nobody. It's too much, too personal, it brings you too close. But he wouldn't let it go." He turns away from me for a moment, eyes burning, mouth pursed. "He wouldn't let *you* go," he adds, but the words are so light, I can almost convince myself I didn't hear them.

Aaron moves around the front of the van and climbs inside, starting the engine and waiting there for me to join him.

To prove my own point, I wait on the curb, watching him through the window until I'm sure he's about to break and take off without me. I climb in at the last second, and we suffer the rest of the drive to the school in silence.

Three years earlier ...

The pageant meeting takes place in the cafeteria at seven, so I beg my old neighbor, Mrs. Kentridge, to watch Heather, and then head for Prescott High. The cool evening air is settling in quick, but the shivering doesn't bother me, the rain doesn't bother me. No, the only thing I'm thinking about is how this pageant could change my life.

The winner gets a full-ride scholarship to Everly All-Girls Academy in Maine which is about as far away from Prescott as one could get. I'd be flown there, first-class, get my own dorm, fully paid tuition, and I could finish my high school career out somewhere better than a drug-infested shithole in an asbestos-ridden building.

Penelope said she'd take care of Heather for me, and even though I don't want to leave my sisters, I can't take it anymore. I can't take my mother or my stepdad or Principal Vaughn and the way his eyes glide down my bare legs during PE.

I'm at a breaking point.

Exhaling sharply, I take the steps up to the front of the building two at a time, and head for the security office to check in and gain entrance to the school. As soon as I do, I hit the front hall and pause, waiting as the security guard's door slams shut and I'm left alone in a dimly lit building crawling with memories and pain.

Before I even see him, I know somebody's watching me.

"Hello, Bernadette," Victor says, stepping out of one of the classrooms and making his way slowly toward me. It occurs to me that we haven't spoken since Aaron broke up with me. Aaron. Sweet Aaron. Aaron whose heart was

ripped out by tragedy, who has nowhere to go but to the devil himself for help.

"What do you want?" I ask warily, hyper conscious of the fact that we're alone together in here, that bad things can and have happened at Prescott High. A girl was raped in one of the classrooms just after a football game. It happens, and nobody cares.

My hands begin to shake, but I don't run.

I want nothing more than to simply skip down this hall and slide into a seat at the pageant meeting. I've never thought of myself as pretty, or if I did, then I hated the world for it. Pretty girls get looked at; they get hurt. But if I can use the curse of this face and this body, and turn it into a blessing, I will.

Victor walks up to me, and even though I'm tall, he's taller. I have to look up at him. He reaches down and brushes some white-blonde hair behind my ear, his fingers trailing across my skin, leaving scorch marks. My breath catches. Does he know that I've always watched them, him and his friends, that I've always wondered what it'd be like to be a part of something, to belong?

"Do you know Kali Rose-Kennedy?" he asks, and my face flushes.

Oh.

Of course he's not here to talk to me. But for a moment there, I breathe a sigh of relief. Victor isn't here to hurt me: he's just here to ask about my best friend.

"We've been close since second grade," I say, shrugging my shoulders loosely. Kali will be at the pageant tonight, too. We're doing this thing together, me and her. In fact, she's probably already waiting for me ...

"I should go." I start to move around Vic, but he puts an arm out, palm flat against a locker and looks at me with something almost akin to sympathy in his dark gaze. Whatever I think I see though, is gone in an instant.

From one of the classroom doors, three of the other boys appear, the ones who make up the rest of their new gang: Havoc. The only one who's missing is Aaron. My stomach clenches, and my heart picks up speed. It's hard to swallow now, and I feel faintly dizzy, standing in this dark, dingy hallway wondering what's going to happen to me.

"Bernadette," Victor says again, and this time, I can't decide if he's using my name as a blessing or a curse. "Grab her."

The other boys—Oscar, Hael, and Callum—come at me so fast I don't have a chance to run, snatching me by the arms at the same moment Vic steps forward and slaps a piece of duct tape over my mouth. The fear is very real as they drag me backwards and out the front doors.

I make the stupid, stupid assumption that the on-duty security officer will save me, but he doesn't. Instead, I'm pulled down the steps, feet kicking at the ground as I struggle.

The last thing I see before I'm thrown in a van is Aaron, bursting from the front doors of the school and staring down at with me with an expression that's equal parts horror and helplessness.

I pray for him to help me. To what god, I'm not sure. None of them have ever taken much pity on me before.

But he doesn't.

He doesn't move.

He just looks at me as the boys yank me into the car, and then, when our eyes meet, he jerks his gaze away like he can't bear to watch.

The van door closes, the engine starts up, and I start to live the first day of my new nightmare.

Prescott High is housed in an old building near the train tracks, with a wide brick front porch and two huge columns lined with cracks. One day, the damn thing is going to pitch forward in a pile of rubble and asbestos, poisoning the earth and everything around it. But I won't care. Even if I'm crushed beneath the debris.

Good riddance.

As usual, I spend a good fifteen minutes passing through security, and take off down the hall before Aaron is cleared to follow after me. As I do, I can sense a strange sort of tension in the students. They're all still looking at me—a byproduct of my deal with Havoc—but they're less ... fearful, and more curious.

Curious to see what happens, maybe, when I stop in the girls' bathroom and find Billie and Kali waiting for me.

"Hey, bitch," Billie says, appearing from behind the door and putting her back to it, effectively pinning me between her and Kali. The latter is standing across from me, green-streaked black hair piled on the top of her head, her pretty face twisted into a scowl.

"What'd you give Havoc to turn them into your dogs?" she sneers, moving toward me in her too-high heels. *Idiot.* She should know not to bring heels to a boot fight.

Shifting, I push an arm against one of the stall doors to make sure there aren't any other girls in there waiting to jump me.

Well, fuck my mom and call yourself Neil Pence, there are. Two girls step out from the stall, taking up a position on either side of me as the remaining three doors open and seven more bitches appear to take up the mantle of Kali's cause.

The only people at Prescott High stupid enough to pick a fight with me are the ones who don't know how to pick a winning side.

I put my back to the first stall, keeping all the girls in my field of vision.

"Guess that's my business and nobody else's, huh?" I quip, raising a brow and waiting to see what Kali's planning on doing here. I'm loath to actually hit her just yet because she has a tendency to be the bully but play the victim. Getting expelled from Prescott High would be bad for me on so many levels. For one, I'd like to get my goddamn diploma, so I can start at the community college. And two, Mom will find out, and then she'll kick me out of the house and Heather might end up alone with the Thing …

"Do you want to know what they asked from me?" Kali continues, brushing a freshly manicured hand over the pink rose tattoo on her arm. The line work is total shit. If my artist had mangled me as badly as hers did, I would've kicked his ass.

"Don't give a shit," I say, even though I'm burning with curiosity. Then again, what if I find out her price was something small, something insignificant. I'd have to face up to the fact that the Havoc Boys destroyed my life for trinkets.

"They wanted me," Kali says, pausing in front of the mirror and leaning in to fix her lipstick. It's bubblegum pink, just like her shirt, nails, and hooker heels. She's got on cut-off shorts that show off her ass, and she flashes this smile over her shoulder like she thinks she's hot shit. "They made me their little toy, and you know what?"

I stand quiet and still as her words sink, but even when I feel the anger rise hot and itchy to my skin, I refuse to give into it. God knows this wouldn't be the first time Kali Rose has lied.

"What, Kali?" I ask, crossing my arms over my black tank and waiting for her to spew whatever venom is tainting those sugar-sweet lips. One brow goes up again, but I make sure to tap my foot impatiently.

"I *loved* it," she says, spinning around to smirk at me as Billie chuckles from her guard position near the door.

I smile.

"Doesn't surprise me. You *are* a whore, after all." I shrug my shoulders, but if what she's saying is true … Jesus, for Havoc's sake, I hope she's lying. Those boys do not want to know what I'll do to them if I find out she isn't.

"They're talented lovers, don't you think?" Kali continues, choosing to ignore my insult as she sashays toward me, reaching out to tease the pink-tinged ends of my hair.

"Wouldn't know," I continue, forcefully pushing her hand away. "So, if that's what you're here to talk about, sorry, but I won't be able to contribute."

"Please, the whole school knows they asked you to be their little fuck toy," Kali spits, face darkening. She's always loved playing games. It's hard for her when others don't follow along with the charade. "Why else would they let you join their little gang? Are you knocked-up or something? I don't see how else you'd get Vic Channing to put a ring on your finger."

I laugh—can't help myself—and Kali's face tightens even further.

"Maybe Havoc let me join their gang because they realized I'm not some desperate, diseased snake looking for her next victim to infect with venom? And maybe Vic asked me to marry him because he'd been around a worthless, lying bitch before and knows how to spot a real woman." I smirk and plant one hand on my hip. "Now, I came in here to piss. Get out of my goddamn face before I show you one of the reasons why the Havoc Boys took me on."

"Billie," Kali snaps, and like some sort of trained show bitch, Billie Charter whips a knife from her belt and comes at me. She thrusts the blade forward, aiming for my stomach. Luckily, I've got the stall door open behind me, giving me enough room to duck out of the way, falling into a crouch.

But holy shit, I must've underestimated that white trash bitch because she slams her elbow down on my head, making me see stars. I throw myself at her midsection and she stumbles back, but not before bringing the knife down on my right arm and slashing me from shoulder to elbow.

Blood blooms, splattering across the tiled floors as I

rise back to my full height and punch her as hard as I can in the face. Kali is there, on my right side, moving in like she thinks she has a snowball's chance in hell of touching me, her army of trashy assholes right behind her.

I slam my boot down on her peep-toe heel, and she lets out a wail that echoes in the graffiti-covered little room. Nothing good is going to come of me staying in here, not when Billie has a knife, Kali is insane, and there are nine other girls just waiting to get their hands on me.

Besides, I'm damn near positive this is a set-up of some sort.

With one last shove to Billie's chest, I manage to skirt her knife and slip out the door, taking off down the hall with blood oozing from my wound. A quick stop at my locker grants me a black hoodie that I can slip on to hide the blood.

If I go to the nurse's office, there'll be inquiries. I'm not about to bring the administration into this. Lord only knows how fucking corrupt they are.

Just around the corner, I bump into Vic.

He snatches me by the arm, and I hiss in pain, his fingers squeezing the sleeve of my hoodie until blood soaks through and coats his fingers in ruby red.

"What the fuck is this?" he snaps at me, drawing his hand back to look at the blood. With a clenching of my jaw, I turn away. *They wanted me; they made me their little toy.*

"What did Kali pay you guys to torture me?" I ask, looking back at him, my expression stern. "If I'm a Havoc Girl and not just some side piece for you guys, then I deserve to know."

"Jesus Christ, Bernadette, did Kali do this?"

"Kali and Billie," I admit, knowing there's no way to get out of this without telling him the truth. My eyes meet Vic's dark ones, and I swear, as black as they are, even more shadows race forward to crowd his stern gaze. "Plus nine other faceless idiots whose names I don't know. Now tell me: what did she pay you?"

"Later. This isn't the time." He pushes up the sleeve of my hoodie to examine the wound, his eyes narrowing. His smell surrounds me, almost cloying in its toxicity, and I can't help but remember our kiss on the jailhouse roof. What was it he said? *"We need each other, you and me."*

My pulse begins to hum, and I swear, the whole universe hones down to a single, fine point, like we're resting on the tip of some dark god's ballpoint pen.

"This is deep," he murmurs, swiping a thumb over the blood and making me cringe when a sharp, hot burst of pain shoots through me.

"I don't want to see the nurse," I declare, and Vic knows why. He knows all about Principal Vaughn, and his naughty nurse. "But I'm not sure I can fake my way through class; it hurts too much."

Shit, was that me being honest? I wonder, and Vic nods once, nice and sharp.

"Follow me," he commands, pulling my sweatshirt sleeve down and stalking off across the now empty hall. At some point, the bell must've rung, and I just didn't hear it. There are a few security guards on campus, but not nearly enough. Our shitty ass public school doesn't have the funds it needs to keep this jailhouse running properly.

We make it outside to the courtyard without any issues, the chain-link fence with its barbed wire looming over us. A few kids look up, smoking cigarettes in the shadows, but at least they're not stupid enough to come at us the way Kali and Billie were.

Victor knows exactly where the hole in the fence is, shoving aside a dumpster and gesturing for me to step out before he does, pulling said dumpster back into place again before he takes off, expecting me to follow.

His bike is parked down the block, just out of sight of the security office. Not that it matters. I've seen how Havoc can manipulate the staff at Prescott.

We pause for a moment as Vic pulls out his phone, taps out a quick message, and then gestures for me to get on his bike. Even though my arm is throbbing like crazy, and I'm starting to feel dizzy from the blood loss, I climb on behind him, wrapping my arms around his taut waist.

This inescapable feeling settles over me like somehow, someway, this man is part of my goddamn destiny. Maybe in a good way, maybe in a bad one, I can't tell. But it's impossible for me to ignore it, the way my body reacts when I'm around him, the way my breath catches, my hands shake, my heart thunders.

Closing my eyes, I let the wind sweep over me as we zip through the streets of Springfield and end up at Vic's house. It's not exactly a safe haven, but kids like us, we have nowhere else to go. There is no perfect little nest for us to crawl into when we're afraid; we take what we can get.

Vic climbs off the bike, and I follow after him, into the dim interior of the shitty little house he shares with his father. It's much the same as it was last time I was in here, but with a few extra liquor bottles on the floor. He kicks them out of his way with a curse, moving into the bathroom and pulling out a first-aid kit from under the sink.

I wait warily in the dining room for Vic to come back.

"Sit," he commands, pulling out a chair and indicating with his hand that I should sit in it. I do, but only because I'm starting to sway where I'm standing, and all I want is to close my eyes for a moment. "Tell me what happened, every detail."

"Stopped in the bathroom to pee, ended up with Billie on one side and Kali on the other, seven of their minions crowded in next to the sinks. Kali taunted me for a bit, and then Billie whipped out a knife. Not much else to tell."

"Taunted you how?" Vic asks, pushing my sweatshirt sleeve up my arm and smearing blood everywhere. He examines the wound for a moment, curses, and then gets to work with some antiseptic wipes. They sting so goddamn bad that I have to bite my lip to keep quiet.

I'm not letting Victor Channing know how much it hurts, no way.

"Kali claims you made her a similar deal to the one you gave me: her body for your cooperation in turning my entire shitty life inside out." My voice quavers a bit as Vic pinches the edges of the wound, trying to get a read on how deep it is. He scoffs at me as he tosses the wipes aside, snatching up a curved needle and some thread.

My brows go up, but I'm determined not to show how

afraid I suddenly am. Stitches? I've had stitches before, after the Thing punched me as hard as he could in the side of my face. There's a scar, just beneath my hairline. I was so young that the memory's blurred around the edges, but I remember it hurt like a bitch. And that was *with* numbing agents.

"Here," Vic says, pulling a flask from the back pocket of his pants and passing it over to me. "Take a swig of whiskey and get ready to hurt."

He kneels down beside me as I unscrew the flask, taking it in my left hand as I turn my gaze away and throw back a burning swig. The alcohol sears my throat going down at the same moment Vic shoves the needle into my skin.

"Fuck." The word manages to slip past my carefully sealed lips as my eyes close against the pain. *In and out,* Vic pierces my skin over and over again, sealing me up, and cutting off the flow of blood. The flask is empty by the time he finishes, cutting off the end of the thread and tying a tight knot.

"We'll need to take these out in a week or two," he says, his voice dark, his thoughts far away. I watch as he rises to his feet and heads into the kitchen to wash my blood from his hands.

"Are you going to tell me about Kali or not?" I ask, because I can't take the dark little demons inside my head. They *know* that Kali Rose is a liar. But yet, I can't get them to stop.

"Now isn't the time," Vic says, and the deep, authoritative way that he speaks just infuriates me. He doesn't just get to decide the fate of the whole world like that. "I'm taking you back to school."

"Not until you tell me about Kali," I say, just as the skies open up and rain begins to pour from the clouds. Slowly, Vic glances over his shoulder at me, carefully drying his hands with a dishtowel. He tosses it into the sink, and then turns toward me, moving slowly across the ugly carpet.

"If I tell you that now isn't the time, then it isn't." Vic's face is hard as he stares me down. "I thought we'd moved past this bullshit: what I say goes in Havoc. It's how we function, how we succeed. It's how we stay *alive*."

"I can only take so much," I whisper, my voice darkening as I swipe a hand over my stitches and cringe at the sudden rush of pain. It'll scar, that mark. *I'm going to fucking destroy those bitches.* But then it occurs to me that the boys will probably destroy them first. "How can I go back to class with Kali's voice echoing in my head, her fucking taunting ..." I turn away for a moment, painfully aware that Vic and I are alone again. Last time, he kissed me and told me we needed each other. What'll happen this time? "Did you really ask to fuck her in exchange for torturing me?"

Vic snorts and when I glance back, he's shaking his head at me, raking his fingers through his dark hair.

"Jesus Christ, Bernadette," he says, turning and heading for the front door without answering me. I lunge forward and grab onto his arm, digging my nails into the inked muscles as he stops and stiffens up.

"I have to know why you did it," I grind out, hating the way my voice sounds, almost like I'm begging.

"Nobody else wanted this but Vic. Nobody. It's too much, too personal, it brings you too close. But he wouldn't let it go."

I'm not really sure if I'm even asking him about Kali anymore, but he doesn't know that.

"You think we'd make a deal that big for something so simple as a fuck buddy?" he asks, glancing over his shoulder to look at me. "And with Kali, of all people? I'd hardly need to make a deal to get her to fuck me."

"You made a deal to get me to fuck you," I blurt, and apparently that's the wrong thing to say. In an instant, Vic is on me, slamming me into the wall next to the front door.

"You want me to screw you, Bernadette? Will that make you feel better? Will that get you over your self-destructive bullshit?" Vic reaches between us and cups me through my jeans, sliding his thumb over the seam in the denim, teasing an ache into my flesh that wasn't there before.

A gasp slips past my lips, and his mouth twists into an awful smirk.

"That's what you've wanted from moment one, isn't it? To let the man you hate more than anyone fuck you into a mattress. That would complete the cycle, wouldn't it?"

My breathing is coming in harsh pants, and even though I hate myself for it, I wonder if Vic might actually be right.

His finger traces up and down the seam in my pants, stroking my core into a hot frenzy. He's so slow, so meticulous, so not like I'd expected. Those ebony eyes of his bore into mine, our harsh breaths mingling. This time, when I reach my hand down to the crotch of his jeans, he's hard beneath the fabric.

Vic takes me by the wrist and slams my hand into the wall, making me groan.

He looks me in the eyes as he continues to stroke me with his other hand, watching as I come apart beneath the firm, commanding brush of his fingers. I haven't been touched like this in years, not since Aaron. And the few guys I've slept with since, I can barely remember their faces let alone their names.

The way Vic is holding me right now is a warning. When he lets go suddenly and steps back, I feel like I should know better. Every instinct in me says to leave this alone, to back off, to let it be.

"If nothing happened with Kali, why not just tell me?" I demand, breathing hard, shaking. "It's okay. You used her. You're using me. You don't give a shit who you destroy or step on or fuck up, do you?"

In the span of an instant, Vic is on me, spinning me around and shoving me against the wall. He tears the button of my jeans, the tiny piece of metal pinging against the tiles of the kitchen floor. My fingers curl against the hideous orange and yellow wallpaper as he wrenches my jeans down my hips, exposing my ass and the violent heat of my aching core.

The sound of his zipper coming down turns my insides to liquid, and I bite my lower lip.

The feel of his cock is a surprising warmth against my ass, but when he moves to push inside of me, it happens so quick that I'm barely able to take a breath before he's filling me up. A cry escapes my lips that I can't hold back, no matter how hard I try. It's been so long since I had sex, and I most definitely don't have a safe place to touch myself, so although I'm wet enough, my body's too tight and Vic is too big.

Pinning my arms above my head, Vic pushes himself inside of me with a rough grunt, and I close my eyes against the brief rush of pain. It fades quickly enough, replaced within the span of a few thrusts to hot, blinding pleasure.

The feeling of having Vic inside of me is equal parts elation and hatred.

I hate him.

I want him.

And I don't know why.

Victor fills me up with his thick, hard length, taking over everything, shattering me to pieces with his body.

Even though I don't mean to do it, I find myself pushing back and into him, hot lashes of pleasure tearing through me like a storm. My hips seem to move of their own accord, rocking back against him as he drives into me.

I'm too taut, too hyper-aware to have an orgasm, but Vic comes inside of me with a ragged groan, his hot breath against my neck, the searing warmth of his hand pressing into my hip. When he steps back, I'm too liquid to do anything but sink to the floor, my forehead against the wall, body shaking.

He just stands there; I can feel his presence behind me, this all-consuming demand that I both hate and crave at the same time. The way I feel about Victor Channing, it makes no sense.

"Get up," he says, but not unkindly. "We need to get back to class."

That's right.

Couldn't possibly risk losing his inheritance, now could we?

Using the wall for leverage, I haul myself up, but there's a mess between my thighs that has to be cleaned up. Without looking at Vic, I breeze past him toward the bathroom. *He didn't use a condom,* I think as I strip down and take a quick shower, careful to keep my hair from getting wet.

It's hard to bring myself to care.

Instead, I open the door in nothing but a towel.

"I can't wear these," I say, tossing the underwear and jeans his direction. They land in a heap at his booted foot as he regards me with dark eyes, his expression impossible to read. Impossible. Just fucking impossible. "I'm not going back to school in cum-stained clothing."

"Nobody asked you to," Vic snaps back, snatching the items from the floor and disappearing into the kitchen. A few moments later, I hear the rushing sound of water in a washing machine. When Vic reappears, he can barely look at me, storming past and up the stairs, taking the steps two at a time.

I lean against the doorjamb and close my eyes, completely numb.

I don't feel a thing.

That is, until I feel his heat, his gaze, watching me. Always watching me.

Warily, I crack my eyes and find him there, staring at me. For the briefest of seconds, the expression on

Victor's face matches mine. But that doesn't mean it's any more explainable or understandable. He's an enigma, a lone planet floating in a faraway galaxy. Yet if I can discern anything from this moment, it's that as soon as he's within my orbit, I don't feel numb anymore.

"Here." He hands over a pair of underwear that look brand-new as well as a pair of Prescott High gym shorts. They're his, so far too big, but at least they have a drawstring. I step back and close the bathroom door, slipping into the undies—dude undies, but oh well—and the shorts. "How are your stitches?" is what he asks me when I open the door back up.

"Fine," I say, but they're bleeding a little. I mean, he *did* throw me into a wall.

Vic grunts and grabs an extra hoodie from a hook near the door, chucking it at me the same way I chucked my dirty jeans at him, and then we head outside to his bike. I have to hide a small grimace when I straddle it, that ache between my thighs burning now that the adrenaline of the moment has faded.

Neither of us says a word until we arrive back at the high school, parking a block away and walking back.

Hael meets us out front.

Must be lunchtime. Seniors are the only ones allowed off-campus during lunch. Either that, or the Havoc Boys have paid off the new security guard to look the other way when they break the rules, the same way they did the last one.

"Where the *fuck* have you been?" Hael demands, sliding his palms over his red hair, muscles in his inked arms bunching with the motion. "Shit is going *down.*

Those Ensbrook and Charter fuckers are all over our dicks."

"I told you to wait until I got back," Vic snaps, ice-cold, iron-clad.

Fuck, I hate him.

And yet ... when I close my eyes, I can feel him buried inside of me, and that heat I work so hard to fight back begins to creep into every single cell.

Luckily, Hael is too flustered to notice either of our strange behavior, or the fact that I'm wearing Victor's gym shorts. His goddamn name is written across one leg in Sharpie—a school requirement since we have so many problems with theft.

"What happened?" Vic demands as we start toward the front steps where Oscar, Callum, and Aaron are waiting. Unlike Hael, Aaron notices the shorts right away, and his gaze flicks up to my face and the slightly damp tips of my hair.

His mouth purses into a thin, hard line.

"The Charter crew won't let us near Billie or Kali," Callum says, his voice that rough, broken sound as he flips his hood back, revealing mussed-up blond hair. "And they're spreading rumors about Bernadette." He looks at me with bright blue eyes ringed in thick liner, and then turns his attention over his shoulder as the front doors of Prescott High open and Mitch, Logan, Kyler, Danny, and Timmy step out. Two Charter boys—Mitch and Logan—and the three Ensbrook brothers. Two families, all trash.

My lip curls.

"What kind of rumors?" Vic asks, as if he hasn't

noticed the horde of assholes descending the steps toward us.

"That she fucks her stepfather. That she's joined us in order to rat our crimes out to him." Oscar says all of this without skipping a beat, his gray eyes raking my body from head to toe. I can tell right away that he knows about me and Vic in an instant. Unlike Aaron, he isn't surprised, and he doesn't care. I also note that he's wearing his original glasses again, like maybe the ones he wore to deal with Don were throwaways, so they couldn't be identified.

I open my mouth to defend myself, but Vic is already sweeping past the other Havoc Boys to face off against Mitch—the apparent leader of this new rebel group. For three years, Havoc has ruled these halls with an iron fist. I can hardly believe what I'm seeing as Billie and Kali bring up the rear of their little team.

"What did Kali pay you to get her dirty work done?" I whisper loud enough that only Aaron can hear, standing on my right side with his teeth gritted, and his hands curled into fists at his sides. He barely slides those gold-green eyes of his over to me, the angry scowl on his face twisting down into a frown.

"She betrayed every person she knows to us, including her cousin who was fucking a well-known local judge." Aaron exhales and closes his eyes for a moment. He acts like I've just taken a sledgehammer to his skull. "Kali's cousin was pissed off at us for a turf war we got into with her brother at Fuller High, and sicced the court system on me. I barely managed to keep the girls from ending up in foster care."

My brows go up, and I feel this sharp ache inside my chest as I turn back toward the scene in front of me.

"Do you think this is a game?" Vic asks as I let my eyes wander the front of the school, searching for any of the on-campus cops. There are none in sight. So *somebody* paid them to look the other way. Could've been Havoc, or maybe their newfound enemies. "Your girl cut mine up with a knife."

Mine.

That word does all sorts of strange things to me. Rage fills me in this unstoppable inferno, and I find myself stepping toward Callum. I haven't forgotten that he keeps a knife in his pocket. He stiffens up slightly when my hand dips into the front pocket of his hoodie, but he doesn't stop me as I draw it out, sidling up beside Vic.

His dark gaze briefly flicks to mine, but he quickly returns his attention to Mitch.

"What's your point? And why are you suddenly so protective of *Bernadette Blackbird.*" Mitch scoffs my name like I'm worth less than dog shit. "Didn't you torture the shit out of her during sophomore year? Is that your thing, Bernadette, to fuck the people that treat you like crap? Must be why you like your pedo stepdaddy so much."

Without thinking, I find myself darting forward, the knife slipping from inside my palm. Nobody expects me to move, so I find little resistance when I bounce up the steps. Swear to god, there's nothing going on inside my head when I slam the blade into Kali's shoulder. She lets out a scream as the metal sinks in, and blood blooms bright on her pale skin.

In a split-second, the world erupts into chaos. Kyler comes at me, Callum skirts around the side and tackles him. Billie grabs Kali as she collapses back, but I'm already retreating, stumbling down the steps as the two groups clash.

It only lasts a minute or two, but by then there are crowds of students watching from the first and second floor windows of the school, cheering on one side or the other. The entire campus security staff as well as our personal pair of cops appear and a few, brave teachers approach, tearing the two sides apart.

"Oh, honey," Ms. Keating says as she kneels down beside Kali and pulls out her phone, dialing up 911. Me, I'm just standing there as the rain starts to come down on top of us in thick sheets.

"Who did this?" Principal Vaughn roars as the boys walk off the fight on opposite sides of the brick walkway. He's pointing at Kali who's moaning and milking the moment for all it's worth. She's no more injured than I am, but I have a feeling that things are not going to go as well for me as they did for her. *She* is not above tossing me to the administration for punishment.

I open my mouth to admit to it before Kali can get the satisfaction, when I hear Hael's voice.

"I did—" he starts, but Aaron's own words drown him out.

"It was me," he announces, and our eyes meet across the rainy courtyard. "It's my knife."

The cops cuff him quick and take him away in the back of a squad car while the rest of us are shuffled into Mr. Vaughn's office.

With one student on their way to juvie, one on the way to the hospital, and eleven more crowded inside the narrow space, our corrupt asshole of a principal doesn't have much choice but to assign us all two days of suspension starting tomorrow, followed by two weeks detention, and then cut us loose.

Prescott High cannot afford to expel thirteen students and lose all that state funding.

Besides, I know Principal Vaughn is still actively recruiting girls for his little side project.

And I'm willing to bet that he's not forgotten how much I know about that.

CHAPTER
TWENTY-ONE

The last two classes of the day are a serious drag. I can feel all the eyes on me, the wandering gazes that take in Vic's gym shorts, that linger too long on my face. They're all wondering why I'm shacking up with the boys that everyone is afraid of, wondering why I let a man I hate put his cock in me, wondering why I love it.

After class, I head outside and find Hael waiting for me.

"Let's go," he says, jerking his head toward that cherry red sportscar of his. My fingers trail appreciatively along the shiny paint job before I climb into the black leather front seat, trimmed with red detail. It smells like new car and Hael Harbin in here.

"Am I in trouble?" I ask, and one of Hael's dark brows goes up.

"With who?" he asks, his voice so cocky and self-assured. I wonder if it's all a front or if he's as sure of himself as he pretends to be. "With Vic?"

"With Havoc," I correct, because I can't stand to hear Victor's name right now. I shift on the seat, and the ache between my legs intensifies. My body wants more at the same time my heart is repulsed by what I've done.

"Why would you be?" he wonders, genuinely curious, his honey-brown eyes shifting my direction. Too pretty to belong to a jerk like Hael. "Yeah, maybe stabbing that bitch in front of the whole school wasn't a good choice, but you're new. You'll figure things out."

"Thanks for trying to take the fall for me," I grind out, even though the words make my mouth hurt. Hael just gives that braying laugh of his and runs his fingers through his bloodred hair.

"Don't thank me. It's my official job, to be the fall guy. But Aaron just *had* to step in there and defend his sweet, little ex." He laughs again as I tighten my mouth into a thin line, and we pull up in front of Aaron's house. Vic's bike is already parked on the curb. He leans against it, smoking a cigarette and staring into space.

He barely looks at us as we get out.

"Well?" Hael asks, as I notice one of the neighbors staring at us from across the street. We look too out of place in this perfect suburban neighborhood, like some sort of incurable blight. It's only in that moment that it occurs to me what I've just done.

I've risked Aaron's safety with his sister and cousin.

He's just taken the fall for me.

The color blanches from my face, and I feel suddenly dizzy.

"Oscar and Callum are picking the girls up from school. Then we need to take Sophia to the police station to sign off on Aaron's arrest."

"Sophia?" I ask, but Vic doesn't bother to look at me. It's like we never had sex, like that moment never happened. Good. That's how I want it anyway.

"Sophia is this old druggie recluse we pay when we need someone to pretend to be Aaron's mom," Hael says with a shrug. Vic's face tightens up, but he doesn't correct his best friend. Instead, we stand there in the drizzle and wait for the minivan to show up.

"Bernie!" Kara shouts, leaping out of the van and racing over to throw her arms around my waist. Guilt surges anew, and I feel a pit form in the bottom of my stomach. I'm guessing the boys used 'Sophia' to get the girls out of school, too.

Ashley gets out of the car next and then stands awkwardly near the garage, like she isn't sure what to do. I have a feeling that I'm going to need to swallow my guilt at getting the girls' brother/cousin locked up and deal with this.

"If we can get my sister out of her after-school program, I can stay here with the girls while you guys deal with Aaron."

Vic nods and gestures in Hael's direction.

"Take Bernadette where she needs to go; I'll stay with the girls until you get back." And then Vic moves forward and lifts Ashley off her feet. The smile that blossoms on her face … it does something strange to my insides. I can't stop staring at the little girl giggling in Vic's strong arms.

"Alright, let's scram, Blackbird," Hael says, flicking his cigarette into the grass and grinning like he wasn't just suspended, like his friend didn't just get dragged away in cuffs. I follow after him, murmur some vague directions, and then we sit in silence with the rain pelting the windshield.

"Why did Aaron do that?" I wonder aloud, almost without meaning to.

"Seriously?" Hael asks, his fingers tightening slightly on the steering wheel. "You're really asking that question?"

I glance over at him as he flicks on the blinker and turns into the parking lot of Heather's school. Her after-school program technically runs for another hour, but I don't want her taking the bus home if I'm not going to be there. Quickly, I tap out a text to my mom, telling her that I'm taking Heather to the mall.

Hopefully she'll be out at one of her parties until late and won't notice that we don't come home.

"Aaron's in love with you," Hael says, and my head jerks up from the screen of my phone to look over at him. He's staring at me like I've lost my fucking mind. "You seriously didn't know that?"

"How would I know that? He dumped me to join Havoc. He tortured me for half a year."

"I barely managed to keep the girls from ending up in foster care."

I bite my lower lip to hold back a sound of frustration. Today has been … less than stellar, my arm still hurts like a bitch, my body still remembers the feel of Vic, and now I've added worry about Aaron on top of it all.

Besides, if my mom actually checks her phone messages and finds out that I've been suspended, who knows what kind of shit will go down?

"Mm." Hael doesn't bother to respond. Instead, he turns the engine off and lets the rain pound the windshield. "You finally got Vic to crack, huh?"

"Excuse me?" I pause with one hand on the door handle, my gaze landing on the ridiculously smug expression on Hael Harbin's face. "What makes you say that?"

He reaches out and grabs the edge of my shorts, giving them a little tug.

"How was it then?" he asks, and then quirks up one corner of his mouth in a cocksure sort of smile, like he already knows the answer to that question. "The sex, I mean. Did you like what he did to you, Blackbird?"

"Fuck you, Hael," I snap, climbing out into the rain and taking off for the doors of the library. They're locked, so I knock and wait patiently for one of the staff members to open them. I've been authorized as Heather's emergency contact since I was sixteen years old, a blessing I don't dare risk. If Mom or the Thing wanted, they could take away my authority to pick up my sister. It's a threat and a punishment I don't think they've thought of, a secret that I keep carefully guarded.

"We're working on creative writing," Heather tells me excitedly as I smooth her hair back and adjust her ponytail, thanking the teacher and apologizing for barging in before the end of class.

"Oh yeah?" I ask, my mind a million miles away. *Why did Aaron risk everything to stand up for me today? Because he's in love with me? Hael is full of shit. There's just no way. Sacrificing me for the sake of his sister and cousin, that's what makes sense. No wonder Kali was able to hire Havoc ...*

"My story's about a YouTube star who videos unicorns and nobody believes they're real," she continues as we near Hael's Camaro. "Whose car is this?" she asks me, standing back as I open the door and pull the front seat forward. When she spots the red-haired asshole behind the wheel, her suspicion rachets up another notch. "I'm not supposed to get in cars with strangers."

"Heather, please, not today," I say with a tired sigh, but she still doesn't look like she's about to budge. "You're having a playdate with Kara and her cousin, Ashley. You remember Kara, don't you?" After a moment, Heather nods and finally moves forward, handing me her backpack. I toss it on the floor as she climbs into the back and fastens her seatbelt. "Heather, this is Hael."

"Hi Hael," she says suspiciously, and he quirks a dark smile.

"Hey cutie." He turns on the car and revs the engine, making Heather grin. "You like sportscars?"

Heather nods, pretending to examine the interior of the Camaro.

"This one seems pretty nice," she admits reluctantly, and Hael laughs, hitting the gas and sending us flying down the wet road through massive puddles, spraying water in waves across the empty sidewalks. Heather laughs, but I frown. I'm not about to believe that these boys, who made me fear for my safety on a daily basis, are suddenly angels with kids.

Hael takes us the back way toward Aaron's, splattering mud across the shiny surface of his car and making

Heather giggle uncontrollably. When we get there, Vic's waiting with the girls in the living room, and every warning bell I have goes off when his dark eyes land on my sister.

He's the biggest monster of them all, the leader of the monsters, the one who paints nightmares in the dark with a brush of shadows.

My hand tightens on Heather's shoulder, and she lets out a small sound of pain.

"Relax, Bernadette," Vic says, rising to his feet, his full mouth etched into a tight frown. He comes up to stand beside me, and growls into my ear. "Don't worry: I'm leaving." Snatching one of Aaron's leather jackets off the hook, Vic opens the front door and glances over his shoulder at Hael. "Stay here until I say otherwise, and don't worry about your mom. I'll handle her."

"Yeah, I hope so," Hael grinds out, but Vic just slips out the door and slams it behind him.

Only then do I release Heather's shoulder. She rushes forward to join Kara and Ashley at the table where, apparently, Vic had started them on an art project of some sort. There are bits of colored paper everywhere, bottles of sparkly glue, and sequins galore. Also, they're filming the whole thing with Vic's phone, intent on making a YouTube video.

My jaw clenches and I sweep a hand over my face.

"What's your problem with Vic anyway?" Hael asks, standing far too close. His hands are in the front pockets of his jeans as he sweeps his eyes over me. *Stay here until I say otherwise.* What the hell does that even mean? Eventually, I'll have to come home from 'the mall' or else my mother will lose her shit. Speaking of, I wonder what's up with Hael's mom?

"Problem?" I echo, turning to face him and refusing to give into the memories nipping at the edges of my tired brain. Hael Harbin once held me down while Aaron stripped off my homecoming dress and gave it to Kali to wear. The two of them left me alone on the side of the road in heels, panties, and a strapless bra. And he wonders what my problem with Vic or any of the Havoc Boys is? A caustic laugh escapes me, but I'm just too exhausted to deal with my emotions right now.

I'm the one that wanted this, that said the word for the whole school to hear. *Havoc.* That was my choice.

"Forget it," Hael says after a moment, still studying me. "Do you mind watching the girls while I step outside to make a phone call?"

"Be my guest," I say, and only once he leaves and I'm alone for a moment do I take a breath.

During my sophomore year, I sometimes wondered if Havoc would kill me.

Now that I'm one of them, I'm damn near sure of it.

CHAPTER
TWENTY-TWO

The next morning, I wake up on Aaron's couch, groggy and confused and panicked. At some point yesterday afternoon, I must've fallen asleep. Sunlight spills across my face as I shoot up to a sitting position, my heart thundering, and look frantically around for Heather.

When I find her sleeping on the couch across from me, sprawled across Hael's chest with Kara and Ashley beside her, I almost choke.

The front door creaks open and Aaron appears, wearing the same clothes he was in yesterday. He pauses for a moment and glances over at me, green-gold eyes rimmed with dark purple circles of fatigue.

"I ..." I start, but then Vic follows in behind him, and I clamp my lips shut against the spill of words that are suddenly so desperate to escape. *We need to talk. Why did you do it? Are you insane?!*

"We're having breakfast with my mother today to talk

about my suspension," Vic says as Aaron sweeps past and disappears up the stairs. "Hael and Aaron will watch your sister for you while we go."

"I can't leave her here with them," I blurt automatically and one of Victor's brows goes up. My stomach twists with anxiety, but I know it's not about leaving Heather with Hael. Glancing over at them, it's quite clear she's more than comfortable here. Fuck. No, all of that anxious energy inside of me has to do with Victor and the fact that he screwed me against a wall yesterday.

"Really? Why not?" he challenges, but I have nothing to say to that, and he knows it. "Here. Wear this." He tosses a bag of new clothes my way just before the front door opens again and Oscar and Callum appear. Oscar gives me a curious look and quirks an almost disturbing smile while Callum breezes past and heads straight for the kitchen.

"You look ... ruffled," Oscar says, his voice a smooth purr that doesn't belong in this dark world we live in. He sounds like a fallen prince or something. "I think I like you better this way: vulnerable, messy, and wearing Victor's gym shorts."

"Fuck you," I snap, rising to my feet and heading for the downstairs bathroom. Once I'm locked away inside, I dig through the clothing in the bag and find a black skirt, white blouse, red heels, and some jewelry that I'm just betting is stolen. There's also a new lacey bra and some panties with a fancy crisscross in the back that will most definitely show off my crack.

My mouth tightens into a thin line, but I put the

clothes on anyway. There's even some makeup—*expensive* makeup—a toothbrush, and a comb in the bag that I use before I freshen up my eyeliner and lipstick. A small bottle of ibuprofen falls out of the bag, and I frown. I'm guessing Vic got this for me because of the knife wound ... but I need it a bit more for the ache between my legs. I pop two pills, check my appearance in the mirror—I look like a fucking secretary—and call it good.

I say goodbye to Heather, but she barely stirs on Hael's chest, and then head outside to join Vic at his bike.

He's smoking another cigarette, offering one up to me in long fingers. He's dressed up in another yuppie outfit, hair slicked back, the tattoos on his arms impossible to miss despite the disguise.

"Callum's knife, huh?" he asks casually, still barely bothering to look at me. Some part of me wants to start another fight, just to get him worked up, to draw that focused attention of his over to me. "That must've felt good, to stab Kali like that."

"I messed up," I admit, reaching up to run my fingers down my freshly braided hair. "How much is Aaron going to pay for my mistake?"

"Kali was barely injured, and we know some people down at juvie." Finally, Victor moves his dark gaze over to me, and I shiver beneath the intensity of it. "No harm done. But next time, talk that shit over with me before you do it. If you want to jump Kali, we can make that happen. I'd just prefer nobody else knew about it."

There's a brief moment of silence before Vic tosses his cigarette into the grass, and I follow suit. He mounts his bike, and as I'm sliding up behind him, I can hear his deep voice rumble through me.

"Are you on birth control?" he asks, and I grit my teeth. Of course we can't just let yesterday go, can we?

"No."

Another moment of silence before he grunts, and then kickstarts the engine. We take off, my cheek pressed against his back, my heart thundering in my throat. It's too much, to be pressed up against him like this. *You goaded him into fucking you yesterday,* I tell myself, and I can't decide if I'm truly a glutton for punishment or if I was testing him because I didn't think he'd actually do it.

Either way, those thoughts keep me distracted as we weave through the middle-class areas of Springfield, and into the prestigious Oak River Heights district. If the neighborhood, shopping center, or school has the word *oak* in it, you know you've reached one of the ritzy areas.

We pull up outside a pretentious white Greek revival style mansion with a two-story porch and a massive oak tree in the front yard. When the city was first founded in 1890, that was one of the ways the rich designated themselves and their businesses, by planting oak trees in and around their properties. Thus, the theme of including the word *oak* in the naming of certain locales.

"Your mother lives here?" I ask, and Vic shakes his head, climbing off the bike and looking up at the house with a scowl that breaks through that fine control of his.

"Her new boyfriend owns this place." Vic glances over at me, that hot anger of his making my skin prickle. "He comes from old money, but when his parents died, they left everything to their daughter. The asshole got nothing, so he's putting pressure on my mom to make sure she takes over my inheritance. After all, how are they supposed to live their fancy lifestyle if neither of them has any money left?"

I glance up at the house again, but I can tell that Victor's gaze is still on me, tracing the sweetheart neckline of the blouse I've got on. When I close my eyes, I can feel the rough press of his cock at my opening, the sensation of his hot, hard flesh filling me up.

"Do you want to stop and get a morning-after pill when we're done here?" he asks me, and my brows go up.

"I get a choice in the matter?" I ask with mock surprise, turning my attention back to him. "Aren't you supposed to just order me around and tell me you'll shove one down my throat?"

Vic's jaw clenches, and he looks at me like I'm the worst thing that ever happened to him, like he's seriously regretting the deal we made.

"Is that what you *want*, Bernadette?" he snaps, turning to look at me. "You want me to order you around and treat you like a whore? Because I can, if you're so goddamn excited about the prospect." Victor steps toward me and pushes me into the tree, setting his forearm against the trunk as he leans over me. "Why are you so determined to make this *suck*?" He snaps this last word out like a whip. "I'll remind you: you came to us. You called Havoc; you made a deal. I gave you more than enough chances to change your mind, to run, which is more than I've ever given another client."

"Why?" I ask and he goes almost completely still above me. I'm shaking now, but for whatever reason, I can't figure out why. Why I want him to hate me. Why I keep provoking him.

I'm scared to belong because I'm scared of being rejected.

The thought pops into my head before I can banish it, and Victor exhales, his breath ruffling my hair.

"We're gonna be late." The words come quiet and soft, not at all like I was expecting. He pulls away from me and turns toward the house, leaving me with my back against the tree, my knees weak. After a moment, I follow after him. As I step up on the front porch, the front door opens to reveal a butler.

Huh.

I didn't know people actually had butlers anymore.

The man ushers us inside and leads us to a solarium on the far side of the house where Ophelia's waiting, her hands folded carefully over one knee, her dark eyes watching the pair of us as we step into the sunlit room. There are well-tended plants along all the walls, green tendrils draped over ceramic pots, flowers blooming and filling the air with sweet perfume.

The table itself is set with a silver tea set, a coffee pot, and various platters with cut fruit, pastries, and breakfast meats.

"Have a seat," she says, and her smile is downright poisonous. There's a special sort of gleam in her eye that infuriates me from moment one. Or maybe it's just her son, crawling under my skin, making me bleed emotionally?

"Mother," Vic says, leaning down to press a cold, clinical sort of kiss to his mom's cheek. What did he call her? The egg donor? I feel like that better encapsulates the scope of their relationship. *She's jealous of us.* When Vic first said that, it didn't quite make sense to me. Seeing Ophelia sitting there in her floral skirt, hair perfectly coiffed, her face painted on ... I start to get it. Maybe she feels as numb as I do most days, but there's no pain in her life to temper it, just ruthless greed. "How long has it been since we had breakfast together? When I was in the womb? Or just before that?"

"Funny," Ophelia says, but I'm damn near positive her son is telling the truth.

Victor pulls out a chair and indicates for me to sit in it. I'm loath to get that close to him right now, but I sit, if only because I know that losing out to Victor will kill Ophelia. And I really don't like her. We spent one lunch together, and I know that for a fact.

I reach out for a croissant as Vic sits beside me, pulling his chair so close that our knees touch. Heat travels through me, this violent surge that takes over my entire body and makes it hard to breathe. I shouldn't be having such strong reactions to him over so little. Clearly, I've gone mental.

Ophelia notes our closeness, and her carefully crafted smile slips a fraction of an inch.

"What's this I hear about you getting expelled?" she asks, lifting her coffee to red-painted lips. Her dark hair is smoothed back into an intricate up-do, one that most girls and women only wear to proms or homecomings or even weddings, not to a casual breakfast with their kid.

That's the first sign that she's afraid of Victor.

She wouldn't bother to put on her armor if she weren't.

"Not expelled, Mother," Vic says, resting a big hand on my naked thigh. His fingers slide back and forth, stroking me and making it extremely difficult for me to focus on the conversation at hand. His flint-like eyes are locked on hers in challenge, his purple-black hair slicked back, one tattooed hand resting on the table. "Suspended. And only for two days. Don't worry: I'm right on track to graduate."

"That's not exactly how your principal described things to me on the phone," she insists as Victor's fingers trail just a bit higher up on my thigh than appropriate. *Shit.* I'm trembling again, and my hands shake as I polish off my croissant and reach for some coffee instead. If I were a smart girl, I'd push Vic off with a giggle. You know, play the part but show him I'm not a slave to the tension between us either.

Instead, I sit there with my back ramrod straight, my heart thumping so loud I can barely hear the stiff back and forth of their conversation, and I do my best not to actively groan when those hot fingers brush against the front of my panties.

I sip the coffee, hot bitter liquid splashing against my tongue as I try to tell my body to ignore the sweeping surge of pleasure from my core. Already, I can feel liquid pooling between my thighs, and find myself shifting in my seat.

"Principal Vaughn?" Vic asks with a hoarse laugh, his full lips twisting into a smirk. "You'll have to forgive him. Sometimes he gets a bit busy running that child sex-ring of his, and gets confused. You know, like how he thought I had drugs in my locker last week."

Ophelia's nostrils flare, but whatever retort she was about to spit out is cut short by the appearance of an older man, his salt and pepper stubble well-groomed, his eyes wandering a bit too much for my taste. He stares at the low-cut shape of my top, eyes tracing the tattoos there with interest before he actually remembers that his girlfriend is in the room with us.

"Ophelia," he purrs, sinking down to give her a kiss on the mouth. She pulls away from him slightly, a frown working its way onto her face. I can hardly believe Vic just dropped that bomb about Principal Vaughn.

My mouth gets dry, and I suck down another gulp of coffee to keep my throat from closing up. Victor's fingers play a dangerous game, stroking the silken flesh of my inner thigh, working closer and closer to that desperate heat. The first deliberate stroke is almost too much. I set the coffee cup down on the saucer so loudly that it clinks and both Ophelia and her beau turn to look at me.

Vic, however, keeps his attention straight forward, his mouth a cruel twist of lips.

"Aren't you going to introduce me, Mother?" he asks, the dutiful son act slipping slightly. There's an edge of danger in his voice that says he's ready for whatever it is she wants to throw at him. "I'm your only son, after all."

"Tom Muller," the man says, introducing himself. He's polished and well put-together, but with a total sleazebag vibe, like he has a punch card for young girls' cherries. He holds out a hand which Victor doesn't take, and then turns his attention to me. "And you are—"

"Don't talk to my fiancée," Victor growls out, clenching his teeth, his fingers stiff against the wet silk of my panties. I bite my lip so hard it bleeds, mixing copper into the bitter taste of coffee on my tongue. "She doesn't like you."

"The girl can speak for herself, can't she?" Tom asks, smiling at me like a used-car salesman.

"I don't like you," I repeat, and his face falls, the illusion of niceties shattering into a million pieces. Does his sleazy act really work on anyone at all? When I flick my attention back to Vic and find a dark shimmer of satisfaction in his gaze, I almost wonder if he's had bad experiences with his mother's boyfriends around his own girlfriends before. "How long do we have to sit here and pretend like your egg donor isn't purposely trying to sabotage you to steal your inheritance to fund her slutty boyfriend's pretentious lifestyle?"

"Just long enough to figure out how far she's planning on taking this. I'm nearly eighteen and she has yet to find something that'll derail me. What's next? You sell all your fancy clothes and hire an assassin?"

I'm staring right at Victor when he slips his fingers under the edge of my panties and pushes them into the molten heat of my core. I'm shaking so bad now that Ophelia and Tom are bound to notice.

"Don't be ridiculous," Ophelia snorts, sliding her hands along her thighs to smooth out her skirt. "I don't need your money, Victor. I'm just trying to make sure that when and *if* you receive my mother's money that you won't blow it all on drugs and nonsense."

My entire world seems to shrink down to a fine point, my senses hyper focused on Vic and his fingers as he pushes them inside of me and then pulls out, teasing wetness over my clit. Ophelia's looking right at me now, chastising me for calling her an egg donor, and for purposely trying to create tension between her and her son.

I barely register any of it.

The whole world falls away around me until I feel this burning ache inside of me that starts in my spine and unfurls through me like a whip, striking all the cold, dead parts of me and bringing them to brilliant, painful life.

"Excuse me," I choke out, shoving back from the table and stumbling to my feet. I smooth my skirt out as I go, taking off into the labyrinthine halls with no clue as to where I'm going.

As soon as I find a bathroom, I slip into it and start to shut the door.

Vic is there though, blocking the door with his forearm and pushing his way in. He slams it behind us, flicks the lock, and turns to me, lifting me onto the counter. My hands go around his neck and find his skin just as slick with sweat as my own.

Our mouths hover close, but for whatever reason, I just can't make myself close that distance to kiss him. Instead of fucking me into the counter like I'd expected, Vic continues teasing me with his hand until I'm trembling so hard I can barely keep my fingers clasped behind his neck. He looks right at me with those ebon eyes of his, pushing his own fingers deep inside of me and using his thumb to stroke my clit.

"Wait," I start, because I feel too exposed right now, too vulnerable. That numbness is fading away, and I'm feeling too much, too quick.

"Wait?" Vic asks, flicking his thumb against me and making me cry out. "What are we waiting for, exactly?" His voice is deep, low and edged with a crack that I want to reach out and push on, just to see if he'll break. "It's just an orgasm. Tell me you've had an orgasm before?"

"I—" I start, but then Vic is moving his hand again, manipulating me like a puppet. "Of course I have."

"Good. Then I don't have to kick Aaron's ass." Vic presses his hot mouth to mine finally, tackling that pesky space between us, stirring up an entire universe of emotions in me. My body finally loses the fight against itself, and I shudder with a climax, pleasure cascading over me and destroying what little self-control I have left.

Victor pulls back slightly, one arm still around my waist, his mouth just a fraction of an inch from mine. The way he smiles at me stirs up motes of anger in the dusty storm of my feelings. I reach out for his pants, and he jerks back, letting go of me and leaving me cold.

"No," he says, and there's a sternness in his voice that makes me want to snap back. How is this fair, for him to take away my protective layer of numbness and leave me aching? My anger rushes to the surface to protect me, and I scowl.

"Let me perform my duties," I grind out, gesturing at his hard cock. "Like you did yesterday."

Victor grits his teeth, his jaw clenching with anger. There it is, I've done it, I've thoroughly pissed him off. He hates himself for losing control; it proves he isn't some sort of dark god, that he's actually human.

"When we're finished here, you can go back and perform your *duties* for Hael. He's chomping at the bit to fuck you over the hood of his Camaro. Have at it." Victor tears the door open and storms out.

I'm still sitting there shaking when I hear the snarled snippets of argument from the hall. I quickly clean myself up and slip out, only to find Vic toe-to-toe with his mother.

"Go on, son," she challenges as Tom hovers nearby, clearly outmatched by the other two people in this room. "Hit me. It'll make you feel better."

"And risk my inheritance for the pleasure?" Vic steps back, his hands tucked into his pockets. They'd have to be, I guess, since he didn't wash them. "No thanks. I'll wait until I get my money and then pay someone to do it for me. That's how you like things done, right? Use cash to get somebody else to do your dirty work for you?" Victor glances over his shoulder at me. "Come on, Bernadette. I think we've overstayed our welcome."

Ophelia grabs my arm on my way out, her fingernails digging into my skin the way my mother's used to. Vic notices and starts to head toward us with a violent sort of purpose in his stride, but I've got this. I don't need his help.

"You're either here for the money, or else you're actually in love with him." Ophelia barks this last part out on the end of a harsh laugh, like the thought of anyone loving her son is absolutely ridiculous, completely unfathomable. "Regardless, you're going to suffer for it. Victor is the spitting image of his young father, and look how that turned out? Once upon a time, I was as naïve as you are now. Don't let him be your greatest mistake."

"Enough," Vic snaps out, but I'm already tearing my arm from her grip, cringing as her nails catch on the stitches in my arm. I swear, I don't breathe again until I get outside.

"I want another name scratched off my list," I gasp, spinning on Victor, his face unreadable, his mouth in a flat line. "Like really scratched off. I don't mean just a dead Range Rover, but ... the whole thing. I want to see progress."

He stares at me for a long, quiet moment, and then nods his head once.

"A deal's a deal," Vic agrees, straddling his bike. "Get on, and let's go."

CHAPTER

Vic takes me back to Aaron's house and then has some sort of caucus in the front yard with Callum and Oscar.

"What happened to Don?" I ask Hael because I feel like he's the most likely to tell me the truth. "I have a right to know that, don't I? I mean, this is my deal after all. This time, I'm the goddamn client."

Hael raises a brow as the sound of little girl giggles drifts down the stairs toward us. The three of them are upstairs with Aaron, dressed in sparkles and glitter, playing some sort of fairy-tale game where Heather is the knight and the other two are damsels in distress. I'm glad to see my little sister playing the role I always wanted for myself.

"Vic hasn't told you?" he asks, and I shake my head. "Your friend Donald was expelled from that fancy school, along with several friends of his. Several other girls came forward with the same story you told. He's being

217

investigated by the DA." The edge of Hael's sharp mouth curves up in a not-quite-smile. "Nothing'll ever come of it, I bet. That's what happens when you have money the way he does, but Vic says we can go for him again once we get his inheritance. Then we can fight on the same level." My mouth parts in surprise, but I do my best to hide the reaction. "Anyway, we broke a dozen bones that'll never heal right. That face isn't so pretty anymore."

"You guys really are thorough, aren't you?" I ask, and Hael shrugs. Loose, cocky, uncomplicated. Not like his idiot boss. *He's chomping at the bit to fuck you over the hood of his Camaro. Have at it.* Right. And what would Vic do if I took him up on that offer? "What's the story Donald's telling now?"

"Dunno. Don't care. Just so long as nothing comes back on us." Hael's phone rings, and he glances at the screen with a tightness in his face I haven't seen before. He just seems to swagger through life, uninhibited, careless. When I lean forward and catch a sneak peek at his screen, I see that double-edged sword of a word again. Mom.

"You don't like your mother?" I ask, and Hael glances up toward me, his face hardening. "Do you like yours?" he retorts, and I shake my head.

"You know all about my mother," I tell him, remembering that night we spent together in the homeless shelter. I was so scared, but Hael wasn't. He covered both our heads with his blanket, wrapping us up in our own private cocoon. *Don't be scared, little bird,* he'd said, smiling a gap-toothed smile at me. *We can tell stories until the sun comes up.* I remember thinking he was the bravest, most beautiful person I'd ever met. "But all I know about yours is that she has a problem with prescription drugs."

"Mm." Hael ignores the call and tucks the phone away, lifting his chin in my direction. "How was breakfast?" He sweeps a tattooed hand over his red hair, studying me with eyes the color of honey and almonds, brown with a hint of gold.

Chomping at the bit, huh? I lick my lower lip, the temptation and the challenge of getting Vic's best friend in bed warring with my sudden and desperate need to be alone. I've been alone most of my life, and this whole Havoc thing ... it comes with a lot of togetherness.

"Breakfast was a nightmare. Vic fingered me under the table while at the same time confronting his mom about her underhanded bullshit. Also, her new boyfriend is a total sleaze."

Hael's brows go up, and he smirks.

"Well, okay then. Sounds like a typical Havoc sort of breakfast meeting. Why is he all stormy and sulky and shit then?"

"He fingered me and then refused to let me touch him," I say, staring intently at the coffee table and wondering why I'm spilling all of this information to Hael. Finally, I look up. "Can you take me to the drugstore? I need to get a morning-after pill, and I don't have any money."

Hael looks at me and then nods slowly.

"Yeah, okay." He stands up just as the front door opens, and Callum, Oscar, and Vic walk in.

"Where are you two headed?" Oscar asks casually, and

I get the idea that it's his job to keep track of everyone on a daily basis. It's not a casual question. Hael and I are not going to walk out of here without an explanation. "Off to the drugstore to get a morning-after pill," I say blandly, shrugging my shoulders. "Victor came inside of me yesterday, and I'm not about getting pregnant."

"Fucking Christ," Vic snaps. "I'll take you."

"I'd rather go with Hael," I say, putting my hand on the cocky asshole's arm. "Is it okay if Heather stays here while we're gone? Shouldn't be long."

"You're too much, Bernadette," Vic growls, stalking past me and disappearing into the dark hallway that leads back to what used to be Aaron's parents' bedroom.

"You like pushing his buttons?" Callum asks, chuckling, that rough voice of his soothing in a strange sort of way. It's like, he's internalized all his shit, and the only time it ever comes out is in an ambient sort of darkness in his voice. "That's a risky ballgame. You've got big ovaries, Bernadette Blackbird." With another burst of laugher, Cal slips past me and into the kitchen.

"Don't stay gone long. We have projects to work on." Oscar's eyes catch on mine, these gray shadows that terrify me even more than the endless black of Vic's irises. "And only two days off of school to do it in."

I move past him and head outside, beyond grateful to find a bit of peace in Hael's car.

"Aren't you dating some girl from Fuller High?" I ask, and Hael shrugs. It's neither a yes nor a no, but I'm too pissed off to care. If he has a girlfriend, that's his problem. Thursday means getting back to school, walking up the front steps of Prescott High and knowing that I'll be navigating a minefield of social politics. "Bet she's a hot piece of ass, for you to cross the Fuller-Prescott line for her."

Hael laughs, this loud, braying sort of sound that I actually kind of like. It's an uninhibited, wild kind of laugh.

"That's pretty much all she is," he says as he pulls into the parking lot of a nearby drug store. I figured he'd idle in the lot while I ran in, but he turns the engine off and pockets the keys, glancing over at me as rain spatters the windshield in big, fat drops. "I'm pretty sure I hate her. Maybe I've always hated her?"

"You screw people you hate?" I ask, and he cocks a brow at me.

"You slept with Vic."

He has a point.

Instead of answering, I smile and push open my door, heading out into the rain and ducking into the front entrance. The place smells like bleach and everything is too white and too sterile. For a moment, I just stand there, wondering where I'm supposed to go and what I'm supposed to do. It's not like I've ever needed morning-after pills before.

"You're right," I say as Hael comes to stand beside me, a sea of color in an otherwise colorless building. "I hate Vic."

Hael works his jaw for a minute, like he's thinking about something, and then gestures with his chin toward the back-left corner of the store.

"Come on, little bird," he says, and I bristle at the nickname, following along behind him. I don't need a guy to tell me about morning-after pills; I have Google. I try to surreptitiously pull out my phone to do some quick research when Hael grabs my hand and yanks me along after him. "Ahh, here we go." He pauses in an aisle filled with tampons and pads on one side, condoms and lube on the other. "Here we go. You have a brand preference?"

"Fifty bucks?!" I choke, grabbing one of the boxes with my mouth hanging open. "For one pill?!"

A couple holding hands starts down the aisle toward us and then pauses, looking unsure.

"Oh Shnookums," Hael says, pulling me into his arms and nuzzling my ear. My entire body lights up with flame, even as my muscles stiffen up and my fingers clench tight around the box in my hands. "It's okay. I'm a gentleman. I always pay for emergency contraceptives after coming in my girl." He pauses and glances over like he's just seen the other couple. "Oh, don't mind us. We're just grabbing supplies for our next fuck-fest."

The couple makes a very hasty exit as Hael chuckles, and I elbow my way out of his arms.

"Seriously?" I ask with a dramatic eye roll, putting the box back and selecting a slightly cheaper generic version instead. Thirty-five bucks. Vic better reimburse Hael for this. "Alright, let's go."

Hael plucks the box from my hand, puts it back, and then grabs four of the expensive name-brand pills.

"Just in case," he says, lifting them up. "And then because you two are idiots ..." He grabs a box of condoms next, hesitates for a second, and then snatches some lube. "Alright, let's go."

"I can make my own healthcare decisions," I growl as

I follow him down the aisle. Hael pauses and lets me catch up, raising his eyebrow again.

"Okay, Blackbird. You don't want this stuff?" He holds it out to me, and I frown.

"I'm not paying you back for any of it. This is Vic's problem."

Hael chuckles and shakes his head at me, heading for the front counter and tossing the shit down on it like he's not at all ashamed to be spending more than two hundred bucks on sex paraphernalia. The woman behind the counter blushes and bites her lip in his direction.

"He's seventeen," I tell her, and she quickly drops the flirty act, ringing the items up as Hael glances over at me and narrows his brown eyes.

"Thanks a lot, Blackbird." He grabs a water bottle from the cooler next the counter and adds that to our tab.

"You're welcome," I tell him with a sharp smile, collecting the bag and heading for the door with Hael on my heels.

"Did you know in some states, they won't let people under eighteen buy morning-after pills without a prescription? Like for real. That's some psycho *Handmaid's Tale* bullshit right there."

"How do you even know that?" I ask as he unlocks the doors, and a pair of Fuller High girls waltzes by, looking him up and down. Good lord. I'd hate to go out in public with Hael on a regular basis. He gets plenty of attention, and returns it right back, tossing a wink their direction before he finally climbs into the Camaro.

"I know all sorts of fun things," he says, looking over at me with heavy-lidded bedroom eyes.

"Vic says you're eager to fuck me over the hood of your car," I say, and Hael lifts both brows this time. "Is that true? Because he basically ordered me to have sex with you."

"He did?" Hael asks, sounding a bit perplexed. He blinks at me and the bedroom eyes fade. "Huh."

"Huh, what?" I ask, feeling my skin get hot and itchy as I pull out one of the boxes and the water.

"Nothing," Hael says absently, gunning the engine and drawing every eye in that parking lot. The women are lusting after Hael, the men after the car. It's pretty pathetic. But I can't say I totally blame them. It is hot. The Camaro, I mean, not the man.

━━━━━━━━━━━━━━━━━━

When we get back to the house, Vic is smoking weed outside with Cal while Aaron entertains the girls and Oscar sits perched on one of the chairs in the living room, fucking with his iPad. Always with the damn iPad.

He glances back at the two of us, gray eyes sharp. He doesn't miss a thing, this guy.

"Did you get the pills?" he asks, and I frown. It's not really any of his fucking business, is it? "And did you take one?"

"None of that is your business or your choice," I snap back, my fingers curling around the handle of the bag. Oscar adjusts his glasses and smiles at me. It's not a very nice smile.

"Not my choice, no, but my business, yes. A baby

complicates things."

"You know what would complicate things?" I ask, stepping forward and dropping the bag on one of the side tables. Aaron and I once carved our initials on the underside with a pocketknife. His mother was furious when she found out, even though you can't see it unless you get down on the floor. "If I kicked your ass and choked the life out of you a second time."

Oscar's face darkens, but before he gets a chance to reply, the back door is opening and Vic is stepping inside. He's goddamn huge, and not just physically. His personality and presence takes up the entire room and sucks the air right out of me.

"What the hell is going on in here?" he asks as Callum slips past him, grabs that black bag of his, and slips right back out. He winks at me before he goes, and I frown, wondering where the hell he's off to.

"Oscar thinks it's his business whether or not I got the pills and whether or not I take them." I lift my chin up, expecting resistance, but Vic just sighs and gives Oscar a look.

"Leave her alone," he says, and although the words sound tired, the order is there. It's not a fucking request. Oscar grits his teeth and stands up, reaching up to push ebon black hair from his forehead.

"It's not often we have two days off during the week. I say we take advantage of it." Oscar looks at me like he wishes I'd keel over and die. Hael just whistles under his breath and slips past me, heading for the kitchen to grab a beer. "Let's go get the wedding dress."

"The wedding dress?" I ask, feeling my stomach dip.

"I ..." I have no good excuse to get out of this. This is what I signed up for, isn't it?

"Do it," Vic says, closing the sliding door and locking it. "Let me get changed first."

"You can't pick out the dress with me," I scoff, feeling my palms get sweaty. "It's bad luck."

"Bad luck?" Vic echoes, and Oscar smirks, noting his boss' discomfort and probably enjoying it, too.

"Bernadette is right. It's bad luck to see a bride in her wedding dress before the wedding. I'll take her." Oscar tucks the iPad under his arm. "Assuming she won't try to choke me while we're out."

"Don't press your luck, and I won't have to," I retort, crossing my arms over my chest and returning Oscar's hard stare.

"I really can't go?" Vic asks, looking confused as fuck. He glances between Oscar and me, his gaze lingering on my lips. I wet them subconsciously, and he closes his eyes. Maybe, like me, he's thinking about our quickie and wondering what it'd be like if we both gave in, if we took our time. "Fine, what the fuck ever. I want this wedding done right. Go."

He opens his eyes again and looks right at me, but I can't hold his gaze. When I do, I feel my armor start to break apart, and all these little worries and fears and wants and desires begin to creep in and tease my aching flesh.

"Let's go," Oscar says, giving Hael's beer a look. "Give me your keys; I'll drive."

"Don't you fucking scratch that fresh paint," Hael warns, but he hands over the keys to his precious Camaro like it's nothing.

I consider saying goodbye to Heather, but then I hear her faux screaming something about dragons and decide to let her be. Sometimes, you just want to be left alone inside your fantasy.

I fully expect our 'shopping' trip to take place in a trailer full of stolen goods, much like it did when we went to get the luncheon dress. Instead, Oscar takes me to a proper bridal shop. I end up standing on the sidewalk outside the doors, soaked in sweat and shaking with nerves.

This is a job, I tell myself, but like the sex with Vic, it doesn't feel that way at all.

"Problem, Bernadette?" Oscar chides, standing next to me and smirking in that irritating way of his. He's of the devil, I'm certain of it.

"No," I snap, more for my own benefit than for his, and then I push in the front doors, a small bell tinkling happily as I move across the shiny wood floors and pause in a sea of white. Why do people get married in white again? Oh, that's right. It's supposed to denote virginity. I have to hold back a snort of nervous laughter.

"Don't worry about the price of the dress," Oscar says, leaning down and putting his lips awfully close to my ear. His breath feathers against my skin, and I shiver. He barely spoke to me on the way over here, and I get the feeling he doesn't like me much. "Just pick something that calls to you."

"Calls to me?" I ask as a perky sales attendant in a khaki skirt and pale pink blouse flounces her way over to me. Her smile is practically plastered on, but I can see it straining at the edges as she takes in the pair of tattooed kids in her shop, undoubtedly here to waste her time.

"Hello there," she says, never allowing her professional façade to drop, despite the fact that she's certain we're not going to buy anything. "Can I help you with something?"

"We're here to get a wedding dress for my lovely companion," Oscar says, placing his hands on the small of my waist and making me shiver. I can feel each one of his fingertips pressing into that tantalizing bit of bare skin between the bottom of my shirt and the top of my jeans. "She's a size eight in commercial clothing. Thirty-eight, twenty-eight, forty measurements."

I grit my teeth and resist the urge to elbow him in the stomach. I have a feeling that if I do, we'll throw down, and I'm not ready to throw down in the middle of a bridal shop.

"Well, I'm here to help. Are we looking for an initial consult or—"

"She knows what she likes, and we need to find a dress today," Oscar says, down to business as usual. The woman turns her attention to me and folds her hands in front of her khaki skirt, seemingly unbothered at being interrupted. I'd have punched Oscar in the balls for that.

"What sort of styles are you into, honey?"

"The most expensive ones," I say, and Oscar lets out a low laugh as the woman tries to keep smiling through my deadpan disinterest.

"Sure, of course," she says, blinking through her confusion. Have to give her credit though. She was born for customer service. "I'm Zoe, by the way. Just follow me."

"Planning on re-selling the dress after the ceremony?" Oscar asks, and I shrug. No point in trying to hide it.

"Something wrong with that?" I ask, but he just makes this clucking sound under his breath and releases me, leaving these little warm spots where his fingertips pressed into my skin.

We follow after Zoe to the back corner of the store— probably to get us out of view of any other customers that might happen in—and she shows me a rack of dresses wrapped in plastic.

I notice that some of them are slightly off in color, in various shades of champagne or gold or whatnot. I mean, they're close enough to white.

"These are from a French designer," she begins as I search for the tag on one of the dresses. *Fifty-five hundred bucks?! For a dress. Holy crap.* My fingers touch the tag, and something inside of me shifts. I don't really care about weddings or ceremonies or tradition, but buying a dress with the sole purpose of reselling it makes me feel like a total asshole.

"Do you have any black dresses?" I ask, lifting my gaze from the tag to Zoe's surprised face.

"A black wedding dress?" she says, like I've just suggested she cut off her own fingers and use them as lace on my gown. "I, um." She pauses again, clearly thinking on her feet. Zoe snaps her fingers. "Okay, I have an idea. I'll set you up in a fitting room."

"A black wedding dress?" Oscar repeats, the sea of white gowns reflecting in the lenses of his glasses. "Aren't we the little rebel?" He gives another one of those deep, low chuckles. "Ophelia will hate it." He pauses a beat as we head toward the fitting room. "But Vic, he'll love it."

Zoe leads me into a room, and then scurries off excitedly, like she's just thought of the perfect dress. I don't bother to wait for her, undressing and kicking off my boots, pants, and jacket. I stand there for a moment in the lingerie Vic gave me, my eyes narrowed on my own reflection.

Tattoos trace over my right hip and down my thigh. Both arms are coated in ink, and I've got pink demon wings across my chest. My pink-tipped white-blonde hair hangs just past my breasts, and the rings in my belly button glint in the fancy studio lighting of the fitting room. Every inch of me is marked in invisible scars, wounds that bisect my soul but not necessarily my body.

There's a light knock on the door.

"Come in," I say, glancing over my shoulder as Zoe slips in the door with a dress draped over her arm. Her pale blue eyes sparkle as she hangs it on a hook and unzips the opaque white garment bag.

"I think I've found the perfect dress for you," she says, beaming at me as she reveals the glittering black fabric. It looks like the sky on a velvety country night, when the Milky Way is a splash of stars against the cosmos. "This is a Lazaro gown," Zoe continues as she takes the dress from the bag and holds it up. "Strapless sweetheart neckline with a lovely pleated skirt. There's an optional feathered piece that goes around the neck as well. We can try it with and without."

Zoe brings the dress toward me, and as she walks, it shimmers and glitters, like the designer reached up and cut the fabric from the stars.

I know as soon as I see it that I've found the right dress.

You're seventeen, Bernadette, and this whole marriage is a sham. You haven't found shit.

I tell myself that this is a business transaction, and that it'll all be worth it when Havoc neutralizes the Thing, when Heather is safe. And yet, I'm not really suffering much, am I?

Zoe helps me into the dress, using plastic clips to gather the excess fabric at my waist.

"Of course, we'd have it tailored to fit you properly," she says as I stare at myself in the full gown, and find the breath knocked right out of me. All of a sudden, I'm swept away in a fantasy of Vic climbing on top of me in this dress, his hands gliding over the shimmering fabric, his lips kissing my bare shoulders.

Jesus Christ.

I'm really losing it, aren't I?

As I'm standing there, shaking and falling to pieces on the inside, Zoe brings the feathered accent piece over and lays it around my neck. She hooks it together in the back and steps away so I can see myself in the three giant mirrors on the wall in front of me.

"How are we feeling?" she asks after what must be several moments. "Any thoughts? We could even try this same dress in ivory or champagne." When I don't respond, Zoe steps up on the dais next to me and places gentle fingers on my arm. "Do you think your mother might want to come and see you in the dress?"

"My mother's dead," I lie, and Zoe blinks her big, blue eyes at me.

"I'm so sorry, I didn't mean—"

"It's fine," I say, turning to look at her and lifting my fingers to the feathers that lie across my inked chest. "I like it. I'd like to see what my friend thinks first. He's actually a very well-known drag queen in the Portland area, so he knows his designer gowns."

"Oh, yes, of course ..." Zoe trails off and nods. I bet she's wondering how old I am, if I can actually afford this dress, if I'm going to try to steal it. But she dutifully leaves the dais and opens the door for Oscar to come in. "I'll be right outside when you're ready. Just let me know what you need."

Oscar's gray eyes home in on my reflection in the mirror, narrowing to stormy slits as Zoe pulls the door closed softly behind him.

"Well, you got one thing right: I do know my designer gowns." He moves toward me, up the steps of the dais, until he's standing directly behind me. His inked form in that stupid suit of his looks pretty much perfect against my own tattooed body. "This is perfection." Oscar hovers his hands over the black feathers on my shoulders, making the fine hairs on my arms stand on end. "Victor will be pleased."

"Victor ..." I start and then scoff, trying to turn around. But Oscar grabs hold of my shoulders and keeps me in place, those intense eyes of his framed by the thick, dark rectangles of his glasses. They should make him look nerdy or businesslike, but with the ink crawling up his neck and flowing over his hands, they don't. Paired with the darkness simmering in his gaze, they just make him look villainous. "Do you suck Vic's dick for fun? What do *you* really think of the dress?"

I try hard not to think about Oscar Montauk in elementary school, or how he once helped me make a dress out of construction paper. I got in trouble for wearing it to recess without anything underneath. Seems fitting that he'd be standing here with me, although I'm pretty sure he hates me now.

"What do I think of the dress?" he asks, skimming his hands down my bare arms. I close my eyes and wet my lower lip. When I open them, he's frowning at me. "I think it needs to serve one purpose: getting you down the aisle to marry Vic."

"You're such an asshole," I snarl, wrenching from his grip and turning to face him, my heart thundering in my chest. Oscar looks down at me with absolutely zero emotion in his expression. But his pants ... I can see the hard shape beneath his slacks. Lifting my eyes back to his, I put a challenge into my gaze. "If you care so little about it, why are you hard for me?"

"I can't control my body," he says, leaning toward me and putting his mouth right up against my ear. His hands skim my waist. He's touching me while I wear a wedding dress meant for another man. Is that wrong? Is this akin to cheating? But I'm supposed to be Havoc's girl, right? I'm supposed to screw all five of them. Isn't that the point? "What's your problem? How can you fuck a man who treated you so poorly? Vic annihilated you during sophomore year, and yet you're panting after him like a bitch in heat."

I draw back and slap Oscar as hard as I can. The crack of flesh on flesh echoes around the quiet room as he snatches my wrist in an iron-clad grip and pulls my hand away. There's a smile on his face now that wasn't there before.

"Everything okay?" Zoe asks, peeping in the door with a nervous look on her pretty face.

"It's fine," I say, staring back at Oscar, refusing to drop his gaze. "We'll take the damn dress."

It isn't until Wednesday that my mom finally checks her messages and finds out about the suspension. I wake up to her call, lying in Aaron's bed with Heather beside me. Staying here, I find that I sleep like the dead. It's nearly noon. I can't remember the last time I slept in this late.

Even though I know I shouldn't, I answer it.

"Hello?"

"What the hell did you do now?!" Pamela shouts, and I can hear in her voice that she actually cares. Not about me, obviously, but about the stain on her reputation that I might cause by being suspended. Springfield isn't a small town per se, but people do talk. And Mom, I think she'd sacrifice me to a sea of vengeful gods if it would grant her the money and status she had back when my dad was still alive. "Why am I getting calls from the school telling me your ex-boyfriend *stabbed* somebody and that you were involved?"

"I'm fine, thanks for asking," I say as I sit up, and my sister stirs beside me. My arm aches where Billie cut me, and I find my fingers subconsciously teasing the edges of the wound. "It's just a two-day suspension, no big deal. I'll be back to school tomorrow."

"And where are you now, exactly? I'm coming to pick Heather up." Pamela sniffs, and I can just imagine her checking her nails for any signs of imperfection. Imperfection should be buffed away and forgotten about, covered up, replaced. That sick, hollow feeling in my stomach opens up, threatening to swallow me whole.

"She's at her friend Kara's house," I say, which isn't even a lie. Not that I give a crap about lying to my mom. She long since lost the privilege of my honesty. *"When you've been lied to by everyone around you, when you have nothing else, you realize the one currency you can carry is truth."* I lick my lips and wonder when Vic's words started to get inside my head like that. "I'll pick her up in a bit and we'll be home in time for dinner, okay?"

It literally makes my mouth hurt to be that nice to her, but it's the only way I can diffuse the situation before she starts making threats.

"Well, we'll talk about this suspension thing when you get home," she says absently, her attention wandering when I don't prove to be the target she wants me to be. "I had a few calls about some classes you missed, too. If you don't want to finish your senior year, fine, I didn't, but I had your father all lined up and turns out I didn't need a degree." She pauses as I close my eyes, quietly seething. A deep inhale brings Aaron's scent into my lungs, and I feel myself calming against my own will. Ugh. Who knew I was such a sentimental bitch?

"I had a bad period and cried in the bathroom during those classes," I say, not caring if the missed days match up to a proper cycle. Pamela won't pay enough attention to notice.

"Okay, honey," she says, clearly bored with me already. "Be here at five, or I'm calling your father."

She hangs up, and I find myself clutching my phone so hard my knuckles hurt.

"He's not my fucking father," I grind out, slipping out of bed and throwing on a hoodie, so I can go outside and smoke. It doesn't occur to me until I actually step out the back door that it's Aaron's hoodie I've got on.

Speak of the devil ...

"Morning," Aaron says, sitting in one of the outdoor chairs and smoking a cigarette of his own. He offers me a light, and I take it, curling up in the chair next to his. My eyes stray to the freshly mowed lawn and the mulched flower beds with the green-leafed rhodies in them. Everything else is orange, red, and brown, the full array of fall colors spinning around us as the maple next to the fence sheds its leaves.

"Sorry about the hoodie," I say, inhaling and holding the smoke in my lungs for several long seconds before I blow it out and let it kiss across my lips. "I was mad, and I slipped it on without thinking."

"You know I don't care if you wear my hoodie, Bernie," he says, dressed in a red zip-up sweatshirt and black sweatpants. His gaze is on the yard, but his focus is elsewhere. I wonder what he's thinking about?

"Um," I start, feeling my own pride kick me right in the throat. Aaron turns to look at me, green-gold eyes swirling with emotion. If I were to really look into them, I bet I could get lost in that gaze of his, tumble down into the endless depths of verdant flecks and hazel sparks. "Thank you."

"For what?" he asks, but we both know what I'm talking about. My eyes narrow. The asshole just wants me to say it. Fine. I'm not too prideful.

"For taking the fall for me," I say, and Aaron's entire body goes stiff. "You risked a lot doing that …"

"Not really," he says, but we both know that he did, and I can't figure out why. He tossed me aside once in order to protect his sister and cousin, so why change up the act now? I study him, that wavy chestnut hair I always loved playing with, that full lower lip I could tease with my tongue, that inked body I no longer recognize as belonging to the boy who took my virginity during freshman year.

"Tell me about Kali," I say, feeling my breathing quicken. I try to focus on my cigarette, using the inhales and exhales of smoke to calm my pulse. "Tell me everything."

"Bernadette," he starts, sounding tired. I guess he would be. Somebody has to mow this lawn and pull the weeds from those flower beds. Somebody cooks the girls breakfast, makes their lunch, worries about dinner. Somebody puts those cute little braids in Ashley's hair, the ones with the pink and blue ribbons. My heart contracts painfully, and I close my eyes. "Why bring up the past?" he continues, his voice far-away, almost dreamlike. "It's over and done with."

"I have a right to know why you bullied me," I say, opening my eyes back up. "I have a right to know why you decided to smash an already cracked vase."

"I told you: Kali had the info I needed to keep my sister and cousin safe."

"Really? And you just became her bitches for half a year?" I shake my head. "No, you're fucking lying to me." I gesture at him with the butt of my cigarette, the black sleeve of the hoodie falling over my fingers. "You'd have just kicked her ass to get the information you wanted. It must've been something else. Why can't you just be honest with me? I thought we were in this together now."

"We are, I just ..." He turns to look at me, and there's an expression hiding just behind the mask he's wearing, something he wants to say, but doesn't. "When did you and Vic fuck?" is what he chooses to ask me instead.

I just stare at him.

"And seriously? No condom?"

"You know what, Aaron?" I say, flicking the still burning cigarette butt into his lap. He curses and flicks it off onto the pavement. "Fuck you."

I head inside, grab Heather, and then kick Hael's shoulder with my foot as he snores on the couch.

"Take me home," I demand, and surprisingly, without complaint, he does.

CHAPTER

Thursday at Prescott High, always a treat to be here. At least now that I have a reputation for stabbing someone, it's become interesting. And no matter how bad it gets here, it's always better than being at home. That dinner with Pamela last night nearly suffocated the last vestiges of life from my body.

"Told you: she belongs with Havoc," a girl says as I sweep past. "She's fucking ruthless."

"I can be," I say, pausing and turning toward her, loving the way her eyes widen just before she scurries off with her friend in tow. "Bitch."

I keep on going, avoiding the downstairs bathroom and heading for my first period English class instead.

"Head's up: the Ensbrooks and the Charters are out for Havoc blood," Stacey calls out as she sashays down the hall with bored, half-lidded eyes and too many rings on her right hand to simply be decorative. "Watch your

239

back, Blackbird." She takes her posse into the restroom as I grit my teeth and exhale, pushing open the door to Mr. Darkwood's class.

Everyone turns to look at me, including Kali, one hand wrapped over the bandage on her arm, her doe eyes wet with fake tears. Part of me wishes the boys would kill her. That's how dark my life has become. But the thing is, her betrayal helped seal my own coffin years ago. It's natural for me to want her dead, isn't it?

"Oh, look," Kali says, sniffling and rubbing at her nose. "It's Havoc's little bitch."

For years, the Havoc Boys have worked their asses off to get control of this school. It's why I hired them. But it only takes one dissenting asshole to break that control, to let the world know they're not as scary as they pretend to be.

And now I'm one of them, right?

I stride forward in my acid-wash jeans, cropped sweatshirt, and boots, and I don't skip a beat before I pull back and sock Kali Rose as hard as I can in the face. Blood spurts from her nose as she rocks back, but I'm not done, snatching the front of her pink sweater and yanking her back toward me.

"Are you fucking serious? Your name is already on my list, but how deep, exactly, the boys dig your hole is up to you." I let go of her and shove the sleeve up on my sweater. It bares my midriff and all my ink, but also hides the raw, angry wound on my arm, closed up with Vic's perfect, tiny black stitches. "You ordered Billie to cut me, and I handled it just fine. I cut you, and you run off to the hospital sucking on Ms. Keating's tit."

Kali's face fills with rage, but she knows I've backed her into a tight corner here. If Mr. Darkwood comes in and she tattles, all of Prescott High will know she's a goddamn snitch. And then I won't have to wait for the boys to get my vengeance; somebody else will do it for us.

"You talk shit about Havoc, you pay the price." I stand up straight, and fix my sweatshirt sleeve, letting my gaze travel around the rest of the room before I take my seat.

Kali's still sitting there, holding her bleeding nose and staring at me. But behind that lick of fear in her eyes, there's rage. She isn't done with me. Good. Because I'm not done with her either.

When Mr. Darkwood comes in, Kali asks for the hall pass to clean up her bloody nose, and I sit down to work on my poem.

Confucius says dig two graves before embarking on a journey of revenge.
But what if that revenge is the only thing keeping you alive?
And what if the people you're seeking revenge on deserve it?
If Batman had just killed the Joker from the get-go, how many more people would still be alive?
Sometimes the bad guys have to die, so if I have to dig two graves, so be it. Better than digging three.

I title the poem *Heather* and turn it in, heading for my next class when the bell rings and pausing in the restroom just long enough to wash the blood from my knuckles.

"I would've paid to see her face when you hauled off and punched her," Callum says with a chuckle, smoking a cigarette and alternating drags with sips of his Pepsi. His blue eyes scan the cafeteria, looking for trouble. "I bet it was goddamn gold."

"She's not afraid enough," I reply, staring out across the room. The first few weeks I hung out with Havoc, it was like they were gods. But now, with this bullshit between the boys and the Ensbrook-Charter brothers, I can feel a shift. People are waiting, watching. This school is a den of lions, and if we don't deliver a little fresh meat, that reputation is all but done for.

Victor doesn't seem to care, scribbling diligently on some homework he missed during our suspension. I grit my teeth, and ignore him, focusing on Oscar as he continues to make notes on his iPad.

"You asked me who I wanted to hit next? I want Kali." Oscar pauses briefly to look up at me, adjusts his glasses, and then refocuses his attention on the screen.

"Excellent. Let's clear up this little mess at Prescott, shall we? I imagine we can creatively incorporate Kali into the whole thing, and wrap this up into a neat, little bow."

"Halloween night," Vic says absently, still scribbling answers down on a worksheet. "We'll deal with them all then. Horrible things happen on Halloween." He stands up suddenly and tucks his pencil into the pocket of his dark blue jeans. "Oscar, figure out where all the best parties are gonna be. Aaron, take Bernadette home after detention. Callum, Hael, you'll stick with me and we'll track their habits."

"Take me home?" I echo, turning to look at him. "I'm supposed to be a part of this group, aren't I? I want in on this."

Vic looks back at me with a raised brow.

"According to you, you're just a fuck-buddy for us to use as we please. Why don't you stick with that role since it seems to interest you more?"

My mouth drops open as he takes off through the cafeteria, and I have to resist the urge to run after him. Not only would that give him the false impression that I give a crap about what he has to say, but it would only damage Havoc's reputation even further for us to reveal conflict in public.

"Are we really Havoc anymore with Bernadette here?" Callum muses, reaching up to ruffle at his blond hair under his hood. "More like Havoc B. Bhavoc. Covahb. There really isn't a great configuration to add a B in, is there?"

"Shut up, Cal," Aaron growls on the end of a sigh. "Leave it alone." I glance his way and meet those pretty green-gold eyes of his. We haven't spoken since our little squabble yesterday, but I need to know more about the whole Kali thing. Understanding why he betrayed me, why they all betrayed me, that's important. "I'll pick you up out front before I get the girls, but don't take too long. I don't like the idea of them waiting for me."

"Don't worry about it," Hael interjects, and I glance over to find him watching me. "I'll take her home."

"But Vic—" Aaron starts, and Oscar finally lifts his attention up from his screen.

"Forget about Victor. I'll tell him it was my idea." Hael flashes a grin and rises to his feet.

Oscar goes back to dicking around with his iPad, and I push up from the table just as the bell rings. Clearly, Hael has an idea in his head, one that I'm hoping matches up the idea in mine.

Trouble.

We're both thinking of starting trouble.

After class gets out, I find Hael behind the school, sitting half in his car and smoking a joint. Cigarette smoke seems to permeate everything, gets stuck in fabric and hair and furniture, but marijuana smoke dissipates better, stinking the place up for a brief while and then disappearing like it was never there.

He watches me as I move across the parking lot to stand beside him, the look in his eyes confirming that we have the same idea in mind.

"You can go back and perform your duties for Hael."
Victor invited me to do this. It's all on him.

"Thanks for offering me a ride," I say, leaning on the roof of his pretty car, fully aware that the move puts my inked midsection right in his face. On the outside, I'm all bravado and sex and cunning. Nobody has to know that I'm a little bit afraid, that sex has always been this double-edged sword for me, wielded as a weapon, a threat, a promise. I can tell myself all I want that it doesn't mean anything.

And yet it does.

If I fuck Hael today, it'll mean a whole lot of somethings.

I'm taking control of my sexuality, I tell myself, but even then, when Hael lifts up a hand and places it on the curve of my waist, my nerves rankle a bit. But then he slides his palm down my skin, and I shiver. His hands are soft as fucking silk.

"Tell me how a mechanic has such soft goddamn hands," I murmur as he curls his fingers through one of the belt loops on my jeans and tugs me forward, knocking me into his lap. Hael's coconut smell drifts around me, mixing with the skunk-y hint of weed, and his lips curve into a sharp smile.

"Motor oil," he says, and I cock a brow. "Gotta get it off somehow. If you start with coconut oil, that'll take off the majority. But there's always some stubborn stickiness. Little bit of dish soap, and a sugar scrub with a pumice stone knocks off the rest." *Ah, so that explains the coconut smell then* ... Hael reaches up a hand to brush some pink-tinged hair back, sliding a single fingertip along my collarbone. "Can't be touching pretty girls like you with oil-covered hands."

"Right." A snort escapes me, but I don't move, letting him curl an inked arm around my waist and tug me just a bit closer. "So, I know why I'm out here. Why are you?"

"What do you mean?" Hael asks, tossing the butt of his joint to the ground and crushing it out with his boot. His words are innocent enough, but there's a devilish curve to his mouth that says he knows otherwise. "Giving you a ride home is hardly a hardship. Are you sure you don't want to sit in my lap on the way?"

"Vic is your best friend," I say, and Hael gives me a weird look.

"So?" he says, acting all innocent as fuck when we both know there's an underlying reason for us both being out here. "What does any of this have to do with Vic? I mean, other than you trying to piss him off by screwing me. Won't work, you know. There's a reason we wanted a Havoc Girl, after all."

My mouth purses into a thin line.

"Yeah?" I quip, my voice turning hard. "And what, exactly, was that reason?"

Hael snorts a laugh and scoots back in the seat, dragging me along with him. He's already got the damn thing pushed back as far as it'll go, leaving me with barely enough room to breathe between his body and the steering wheel when he closes the door on us.

"Ask Victor, you two are so damn close," Hael says, eyes sparkling as he puts one hand on either of my hips.

"I'll admit something. I just had a real bad break-up, and I'm horny as fuck. My motivation is to let Brittany know that I'm banging a girl twice as hot as she is." He shrugs his shoulders and gives me a look. There's something that doesn't quite ring true about his statement, but what does it matter?

"Brittany, huh?" I say, putting my hands on his shoulders. He's wearing a black wifebeater, so his tattooed skin is bare, scorching beneath my palms. "She the cheerleader from Fuller High?"

"Yep." Hael slides his hands up my waist and under my crop-top sweater, pushing it up and out of his way. I'm aware we're sitting just behind the school, in a place that anyone could stumble on us, but I don't really care. I mean, that's sort of the point of all this, isn't it? I'm a Havoc Girl. Havoc rules this school. God help anyone that peeps in on us. Anyone that isn't Vic …

Because I want him to see.

He challenged me, so here I am. Here I fucking am.

Hael tosses my sweater aside and then runs his hands over the lacey cups of my bra. It's the one that Vic gave me in the bag of clothes the other day, and as much as I hate to admit it, it fits a million times better than the ones I was wearing before.

"Damn, girl," Hael growls, running his thumbs over the pert points of my nipples. Hard to believe this is the same kid who held my hand through a whole night in the homeless shelter all those years ago.

I let my head fall back and try to remember how to breathe. My heart is racing so fast I feel dizzy, and my pulse is thundering so loud in my head I can hardly hear the radio when Hael leans forward to turn it on. I recognize the song *Fire Up The Night* by New Medicine.

Hael's hands are pure fire as he skims them over my aching skin, working my nipples through the lace with his thumbs. Unlike Vic, Hael Harbin is in complete control of himself. I can feel his confidence when he slips the lace over my breasts and then palms the full mounds with a groan.

"Damn, Blackbird, you've got some nice tits," he grinds out, leaning forward and giving me this wicked look before flicking his hot tongue out to taste my nipple. My back arches automatically, offering my breast to his hungry mouth as he sucks greedily and then gently bites the hardened peak. A gasp slips out of me, and I find myself curling my fingers in his hair to gain some semblance of control.

My head is bowed over because of the low roof, so I end up wrapped around Hael as he teases both nipples until they're painful and aching. When he pulls back, the wetness on those pert pink points makes them feel icy cold, and I put his hands right back where they were.

"Let's get some of these clothes off," he purrs, reaching down to undo the button on my jeans. As soon as he does, he slips his hand in to see what we're working with here. Lucky for him, I'm soaked through already. "Fuck," he groans as I grab his wrist and push his inked hand under the silken fabric of my undies, the same ones Vic gave me that I washed last night.

Hael's fingers tease my folds as he looks up at me

with eyes the color of honey, and runs his tongue over his full, lower lip. I won't lie: I've wondered before what it might be like to fuck Hael Harbin. And I have to say, so far I'm not disappointed.

Using my own wetness for lube, Hael works my clit with his thumb, this strong, steady pressure that has me quivering and sweating before the song's even over.

Scrambling for the door handle, I press down on it and push Hael's hand away at the same time.

He must know what I'm up to because he just grins as he strips off his shirt and chucks it into the back seat. There I am, bare-breasted and stripping my jeans off in a deserted parking lot, my heart thundering like crazy as I wonder who might be watching.

When I climb back in, shoving my jeans into the passenger seat, I find that Hael's already one step ahead of me. He's not only undone his own pants, but he's in the process of fanning out a sea of condoms for me to look at.

"Your choice, baby," he says as I straddle his thighs and yank the door closed behind me, trapping us together with the smell of leather and sex. "I've got different colors, ribbed options, different flavors ..."

"Don't get too excited," I say, snatching a red condom that matches his hair. There's a hitch in my voice, a breathless sort of quality that belies my insistence that this is all a chore, that I'm doing this out of duty. I'm here because I want to be here. "There's not nearly enough room in here for a blow job."

"Tomorrow morning then?" he asks, as I reach down

and wrap my hand around his shaft, giving it a squeeze. "I'll pick you up before school?"

I meet his eyes and then lean forward, letting a bit of saliva well up on the edge of my lips and drip to the head of his cock before working him with my fist. He's got a piercing on the tip that I tease with my thumb, mimicking the way he touched me first.

"Maybe." I look down at Hael, lounging back on his red and black leather seat, ink tracing his muscular arms. He doesn't have nearly as much work as, say, Oscar, but it's impressive, for someone who's not-quite-eighteen to be sporting so much skin art. Technically, it's illegal to get tattooed under the age of eighteen in Oregon, but illegal doesn't mean impossible. I'm sure he has his contacts the same way I have mine. "Put this on," I say, handing over the condom and giving him a few last pumps with my fist while he opens it.

It occurs to me that we haven't kissed yet.

It occurs to me … that maybe I don't want to.

There's a certain distance here that I can handle. I can stay numb on the inside while my body burns on the outside.

Hael finishes slipping the condom on, and then reaches out for my hips, dragging me just a bit closer. The space is so confined that my knee is digging into the door on one side, the gear shift on the other, but it doesn't matter. When Hael pulls my panties aside with two fingers and encourages me to slide over him, I don't have to think. I don't have to feel my emotions breaking into pieces and cutting me up from the inside.

The music continues to blare from the speaker, one sexy song after another. I realize Hael must have some sort of playlist set up. None of this is random.

I position him at my opening and start to settle back. He stops me by squeezing his inked hands against my hips.

"You don't have to kiss me, but I want you to look at me," he growls out, drawing my eyes up to his face. Hael smirks and then releases some of the pressure on my hips. "That's better. Now, ride me, baby."

I slide down, taking every last inch of Hael into me. He's not as big as Vic, so it's a slightly more comfortable fit. A small gasp slips past my lips as he adjusts my hips and makes it so that we're completely joined together, encouraging me to move by leaning forward and biting my neck just enough that it rides that line of pleasure and pain.

"Say something, Bernadette," Hael whispers, his voice husky with pleasure. "I want to hear your voice." His request hits me like a brick to the chest, and for a moment, it's all I can do to sit there, feeling his hard length inside of me. *My voice? Why?*

"Shut the fuck up," is all I can think to respond with, and Hael laughs, letting me push him back with a hand to the chest. I curl my nails against his skin, satisfied when my fingernails leave welts. His brown eyes darken with lust as I work my hips, making the poor Camaro rock beneath us.

Hael moves his hand back to that sweet spot he found earlier, teasing my clit and obliterating the rest of me.

There's nothing but my body, wrapped around his, two hearts beating while two bodies flame.

With his free hand, Hael holds my hip, kneading his fingers against my inked flesh. There's a pink dragon wrapped around a lotus blossom tree, the petals of the flowers bleeding into her scales. The piece cost over a thousand bucks, but I stole the money from my mother's wallet the day before her big Vegas trip with her girlfriends and let her blame it on the Thing.

It was money well-spent.

A sigh escapes as my body begins to tighten around Hael, my climax coming too quick and too hot to stop. The bright hot ache of perfect agony explodes in my core, and I lean forward as the pulses overtake my body. With a growl, Hael rocks his hips up, pushing himself into me again and again. My bare breasts are against his hard chest, and the urge to kiss him is overwhelming.

But I don't.

Instead, I dig my nails into his shoulders as another orgasm washes over me, consuming what little decorum I've got left.

"Fuck, fuck, fuck," I groan, panting as Hael lets me fall over the edge, his own climax not far behind. He grunts against my shoulder, his body slicked with sweat, shuddering as he spills himself into the condom.

For almost two whole songs, we just lay there panting.

"Shit," he grumbles, and then pushes me over into the passenger seat—not unkindly—before exhaling and swiping his hands down his sweaty face. "Well, that was fun." Hael looks me over appreciatively.

At least I can see that his hands are shaking, that I've had some effect on him. He sits up and turns the ignition, letting the Camaro rumble to life beneath us before bothering to remove the condom and fix his pants. He ties it off, and then climbs out to chuck it in the dumpster before coming back.

I don't say a thing, just slip my clothes on in the tight space, my body throbbing and humming, my breath still coming in pants.

"Off we go," Hael says, revving the engine and peeling out of the parking lot with a squeal of tires. He takes me straight home, and, seeing as it's a ten-minute walk, it's all of a two-minute drive. Neither of us speaks, both lost in thought. My mind is obsessively turning over Victor's words. No clue what Hael is fixated on.

He pulls up in the driveway, parking next to my mother's car.

Fuck.

She's always home when I most need her to be away.

"Need any backup going in there?" Hael asks, his inked hands on the steering wheel. He glances my way and gives me this cocksure little smile. "I'm happy to throw your stepdad against the wall again if needed."

"No, I'll be fine," I say, because really, I just sort of need to get away from him. There's this strange churning in my stomach that I can't explain, that almost feels like guilt.

"Alright then," he says, watching as I gather up my backpack and open the door. I notice he doesn't try to be a 'gentleman' this time. "Bring your stuff for a sleepover tomorrow. If you need to make arrangements for your sister, Aaron's hiring a babysitter."

Without responding, I slip out and head inside, slinking up the stairs before Mom can assault me on them, and then settle myself in to wait for Heather's bus. Luckily, the after-school program has one that brings her straight home.

Meanwhile, I have a moment to nibble on my lower lip and think about what just happened.

I just had sex with Hael Harbin.

I'm also certain I've just pissed Victor off.

It's going to be interesting, seeing what tomorrow brings ...

CHAPTER
TWENTY-FIVE

The next morning, Hael picks me up just after Heather gets on the bus, smoking a cigarette out the window of the car. He eyes my leather pants and jacket as I climb in, and makes a sound of appreciation under his breath.

"Lookin' good this morning, Blackbird," he tells me, starting the car and taking me just a few blocks away before he pulls into the driveway of a vacant house with a *For Sale* sign in the yard. After climbing out, Hael walks across the street and sticks something under the rear bumper of a white Kia Sportage.

"What the hell was that all about?" I ask, and he shrugs.

"Vic'll explain tonight," he tells me, and then his eyes rove my body again. "You give a fuck about missing first period? Because I don't."

"It's sort of like high school roulette," I explain, shrugging one shoulder. "You know those automated calls they send out when you miss class? If my mom happens to answer one, she might tear me a new one. If not, all is rainbows and unicorn shit."

Hael grins at me.

"Want to take a risk?" he asks, and I feel this heat creeping up into my chest. I swipe some pink-tinged blond hair behind an ear and shrug.

"Maybe at lunch?" I retort, acting like I know way more about this sort of shit than I really do. How many blow jobs have I given in my life? One? Two, maybe. But there's this challenge coupled with eagerness in Hael's face that I want to see through. I just can't risk missing anymore class, not when Pamela is still a threat. Sending Havoc after her is an option, but I was sort of saving her for last, after the Thing had been dealt with. I'm hoping that whatever the boys come up with, it neutralizes him as a threat.

I just want my sister safe, that's the only thing that matters.

"Lunch then," Hael replies, stroking a thumb down the seam in his jeans and giving me a devilish sort of grin in response. "Meet me in front of the cafeteria."

"Deal," I say, leaning back against the door to study him. I swear, it still smells like sex and sweat in here. "But don't think I'm not expecting you to return the favor."

"Oh, I see how it is," Hael growls as he pulls us out of the driveway and starts off toward the school. I always know when we're headed in the direction of Prescott High because the houses get considerably less nice, smaller, and much closer together.

"Am I not allowed to ask for reciprocation?" I quip, crossing my arms over my chest.

"Ehh, on the contrary, I think that's how a Havoc Girl *should* sound," Hael says, parking in his usual spot, right next to the dumpsters and just outside the perimeter fence. It's the exact same spot we fucked in yesterday. "But don't worry." He leans over to take off my seat belt and puts his hot mouth right up against my ear. "I give as good as I get."

Hael climbs out, leaving me to follow along behind him and around to the front of the school where we both endure the usual pat-downs, metal detectors, and rude inquiries intended to make us feel like fucking terrorists.

As soon as I get in the hall, I can feel it, his eyes on me.

"What?" I ask as Vic steps out of the shadows of one of the classrooms, and Hael freezes up. Maybe our having sex isn't as much the non-issue as he made it out to be? But Victor doesn't say a word, sweeping up the hall toward his first class and carrying a dark shadow with him that makes me shiver.

"Fuck me. We might be in trouble," Hael murmurs, but then he just shakes it off and keeps going, leaving me to brave my English class alone.

Kali isn't present today which is a goddamn blessing. I swear, I can still see a drop of red blood on the floor near her desk. It makes the class a little easier to get through as Mr. Darkwood returns both of my poems covered in red marks and asinine suggestions that I'll never take. My poetry might not be good, but his is lifeless, rigid to form, and dull as drying paint. I ball both of the pages up, chuck them, and then start over again.

Guilt tastes like ash on my tongue.

I'm tasting the remnants of yesterday.

But a cherry-red Camaro can't take away the question in your eyes:

Who are you? And what have you done to me?

Victor Channing is not in a good mood when I pause outside the cafeteria and find him standing there. He's waiting, maybe? I guess we've all been eating lunch together every day since I joined Havoc.

What'll it look like if Hael and I both disappear, as we'd planned?

I stand there awkwardly, trying to think of what to say. Vic seems quite content to keep silent, staring at me and refusing to avert his gaze. Luckily, Aaron, Oscar, and Callum show up before the stifling silence chokes me to death.

"Are we intending a funeral?" Callum asks, trying to lighten the mood with one of his deep, dark chuckles. "Because the atmosphere is tense as fuck."

Hael appears, swaggering down the hall like he owns the world, and wearing a cocky take-no-shit smile.

Vic doesn't smile back.

"After school, we all head straight to Aaron's. Is that

clear? Any other deviations from the plan I should know about?" he snaps, and Hael's smile disappears.

"No boss," Callum says, lifting his hands up in a placating gesture. He exchanges a look with Hael who at least has the good grace to cringe, running a hand over his red faux hawk.

"About yesterday—" he starts, but Vic is already pushing his way into the cafeteria, and Aaron is staring at me like he's never seen me before.

"Interesting," Oscar observes, slipping in after Vic. Callum looks between the three of us, pushes his hood off his blond hair, and then chuckles again.

"Jesus Christ," he says, and then he leaves, too.

The dynamic between Hael, Aaron, and me isn't pretty.

Aaron is clearly furious, but doesn't know what to say.

"We're gonna go take care of that errand and then smoke by my car," Hael says, his voice neutral, edging on the verge of a challenge as he stares Aaron down. "That cool?"

Aaron just stares right back at him. They're about the same height, same build. If a fight were to break out, it'd be a close one. But we really don't need to show any discord on campus.

I should just suggest we eat in the cafeteria. That'd be the simple solution to a tense afternoon. But somehow, Aaron's and Vic's attitudes make me want to leave with Hael.

"Smoke, huh?" Aaron asks carefully, and then laughs,

this caustic, awful sort of sound. "Right. I bet that's what you did yesterday. Smoked." He shakes his head and shoves his shoulder into the swinging door, the one covered in Sharpie and stickers. There are more penises drawn on that door than there are in the entire student body.

"Am I in trouble here?" I ask Hael, turning to look at him. His gaze is on the cafeteria door, jaw tight. He moves his honey-colored eyes over to me, but he can't seem to force that cocky smile onto his face. "I thought this was part of me joining Havoc. I recall Vic using the word 'plaything'." My own jaw is clenched when I say that. It's a cop out, I know. Me and Hael, this has nothing to do with me trying to be a good Havoc Girl and perform my duties, and everything to do with trying to piss Victor off. Apparently, I'm succeeding. "Are we not allowed to fuck each other?"

"Maybe we're just not fucking each other to their specifications?" he muses, shaking his head. "Whatever. If Aaron or Vic are mad about it, they can friggin' talk to me." Hael tucks his inked hands into his pockets and then gestures with his chin. "You coming, Blackbird?"

I follow him down the hall, opposite the direction of the front doors and straight toward the principal's office.

Hael has the keys which doesn't surprise me; I bet Havoc has access to every room on campus.

"Here?" I ask, and he laughs, this shit-eating, I-own-the-world asshole sort of laugh. It makes me want to punch him, not suck his dick. "We'll get caught. And there are cameras."

"The cameras," he says, pointing up at one in the corner with a blinking light. "Are cheap ass, battery-run fakes that Vaughn got from Wal-Mart. You think he really wants cameras in here? Isn't this where he propositioned you?"

My mouth flattens into a thin line.

It is.

Hael's right. I open my mouth to ask him how he knows, but he's already way ahead of me, sitting in Vaughn's chair and leaning back. He crosses his arms behind his head and looks me over.

"He propositions all his victims in here," Hael says as I close and lock the door behind me. *Fuck, this is risky.* But really, what can Principal Vaughn do if he catches us in here? We know all his secrets. It's just a matter of time before the cliff edge he's standing on comes tumbling down.

"How many girls has he asked?" I say, but Hael just shakes his head.

"No time. Don't worry about that right now." He grins at me, and I hesitate just a brief second before letting the subject go. Hael's right, we're running on limited time here. I know on Fridays, Vaughn holds a staff meeting in the teachers' lounge. He's usually on his way back to his office when I start heading for fifth period.

So we've got ... twenty minutes, tops.

Also, I know this isn't the last we'll be talking about Vaughn and his cam girls. I might've been one myself, if I hadn't already been burned, if I didn't already know better.

"Let's defile Mr. Vaughn's office," Hael suggests, and then he leans forward, those honey-brown eyes of his glittering with mischief. "You want to go first? I'm dying to see what tough-as-nails Bernadette Blackbird looks like when she's getting proper head."

I wrinkle my nose, but my palms are sweating, and the thrill of being in here when I know it would infuriate Vaughn is almost as alluring as the prospect of Hael on his knees. *Wow. Where did that thought come from?* I'm supposed to be Havoc's plaything, right?

"I'll go first," I agree, and Hael slides off the chair and onto his knees, gesturing at the vacated seat with an inked hand.

"Ladies first." I kick off my heels and sit down as he turns to face me, flicking the button on my leather pants and curling his fingers under the waistband. "Leather pants, man's conundrum. Makes a woman's ass irresistible, but also a pain in *my* ass when it comes to getting them off." He starts to peel the fabric down my hips as my heart thunders in my chest.

"Don't tell me *Brittany* often wears leather pants," I say with a bit of a curl to my lip. I have no idea why I bring up the peppy cheerleader that Hael's been dating, but he doesn't seem to mind. In fact, his cocksure grin gets a little crueler, a little sharper, and I realize that maybe while I was using him yesterday to punish Vic, he was punishing Brittany.

"Not frequently," Hael agrees, tearing my pants off and slinging them over his shoulder. He parts my knees and then leans in, running that wicked hot tongue up my inner thigh. My hands curl around the ends of the arm rests, and I find myself staring up at the drop ceiling above our heads. "Look at me," Hael commands, just like he did yesterday.

My gaze drops to his, and I realize that even in this position, I'm not in charge. He is. And it pisses me off. But then he slides his thumb up the crotch of my underwear, and I can't find the energy to be angry. Instead, my skin gets hot and a bead of sweat trails down between my breasts as Hael leans in and presses his mouth against my core in a naughty kiss.

"Eighteen minutes," I remind him, and he laughs, yanking the panties to the side with two fingers and tasting me between the thighs the same way he tasted my tits yesterday. A sharp exhale escapes me as I grab hold of his bright red hair and pull him closer, encouraging him to move faster. Straight ahead of me, I can see the clock on the wall ticking down the seconds.

Hael's tongue dances a wicked little jig against my body as he slides his left hand under my right thigh, gripping my ass and squeezing hard. He waits until I'm trembling before he finally pays any attention to my clit. The tip of his tongue flicks across it at the same moment he enters me with two fingers, curving them against my aching insides and drawing a climax from me that's like magic. One-part skill, two-parts the thrill that we might get caught.

"Five minutes left," he says, smirking at me and running his tattooed arm across his mouth. Hael chucks my leather pants at me in challenge. "How good are you,

Blackbird?"

"Better than you," I mock, but Hael gives that braying laugh of his, like he doesn't believe that for shit. I guess, seeing as he gave me an orgasm in thirteen minutes, he can act like that. I struggle into my pants, slip my heels back on, and then turn to find him already situated in the chair.

Hael occupies it like he's the king of the school, one elbow on the armrest, inked fingers resting beneath his chin. His smirk is lazy and self-assured, his posture dripping arrogance, and his gaze flaming with heat. With those sexy bedroom eyes of his, and that sweet coconut smell, he's practically irresistible.

Dropping to my knees, I tear the button on his jeans open and look up at him, freeing his cock and feeling my breath catch in my throat. *Better than you,* I said, but really, that's a load of crap. I barely know what I'm doing.

My hand wraps the base of Hael's cock while he threads tattooed fingers in my hair, guiding my mouth to exactly where he wants it. My dark purple lipstick is gonna stain, but maybe that's what he wants? I don't worry about it as I take the head between my lips and slide forward, enveloping his hard shaft in the heat of my mouth.

The groan that escapes Hael's lips makes my already over-excited body tingle as I swirl my tongue around the tip and feel his hips buck up off the chair.

"I won't lie, I've wondered what your mouth might feel like," he says, his fingers pressing a little firmer against the back of my head, encouraging me to go faster, take him deeper. "I used to grill Aaron about it."

I ignore him, working him with my lips and tongue, wondering how many minutes we have left. *We must have at least three, right?* My right hand grips the base of Hael's dick while my tongue does most of the hard work, swirling around him and working these deeply satisfying groans from his throat. He helps me along, hips bucking up off the chair to create more of that wet, hot friction.

I'm so into it, I consider reaching down to stroke myself through my pants when I hear the sound of a key in a lock and start to pull back.

"No, wait, I'm almost there, baby." Hael holds me still as he groans, thrusting up into my mouth and coming hard before I get a chance to pull away.

"What the hell is this?" A startled male voice snaps the wild tension in the room as I struggle to swallow and wipe my lips at the same time. Hael is buttoning up his jeans like he doesn't give a shit and standing up. I turn to follow his stare and find Principal Vaughn, red-faced and shaking with one hand on the doorknob of his office. "I let you off easy last week, but we're looking at expulsion for something like this."

"Hello Vaughn," Hael says, reaching into his pocket and pulling out a flash drive. He tucks it into the front pocket of the principal's white button-up shirt and smiles. "Take a look at what's on that drive, and then get back to us with your plans." Hael turns and offers up an inked hand for me to take. I do, narrowing my eyes on him, my heart beating so fast I feel dizzy. But I meet Principal Vaughn's wide-eyed stare head-on. I hate this man for so many reasons, the least of which is that, when I came to him with allegations about my stepfather, he went and called the Thing personally.

Invited him to pick me up.

Called me a liar.

Called my sister a whore.

I'm shaking with rage now as Hael drags me a step forward, and then pauses to put his hand on Vaughn's left shoulder.

"Watch the videos and decide how you want to repent. Maybe next time it won't be just your car that we blow up."

Hael yanks me out the door and into the hallway, shoving me into the cinder block wall and leaning over me. His mouth hits mine before I can even think to turn away, searing through the haze of anger and leaving me panting.

"I wanted to see what I'd taste like on your lips," he says, and then he laughs again and pushes off the wall, disappearing down the hallway toward his next class. Everyone's staring at us, but it doesn't matter.

At Prescott High, everyone knows ... you don't mess with Havoc.

CHAPTER

I head down the front steps after school to find Hael waiting for me in his car on the curb across the street, music blasting from his speakers, one tattooed arm hanging out and tapping a rhythm against the cherry-red metal.

Like a good girl, I look both ways before I cross, skirt around the hood, and slip into the passenger seat.

"Waiting for Oscar and Callum," Hael explains when we don't take off right away, smoking a cigarette and blowing gray smoke out the open window. He offers me the pack, and I take one, careful to avoid our fingers touching.

I let Hael Harbin go down on me in the principal's office, I think, and then pull in a deep inhale to banish the thoughts with nicotine. *And all for the sake of revenge.* A small smile curves my freshly painted lips. I mean, there are worse ways to ensure the downfall of one's enemies.

Oscar appears in his suit, Callum right behind him,

wearing a baggy blue hoodie with the sleeves cut off, like always.

They head across the street and I start to get out, but Hael beats me to it, climbing out and lifting his seat up so the other two boys can crawl in the back. They look ridiculous back there, like we're in some sort of clown car or something. It's far too small for them, but nobody complains.

"Can we please grab something to eat on the way to Aaron's? I'm fucking starving," Callum groans, that throaty voice of his giving me the chills. He curls his fingers over the back of my seat and peers at my phone as I tap out yet another lie to my mother. His smell drifts over me, this pleasant mix of shaving cream, talc, and aftershave. "Maybe the drive-in?"

"If it's not sanctioned by Vic, I'm not doing it," Hael says on the end of a forced laugh. "Pretty sure Blackbird and I are in enough trouble as it is."

"For fucking in your car behind the school, or taking your lunch assignment to a different level?" Oscar asks, and I can see in the rearview mirror that he barely lifts his eyes from the screen of his iPad.

"Lunch assignment?" I ask and Callum chuckles, low and dark. There's some deep-seated pain in that laugh, but also a grudging sort of acceptance. *The darkness is where I live; I've learned to be happy here.*

I shiver.

"You know how hunters send their dogs in to flush out the prey?" Callum asks, and I glance back to give him a questioning sort of look. "Hael is the dog."

"And who's the prey?" I ask, just before I come up

with the answer on my own. "Principal Vaughn." I hit send on my text and wonder how long my luck's gonna hold before Mom starts after me for being gone all the time. That, and because I've always got Heather with me. Always. Once she's done with her after-school program, we'll go pick her up. "I thought we were going after Kali next?"

"Kali's tied up with the Ensbrook and Charter brothers," Oscar explains in that Lucullan smooth voice of his, like some sort of dark angel. Finally, he turns off the screen of the iPad and sets his inked hands over the top of it. "It's going to take a bit more finesse. Principal Vaughn is becoming a problem."

"He hauled Vic into his office yesterday and nailed him with weekend janitorial duty for a dress code violation," Callum explains, and Hael makes a sound of surprise, his hand tightening on the wheel.

"Why is this the first I'm hearing of that?"

"Maybe because you guys were too busy screwing each other to check the group chat?" Callum asks, leaning over me again and snatching my phone. He hits my text messages and pans up the long list of speech bubbles to one from Vic, timestamped for early yesterday afternoon. Oops. I was a little distracted last night when I glanced at the messages. I'm not used to actually being a part of a group chat that's worth checking. "Now, Bernadette, ask him if we can't swing by the drive-in? If you ask, I'm sure he'll say yes." Cal chuckles again, and I frown.

"I'm not following the joke," I say, but Callum just laughs and neither of the other guys offer up an explanation. Instead, we head straight to Aaron's, even as

Callum bitches incessantly about being hungry. Vic is already waiting for us in one of the chairs on the lawn, smoking a cigarette and frowning so deeply I wonder if the expression might end up etched into that pretty face of his.

"Boss, let's order food," Callum says, and Vic carefully lifts his dark gaze from me to his friend. Cal puts his hands in a prayer position and waits until his leader casually sighs and nods once. "Pizza, I think. Yeah, I'm feeling pizza."

I study Callum as he slips his hood off. He's always wearing baggy tops, but his legs are muscular and trim under his black shorts, and he's got a much leaner build than most of the other guys. A series of deep scars mars his legs, the wounds old, the flesh shiny and healed over, but a clear sign of past trauma. I wonder what happened to him?

"He eats like a horse and still has a dancer's body," I grumble as Callum disappears into the house, and I notice that Vic stiffens up slightly beside me, glancing my direction. "I'm a little envious."

"How so?" Vic asks, his voice dark, sharp, dangerous. A hot thrill chases up my spine as he rakes that ebony gaze over me. "You're in perfect shape. Don't you think so, Hael?"

Hael pauses next to us as Oscar sighs and slips in the front door, leaving the three of us alone on the lawn. "I mean, you got a good look yesterday, didn't you? And again today?"

Hael's honey-colored eyes shift my direction and he licks his lower lip, flexing his tattooed fist around his car keys.

"She has a perfect body," he agrees, looking from me to Vic, like he's waiting for the other shoe to drop. Victor just scoffs, flicks his cigarette into the grass, and stands up, heading into the house and leaving the two of us behind. "Fuck," Hael murmurs, gritting his teeth. "We're in trouble; he's pissed."

"Why?" I ask, and Hael looks at me like I'm a crazy person. He opens his mouth like he's about to answer me when Aaron pulls into the driveway, and Kara spills out the back door of the van with her cousin in tow.

"Movie night and popcorn!" she yells, pausing next to me and grinning. "Our favorite babysitter is coming over tonight."

"So I hear," I say, pretending that I don't feel her brother's eyes on me, taking me in, judging me. I stroke Kara's hair back, the same, wavy silken texture as Aaron's. "Do you mind if Heather joins you guys?" Kara's grin lights up her face as she glances back at Ashley, shyly clinging to Aaron's pant leg.

"She can join. You, too, if you want."

"I appreciate that," I say as Aaron picks Ashley up and carries her past me, tearing his gaze away and acting like he doesn't see me standing there. Whatever.

"Ladies first," Hael mimics, repeating his words from earlier. I turn to find him with his arm out, gesturing for me to head inside. I do, and the normalcy of Aaron's house falls over me like a curtain. There's no tension in these walls, no hate, no ragged screams broken up only by dry wall. No *Thing*.

"Where are we off to tonight?" I ask Oscar, pausing in

271

the living room as Callum slumps on the couch and orders pizza on his phone app, Aaron disappears upstairs with the girls, and Hael gets himself a beer from the fridge.

"We have too many open business transactions," he says, looking at me through his black-framed glasses and smiling. Someone with glasses shouldn't look so scary, but Oscar Montauk, well, he manages to pull it off just fine. "We're going to start cleaning things up."

"I thought you guys preferred to be direct. Isn't that what you said to me on day one? *Don't beat around the bush. We* really *don't like it.*"

Oscar lifts a finely curved brow and then reaches up tatted fingers to touch his equally inked up neck.

"Good point. We're going to follow Principal Vaughn and see if Hael's gift has stirred him to action." Oscar pauses to listen to the girls' giggling upstairs, and then turns to look at me, a smirk curving over his wicked lips. "The flash drive had a few select videos of his cam girls on them, just to remind him that we know all his dirty, little secrets."

A frown takes over my mouth, and I exhale, memories washing over me. I push them down and let cool, icy numbness seep back into me. I can tell the story, without reliving it. It's a specialty of mine, disconnecting.

"Principal Vaughn is a monster of the worst kind," I say, thinking about his hand on my knee, rubbing, caressing. "He waited until I was at my lowest before he decided to invite me into his bullshit."

"What happened, exactly?" Callum asks, looking up from his phone, the light playing across his relatively delicate features. If it weren't for the scars, and the hard muscles in his shoulders and chest, he'd have that pretty, preppy sort of look. "If you don't my asking. Everyone deals with trauma differently. I have a tendency to re-live mine over and over inside my head. Talking about it gets it all out." His blue eyes flash and he licks his lips, blond hair disheveled from his hood, legs crossed on the velvety couch cushions.

"Well, you all know the beginning of the story," I say dryly, gesturing in Callum and Hael's general direction, my eyes narrowing. "You guys decided to turn my life into a living hell with Kali Rose's help, and I went to Principal Vaughn to report the bullying." A dry laugh escapes me, and I run a hand over my face as Aaron comes down the stairs. If he's going to act like I don't exist today, I'll return the favor. I continue with my story, perching on the back of the larger couch. "You assholes did … whatever it is that you do, and my accusations were buried in bullshit. Then my sister died, and …" I trail off, and there's this hitch in my chest that makes it impossible to breathe.

When I think about Pen, I lose myself.

To sadness.

Regret.

Anger.

Rage.

My hands begin to shake as Aaron moves into the living room and offers me a cold beer. I take it and we exchange a wordless look, both of us holding onto our emotions so tight that we may as well be on different continents.

I remember the day Penelope died. I also remember how the bullying stopped. That was the day the Havoc Boys left me alone for good. That is, until I marched up to Victor Channing on the first day of school and called out that word.

Havoc.

They create it.

They revel in it.

They dispense it.

"We threatened Principal Vaughn with photos of him fucking the school nurse in his office. It was a serious enough offense that he buried your report, but not enough to keep him off our asses forever." Aaron sits down in the burgundy chair between the two couches and sips his beer, his expression distant and focused on the fireplace instead of my face. Callum, Hael, and Oscar, however, are all staring at me.

Victor is nowhere to be seen, but for some reason, I feel like he's listening.

"After Penelope died, I went to see Principal Vaughn —Ms. Keating didn't work at Prescott then or else I would've spoken to her." I knock back a third of my beer in a single gulp and swipe a tattooed hand over my mouth. "I reported my stepfather for molesting ... for *raping* my sister. And instead of helping me, Vaughn called the Thing and told him everything I'd said. Then he put his hand on my leg and asked me if I wanted to escape."

My eyes close briefly, and I feel that familiar anger taking over. His hand was so sweaty, almost lukewarm, his tongue sliding over his thin lower lip. Even the look in his eyes was a violation of sorts.

"You don't have to live this life, Bernadette, not if you don't want to. Would you like to escape? To make something of yourself? I know an easy way for a girl like you to make money."

"I told him I wasn't going to be a prostitute, that I was fully aware that was an option." I sigh again, and my body just feels so damn heavy ... "He mentioned I could work from the safety of his cabin, on camera, that—"

"Enough," Vic says, appearing from seemingly out of nowhere. He's just suddenly standing near the bottom of the stairs, face dark, features hard. "The Kia Sportage is on the move."

"Kia Sportage?" I echo as Oscar smiles.

"Vaughn's wife's car," he says, and then glances my way. "*Not* the nurse. His actual wife. She's staying in Connecticut with her ailing mother. Meanwhile, her inglorious husband is using her car now that we've blown his up."

"He's heading for McKenzie Highway. Clearly, he's on his way to the cabin." Vic's jaw works in irritation.

"Well, that was fast," Hael says with a somewhat nervous laugh. He's still stressed about Vic. I meet the eyes of Havoc's leader, and he returns my stare with a stony one of his own. "Do you think he's taking a new girl up there? Or just getting rid of evidence?"

"No clue," Vic says, pausing as the girls' laughter rings through the house again. I can hear a movie playing, and figure they've started their movie night early. "Let's get Bernadette's sister over here and get ready to go."

"I'll take Bernadette over to pick her up," Hael starts, and the whiplash look he gets from Vic makes me stand up and take a small step back.

"Like hell you will. Aaron, take her over there in the minivan and grab that babysitter of yours on the way."

Aaron stiffens up, but he doesn't argue, setting aside his half-finished beer and rising to his feet.

"Are you pissed at me?" Hael asks, narrowing his eyes, his hand clenching around his bottle. "Because if you are, you can just say it." He stands up and turns to face Vic, but it doesn't seem like Vic's interested in a conversation. He just brushes his friend off like it's nothing.

"Everybody else, get your shit together. You know the plans for Vaughn."

"Jesus," Hael grinds out, but he takes off in the direction of the kitchen and a moment later, I hear the door to the garage opening.

"Let's go," Aaron says softly, snatching his keys from the hook and heading outside into the crisp autumn air. The red, yellow, and orange leaves remind me that I need to get Heather's costume together. This year, she wants to be some superhero I don't know much about.

As soon as I climb in, Aaron's turning up the radio, his inked hands tight on the steering wheel as he reverses out of the driveway and starts off in the direction of Heather's school. She's gonna be mad at me for picking her up early again. Better than letting her ride the bus home to Mom and the Thing without me there.

Speak of the devil ...

My phone bings with a new text message, and I pull it

from the pocket of my jacket to check. Sure enough, it's from my mother.

You've been gone enough lately. Come home tonight, and we'll have family dinner with Dad.

I can't seem to control the scowl that takes over my face, gripping my phone so hard I'm afraid the cracked screen is finally going to give up the ghost and snap in half.

"Your mother?" Aaron asks after a moment, and I shrug one shoulder, reaching up to splay my fingers against my forehead. Pink and white-blond hair falls around my face as I try to figure out how to respond.

"She wants to have family dinner. She wants me to sit at a table with a man who raped her daughter." I lift my face up and look over at Aaron, studying his clenched jaw and tense shoulders. *"You should've taken off when you had the chance, gone to live with that grandmother of yours,"* he'd said, but doesn't he know that even if I *could*, that I wouldn't? How can I live a normal life ever again after all the crap I've been through? How can I just move on knowing the monsters that tormented me are still living in the shadows, waiting for fresh prey? Maybe Batman was a 'good guy' because he never killed anybody, but I think he's a pussy. Kill the Joker, save the people. Maybe there are no such things as good guys? Maybe there are only people who put their moral compass above practicality that *think* they're good guys?

And then there are people like the Havoc Boys, rotten to the core, but who, in the darkness of their shadowed deeds, can change lives for the better.

"Your mother's an idiot," Aaron says, his voice almost

normal for once. "But don't worry too much about her— or the Thing. We've got plans in the works."

"What are you going to do to her?" I ask, because this has been bothering me all summer, every sunny day when I sat by the creek with Heather and mulled over this decision in my mind. *Havoc.* Just that one word, and my fate was sealed. "Wait. Don't tell me, I don't want to know."

"Are you worried we'll hurt her?" Aaron asks after a few moments of silence. There's a song on the radio called *Gasoline* by I Prevail, and I feel like it encompasses the Havoc Boys perfectly.

"I'm worried you won't hurt her enough," I say, and then I turn my phone off and shove it into my pocket. She might call the police again, but oh well. I told her we were staying the night at a friend's house and not to worry. She can't exactly report me as a runaway with that text between us. If she does, I'll ... sic the boys on her.

I close my eyes and scrub at my face with my hands.

We don't talk again, stopping at Heather's school while I apologize profusely to the after-school program director, and then lead her out to the van. On the way back, we stop by some random girl's house, and a peppy teenager hops into the back to sit next to Heather. Apparently her name is Jennifer Lowell, and she goes to Fuller High. She's eighteen, a senior, and as soon as she graduates, she's running off to the University of California San Diego, blah, blah, blah.

Eventually, I tune her out and Aaron turns up the music. I don't think he's particularly interested in her babbling either.

When we get back, the girl bounces into the house and greets Hael with a warm smile.

"Brittany's been asking after you," she says, and I clench my jaw.

"Maybe she should've thought of that before she dumped me again?" Hael challenges with a raised brow. "The girls are upstairs by the way."

"Brittany says you blocked her on, like, everything. Do you want me to give her a message?" Jennifer presses, biting her lower lip coyly. "Or … maybe you're just done with Brittany altogether?" She reaches up and trails a pink sparkly nail down Hael's chest.

He just stands there and lets her do it, too, which fucking pisses me off.

"What are you gonna do, Havoc Girl?" Vic whispers, pausing next to me and following my gaze across the room. "Let another bitch touch your boy?"

"He's not my boy," I say dryly, and Vic shakes his head.

"Suit yourself." He heads outside, and I find myself moving across the room. I slap Jenn's hand away from Hael's chest and give her the deadliest glare I can manage. It must work because she takes a full step back, eyes wide, and stops popping her damn bubblegum for a minute.

"You're here to watch the girls, not hit on the Havoc Boys. Keep your fucking hands to yourself and do your job."

"We've got some good shit this week," Callum says, lifting up a baggy of weed. "You want to get paid?" He tosses it to her and grins. "Do what the Havoc Girl says and keep the kids safe. Our guys will be patrolling the neighborhood. You need anything, you've got Vic's number."

"Got it," Jenn whispers, averting her eyes as I give Heather a goodbye kiss and follow Callum out into the cool evening air.

"Your guys?" I ask, and he shrugs one loose shoulder.

"We don't operate alone, you know that. right?" He glances my way and throws up a crooked smile. "The five of us, we're the core of everything, but we work well with others, provided they know who's boss."

"Vic?" I ask dryly, and Cal shrugs again.

"Vic," he agrees, moving over to the minivan. We all pile inside, and I end up in a captain's chair in the middle row, opposite the asshole in question. Aaron drives, Hael sits in the passenger seat, and Oscar and Callum occupy the back row.

"Off we go," Vic says as I glance around and realize how much stuff they just loaded in here in the last ten minutes. "Last chance, Bernadette: are you sure you want to go?"

I look him dead in the eyes, and I nod.

Initially, I thought I could get my vengeance while keeping my hands clean.

What I didn't realize was that my fingers were dipped in crimson the moment I said yes to Havoc's price. I may as well enjoy the bloodshed.

CHAPTER
TWENTY-SEVEN

The drive to Principal Vaughn's is a lot longer than I expected. I stop staring at the clock thirty minutes in, my fingers dancing across the dark surface of my phone. It's tempting to turn it back on and see if my mother's texted me again, but I don't think my nerves can handle her bullshit on top of everything else.

"Where is this cabin anyway?" I ask, and Vic glances my way, his face dark and unreadable in the shadows of the minivan. Nobody's talking much, the tension palpable. I just can't decide if it's because we're hunting our pervert of a principal, or if it's something more ... *me* related.

"Middle of butt-fuck-nowhere," Vic supplies finally, tapping tattooed knuckles against the window as he stares me down. I meet his gaze unflinching. *I'm not afraid of you,* I say with my eyes, but maybe that's a lie? "There's a turn-off just after McKenzie Bridge."

I bite my lower lip and turn toward the window. On

either side of us, there's nothing but trees and pure, obliterating blackness. That night the boys dropped me off on the side of the road, I think it was out this way somewhere.

A ripple of anxiety washes over me as I realize that I'm in a minivan full of strong, ruthless men. Out here, there'd quite literally be no one to hear me scream. They could do whatever they wanted with me.

"What's the plan?" I hear myself asking instead, feeling like my voice is somehow detached from the rest of me. Numbness. I gather it around me like a blanket, and make sure to stay well away from Victor Channing.

"Assuming Vaughn is there," Vic begins, and Oscar interrupts.

"He's there." His words are absolute, like he truly believes he's never made a mistake in his entire life. "But the real question is if he's alone or not, if he brought the nurse, or if he's got a new girl."

"What about the nurse?" I ask, trying to remember her name. Whitney, was it? Whitney … something. The whole Prescott student body calls her the Nurse of Yes-Scott High, which, if you know that Principal Vaughn's first name is Scott, is actually a pretty clever saying. There's not a damn kid on campus who hasn't overheard *yes, Scott, yes!* coming from the nurse's office on occasion.

"What about her?" Vic asks, still not looking at me. In fact, I'm pretty sure he's glaring at the back of Hael's head.

"If she is there, then what?" I press. "Does she get

hers, too?"

"She wasn't on your list," Oscar says matter-of-factly, "and we have too much on our plates to take on charity work. If the nurse is there, we'll knock her out and tie her to a tree until we're finished with Principal Vaughn."

I purse my lips, because they all know that Nurse Whtiney is just as culpable in all this shit as Vaughn is. She recruits girls, too, vulnerable girls who come to her to ask questions about birth control, or STDs, or finger-shaped bruises she should be reporting. Instead, she picks out the weak ones and coerces them into the cam business to make porn for her and her boss. She drives a Lexus, by the way. Should've had Hael blow that one up, too.

"And if there's a girl?" I continue, turning to look at Oscar. Vic might be the boss, but Oscar's the logistics of the Havoc operation. He pushes his glasses up his nose with a tattooed middle finger and smirks at me.

"We give her the keys to the Kia Sportage and send her on her way. You don't think we'd hurt an innocent girl, do you?" he taunts, and my hands curl into fists. "I mean, not unless we were hired to do it."

"Fuck you," I growl back, and Oscar laughs, this genteel laugh that's so at odds with his tattoos. "Now what's the plan with Vaughn? Be direct, remember?"

Oscar leans forward, his raven-black hair sliding across his forehead, gray eyes catching the light from the dash up front.

"We're going to put him in his underwear and degrade his ancient ass on a live feed." My brows go up, but I have to admit there's a certain sense of poetic justice in Vaughn's sentence. "After that, if he's lucky, we release him into the woods with no phone, no pants, and no shoes. We'll set the cabin on fire, and then send his signed confession to the cops."

"How are you going to get him to confess?" I ask, and Oscar doesn't hesitate before pulling his revolver out of his jacket. He smiles at me as he slides his thumb along the barrel, but it's not a very nice smile, not at all.

"With this." The matter-of-fact tone in his voice never changes.

"Anything about the plan you don't like?" Vic asks me, and a shiver takes over me. The memories of him touching me aren't nearly as faded around the edges as I'd like. Instead, when he talks, they burn. *His body pushing inside of mine, taking over me, his fingers dancing a dirty rhythm over my core.*

I grit my teeth.

"I like it," I say, glancing over at Callum. He's leaning against the window, watching me with those blue eyes. I remember in elementary school how we had to do square dancing lessons on Fridays. I hated it. I used to cry and sit in the corner with my hands over my ears. And then one day, I saw Callum dancing with another little girl from our class. He looked so happy doing it that I got up and hesitantly moved over to stand near him. He held out his hand and smiled at me, and I joined in. The dancing wasn't so bad as I'd thought, and for a while there, my life got a little less dark.

I'll never forget that.

Doubt he remembers that moment though.

"After this, can we get something to eat?" Cal asks, and Hael and Aaron both groan.

"Seriously?" Aaron snaps, just before he reaches over to turn off the stereo. He turns onto a gravel road and shuts off the headlights, leaving us in total blackness. How he navigates that winding, mountain road is beyond me, but I'm on pins and needles the whole time, my fingernails digging into the sides of my seat.

A good twenty minutes later, we make a slow, tight turn between two large trees, and I spot the white Kia Sportage under the dim glow of a porch light.

"Bingo," Hael murmurs, and the tension in the van seems to snap, a new energy taking over the group, just like the night we broke into Oak Valley Prep.

"Time to kick some ass," Cal says with a low, hoarse laugh as Vic throws open the sliding door, grabs a black duffel from the floor, and hops out. I follow after him, unsure of what my role here is, exactly.

"Break the door down," Vic says, slinging the duffel over his shoulder. "More impactful that way."

"Consider it done," Hael says, and both he and Callum move forward and up the front steps of the porch. There's only one car here tonight, so I'm guessing Miss Yes-Scott isn't entertaining her boss tonight.

Both boys put their boots up to the door and kick in unison, knocking the wood off its hinges and sending it crashing to the floor. A high-pitched scream follows, accompanied by Vaughn's distinct bellow.

"What on earth—" he starts, followed by a grunt. I

chase after Vic, Aaron, and Oscar, stepping on the broken door and finding a cozy cabin lit with a fire, Principal Vaughn bent over and already bleeding from the face, and Ivy freaking Hightower naked on a bed in the corner.

She's covering her body with a blanket, her painted lips open in surprise as she gapes at us.

"Clothes, keys, now get the fuck out," Vic says, tossing a pile her way and snatching some keys off the counter of the kitchenette near the door. He chucks those in her direction, but she's so out of it that she doesn't catch them before they hit her in the face.

"What's going on here?" Vaughn manages to grind out before Cal and Hael shove him into a chair next to the fireplace. He looks up, red running from his nostrils, one hand trying to cup the liquid as it drips from his chin.

Vic tosses the duffel onto the floor and moves over to stand in front of our principal, bending low, and staring the older man straight in the face.

"You've conned your last girl, Vaughn." Vic smiles, and it's even less pretty than Oscar's. "And you've fucked with Havoc for the last time."

"Are you going to kill me?" Scott Vaughn asks, beginning to shake. It doesn't escape my notice that his first thought is that he's going to die. That's the power of Havoc.

"Probably not," Vic says, standing up straight as Ivy yanks her dress over her head. There are handcuffs dangling from the headboard, a pink vibrator lying atop the white blankets, and a camera on a tripod near the end of the bed.

The footage is streaming onto a laptop that's sitting on the counter. Oscar moves over to it right away and cuts the feed.

"It's not live," he calls out, and Vic grunts.

"After we're done here," Victor says, cocking his head to the side. "You might wish you were dead though. Boys."

"Alright, princess, are you deaf? The man said get out." Hael grabs Ivy by the arm and yanks her from the blankets, dragging her toward the door.

"Am I still getting paid for tonight's session?" she asks, and Hael laughs, shoving her outside and then glancing over at me with his signature smirk in place. Hard to believe I had his dick in my mouth just a few hours prior, huh?

"And where's the reward in altruism, huh? Do you hear this bitch?"

"She's an anomaly," I say, moving over to the door to stare Ivy down as she fumbles with Vaughn's keys and unlocks the doors to the Kia.

"Can I at least have my purse?" she snaps, turning around to face me. Maybe she thinks having me here makes her safer? It doesn't. I have no control over what the Havoc Boys do.

I grab the pink purse from the floor near the umbrella holder and move down the steps, shoving it against her chest, and refusing to let go until she looks me in the eye.

"If you tell a soul about what happened here tonight, you're next." Ivy tries to take the purse from me, but I keep hold of it. "I mean it. I'll send Havoc after you, and you won't like what happens."

"Okay, okay, I got it," she says, her expression mollifying as she cringes away from me. Despite what Hael thinks, I do feel sorry for Ivy. She's always cared far too much what the world thinks about her, and she's so desperate for attention that she was probably easy pickings for Vaughn. As far as the money, of course she wants to be paid. She lives in a double-wide with her dad and three sisters. This could be rent she's losing out on. "Wait," I say, just before she climbs in. I pound back up the stairs as Hael stares at me like I've lost my damn mind, and I find Vaughn's wallet in his discarded pants.

The boys have already started stripping him, but I don't look his way as I take the wallet and empty it of cash and credit cards, heading back outside and handing them over to Ivy. She stares at the wad of money for only half a second before she snatches it from me.

"Thank you," she murmurs, and then she climbs in the car and gets the fuck out of there, spraying gravel in her haste.

"You are one, weird chick," Hael murmurs, studying me as I come back up the steps and move across the broken door. He waits for me to pass, lifts it up, and sets it back in place as best he can.

"We'd make you get naked, like you do your girls, but nobody wants to see that," Vic says, turning to look at Aaron who's now manning the camera. "Can you work that thing, or do you want to use our phones to film?"

"I've got it," Aaron says, as Oscar moves over to stand in front of Principal Vaughn with a notebook and pen in his hand.

"I want you to write out your bad deeds, and then I want you to sign it," Oscar tells him, waiting until Vaughn takes the items from his hand before moving away. "Oh, and don't skimp on the details. We'll know if you did." Oscar pulls his gun out and sets it on the counter, playing around with the laptop again before he presses play on a video. A girl that I vaguely recognize from our school starts to strip on camera, and I look away.

"A confession signed under duress is useless in court, you know," Vaughn says as the pen hovers over the page and his eyes dart around the room in fear, coming to land on mine. "What is your stepfather going to think of all this?"

"He'll probably just be disappointed he doesn't get to watch anymore of your illegal, underage porn videos," I say, completely deadpan. That numbness inside of me is burning at the edges with a righteous rage. "Start your note with *I'm sorry*. More people need to learn how to say those words without gagging." I nod my chin at him, and Aaron flinches. The words weren't directed at my ex, but hell, they sure are poetic, aren't they? "Do it."

Callum stands beside our principal, one hand tight on the man's shoulder as he reads over the words. I take a seat on a small bench next to the closet and wait patiently, my mind racing with all the ways this could go horribly wrong and bite us in the ass.

"Don't worry," Aaron says, leaning against the wall next to me and lighting up a cigarette. "We've been at this long enough to know how to cover our bases, Bernie." He doesn't look at me, his attention focused on Vaughn.

After a good fifteen minutes, Callum makes a frustrated sound and yanks the notebook from the principal's hands.

"He's not getting shit done," he says, handing the note over to Oscar.

Oscar reads it and then glances at Vic before picking up his gun and putting the barrel to Vaughn's head.

"Here's what I want you to write: *My name is Scott Anesso Vaughn, and I'm the Principal of Prescott High. For over ten years, I've been coercing young girls into the porn and prostitution industries for pay. I've also slept with many of these girls, the majority of whom were under eighteen. I can no longer handle the burden of this truth.*"

"Please don't," Vaughn whimpers, hand shaking as he sits there in his underwear and struggles to follow Oscar's instructions. "I have kids. They go to the U of O, you know. Both amazing athletes, and—"

Oscar hits him in the face with the gun, hard enough to send blood splattering across the log walls of the cabin, and then pulls the hammer back for emphasis. Vaughn quickly shuts up, finishing his note and signing it with a flourish. He passes it back to Oscar who re-reads it, the flames from the fireplace reflecting off the surface of his glasses. With a curt nod, he withdraws the weapon and Vaughn lets out a sharp exhale of breath.

"Now get up," Vic commands, nodding over to the bed. "We're going to make a little video."

"Please no," Vaughn whimpers, his body limp when Cal hauls him to his feet. "Please, I'm begging you!"

Aaron moves back over to the camera as Vaughn crawls onto the bed, a grossly pathetic sight in his underwear and nothing else.

"I want you to think of all the girls you've brought to this cabin," Vic says as Vaughn begins to weep softly. But I have little sympathy for a pedophile and a pervert, so I stay numb as I watch him cry. Is he really weeping or is it just an act? Probably an act. There's not even a sense of satisfaction in me, watching these evil men like Don and Scott burn, just that same, easy numbness. "Think about all of them, desperate for money to pay rent or buy food for younger siblings or earn a ticket out of poverty." Vic pauses and turns to point at me. "And then I want you to look Bernadette in the eye and say you're sorry for what you've done."

"I'm sorry," Vaughn sobs, shaking. "I'm so sorry."

"We're going live in thirty seconds," Oscar says, and Vic nods, turning back to Vaughn.

"You're going to perform the same way you make the girls do. Whatever the psychos watching this video ask for, you're going to do. Do you understand?"

Vaughn is openly bawling now, but nobody in that cabin cares.

"We're going to live stream him?" I ask, and Cal

nods.

"During live cam feeds, those watching can ask the girl to do certain things and pay in tips for the privilege to see her do it. So Vaughn's going to spend an hour learning what it's like." Cal's mouth curves into a smile. "It's nice, isn't it? Hand-delivering karma."

I don't know how to respond to that, so I turn back to watch the drama unfold in front of me.

As promised, for an entire hour, Vaughn does what the crazy fucks online demand of him. I can't watch most of it, so I let myself outside into the cool, night air. Cal joins me, and we sit on the rocking chairs on the porch in silence.

"Aaron said the taste of vengeance wasn't so sweet as I thought it'd be, that it'd leave the taste of ash in my mouth," I say finally, and Cal glances my way, his hood firmly fixed in place, legs folded on the chair in front of him. "But I don't taste ash. I don't taste anything at all, to be honest with you."

"Mm." Callum glances my way, studying me in the dark. "I felt that way, too, at first. Once you surrender to the dark, it gets easier." He stands up suddenly, his body unfolding from that chair in such a graceful way that I find myself envious again. I've never been clumsy per se, but I've also never been particularly graceful either. Callum makes every movement he makes look like dance.

The front door opens and Aaron appears, limned in light from inside.

"We're done here," he says, and only then do I notice

the blood on his knuckles. He sees me looking and swipes them on his jeans like he's ashamed. Violence. It's what Havoc does, I'm not surprised at all. "If there's anything in the cabin you want, come get it."

Cal heads inside, but I stay where I am. There's nothing in there I want; it's all tainted.

"You beat him up?" I ask, and Aaron shrugs.

"Not as bad as Don," is the only response I get before Oscar appears, carrying the laptop and camera, probably to sell later. Principal Vaughn comes stumbling out next, naked, shaking, and spattered with blood. Hael shoves him in the back and he falls down the front steps.

"Go on, get the fuck out of here," he says as the principal struggles to get to his feet. "Start running, and don't stop." Hael glances my way and a strange expression crosses his face. "You don't want to know what'll happen if we find you."

My entire body ripples with disgust, and I turn away.

"Let's light this baby up," Hael continues, and I hear Vic grunt his agreement. The smell of gasoline stings my nostrils as Callum hooks a hose up to a water pump and turns it on, soaking the ground around the cabin. I guess they're looking to keep the fire contained?

"Come on," Aaron says, and when I don't respond, he reaches out and grabs my hand.

A violent shiver overtakes me, and I tear my hand away from him, moving down the steps of my own accord and standing back while the rest of the boys douse the place.

"Burn it fucking down," Vic commands as we gather

near the minivan, and Cal steps forward with an old-fashioned lighter in his hand, flicking it on and then tossing it onto the front steps.

Flames sweep over the cabin and consume it, leaving nothing but ash in their wake.

Two years earlier ...

Everything I own is lying in a heap in the backyard. I'm the only person home at the moment, standing with one hand on the edge of the sliding glass door, my eyes focused on the admittedly small mountain of clothing, books, and furniture tossed haphazardly on the gravel-covered area near the old shed.

"Boo."

A voice surprises me from behind, and I jump, a strong arm banding around my waist and yanking me into a firm chest.

I know immediately who it is that's holding me there: Victor fucking Channing.

"What are you doing here?" I manage to whisper, fear a hot, wild thing inside my chest. But my body's a traitor because it's not just fear that I'm feeling, it's want. Need. An emotion I never thought I'd be able to associate with the Havoc Boys, not after what they did to me during pageant week.

Not when they ruined homecoming.

Not when they make me question every step I take.

They've turned Prescott High into a nightmare for me.

"We've decided to have a bonfire," Vic says, his mouth too close to my ear. I stay stone-still, terrified of whatever it is he's got planned. That's when I see Aaron come around the corner of the house, a red gasoline can in one hand. He doesn't look at me as he moves up to the pile and drenches it in flammable liquid.

They're going to burn my stuff.

I can only pray they're not going to burn me, too.

"Why are you doing this?" I whisper, but I've asked that question a hundred times, and I've never gotten an answer. Victor just laughs softly and releases me. I stumble away from him as Oscar, Callum, and Hael join Aaron in the yard.

It's Vic, though, who pulls a lighter from his pocket and approaches the pile.

I don't have a lot in life, barely anything, and what I do have, I've worked hard for. I can see my new heels for the winter formal in that pile, the ones I worked two shitty jobs for. They're propped up next to a shoebox full of old pictures, pictures of a dad I didn't get to keep, of me and Pen as babies, of a life that didn't suck quite so bad as this one does.

The leader of the Havoc Boys doesn't skip a beat when he leans over and sets my entire life on fire, the flames catching and licking across the pile in seconds. I just slide to the floor and sit there on my knees watching, waiting, wondering.

Why? Why me?
All I ever wanted was to be one of them.
All I ever wanted was to belong.
But that need, that desire, like so many others, is and will always be a worthless pipe dream; the taste of it is bitter ash on my tongue.

I must fall asleep in the van because I don't remember much between climbing into the car and waking up in Aaron's bed. His familiar smell surrounds me, like rose and sandalwood, and I have to fight back the wave of strong memories.

I lost my virginity in this bed.

Aaron said he loved me in this bed.

I frown and shove the covers off, climbing out of the bed and swiping my hands over my face. My phone is lying on the nightstand, the screen still off, whatever angry words my mother might want to say hidden within.

I leave it there as I stand up and grab my backpack from the floor near the door, pulling out my change of clothes before I creep down the hall to check on Heather. She's passed out, curled up on an air mattress that just barely fits between Kara's and Ashley's beds.

A sigh of relief escapes me as I lean my shoulder against the doorjamb and watch the three of them sleeping. The first real smile I've given in weeks takes over my mouth, and I feel this unsettling sense of contentment.

I could live a life like this, getting up early in a house that's free of hate, showering, making breakfast for the girls ... But I don't let myself hope for it. Hopes, wants, dreams, they can all be destroyed in the span of a single exhale. A ragged inhale. A surprised gasp.

Shaking my head, I push away from the wall and head for the bathroom. It must be early because I don't hear anyone else moving around in the house. Good. I smell like a campfire, and as much as I'm glad that Principal Vaughn got his last night, I also don't need a scented reminder of what happened.

The bathroom is free, thankfully, so I step in and lock it, stripping down and climbing in the scalding warmth of the shower. As I let the heat wash over me, I pretend like I'm scrubbing away all the bad memories, like soap and water can really heal an injured soul.

The sound of the door opening snaps me out of my daze, and I freeze. Did someone pick the lock? Callum could pretty easily if he wanted. Hell, what am I saying? Any of the Havoc Boys could.

Peeling back the curtain, I find Aaron yawning, his dick in his hand as he takes a piss.

"What are you doing in here?" I snap, and he jumps, missing his target, so to speak, and cursing violently under his breath. "Did you pick the lock?"

"No, fuck, no," he grumbles, adjusting his aim as I stand there glaring, my anxious heartbeat shifting into a different rhythm, one that doesn't exactly add up to a guy taking a piss in front of me. But even though I'm naked and Aaron somehow breezed through the locked door, I'm not afraid of him. *He wouldn't hurt me,* I think automatically, but then my cynical mind starts to laugh when I remember.

Right.

He already did.

But ... for what reason?

"I barely managed to keep the girls from ending up in foster care."

"I'm waiting," I say as he shakes off his cock and tucks it away, zipping his pants up and snatching a container of antiseptic wipes to clean up the mess. Wow. A seventeen-year-old guy covered in tattoos scrubbing up stray droplets of pee to keep a toilet clean? Unheard of. He even puts the toilet seat down when he's done, and I can't help but be thoroughly impressed.

"The lock on this door is broken. I've been meaning to fix it, but ... life." Aaron glances over at me, some of his wavy chestnut hair falling into his eyes. He flicks it away with inked fingers. "And I'm sorry. It's early, I'm tired. The girls take forever in the shower in the mornings, so we've worked out a system where I can sneak in and pee if I have to." He scrubs a hand over his face.

"Don't you have a downstairs bathroom?" I ask, and he gives me this look with those green-gold eyes of his.

"It's occupied," he says, narrowing his gaze even further. "We hide the weed in there."

"The weed?" I ask, imagining, like, a small baggy

full of the green stuff.

"Yeah," Aaron says, sounding tired. "We have some people that grow for us, and then they pass it over for drying. I don't want the girls to know what we do, so we hide it in there and keep the door locked."

"Oh." My fingers stay curled around the edge of the shower curtain. "That makes sense in a strange, Havoc sort of way ..."

"It pays the bills," Aaron says, watching me carefully as water drips down my face and sluices between my gently parted lips. "I don't exactly have dental or health insurance for the girls."

"You don't have to justify yourself to me," I say when I realize that he's getting defensive. That'd be Aaron for you. I think he always got off on being the nice guy. Now he can never be the nice guy again. It pisses him off, I think.

My gaze scans his body automatically, taking note of how much he's changed since we were together. His muscles are hard, covered in ink. His sweatpants hang too low, showing off that enticing 'V' on his hips that he never had before. While his personality may have downgraded, his body sure has upgraded.

I lift my eyes to his.

"I want to know everything that happened with Kali," I tell him, and his jaw tightens. "I deserve that much at least, don't you think?"

"I ..." Aaron trails off, and he doesn't look so badass for a moment there, but like the boy who held my hand in a rainy graveyard. "Yeah, you do." He turns toward the door, and something catches in my throat. I think it's the need to call out to him, to ask him to come back, to look him in the eye and see if he still cares about me.

"For the record, I could never go to Nantucket," I say, and he pauses with his hand on the doorknob. "My grandma can't take Heather in; they're not related. Nona's my dad's mother, remember? And I can't leave Heather with the Thing. You know what happened to Penelope."

I can see Aaron's breath slow before he finally turns the knob.

"I'll make pancakes," he says, and then he slips out and leaves me alone to slide down the shower wall.

For the first time in almost two years, I cry.

And it feels fucking great.

CHAPTER

Dressed in cut-off shorts, and a dark pink halter that mimics the color of my hair, I head downstairs and find all five guys in the kitchen, sitting on counters, slouching against walls, all of them with breakfast plates in their hands.

I walk in barefoot and all eyes fall on me, making me shiver. It makes me feel both powerful and terrified at the same time; I can't explain it.

"You look so pretty today!" Kara exclaims which stops me dead in my tracks. I'm not wearing a lick of makeup, and my hair is wet and slightly disheveled. I glance over at her beaming face, but now all three girls are staring at me, and I realize the weight of their stares is a hundred times more powerful than those of the guys.

Men have selfish motivation, want, and desire tainting their vision; little girls have dreams, ambition, and honesty turning theirs crystal clear.

My cheeks flush and the terror fades away.

"Thanks," I say, tucking some hair behind my ear and grabbing a plate. To look at us all, you wouldn't know we humiliated a grown man, beat him up, and set his house on fire last night. I guess that's the point though, isn't it? "What's the plan for today?"

"The girls have been invited to a birthday party," Aaron says, using tongs to put hot bacon on the edge of my plate. "A princess-themed birthday party." That's when I notice he's wearing a crown on the top of his head. Looks weird as hell, considering the tattoos and all. I almost smile. Almost, but not quite.

"That sounds like fun," I say, hugging Heather from behind, her smell calming my nerves. She always smells like soap and the cucumber-melon body spray she borrows from my side of the bathroom vanity. "Are you going to dress up?"

"I'm too old for princesses," she says, wiggling out of my grip. "I'm going as Deadpool."

"Like ... Ryan Reynolds, superhero Deadpool?" I ask, raising a brow as Heather turns a challenging look on me. "I'm not mocking, I'm just asking."

"Aaron has a mask I can borrow," she says, and I shrug. Whatever. It's only two weeks until Halloween, so if she wants to dress up early that's fine with me. "Can you do my hair though? You can just cut it all off with scissors ..."

I give her a look and flip her ponytail with my fingers.

"I'll put it in a bun, and we can discuss cutting it off later—at a salon." *If I had the money for a salon.* I grit my teeth slightly, glancing down at the engagement ring on my finger. When Heather noticed it, I told her it was just costume jewelry for Halloween. But knowing its worth, it's so damn tempting ... "If you're done eating, go upstairs and take a shower. You stink."

She doesn't really, but she could use a shower anyway. Heather frowns at me and sighs but does as I asked. Kara and Ashley follow up behind her and disappear into their room to pick out dresses, leaving me to sit on one of the three stools.

"Here," Vic says after a moment, moving over to the peninsula where the cooktop is and pausing beside Aaron. He tosses an envelope down in front of me, and I stare at it for an inordinate amount of time before I take it and open it up.

"This is like two grand in cash," I say, glancing back up and finding that endless void that is Victor Channing staring back at me.

"Your cut of the money we stole from Donald's safe, after expenses. We keep an account for Havoc related shit."

"Like gasoline?" I ask, and Vic's lush mouth curves into a dangerous smile.

"Like gasoline."

He leaves the kitchen and some of the tension in the room goes with him.

"The girls are going to a party, so what's our plan for the day?" I ask, lifting my gaze from my plate to the four boys in the room with me. Hael won't look at me for whatever reason, but Oscar at least glances my way, looking bored out of his mind.

"Aaron and Hael will be trimming and prepping the marijuana in the bathroom for sale while Callum has a day off, Vic does whatever the hell he wants, and I work on your wedding plans."

The color drains from my face, and I stifle a groan.

Right.

Wedding plans.

Fantastic.

"What's our budget?" I ask dryly, expecting him to laugh in my face. "Aren't we just going down to the courthouse?"

Instead, Oscar smirks.

"Twenty grand, and no. You and Victor will be married in a proper ceremony. Care to join me in making plans?" he asks, and my mouth falls open. "It's not a lot, in theory, but we can make a classic, elegant ceremony happen."

"Twenty grand?" I repeat, feeling my hand sweat where it's wrapped around the fork. "Are you serious?"

"Deadly," he says, and that one word, coming out of that sharp mouth of his, is bound to give me nightmares.

***

The majority of the morning I'm left to hang out with the girls, helping them pick out costumes for the party and arranging their hair into fancy coifs with the help of YouTube tutorials. Aaron comes by at one point and hovers in the doorway, but I guess there's still too much weirdness between us for him to want to join in.

Once he leaves with the girls, I wander downstairs and sit across from Oscar on one of the couches, my still silent phone in my hand. I figure I better turn it on before Mom tells the Thing I've disappeared with his daughter, and I end up with a SWAT team hunting my ass down.

"Problem?" Oscar asks, looking up from his laptop. The shine of the screen catches on his glasses, blocking his eyes from view. I can't tell what he's thinking on a good day, but like this, he's impossible to read.

"I need to check my messages, but I'm dreading looking at them because I just know Pamela's gonna be pissed off, and I hate dealing with her."

"Give me the phone," Oscar says, gesturing toward the coffee table. I set it down and slide it across. He catches it before it falls off the other side and powers it on. Meanwhile, my stomach churns, and I lift one leg up on the couch, wrapping my arms around it and wishing the damn thing would start up faster so I could just get this over with.

He stares at the phone for a moment, and then starts tapping out a text message.

Not two minutes later, he's setting the phone down on the coffee table.

"Well?" I ask as Oscar refocuses his attention on the laptop. He barely pays me any attention, like maybe he never wanted me to join his boys' club after all?

"Your mother said to get your ass home before your

stepfather does or else. There was nothing after the *or else* portion of the conversation." He starts typing and doesn't bother looking at me. "I wonder if it's too gauche to use black lilies for a wedding?" This last part is mumbled, mostly to himself as he taps inked fingers against the bottom of his chin. "I wonder if I care?"

"And?" I press, my hands shaking as I think about picking the phone up again. "How did you respond to that?"

More typing, and then a very distinct pause as Oscar finally glances up.

"I told her that a woman with so much to hide shouldn't be so quick to judge and that her husband wouldn't be home anytime soon because he's fucking his new partner."

I blink a moment to clear the shock and then lunge forward to grab my phone.

Sure enough, that's what Oscar's responded with. The color drains from my face as I read and re-read both Mom's message and Oscar's reply.

Where the hell are you? I'm starting to worry! I have to pause for a moment there to roll my eyes. Worried? She's not worried about me or Heather. We're nothing but accessories in her life, as useful or replaceable as a new necklace or a purse. *Are you with that boy again? The one who hurt Neil? You're better than that, Bernadette. You are not a slut. Get your ass home before Dad does or else.*

And then ...

Heather's safe and attending a friend's birthday

party. You, on the other hand, shouldn't be so quick to judge since your husband's fucking his hot, new partner. Doubtful he'll be home anytime soon. He's busy, after all. See you tomorrow.

I wait there for what feels like an hour, staring at the screen, expecting a reply, and getting nothing.

"She'll be too busy calling and bitching out your stepfather to respond," Oscar says, keys clacking away.

"Is Neil really fucking his partner?" I ask and get the barest of smiles in response.

"No. She's far too classy to let a perverted, married pedophile touch her. In fact, we might use her in his downfall. But your mother doesn't know that."

"They'll be screaming and fighting and then anger fucking all night," I say with a grimace, leaving my phone on in case Heather needs to all me. "Thanks, that buys me another day."

Oscar doesn't bother to respond again, so I get up and head to the kitchen for some snacks, hiding myself in Aaron's room for the rest of the day to binge *The Chilling Adventures of Sabrina* on Netflix.

For the first time in a while, I'm actually somewhat relaxed.

Weird, right? Considering I'm in my ex boyfriend's room in a house full of bad boys with no qualms about making others bleed.

Once it gets dark out, I make another expedition to the kitchen and find Callum coming in the front door, soaked in sweat and wearing sweatpants and a tank top. He's carrying that damn bag of his, the one he always stuffs in his locker at the beginning of the school day. He smiles at me as he passes by.

"What's in the bag?" I ask, tucking my fingers into the pockets of my shorts.

"My shattered hopes and dreams," Callum quips, but he smiles as he says it, softening the blow of what I'm almost certain is the truth. He cocks his head to one side, blond hair sliding across his forehead. His arms are corded with hard muscle, and despite his smaller stature, I trust he'd be a match for Hael or maybe even Vic. Beads of sweat cling to his tattoos as he reaches up to push some hair from his face, blue eyes dark.

They don't match his smile, those eyes. His smile says that everything is okay, but that gaze of his is too full of shadows and heartbreak. Cal takes a step forward and pauses, grimacing as he reaches out to put a palm on the wall, steadying himself.

"Work out too hard?" I ask, and he grins.

"More like ... some injuries just don't heal right," he says as I study him for a moment. Aaron's transformation from good boy to bad was pretty goddamn dramatic, but I think Cal's might be worse. He was always small and shy, huddling up next to Vic on the playground. But whoever that Callum Park was, he's gone now. In his place, there's an entire person made of up secrets and shadows.

I bite my lower lip for a moment, inhaling and finding Cal's talc and aftershave scent mixed with the fresh bite of sweat. Why is it so hot when guys have that fresh sweat smell? I mean, after a while, sure, it's not so sexy anymore, but when they're warm and that tattooed skin is moist ...

I shake my hands out, and Callum's smile turns into a grin.

"Did you really get throat punched by a member of a rival gang?" I ask, and one of Cal's blond brows goes up before he laughs, that smoky chuckle making me shiver.

"Nah. No chance I'm letting some gang banging asshole touch my throat." Callum draws a line across his neck with a blue-painted fingernail. Pretty sure that's his favorite color. He chuckles again and shakes his head. But from what I can remember, his voice used to be this angelic whisper. I get that he's gone through puberty since, but still, that voice of his is so husky and dark. Something must've happened. He taps his fingers against the side of his neck. "Is that the rumor going around Prescott?" I shrug. We both know that it is. Cal leans in and puts his mouth near my ear, the soft, pink curve of his lower lip brushing against my lobe. "You don't like my voice?" he asks, that husky sound curling around me like smoke.

"I love it, actually," I say, turning so that his mouth brushes my cheek and we're staring right at each other. Cal barely talks to me, but not like how Aaron ignores me. It's obvious Aaron is avoiding me, and we both know why that is. But Callum ... he may as well be a stranger.

"Sometimes pain is pretty, to the people who have too much of it," he tells me, and then kisses me on the cheek. "You're gorgeous, by the way." Cal pulls back and heads up the stairs toward the bathroom, leaving me gaping after him and trying to figure out what that last comment just meant.

Pain is pretty. And I'm made of it.

Hael appears from the direction of the laundry room a moment later, reeking of marijuana and soaked in sweat. He grabs two beers from the fridge, offers one up to me, and then leans against the counter, the bare skin of his arms covered in little green pot leaves.

"Trimming is simple work but tedious work, fuck my life," he groans, downing the beer. I'm not a hundred percent sure what, exactly, trimming is. I take it to mean he's trimming pot leaves off the plant.

"Why are they so ... sticky?" I ask as I move over to him, peeling one off of his bicep and finding that even that simple touch between us ignites that fire in my body.

"Dunno, science-y shit. More crystals and terpenes or something. Now you know why good weed's called sticky-icky, huh?" Hael pauses as Aaron comes out of the laundry room, closing the door behind him. There's a bathroom just off of it, and on the other side a door to a poorly converted garage. I mean, there's drywall in there and a carpet over the cement, but it's cold as hell and still feels like a garage. I remember because Aaron and I used to fuck in there sometimes.

He sees me there with my fingers still resting on Hael's arm, and it's like every emotion in his face goes dark all at once.

"I'm gonna shower."

"Cal's in there," I say and Aaron groans, grabbing a beer and then slumping to the floor of the kitchen. It smells like pot so bad in here. I wonder if the neighbors can smell us down the block? I wouldn't be surprised. Good thing weed's legal in Oregon now, although I imagine the boys are growing and selling it in illegal ways ...

I draw my hand back from Hael, and I refuse to think about his dick in my mouth, or me riding him in his Camaro ... *Fuck*. So much for that. It's *all* I can think about now.

Victor appears in the doorway to the kitchen as if summoned, this dark shadow that makes me shiver. I don't look at him, sipping my beer and keeping my attention on the cabinets instead.

"Are you done?" he asks them, and the boys nod. "Good. We'll drop most of the product off tomorrow and keep the rest here for emergencies." He glances my way, maybe noticing the way Hael and I are leaning into each other. I refuse to meet his gaze until he talks to me like a goddamn adult.

"Shower's free!" Callum calls down the stairs, and Aaron groans, rising to his feet and flicking a glance over at Hael.

"Mind if I go first?"

"Have at it," Hael says, and he, on the other hand, has no problem looking right at Vic. I glance back and find that Oscar's gone, leaving the three of us alone in the dark kitchen. The only light comes from the cracked door of the fridge. "Are you finally going to say it aloud? You know Bernadette and I fucked in my car. And we gave each other head in Vaughn's office. You know fucking everything, so why not just say what you're thinking and get it over with? Because both Bernadette and I don't get it. Isn't this part of why she's here? To be our girl? *Our* girl? Or is she just your girl then?"

Victor stiffens up, and I finally gather the courage to glance his way. His jaw is clenched, but he isn't saying anything. Instead, he just slides his dark gaze from Hael and over to me.

"Did you like it?" he asks, and there are so many shadows in his face that I can barely make out his expression. "Screwing Hael in that pretty car of his?"

"You're the one that told me to do it," I snap back, realizing that I'm already shaking. He's doing it to me again, melting that frigid core inside of my heart and releasing a torrent of emotions that are impossible to make sense of. "You practically commanded me to fuck him."

Vic laughs, but the sound is dark, foreign. It puts this gap between us, a yawning chasm that can never close.

"You're right, I did," he says, and then shakes his head, raking his fingers through his hair. "You could barely stand letting me touch you, but the look on your face when you were riding him … Well, shit, Hael must be as good as all the sluts at Fuller High say he is."

"You were watching us?" I grind out, but I'm full of shit because I knew he was. I knew it. And I wanted him to watch. "And don't call them sluts. If anyone's a slut, it's Hael."

"I'm still standing here," he snaps, sounding irritated. "Do you two want me to leave so you can anger fuck each other on the kitchen counter?"

"I want you two in the master bedroom," Vic commands, tearing himself away from my gaze and heading for the hallway. "Now."

"This is insane," Hael growls out, scrubbing at his face with his hand. He glances over at me. "You didn't like him touching you?"

"That wasn't what happened," I reply, feeling the layers of my anger crack and break apart.

When Vic touches me, my shields fall away, and I can't breathe. When he touches me, all I can think about is how I want him to touch me more. When he's not around, all I think about is how to get him back.

It's an obsession I've had for years.

Victor Channing, my dark, little secret want.

"Huh." Hael sets his beer aside and stands up, offering out a hand for me to take. I do, letting him pull me to my feet, and then carefully extracting my fingers from his. We head down the hall together, one of my palms pressed into my stomach, trying to quiet the sudden rush of nervous energy that's percolating through me.

Vic is waiting in a chair near the window, the only light in the room from a single lamp on the table beside him. His hair looks more purple than black right now, an aubergine color that really suits the slightly tan color of his skin. His irises are a deep brown, but, like they often do, they seem black.

The knuckles of one tattooed hand are curled against the side of his face while he rubs a thumb along the side of his phone with the other.

"Take a seat on the bed," he says, and Hael and I exchange a glance.

"What's this all about?" Hael asks, and Vic looks up at him, the anger gone from his face, replaced with something else I can't quite figure out. "What are you doing, bro?"

"Sit down," Vic repeats, and there's this tense moment there where Hael has to decide what he wants to do: listen to the boss of the Havoc Boys or make a statement. Teeth clenched, Hael sits down on the edge of the bed, and I perch beside him. Victor turns to me.

"Do it," he commands. He holds up his phone, and I can tell by the light that he's just started recording. His mouth curves to the side in a cruel smirk. "Fuck my best friend while I watch."

I glance over at Hael to gauge his reaction and find him with a wicked smile on his face.

Victor is … going to film us. He's going to watch.

Hael might not get it, but I do.

Victor really is still pissed, even if he doesn't look it.

I turn back toward him, but all he does is lift a dark brow in question. This is another challenge from him.

"Well? You said you wanted this, didn't you, Bernadette? To do your duties? Here's your opportunity. Do you know why we wanted a Havoc Girl in the first place?" Vic is taunting me now, and I can feel my hands curling into tight fists. "Because we didn't want a girl to

314

come between us. So now we're going to share you."

I open my mouth to say something, but what's the point?

Vic wants to be an asshole? I can be one, too.

Instead of responding the way I want—I'd love to chuck something at his perfect face right now—I turn toward Hael instead, heart thundering.

"Here," Vic says before I can even get started, chucking some condoms at us that he pulls from his jeans pocket. "Wouldn't want to make the same mistake with Hael that you made with me."

"Definitely not," I grind out, snatching one up and turning back to Hael. He's got a cocky smile on his face, like maybe this is all fun and games to him. Fucking is like an Olympic sport to this asshole anyway, so why am I not surprised?

Hael takes the condom and tucks it into his pocket, scooting back on the bed and then pulling me up with him. He rolls us over so that I'm on my back and he's hovering over me, that coconut scent of his enveloping me and mixing with the fresh scent of weed, protecting me from the dark influence of Victor Channing, his voyeuristic ass sitting in the corner.

I should question him, ask him what he's filming us for, but I know he won't post it anywhere. Vic is too selfish for that. This is all for him.

Hael seems to sense that I don't want to be kissed, moving those hot lips of his to my neck. As soon as he makes contact with my throat, I sigh, my back arching up off the bed. His right hand slides up and under my shirt, heating my skin to unbearable temperatures.

He's watching, I remind myself, but that doesn't make the moment less hot. It amps up the tension, and I find myself squirming, wishing Hael would move his hand between my thighs to satisfy that deep ache in my core.

"Not so fast, Blackbird," he purrs, grabbing my wrist when my fingers drop to the waistband of his jeans. He pins it above my head and runs his hot tongue down the curve of my neck, tasting my pulse. "Vic wants a show, not a sprint. Let's give him a proper performance, shall we?"

My fingers curl in Hael's bloodred hair as he kisses his way down my throat, my fingers teasing over his sweaty neck and down his arms. His muscles are trembling slightly from all the work he put in today, but that just makes it even hotter. I can feel every jump of his pulse when I rest my fingers on the side of his throat.

He moves suddenly, surprising me by biting the hardened point of my nipple through my shirt and drawing a long groan from me. His coconut and leather scent is still there, but it lingers under the heavy, sweet scent of weed.

My fingers tease down Hael's rounded biceps and pick some of the sticky leaves off his skin as he works my breast with his mouth, drawing all that lust and need from my core into my chest. My nipples ache as Hael runs his hand up and under my shirt, palming one of the smooth mounds as he kneads the flesh with strong fingers. My eyes find Victor's, his phone in his right hand while his left sits easily on the arm of the chair.

You want me, I think as Hael lifts my shirt up, uncovering my breasts, and moves back in with that strong, hot mouth of his. *And you hate that your best friend's mouth is on my tits. You hate it because you wish it was yours.*

My fingers dig into Hael's hair, and I draw his mouth up to mine.

If I kiss him, it'll destroy Vic. He'll snap. I want to see that, what he does when he comes undone. Before I can think too hard about it, I move in and press my lips to Hael's. He's already a step ahead of me, taking over the interaction with the hot, wild heat of his tongue, chasing my own with strong, possessive strokes.

A strange feeling scatters through me, like shooting stars, taking over my whole body as we adjust ourselves, and I end up in his lap. My arms cross together behind Hael's strong neck as I taste the sweat on his lips from a hard day's work.

Shit.

Kissing him is doing all sorts of strange things to me, like I knew I should have never done this in the first place. Kissing someone opens up your soul to theirs, lets you taste their essence in a way that just doesn't come across with sex. And now that I've tasted Hael properly, I sort of ... like him?

Victor fades away in my awareness as I grind my hips against the hard bulge in Hael's jeans, and his inked hands drop down to cup my ass. He kneads my flesh as I work my body against his, finding this sweet spot where pleasure teases my clit with every forward thrust. With

Hael touching my ass, and his hard, hot body beneath mine, it doesn't take me long to work myself to a climax.

"Oh, yeah, baby, you know where it's at," Hael growls against my ear as he bites my lower lip and groans as I gasp and shudder in his arms, the violent grinding motion of my hips slowing as that unbearable pleasure unfurls inside of me like a lightning strike. Pretty sure I've soaked my panties and shorts straight through. "*Fuck*."

Hael flips me over and then tears my shorts and underwear off, chucking them aside as he leans down to kiss my mouth and struggles with his belt buckle at the same time. I help him free his cock, the long, hard length of him hot and pulsing in my hand. We eat at each other's mouths, totally and completely forgetting that we're being filmed—that we're being *watched*.

My eyes flick back to find Vic's. His gaze has darkened a dozen shades, turning those dark brown eyes of his into an endless ebon black while his left hand grips his cock in tight fingers. He strokes himself while he watches us, jaw clenched tight, the phone still locked onto our sweaty, tangled bodies.

My fingers tease Hael's dick, my thumb sliding over the bead of pre-cum at the tip and working him until he's panting and thrusting into my hand. He snatches my wrists again and pins both above my head, reaching down to guide the head of his shaft to the molten heat throbbing between my thighs.

"Condom," Vic barks out, and I grit my teeth. He can't remember when he's fucking me, but he has enough sense to boss his friend around?

There's a knock at the door, but whoever's on the other side doesn't bother to try the knob. Not that it would matter, since it's already locked.

"Vic, are you in there?" It's Aaron.

"Yeah, but fuck off, I'm busy right now." Victor chucks another condom our way and Hael catches it, cursing as he pulls it out and slides the wet latex over his dick. He doesn't hesitate before he comes down on top of me again, honey-brown eyes dark with need. This time, though, he doesn't hold me like he's trying to piss somebody else off; he holds me like he's glad it's me in his inked hands.

"I want to see your tits bounce while I fuck you," he growls out, tearing my shirt off and tossing it aside. Hael skims his hands over my body, teasing my inked flesh with reverent fingers. He smirks at me, and then grips my hip with one hand, using the other to position himself. "Okay, Havoc Girl, let's see what you've got." Hael thrusts hard and deep, making me cry out as I throw my head back into the pillows. One of my hands reaches between us to touch my clit as he slams into me, bruising my body with the frenzy of his.

When he leans down to kiss me, I rake my nails along his biceps, feeling the ragged line of the scar on his right arm. His warm breath teases my lips as he kisses me again, his mouth firm but gentle while his hips are absolutely brutal.

We've barely been going ten minutes before I'm crying out *again*.

"Oh, god, don't stop, baby," I groan, tugging on Hael's hair as he kisses along the side of my neck. He bites me, too, but it doesn't hurt. Instead, it just draws another orgasm from me, my cunt pulsing along the length of his cock. "No, no, no, no," I whisper, holding him to me. "Don't stop."

"No chance in hell," Hael says, sweat dripping from his body and onto mine. Tiny little green marijuana leaves are stuck all over my skin, but when I breathe deep, all I smell is sex and coconut oil. *Fuck, Hael Harbin is good.*

"That's enough." Vic's cold, hard voice slashes through the heat in the room like a knife, making me groan as Hael pauses, and the delicious rhythm he'd been nurturing in my body subsides. My orgasm flickers on the fringes of my consciousness as Hael glances back at his friend.

"What?" he asks, sounding like he wants to punch something.

"I said that's enough," Vic repeats, his gaze so dark it almost hurts to look at him. His hands are clenched into fists at his sides, the muscles in his arms so taut that I can see his veins. He's put the phone down, and his pants are back on and zipped up. "Get off of her."

Hael's eyes widen, and I feel his body go tense between my spread legs.

"Are you fucking kidding me?" he asks, his voice so quiet, I might've missed the words if I wasn't looking at his lips.

"Do I make jokes very often?" Vic retorts, standing

there near the end of the bed with so much tension in his body he looks liable to snap at the wrong word. "Get off of her and get out."

"You're insane," Hael says, turning back to me. But then Vic is grabbing his shoulder and yanking him back. It's a weird sensation, to have Hael pulled off of me like that, and I sit up, grabbing the sheets as my own anger rushes to the surface.

"What the hell, Vic?" I snarl as Hael tears from his friend's grip, panting and shaking, his teeth bared in a snarl.

"What are you even doing?" he snaps, flinging out his hand to indicate me. "We talked about this. Bernadette is a *Havoc* Girl. Not Vic's girl. If you wanted her to be yours, then why didn't you say so when we were talking price?"

Whoa.

This conversation got real, real fast. Hael tears the condom off his still-hard dick and chucks it at the wall before zipping up his jeans. He rakes his fingers through his hair and closes his eyes.

"Sit back down and—"

"No," Vic says, standing his ground. "Get out."

"I'm not fucking leaving!" Hael yells back at him. "You might be the boss, but she's not just *your* girl."

"She's my future wife," Vic says, still completely frozen in that dark well of shadows he's drawn around himself. "If you touch her again, I don't know what I'll do. I can't be held responsible for my actions."

"Do I even get a fucking say here?" I snap, standing

up from the bed. "I might've agreed to your price, but I'm not some fuck doll for you to fight over."

"You are not a fuck doll," Vic says, but he doesn't move his attention from Hael's face. "But this isn't about you. This is about me. I'm a jealous, possessive asshole, and I wanted to kill Hael for fucking you in his car. He's my best friend, Bernadette. There's a problem here."

"Victor," Hael starts, but Vic just shakes his head.

"Get out. *Now*. This is the last time I'm going to ask."

Hael looks at me and then back at Vic, and there's something in his face that says maybe this one time, he's not going to listen. Maybe this one time, he's going to fight Victor and see what happens.

The tension stretches between the three of us until it's almost unbearable, until I can't breathe.

"Fuck you, Vic. Seriously, fuck you." Hael turns away in a storm cloud of his own rage, unlocks the door, and then yanks it open. He pauses once before leaving to look over his shoulder. "I love you, man, but you almost pushed it too far this time." Hael leaves and slams the door so hard that one of the framed pictures on the wall crashes to the floor and shatters.

For a whole minute there, the room is completely silent.

"Get on the bed," Vic tells me, glancing back in my direction. He stalks over to the lamp and turns it off, plunging us into darkness.

My body is shaking with a mix of frustration and anger. I was *this* close to having a second orgasm, and he ruined it. Fucking Victor stupid-ass Channing.

He turns around to look at me, moonlight filtering between the mini blinds on the sliding doors to his left and limning his large form in silver.

He's jealous, I think as my mind runs through all the ways I could handle this moment. I could tell him to fuck off, openly defy him, and see what he might do. Or … I could let the hot, wild heat taking over my body run wild. Despite his bossy possessiveness, despite the way he treated Hael, I still want him.

Stepping back, I drop the sheet to the floor, and then I lie back on the bed, my knees crossed together, my elbows keeping me propped up.

Victor slips his shirt over his head and tosses it aside before kicking off his shoes, peeling off his socks, and then shoving his jeans down his muscular hips. As my eyes adjust to the light, I notice that he has a condom in his hand. He slips it on before moving over to me and climbing on the bed, his weight denting the mattress and making me bounce slightly.

I can smell him now, that bergamot and musk scent of his, all male, all Vic.

My breath catches as he reaches up with a big hand and cups the side of my face. His entire presence is edged in violence, but his touch is gentle enough.

"I'm apologizing in advance for how hard I'm going to fuck you," he says, and a wash of heat spreads from my core to the hardened points of my nipples, the bruised curve of my lips. "But after, I'll take it nice and slow."

He grabs my hips and flips me over, pulling me back

and into him. I can feel the heat of his body as Vic presses up against me, a sigh shuddering through him as he runs his palm down my spine. I can feel the tension in his hands as he caresses me, and then, it's like a switch has been flipped. Vic grabs my hair and yanks my head back, making me cry out. It doesn't hurt per se, but it rides that fine line.

"I'm having a seriously hard time fucking controlling myself right now," he growls, and his hands tighten on both my hip and my hair. "There are so many things I want to do to you." Vic leans down and kisses my shoulder, swirling his tongue in a circle against my skin before he bites me—*hard*.

"You won't like it when Victor takes you to bed. He's a rough, angry sort of lover."

Aaron's words echo in my head as I shift my body and Vic growls, holding me in place. He's bruising my hip, making my scalp burn, and yet it's not unpleasant. His mouth traces up the line of my shoulder toward my neck, and he bites me again, drawing another long, embarrassing groan from my throat.

Vic releases my hair and curls his inked fingers around the front of my neck. With his other hand, he guides the tip of his cock to my throbbing heat, slicking the length of his body against my wetness.

"We didn't want a girl to come between us and yet, here you are, doing just that. Are you fucking proud of yourself?"

"Screw you," I snarl, gritting my teeth as Victor teases me with his cock. He lifts my head up even further, forcing me to curve my back and push my ass against him.

"You've hated me for so long, haven't you?" he asks, and I realize then that I'm shaking. He's stripping me bare again, and I hate it. I hate it, but I also … I can't explain it, but I want more. His voice is like smoke, curling around and enveloping me. It's sumptuous, lavish, regnant perfection. "What's it like? Having me touch you this way?"

"Eat shit," I gasp as he adjusts himself, his fingers curving under my jaw. He holds me in a tense grip, his anger hot and evident on his skin. His muscles are taut, slick with sweat. A droplet slides from his inked skin and drops onto my own.

Victor crushes his mouth to mine, holding me just where he wants me, taking my lips the way he's taking over the rest of me—body and soul. His kiss is savage, almost brutal, bruising my mouth but inciting this near desperate need for more. Our tongues slick together as he tastes me, biting my lower lip just hard enough to make me bleed. Not that it matters, right: blood in, blood out. And we've already shared blood, cum. We're already intertwined.

"I bet I could make you come on command," he purrs, pulling back slightly, smirking at me in the dark.

I grit my teeth and start to struggle against him, but his grip is complete, his control absolute. *If I asked him to stop, would he?* I only have to think for a split-second before I have an answer to that question: *yes.* Victor was serious when he said I was a part of Havoc, a part of the family. He won't hurt me, not anymore.

A surprise gasp slips past my lips as Vic pulls his hips back slightly and replaces the tip of his cock with his finger, slicking it along the wetness of my core, teasing me. Everything in my body hurts right now. I'm aching with need, like each molecule is fired up and quivering. This isn't helping.

"Stop teasing me and—"

Victor clamps his hand over my mouth at the same time he pushes a single, inked finger into my pussy. A sigh of relief gets caught in my throat as Vic maintains his iron-clad handhold over my face, hooking his finger inside me and drumming up sensations that I've never felt before. I wiggle against him, but I'm seriously trapped here, his hot, heavy body behind me, his hand covering my lips.

"Come for me, Bernadette. That's an order." Victor thrusts his finger deep, slicking it against my aching insides. My nipples are so hard now that I'm frantic for a caress of any kind, but Vic's only touching me as much as he has to. I get nothing extra, even less than I got during our first, fucked-up sexual encounter against the wall. "I want to hear you cry out the way you did when you were sitting on Hael's cock."

A rogue whimper escapes me as Vic inserts another finger, sliding the two of them in and out, nice and slow. It's pure goddamn torture, and he knows it. His chuckle is dark and angry, rife with frustration. No part of him actually thinks this is fun. To Vic, this is a necessity. He slips a third finger in, amplifying the pleasure coursing through me, and then releases his hold on my mouth.

"Ready?" he asks, and then he drops his second hand to my clit, using the natural lube from my body to make it nice and slippery. He works the hardened nub with his thumb in slow but firm circles. I want to resist him, put up some sort of fight, but it feels too good. I find myself falling, collapsing, shattering to pieces. "Let me hear that climax, *baby.*"

Vic flicks his thumb in just such a way that I fall over the edge, shuddering as the orgasm unfurls inside of me like a whip. A sound tears from my throat that I can't stop, that I'm sure the whole house can hear.

It hits me hard and fast, leaving me a boneless, shaking, sweating mess.

"Good." Victor slaps me on the ass and then grabs my hair again, yanking me back toward him. "I told you that you'd mewl beneath me." Before I even get the chance to recover, he's removing his fingers and replacing them with the tip of his cock. With one hand locked on my hip, he drives into me with a fierce growl, hitting the end of me and drawing sounds from my throat I wasn't even sure I could make.

Vic thrusts deep, filling me up completely. My body stretches to accommodate his, but luckily, I'm all warmed-up. If I weren't, his balls-deep thrusts might hurt. He's just too goddamn big for his own good.

A gasp escapes my lips as my hands curl in the sheets, my body rocking forward with each violent thrust. Pleasure courses through me in an unstoppable storm, this torrent of fiery heat that makes me grit my teeth against a scream. I don't want Vic to know how much I'm loving this, how good it feels to have his body inside of mine. It's like he's claiming me with each pump of his hips and yet, I don't hate it.

I ... I love it.

Vic pulls on my hair again, forcing me to push up to my hands. My breasts sway with the motion as he pounds into me, the only sound in the room that of our bodies joining together over and over and over again.

He isn't nice. No, he's rough, wild, forceful. But there's something to it that I find appealing, like I've finally managed to catch Victor Channing with his pants down—both metaphorically and literally. His numbness and his shadows have been stripped away and there's nothing left but emotion. Anger, maybe. Jealousy. Even hate.

But it's all better than being fucking numb.

He groans, this deep, dark sound that's frenzied with need, and I swear, I can hear him coming undone. Victor pounds faster, fucks me deeper, and then comes violently, grabbing my hip in tight fingers and yanking my hair so hard that I cry out. With a few last, wild thrusts he finishes and pulls out, cursing as he tears the condom off and chucks it in the trash.

Vic rakes his fingers through his hair as I turn over to look at him, and then his gaze falls down to mine, stealing my breath away. I can still barely see him, but with the moonlight showcasing the hard, strong lines of his face, I can tell we're nowhere near done in here.

"I'm a Havoc Girl," I gasp out, because that's what he

asked of me. That was the price. But it feels like now, in his shadowed gaze, he's asking me for so much more.

"You're my fucking girl," he says, climbing on the bed as I scoot back until my back is pressed into the mountain of pillows next to the headboard. There's the lingering scent of Hael's coconut oil mixed with the skunk-y smell of weed, but ... when I really inhale, all I smell all over this bed is Vic's musk and amber scent.

"This is your bed when you're here?" I ask, but he's not letting me get away that easily, climbing over me, his knees on either side of my thighs, his hands on either side of my chest, palms pressed into the mattress. Our faces are now only a hair's-breadth apart.

"Bernadette," Vic says, his warm breath tracing over my lips. My scalp is sore, and I can already tell I'm going to be bruised in the morning. "You go out of your way to piss me off, don't you?"

"I didn't fuck Hael to piss you off," I say, holding his stare, my heart thundering like crazy in my chest. But then I hesitate. *"When you have nothing else, you realize the one currency you can carry is truth."* "Not this time," I correct. "And not in the principal's office. Only ... the first time."

Vic's sharp mouth curves into a grin, flashing white teeth in the dark.

"I'm going to devour you, Bernadette Blackbird," he says, and then he pushes back, grabbing my knees and opening my legs to him. I'm powerless at that point to resist; my entire body is in flames, and I need something to douse that heat.

My head falls back into the pillows as Vic puts his lips between my thighs, tasting my desire with a long, hot flick of his tongue. He pleasures me with reckless abandon, no pretense of niceties, just a firm hand on either side of my hips. He isn't worried about getting messy as he takes over my body and I dig my fingers into his dark hair.

I'm too conscious of the sounds escaping my throat, and it's holding me back. Vic seems to sense that, chuckling and raising his face up to stare at me through the dark.

"None of the kids can hear us in here, babe," he repeats, and I wonder if he's mocking me for calling Hael babe earlier. "I promise you that. They're all upstairs, I'm sure, tucked away, snug as bugs in rugs."

"That doesn't mean Hael or—"

Vic drops his face back down, capturing my clit gently between his teeth and then sucking on it. At the same time, he drives two fingers into me, and I feel that pesky climax unwrapping again. Energy bursts through me as I struggle against Vic's grip, another cry escaping my bruised lips as my body collapses back into the bed, the surge of adrenaline fading to a soft relaxation.

I've barely caught my breath before he's climbing over me again.

"Vic," I say, but he captures the side of my face in his hand and kisses me, the taste of my body on his lips. As soon as his mouth touches mine, I'm falling, deeper and deeper into him. Even though I know I shouldn't. Even though he was once the monster in my dark.

Before I can think better of it, my legs are wrapping around him, pulling him close. He reaches between us and guides his bare cock into me, never breaking our kiss.

We begin to move together, me lifting my hips to meet his, him thrusting with deep, slow undulations, his hard body rubbing my clit with each movement. Our tongues slide together in a similar dance, tasting, thrusting, withdrawing. It's all friction and heat and hands. I dig my nails into Vic's back and drag them down his skin, making him groan, marking him. He returns the favor by putting his mouth to my neck, sucking hard enough to leave hickeys. But it just feels so damn good.

"I'm going to mark every inch of this body, Bernadette," he whispers, making me shiver.

Vic fucks me until my body begins to pulse yet again, and then he rolls us over so that I'm on top, putting his hands on my hips and digging his fingers in hard enough to bruise. "Ride me hard," he commands, and I do.

My hips rock back and forth in a frantic rhythm as I throw my hair back, my nails digging into his chest. Vic reaches up, threading his fingers in my hair and then pulling me down. He kisses me hard, biting my lower lip as I work my body against his, feeling his pulse pick up, his muscles tense.

I think about rolling off of him and finding another condom, but when I start to leave, he grabs my hips and holds me there, thrusting his hips up off the bed until I'm groaning and moving again. My body works to pleasure us both, drawing another climax up and out of him, until he's coming hard inside of me, the sound that escapes his throat filling the quiet room.

We're both left panting, me lying on top of him, my head buried in the hollow between his neck and shoulder. One of his hands strokes down my back, almost soothingly, until he cracks it across my ass.

I lift up my head, determined to at least chew him out for that move, but he grabs me by the back of my head and kisses me again, like he can't get enough, like it'll never be e-fucking-nough.

Vic slaps his hand against my ass again, and then pushes me over, kissing his way across my sweaty, naked body. His fingers slip inside of me again, working me up into another frenzy.

"It's not fair. I can't do this anymore," I whisper, wondering if I'm going to survive the night in here with him. Or … if I should leave? But he just laughs at me and keeps going until I'm coming again, drenching his hand and biting down so hard on his chest that I draw blood.

"Are you marking me, too, Bernie?" he taunts, looking down at me through the shadows. I put my hand over the mark I've just made, but I don't know how to answer his question. What *am* I doing?

"I should go," I start, but Vic just shakes his head and leans down, putting his lips near my ear again.

"Did you think I was joking, Bernadette? You're my girl, and you're sleeping in my bed tonight."

And then he mounts me again, and I'm lost to oblivion.

Victor Channing has some serious fucking stamina.

CHAPTER
TWENTY-NINE

I wake up with Vic's heavy arm around my waist, his body curled up against mine. His bare skin is hot, his heartbeat thumping against my back. *What the actual fuck?* I think, looking out of a pair of sliding glass doors into the backyard. With him touching me like this, I feel like I'm falling to pieces. The numbness inside of me is stripped away with every breath he exhales, tickling my pink hair against my shoulder.

"I have to pee," I whisper, pushing his arm off. When I glance back at his face, I can see that he's still asleep. And he's so much cuter this way, too, none of those asshole vibes radiating off of him.

The only usable bathroom in the house now is the one upstairs, so I slip into my panties and Vic's discarded shirt, and make a run for it. Of course, when I get there and slip into the bathroom, it's all fogged up with steam.

"Shit," I curse just before Aaron peeks out the curtain and sees me standing there. He sighs.

"You can come in," he says. "I won't look."

The curtain's tugged into place as I bite my lip and decide I just can't hold it. Cursing, I sit on the toilet and try to pee without thinking about the thin sheet of plastic separating Aaron's warm, tattooed body from mine.

What the hell did I do last night? I wonder, thinking about Hael's hot hands, and the fury on his face when Vic kicked him out of the room. And Vic … Vic. Fucking Vic. I've never had sex like that before, so completely undone. We only managed to use a condom the first time. The rest … "Goddamn it."

"Do you need the shower?" Aaron asks, sighing again.

Do I? Of course I do. I have Vic's cum between my legs, and I'm in desperate need. *Those sheets in the master bedroom are going to be wrecked …*

"That'd be nice, thanks," I murmur, not expecting him to just climb out in front of me. My eyes slide over the hard, wet planes of Aaron's body as he wraps a towel around his hips and leaves the water running. He doesn't look at me as he leaves the room, closing the door behind him. But I saw it. His dick was hard. And I can only assume it was because of me.

With a groan, I hop into the shower, scrub myself down, and climb out.

As soon as I'm dressed, I open the bathroom door to find Vic waiting for me, his forearms braced on either side of the doorjamb.

I freeze, but my heart doesn't get the memo. I can hear it pounding like a war drum.

"Bernadette," he says carefully, running his tongue across his lower lip. His eyes actually look brown today, like some of the shadows have been stripped away. Make no mistake: when he smiles, angels cry. But he looks moderately less scary and that's saying something.

"Are we doing … Havoc stuff today?" I ask, the words husky as I try not to stare at his bare chest or the bitemarks on his neck, the red welts from my nails on his arms and shoulders. I've thoroughly marked Victor Channing, and I haven't spent much time in front of the mirror today, but … I glance to the side and catch a quick glimpse of my face and neck. There are red hickeys on my throat, no doubt about that.

I glance back at Vic, and he shrugs, those muscular shoulders of his moving like well-oiled pistons.

"I think we've all earned a break," he says, his eyes taking me in, absorbing me, wrecking me, ripping me to pieces without even trying. *I'm completely numb without you.* The last thing in the world I want to do is go home right now, but I don't want to be here either.

I need space from Vic.

"Okay." It's the only world that'll come out. I've forgotten the English language.

"Bernadette," he says in that way of his. "Are you trying to run away from me again?"

"I don't …" I pause when I see Hael leaning against the wall, watching us. His honey-brown eyes meet mine, and he cocks a little half-smirk that doesn't quite reach his gaze. "I need to figure out Halloween costumes—for Heather and for me. We're going to a stupid party, right?"

"As relevant as all of that information is," Vic starts, his voice smooth and low, "it's not an answer to my question."

"I don't need to run from you, Victor Channing," I say, slipping under his arm and moving into the hallway. I pretend like I don't feel Hael's eyes on me either.

"You don't? Because you're acting like you can't get away fast enough." He turns to look at me, spots Hael leaning against the wall, and frowns. "What?" he asks, careful to keep his voice neutral.

"Nothing. Brittany wants to meet me somewhere today to talk." Hael rolls his eyes and pushes up off the wall. "But I wasn't sure, what with all those white trash weasels on our dicks, if I should go alone."

"Take Bernadette with you," Vic says, voice still solidly neutral. Guess we're not going to talk about last night, and that's fine with me. "She wants to get away from me; you want to piss Brittany off." He shrugs his shoulders like it doesn't matter, but it does. He said as much last night. "Callum can tag along, too. When you're done, pick the girls up from their birthday party, and take Heather and Bernadette home."

Victor heads down the steps without looking at me, and I can't decide if I just stood my ground or made a crucial mistake.

"You okay?" Hael asks, studying me. I'm dressed in dark jeans and a top that plunges just a little too far between my supposedly G-size breasts. "About last night …"

"I'm fine," I blurt, interrupting him. I'm not ready to deal with last night just yet. "How's Brittany?" I don't mean the words to come out quite that snippy, but there it is. Guess I'm not a huge Brittany fan after all.

Vic would've noticed my tone, not sure that Hael does.

"Oh, same, same, always with the goddamn drama. She fabricates it to keep herself busy." He comes over to stand beside me, and I can feel it, that crackle in the air between us that makes my palms sweat. "You sure you're okay?" he repeats, and I raise an eyebrow.

"Maybe you're the one who's not okay? Getting kicked out in the middle of sex ..." Hael grits his teeth and shakes his arms out like he's shedding his frustrations from last night. I swear, I thought the two of them were going to spatter those walls with blood.

"Victor's intense," Hael says, shrugging again, his brown eyes trained on my face. "Just sayin'. If you need to chat about it ..."

"You're not about to be my coffee buddy," I reply, taking a step back to put some space between us. "That's not really where our relationship's headed."

"Where is it headed then?" Hael asks with a laugh. He puts a hand on the wall and leans in toward me. "Don't pretend you don't fucking like me."

"I like *fucking* you," I admit, tucking my fingers into my pockets. "I just don't want to sit and have a heart-to-heart with you."

Hael laughs again and shakes his head, running his hand over his bloodred faux hawk.

"Sure, sure." He gestures in the direction of the stairs with his chin. "Let's get out of here before Vic changes his mind. Hey Cal!" Hael starts down the steps and hops off the bottom one. "You down for a coffee break?"

I come down the stairs and pause, noticing Callum stretching in the sunshine that's streaming through the sliding glass doors. Just beyond the glass, I can see Vic and Aaron smoking on the back patio. They're both tense, shoulders taut. *I can't wait to get out of here.*

"Were you doing yoga?" I ask, and Cal shrugs, grabbing a wet cloth off the table and swiping the sweat from his forehead.

"Yep," he says, and then he gives me a mysterious little smile that doesn't quite reach his eyes. "When you're smaller, like me," he nods in the direction of me and Hael, indicating my slight frame compared to Hael's bulk, "you gottta stay limber. Makes beating the shit out of meatheads much, much easier."

I raise an eyebrow as Callum yanks on his blue hoodie, grabs a pack of cigarettes from the table, and a Pepsi from the fridge.

"Ready," he says, and off we go.

The coffee shop Hael takes us to is on the 'good' side of town, and I can see as we pull up to the curb that it's a Fuller High spot. They've practically pissed all over it. There are *thank you* letters and photos from all the sports teams, profusely thanking the shop for funding student athletics.

I'm not even out of the car yet, and I'm scoffing.

"If the coffee shop's owners really wanted to help teens realize their potential, they'd give their money to Prescott," I say as Hael turns off the engine.

"Yeah, but then they wouldn't get to preen their feathers and praise themselves for being philanthropists while counting all that cold-hard cash the Fuller kids bring into the café." Hael raises both brows and climbs out, drawing the attention of every snot-nosed, middle-class bourgeois asshole hanging out at the bistro tables on the sidewalk.

I follow along behind him, noting that the students at least pretend to avert their gazes. They're afraid of Havoc, same as everyone else. The only kids from Fuller willing to stand up to the Havoc Boys are the players of the varsity football team. Their turf wars last year were epic.

Hael swaggers up the curb and pauses to hold open the door to the shop for me, pretending to cringe slightly when I give him a look.

"Right, you don't like gentlemen," he says, leaning forward and letting his hot breath tease the shell of my ear. "But don't worry: I'm more than happy for you to suck my dick on campus again." I elbow past him with Callum following behind. He makes a straight beeline to the counter for coffee and pastries.

Me, I find myself staring across a crowded room at what can be the one and only Brittany.

She's sitting there with long, dark hair shimmering

over her shoulders, skull patterned tights, and a plaid miniskirt.

I'm so beyond confused.

But I know it's her by the way Hael's staring, his eyes narrowed, mouth pursed into a thin line.

"She's more nuanced than I expected," I admit, and Hael coughs out a harsh laugh.

"It's almost Halloween, Bernadette," he says, and then he starts off across the café, pausing in front of her and not bothering to take a seat. I could make myself scarce, join Callum at the counter, but it's more fun if I follow.

"I'm here. What do you want?" Hael asks, and Brittany snaps the PopSocket on her phone in, looking past him and over to me.

"Who's this?" she asks, her voice a harsh clip as she looks me over with dark brown eyes, clearly not all that impressed. "Are you off to the Halloween party tonight, too, then?"

"Everyday is Halloween for me," I retort, enjoying the way her face crinkles up. I used to want to be like her, this beautiful, untouchable goddess among teens. I think most little girls entertain that thought at some point or another, the wish to be popular, to fit in but still stand out.

Havoc broke me of that.

The world broke me of that.

"I'm not talking to you with your new plaything in tow," Brittany spits back, and I have to curl my hands into fists to control my temper. Her use of the word of plaything better just be a coincidence. If I find out that Hael told her anything about my deal with Havoc …

He slams one of his tattooed hands palm-down on the table, his usually cocky expression dead-serious.

"Do not talk about or to Bernadette. You hear me? I'll fucking destroy everything you hold dear, starting with that perfect relationship you have to dear old daddy." Brittany's beautiful face cracks into a million pieces at his statement, and her eyes flame as she flicks her gaze over to me again.

Hael notices the path Brittany's attention takes and a cruel smirk curves across his lips. One of his inked hands slides around the curve of my waist to rest against my lower back, pulling me in so that his hot, hard body is pressed up against mine. With practiced ease, he cups my chin with the tattooed fingers of his other hand and lifts my face for a kiss.

His tongue practically sizzles as it slides between my lips, taking over the empty space that Vic left, making all those shiny new emotions inside of me sparkle like diamonds. Heat races through me, curling low in my belly, making my already sore insides throb and ache for more.

As quick as it happened, it's over and Hael is stepping back. He grins as he releases me, but that, too, fades as he flicks a look back at Brittany and frowns.

"You have two minutes starting now. What do you want?"

Now that I'm satisfied that Brittany—who the hell knows what her last name is—looks properly homicidal, I decide to give Hael some space. *Because you can't fucking stand watching her look at him, huh, Bernadette?* I grit my teeth.

"Got you a coffee," Cal says, and I turn around to find him pointing at the only free table in the entire place. There are three coffees waiting, three pastries. I decide I truly don't care enough about Brittany to stick around and listen to her BS on Hael. Instead, I join Callum at his table.

But on the inside ... yeah, my stomach is churning, and my gaze keeps flicking back to them. I just feel anxious, and I can't figure out why. Maybe when Vic mentioned speaking the truth, he didn't just mean to other people—he probably also meant to myself.

"Don't worry about them," Cal says, splitting his croissant in half and looking over at me with bright, blue eyes. "Hael is done with Brittany for good."

"What makes you say that?" I ask, and he shrugs. The tattoos on his right arm are so eye catching, I find myself staring at them instead of his face. He's got these black ribbons twisted around his muscles, the shine and linework on them so crisp that they look real. The ribbons lead to a broken girl lying in a heap in a spotlight. I can't see her face, but her blond hair cascades around it in a curtain, the detail so fine I feel like I could reach out and touch it.

"She cheated on him with one of the Fuller football boys. There's nobody Hael hates more." Callum's voice is low and rough, but in a pleasant sort of way, this husky darkness that traces like velvet across my skin. Curiosity is going to get this kitty killed because I'm *dying* to know the real story behind Cal's scars. "They've cheated on each other before, but this is like, last straw shit for him."

I focus on my coffee and let my eyes wander the

crowd, taking in the designer labels, the fancy diamond tennis bracelets, and the think-their-shit-don't stink VSCO girls with their stupid ass *Save the Turtles* metal water bottles, hair scrunchies, and vacuous facial expressions. If you don't know what a VSCO girl is, Google it. Maybe you'll be as disturbed as I am, having to look at them with their *fair-trade* coffees in their biodegradable cups. Guess they can save the world with paper straws while still driving gas-guzzling cars, using makeup tested on animals, and calling me an asshole for smoking. Good on them.

"How did he even meet Brittany?" I ask, running my finger around the rim of my coffee cup. "I thought Fuller and Prescott were rival enemies to the bitter end."

"On the spring break trip last year," Callum says, eyes darting around the room, taking note of anyone who looks like they might have balls or ovaries big enough to pick a fight with us. We are very clearly the outliers here, dirty Prescott High trash daring to mix with the Fuller elite. They think of themselves as savage royals, but they're nothing but petty cowards and liars. "Prescott High stays on one side of the lake, Fuller on the other. I guess Hael and Brittany got drunk and stumbled on one another." Cal shrugs his shoulders again, dismantling his entire croissant before he eats it.

I take a sip of my coffee, and I'm pleased to discover that it tastes like dirty dishwater. On the other side of the tracks, in this crappy hole-in-the-wall that uses Styrofoam cups (sorry turtles, I want to save the environment, too, but sometimes socio-economic problems get in the way), that has coffee a hundred times better than this hipster hellhole.

"Brittany's using him to get back at her father," Callum continues, realizing that Hael's not likely to want his food, seeing as he's white-knuckled, face pale, jaw clenched and shaking over there. Fortunately, Cal takes care of this for him, once again dismantling the croissant before eating it.

"Who's her father?" I ask, and Cal pauses, looking up at me in surprise.

"The chief of police," he says, and I cock a brow, my hand squeezing so hard on my coffee cup that it dents and hot coffee pours out the top, scalding me. I curse and dab at it with a napkin, thinking about the Springfield police and the depth of their corruption.

"Fantastic."

Callum and I sit in companionable silence for a while, until the front doors open, and three huge dudes walk in. They're all as big as Vic, and it's clear from moment one that they're looking for trouble.

The guy in front is a bit smaller than the other two, so I figure he's probably the quarterback of the Fuller High football team. Who else could these jerkoffs possibly be? I mean, they're the total clichéd package—complete with letterman jackets.

"Oh, hey there Prima," QB-dude says, sauntering over in our direction. He hasn't noticed Hael and Brittany on the other side of the coffee shop. Nah, he's just homing in on the first target he came across. But Prima? What the fuck is that nickname about? "What the hell are you doing on our side of the city, huh?"

Callum takes another sip of his coffee, and I can't help

but notice how much smaller he is than even the leader of these thugs. Not good. I'm willing to step in and fight, too, but it's gonna be a tough one.

"Did you hear my question, you trailer park fag—"

Callum's up in an instant and tossing his steaming hot coffee into the guy's face. The scream QB lets out is legendary, stumbling back into his buddies and scratching at his face with his nails. In an equally smooth follow-up, Cal steps forward and throws a perfect right-hook into the guy's face.

The crowd in the café erupts into booing, tossing insults our way and encouraging their own guys to kick some ass. Hael appears from behind the other two football douchebags, on par with their weight class, and sucker punches first one and then the other, knocking them forward and stirring up the chaos. He opens the door to the café and gestures for us to join him.

Snatching both my coffee and Hael's, I get the hell out of there before the rest of the team shows up and we end up outnumbered in enemy territory.

Cal climbs into the backseat of the Camaro while I take the front seat, and Hael slides in, gritting his teeth, his knuckles white on the steering wheel as he starts the engine and peels away from the curb.

"You okay?" I ask, because he seems nonplussed while Callum is calm as a cucumber.

"Fine," Hael grinds out as I set his coffee in the cup holder and give him a look.

"I thought Havoc was all about transparency? Family first, right?"

"Brittany just told me she's pregnant, okay?" he snaps,

and my eyes go wide. Wow. No wonder Hael is soaked in sweat. At the same time, I feel my stomach churn with that same anxious energy I felt in the café. And it's not because Callum just assaulted a kid with scalding coffee. No, this is about Hael and Brittany.

"Damn it, dude," Cal growls out from the backseat.

"It's not my kid," Hael murmurs, but like he's trying to convince himself as much as he is me.

"You're not the first guy to pull that shit when he realizes he's made a mistake," I say, and Hael punches the steering wheel with his tattooed fist.

"No. I used a condom every time. Whoever's baby that is, it isn't mine."

"Condoms aren't foolproof," I respond, and that anxious feeling in my stomach gets even worse. Vic and I did not use condoms appropriately last night, and I'm not on any birth control. Shit. The last thing I need is a baby in my life. The responsibility, and the weight, that would end me. *At least Hael bought me extra morning-after pills, huh?* Although I'm smart enough to know they don't always work. "It could still be yours."

"It's not," Hael snaps, and that's the end of the conversation.

We head over to Kara's friend's house to pick up the girls. Cal lets Ashley sit on his lap and buckles them in together while Kara gets the middle seat, and Heather sits on the other side. They're all so excited about the party that they talk nonstop on our way back to Aaron's.

As happy as I am that Heather had a good day, I can't get Hael's words out of my mind. *Brittany just told me she's pregnant, okay?* I don't like that. I don't like it at

346

all.

When we get back to the house, the girls rush in and head straight upstairs to fight over the game system in Kara's room while Hael paces the front lawn, raking his fingers through his hair and smoking like a chimney.

"What the fuck is wrong now?" Vic asks, coming out to stand on the front porch, his arms crossed over his chest, dark eyes tracking his best friend's movements.

"Brittany's pregnant," I offer up when Hael stays silent, and Vic's brows go up.

"Interesting."

"Interesting?!" Hael shouts, chucking his half-smoked cigarette and starting another. He's gesturing like a crazy person, and one of the neighbors is already staring our direction. "How is this fucking interesting? This is a nightmare." He throws both his pack of cigarettes and his freshy lit one into the grass and puts his tattooed hands over his face. "I fucking hate Brittany. I hate her. And her father is a nightmare from hell. He'll crucify me. He'll ruin everything."

"Don't be so dramatic," Vic says, tilting his head to one side.

"Dramatic?" Hael drops his hands and gives Vic this look that's half pleading, half terror. "The chief's got that new anti-gang unit just frothing at the mouth to come after us." Hael keeps pacing, and then I hear something I never expected: him cursing in French.

Whoa.

What the fuck?

"Is it yours, bro?" Vic asks, glancing my way and studying me like he expects me to give up my feelings that easily. I smile, just to throw him off. On the inside, I'm screaming and I'm not sure why. My body aches from all the places Vic touched me, and my skin is just as marked with his touch as his is with mine. We owned each other last night, no doubt about that.

"No!" Hael shouts, and then he grabs Kara's pink football from the lawn and throws it as hard as he can against the trunk of one of the trees that lines the edge of the yard. He's not bad, either. Interesting, considering how much he hates football players. "It's not mine, it can't be. I haven't slept with her since the weekend before Labor Day. No way. No fucking way."

"Then calm the hell down, and we'll deal with it," Vic says, his voice smooth and dark. "Why would she claim it was yours? What's her motivation here?"

"I don't know," Hael says, pinching the bridge of his nose and exhaling. "I have no clue."

"She's in love with Hael," Callum supplies, leaning up against the garage door and listening intently to the conversation, arms crossed over his chest. The front door opens and Aaron and Oscar step out while Hael continues to curse and pace in circles across the grass.

"Hey, Mr. Peters!" Aaron calls out, smiling and waving to the old man across the street, his faux smile fading into a very real frown as soon as the neighbor grumbles something under his breath and disappears into his house. "Fucking nosy fossil," Aaron murmurs, lighting up a cigarette. "What's going on anyway?"

"Brittany's pregnant," I say again, like I'm trying to make myself get used to the idea. Why do I even care? *Because the Havoc Boys were always supposed to be mine.* The thought pops into my head, and I shiver. I hate it when my subconscious calls out the lies I tell myself. *Fuck Havoc. I don't care about Havoc. I'm only here for revenge.*

All lies.

They've always been lies.

"Pregnant?" Aaron chokes out with a groan. Oscar just narrows his gray eyes and taps the fingers of his left hand on the face of the watch he's wearing on his right. "Hael, man, come on."

"It's not mine," Hael repeats for the hundredth time. "If I thought it was, I'd ..." He trails off and shrugs. "Jesus."

"Jesus isn't responsible for sleeping with that brain-dead whore," Oscar says, crossing his arms delicately over his chest. "That was all you. Now, what's our plan?"

"Why do you think Brittany's in love with Hael?" I ask Callum, and he shrugs again.

"She has been since the lake trip last year. It's all in her face. She cares too much what Hael thinks. It might not be his baby, but she wants it to be. Maybe even believes it."

"What are you, a fucking mind reader?" Hael asks, scowling at his friend. "Where do you come up with this stuff?"

"So, if she's not in love with you, what's her motivation?" Callum retorts, giving a snippy little smile in response to Hael's glower. "Tell us, we're waiting."

"I warned you not to fuck that girl," Vic says, shaking his head like a disappointed father. He sighs like he's beyond exhausted. Maybe he is, considering how little sleep we got last night. "And now we have yet another problem on our very full plate. Let me think this over for tonight. Go home to Marie. She's threatened to report you as a runaway again if you don't show up tonight."

"Fine," Hael snaps, moving over to his Camaro and climbing inside. He slams the door and peels out of the driveway. Marie ... I feel like I know that name. Pretty sure Marie is the name of Hael's mother. For as long as I've watched these boys across the playground, I've never been able to get close. They're all mysteries, even Aaron. Especially Aaron.

"Take my girl home, Aaron," Vic says, casting one, last glance my way, like he's waiting for me to acknowledge the hot ache between my thighs, the finger-shaped bruises on my hips, and the bite marks on my neck.

Aaron grits his teeth; there's no way he missed the word *my* in that request.

I say nothing, give Vic nothing. Eventually he turns away and heads inside.

And I ... I get ready to return to the gates of hell.

CHAPTER
THIRTY

Neither my mother nor the Thing are home when Aaron drops Heather and me off at the house, so I make the best of it by getting my sister's lunch ready for tomorrow and laying out our outfits.

In the morning, I wake up early and bundle Heather into warm clothes. Fall is in full-swing, and the air is crisp, a layer of frost teasing the pumpkins on our neighbor's lawn. They do fun things like that, the people who rent the other half of this duplex. They go to the pumpkin patch and carve jack-o'-lanterns, rake up piles of leaves and dive into them. They make fall seem fun. For me, it's just another season I have to survive.

Prescott High is in usual form, a fight breaking out between Stacey Langford's girls and some of Billie and Kali's friends. Good. They've been walking around like they own the place. I feel like Stacey's being smart, throwing her towel in with the winning side. Havoc won't forget that.

During English, I listen to Mr. Darkwood drone on and

on, my attention focused on the back of Kali's head as she plays with her phone under her desk. She wasn't involved in the fight this morning. Neither was Billie. Instead, they let their friends fight Stacey's girls for them. Pathetic.

I turn my attention back to the half-finished poem in front of me. It's a haiku this time, because Mr. Darkwood doesn't like originality or experimentation. He prefers neat, clean, and formulaic.

> *She cannot have you*
> *Not when I have yet to taste*
> *Passion on your lips*

Still no good. Lazy writing. I scribble it all out and start over.

> *Bad girls like bad boys*
> *Sometimes they even love them*
> *Not understanding their truth*

Utter horseshit.

I turn the poem in anyway, dreading lunch as soon as I see the look on Hael's face in the hall. He's tight, angry, cagey. When he sits by us in the cafeteria, he may as well be in another universe. And Victor ... Fuck. The way he looks at me makes it feel like my skin is splitting, like I'm crawling out of a cocoon with fragile, wet wings.

As soon as class is over, I bolt. I've biked or walked home by myself for years. I don't need to be babysat every single day. On my way out, I spot Callum heading down the sidewalk in the opposite direction, his black bag slung over one shoulder. Where it is he always disappears to, I don't know.

But I'm curious.

I check my phone. I have several hours until Heather gets home, so I change my direction and start off after him. He surprises me by skipping the bus station and walking all the way past Main Street with its shops and restaurants, an area that used to be deadly to traverse at night but that's slowly been improving as hipster millennials snatch up all the cheap houses on our side of the tracks.

He keeps going, disappearing into the bottom floor of a large industrial building near the warehouse district. I pause outside to read the letters on the glass. *Southside Dreams Dance Company.*

Huh.

I try the door and find it unlocked, moving down a red-painted hallway with various dance troupes featured in framed photos on either side. Once I get to the end, there's a sign that points toward a locker room and another that says *Studios.* I follow that one, ending up in another hallway with glass windows on either side. Studio A and B are empty, but when I get to Studio C, I find a single dancer, stretching his leg on the barre across from the window.

Holy. Fucking. Shit.

My mouth drops open as I find Callum in black leggings, black ballet slippers, and a loose tank that shows off all of his ink. He stretches for a while, unhurried, unconcerned, and then moves over to turn on a stereo. I can't hear the music from out here, but I find myself glued to the glass, fingertips pressed against the cool surface as Cal starts to dance.

What the hell am I looking at right now? I wonder as he does a series of impressive spins, and then balances on one foot, lifting the other leg up so high that I imagine he could touch the back of his head with his toes if he wanted. *Callum Park ... is a ballerina?!*

Only men aren't called ballerinas, are they? But I know literally nothing about the dance other than the basics that permeate common culture. Mom once had aspirations that I'd be a ballerina, forcing me into classes that I hated from moment one. But then Dad killed himself, and we were too poor for her to entertain her vicarious fantasies.

My breath fogs the glass as Cal fills the room with his presence, claiming the drafty warehouse room like it's a stage in Paris. My eyes are locked on his lithe form as he moves; I'm paralyzed. I couldn't look away if I wanted to.

The way he moves, it makes so much more sense now. He floats through life like he's underwater, weightless and fluid. And that dancer's body ... well, I guess it really is a dancer's body, huh?

What a beautiful hypocrisy, I think as I watch his scarred, tattooed form move through space like he's commanding it, the black silken shoes on his feet carrying him up to the sky and then grounding him in the same breath. I've been watching the Havoc Boys since second grade, and yet I never knew about any of this.

"Excuse me," a little girl says, smiling as she scoots past and opens the door to the studio. She's dressed in a plain gray leotard and pink shoes, and I figure she's probably around Heather's age. Callum doesn't stop dancing when she comes in, but he does smile, and gesture for her to start warming up at the barre.

Within a few minutes, there are a dozen little kids in there, stretching and prepping for class. Callum fiddles with the stereo for a minute, dries the sweat from his forehead with a white towel, and then gets to teaching.

The girls run through first position with Cal correcting their form, offering murmured words and gentle adjustments. I should probably leave, but ... I check the time and see that I've still got another hour to kill. If I take the bus from here, it'll take ten minutes to get home, tops. I settle in to watch, loving the contrast of Callum, with the ropey muscles in his arms, his ink, his scars ... teaching these little girls how to dance.

Something in my chest shifts, and I realize that I know little to nothing about him. Nothing at all. *"I felt that way, too, at first. Once you surrender to the dark, it gets easier."* I can't even imagine what he might've been talking about. Clearly, I'm not the only member of Havoc who has unresolved trauma.

After class, the girls (and two awesome little boys) take turns giving Callum hugs, and then slip out of the room, smiling shyly at me as they skip past and head for the locker room.

I consider leaving, but then I realize that Callum's gearing up to dance again, turning on the stereo and moving until his body is trembling and he's soaked in sweat. I notice he keeps putting his hand to his lower back and closing his eyes like he's in pain. At one point, it's like his ankle gives out and he stumbles, hitting the floor hard and then sitting there with his head hanging down, blond hair covering his eyes.

My heart contracts, and I feel like I'm watching something I shouldn't, so I take off down the hall, grab the bus, and head home.

On Wednesday, Callum takes off for the dance studio again, and I follow him.

This time, he teaches a mixed male/female class of teens around our age. It doesn't escape my attention that every girl in that class—plus a boy or two—are hitting on him. I'm surprised to see him act like a professional, ignoring their advances, and focusing on getting the group to perform a rehearsal that has my jaw dropping.

I don't know much about dance, especially ballet, but as an audience of one, I'm captivated.

The dancers exit the room after class, and one boy pauses to put his hand on my arm.

"Cal wants to see you," he says, and I feel my throat close up.

Shit.

Caught red-handed.

I slip into the room and find Callum waiting for me, arms crossed over his chest, a slight smile on his face.

"Hello, Bernadette," he says, watching as I step into the studio, the smell of floor polish and fresh sweat in the air. "Come to see me dance?" he asks, voice neutral but not unpleasant. I shrug my shoulders, glancing at my reflection in the mirror. My leather pants and jacket look so out of place in here. "Take your shoes off," Cal suggests, turning up the music and grabbing a pair of pink slippers from his bag. He smiles at me, but there's a hint of a challenge there that I can't resist.

"Why not?" I say with a shrug, sitting on the stool in the corner and shedding my boots and socks. Not sure what Cal's planning on doing with me. I'm not completely inept on a dance floor, but I'm certainly not trained for ballet.

Callum moves over to the mirror on the far wall, the one that I've just now realized is the window I was looking out from the other side. No wonder Cal never spotted me through it. He pulls the cord on some curtains, blocking the view of any passers-by in the hallway, and then locks the door.

Part of me wonders if I should be afraid.

But I'm not.

Welcome to the family.

I'm part of Havoc now, and unless the boys are playing some kind of fucked-up long game with me then ... No. Not with the way Vic looks at me. No fucking way.

"There's a leotard for you in my bag. You should put it on." Cal moves across the floor in his black slippers and flips through songs on his phone until he finds one he likes. It ends up being *Shatter Me* by Lindsey Stirling and Lzzy Hale.

Slipping my jacket off, I move over to the bag and find a plain black leotard waiting for me. I finger the fabric for a moment before turning my back on Callum and slipping my shirt over my head. I'm fully aware that he can see everything, considering there are mirrors both in front of and behind me, but I don't care.

I peel my leather pants down my hips, and then take off my bra and panties.

When I glance over my shoulder, I find Callum leaning one shoulder against the wall, watching me.

He waits until I've pulled the leotard on and parked my ass on the stool before he closes the distance between us, kneeling down and slipping one pink slipper on my foot. It's not a pointe shoe—like I'd even know what to do in a pair—but it has long, pretty ribbons that tie up my calves.

"Traditionally, these wouldn't have ribbons on them," Cal explains as his fingers tickle the skin on my legs, tracing over one of my tattoos with his thumb. "But every little girl wants to imagine, at least for a moment, that one day she'll be wearing pointe shoes and standing center stage."

"Have you mistaken me for a little girl?" I ask as he slides his palms down my leg and presses his thumb against the arch of my foot, leaving me, for a brief moment, completely breathless. Callum looks up at me with a cerulean gaze, his blond hair stuck to his sweaty forehead.

Today, he's wearing a gray zip-up hoodie with the arms torn off. It's only zipped up about halfway, so I've got quite the view of his chest and abs, these chiseled muscles that contract as he presses his fingers into my foot, simultaneously massaging and stretching first one and then the other. It takes a concentrated effort on my part to hold back a groan. I'm not sure if I've *ever* had a foot massage in my entire life.

"Come on," he says finally, ignoring my question and standing up. He holds out a hand to help me to my feet, and then moves back to the stereo, starting the song over from the beginning.

Cal stands in the center of the room and carefully moves his arms in time to the music, rising up on his toes when the song starts to pick up, Lzzy's voice singing about pirouetting in the dark. Callum follows her softly sung command before moving across the stage and spinning several times, extending one foot, and then looking up at himself in the mirror. He doesn't seem satisfied with what he sees, so when the song picks up even further, he follows along with the pace.

There's a bit of dubstep woven into the pop/classical mix of the song, and when the drop hits, Callum just lets completely loose, taking over the entire room with his energy. What becomes apparent to me as I watch him is that he's dancing from a place of anger.

He whips around the room, his body moving in ways I never could.

When the second drop in the music comes, he takes off for this fantastical leap and doesn't quite land right, stumbling and falling into the wall with a curse. For a moment, he closes his eyes and breathes through it. From what I can see on the opposite side of the room, he's in pain.

But he doesn't stop. Instead, he pushes off the wall and keeps going, captivating me completely. I've never seen a man move like that, especially not when he's covered in ink the way he is. *Damn, he's good,* I think, studying him as he pushes through the pain, muscles trembling, forcing his body to bend to his will.

The song comes to an end, and Callum's left bent in half in the center of the room, his breath coming in sharp pants. When he lifts his head up, he looks devastated, staring at himself in the mirror for a long, private moment while I try to figure out what it is that he wants from me.

"You're a beautiful dancer," I say, and he laughs at me. It's not a nice laugh either. Not at all. *I Don't Care* by Apocalyptica and Adam Gontier comes on the stereo next, and it feels properly morose.

"I *was* a beautiful dancer," he says, limping over to the stool and sitting down heavily on it. His jaw clenches, and he leans over like he's hurting. I don't know what to do, so I just stand there and watch him try to get through whatever it is.

"Are you alright?" I ask finally, and Cal nods, lifting his head up, his blue eyes dark.

"I'm fine."

"How did you know I was watching?" I ask, and he quirks an almost-smile, forcing himself to his feet and exhaling.

"One of my girls asked who the rock star in the hallway was on Monday," he says, flicking his gaze to my face. "That, and your smell lingers in the hallway."

"My smell?" I ask as Callum holds out a hand for me to take. I do, and he pulls me into the center of the room, guiding my body with his. Adam's husky voice slips through the speakers in the four corners of the room as Cal walks me in a slow circle, putting my back to his front, and extending my right arm by sliding his fingers along the length of it until our hands curl together.

"You smell like peaches and leather," he whispers against my ear, his rough voice breaking a bit. Cal pulls away from me and encourages me to spin, slipping an arm around my waist and yanking me close again. I can feel his heartbeat against my chest as he moves us back a few steps, our slippers brushing against the shiny wood floor.

I can't stop staring at his face, at this mixture of elation and desperate agony.

"Why are you so angry?" I ask him as he turns me in another circle and then dips me. I have no idea what I'm doing, but it's not hard to follow the smooth, easy cadence of his movements. It's like the music speaks to him in secret words I'll never be able to understand, and he translates that mystical language with his body.

The song ends, the last notes echoing around the room, and then the power shuts off.

"Fuck," Callum murmurs as I freeze in his arms. "The building manager hasn't been paying the electricity bill on time, so sometimes we get blackouts."

He steps back from me and walks a tight circle around my sweating form. I yank the scrunchie off my wrist and throw my white-blond and pink hair up into a high pony.

"Do you know what first position is?" he asks, and I shrug.

"Vaguely." I put my body into what I think the right position is, and Callum steps forward to make some corrections, his hands gentle as he guides my arms into place and slides a finger down my spine to encourage me to straighten up.

"Good. Second position?" I shake my head because that's as far as my knowledge goes, and even then, it's only from watching movies and TV shows with vague references to dance. Callum shows me what to do by taking the position and waiting for me to imitate it before he moves over to correct me, gently putting one of his shiny black ballet slippers between my legs and encouraging me to spread them apart a bit more.

Our eyes meet, and my throat gets tight.

"You think I'm angry?" he asks finally, and I nod.

"It's in every movement you make," I tell him, and he nods, stepping behind me so that he makes a shadow in the mirror. The only light in the room comes from a dusty skylight up above our heads, and even then, dusk is approaching quickly. Speaking of, I really should get going ... "It's like you both hate and love dance at the same time, like it's the air you breathe but also the poison that's slowly killing you."

"Mm. Third position." Callum takes up the pose, and I copy him. Again, he steps forward to correct me, getting too close, touching me too softly. I can't believe this is the same guy who chucked hot coffee in a football player's face and then punched him in front of two dozen Fuller High students. "Do you know why that prick called me Prima the other day?" he asks, like he can read my mind, his velvety voice making me shiver.

I shake my head, and Cal sighs heavily.

"I used to think dance would get me out of here," he says, and even though it's too dark to see his facial expression, I can feel his emotions in his words. I don't need to ask where here is, exactly. I know he doesn't mean just Springfield, but … poverty. Darkness. Violence. Hate. Abuse. Everything.

He puts his hands on my shoulders, and I shiver, closing my eyes and holding third position with shaking arms. I'm no good at this. But I don't think that was the point. He's showing me his world, and it's a world you can't explain with words.

He readjusts my arms and feet for me, and each place his hands touch leaves a mark that I can just *feel* when I close my eyes, like bright spots of light in the blackness behind my lids. He stretches out my arm, smirking a bit when my breasts brush against his chest. I don't exactly have a dancer's body myself. Too busty, too curvy.

"I don't see why it can't be?" I ask, and Cal laughs again, a dry sound that makes me shiver again. I open my eyes, and find that some cloud cover's moved over, blotting out all the light. We're standing in total darkness now.

"When I was fifteen," he says, moving my body again. I let him manipulate me and find some sort of comfort in it. For a moment there, I don't have to think or wonder what I should do, what my next move will be. I just exist. It's beautiful. "I made the mistake of sleeping with my dance partner." He pushes down on my arms until they're relaxed by my sides. "Her boyfriend and his buddies kicked the shit out of me. They broke my left ankle, shattered my kneecap, fucked up my spine. I can't dance for long without hurting. And there are just some things I can't do anymore …" He trails off, lost in dark memories. "Not only that, but the recovery time put me so far behind. What a way to lose my virginity, huh?"

"What did you do?" I ask, because I know that Callum was already part of Havoc in ninth grade. They'd just formed their little gang, but they were small-time back then. Not so much anymore. I can't imagine they didn't seek revenge.

"I almost killed the ringleader," he says, his voice cracking slightly. "Vic stopped me. If he hadn't, I'd probably be in prison for murder. But he taught me how to get revenge the right way—without getting caught." Callum steps away from me and moves over to his bag, lifting his phone out and turning it on again. He sets it on top of the stereo and the light plays strange shadows across his face. "You did good, coming to Havoc."

When he turns around, he's limned in light. My breath catches, making my chest feel tight as he approaches me in his hoodie, his sweatpants bunched up above his knees. The scars on his muscular calves catch the glow from his phone screen, highlighting the jagged, angry lines.

My heart stops beating for a moment as Cal reaches out a hand for me to take, and I carefully place my fingers in his. *City* by Hollywood Undead starts to play as he pulls me to him, hard and fast. The sudden movement knocks the air out of me as he draws me in against his chest, my back to his front.

"I'm going to personally make sure every person on your list suffers," he whispers, his velvety voice against my ear. Callum walks us in a circle and then pushes me forward, making me spin with my hand in his before he pulls me close again. His legs move against mine, forcing my body to perform a dance I've never seen before but somehow instinctually seem to know.

It's him, that's what it is. It's impossible to resist Cal's movements. In this moment, his body owns mine.

As the somber notes of the song drum past, Callum dips me back and then pulls me up, putting his hands on my hips and lifting me into the air. I'm not exactly a little ballet bird, but he lifts me up like I weigh nothing. We spin around together, my hands on his shoulders, our eyes locked. There's barely any light in here, just the glow from his phone, but it's enough to see the emotions playing out in his gaze.

There are so many, it's like a kaleidoscope of colors—robin's egg blue, azure, cerulean, sapphire.

My feet hit the floor and we're moving again; his hands are all over me, fondling, caressing, guiding. He even slides his fingers along my bare inner thigh, burning me with the strength of his touch, and then stretches my leg up and out. I end up wrapping it around his waist, and we fall into the mirror.

My back hits the glass and our faces get close, too close, lips hovering. We exchange breath, but there's not a lot of oxygen left in this room; it's all been sucked out, replaced with passion and heat and desire.

We're pressed so tightly together that I can feel Cal getting hard against me, but he doesn't act on it. Instead, as the song picks up, he steps back and pulls me with him, spinning me in a wide circle and then stepping close again. He turns me around and then lifts me up by the waist, swinging me into his arms as the last notes trail off.

The next song starts up—it's *The Diary* by Hollywood

Undead. It's much more upbeat in sound, but the words are about people like us, running the streets, feeling desolate and empty. I have to swallow twice to clear the lump from my throat.

Cal is still staring at me, his gaze dark, his body quivering with exertion. Sweat beads on his forehead, sticking his blond hair to his skin. For the briefest of seconds, I feel myself living a different life. Here I am in a ballet studio, in the arms of the most talented dancer I've ever seen, my heart beating out of my chest. It's like I'm looking at an alternate reality, one where the pain of the past no longer exists.

My fingers trace along the side of Cal's jaw, and I feel us being pulled together, our lips desperate to meet, to complete this fantasy we're both living.

And then the lights snap back on, blinding us. The song switches to *Losing My Mind* by Falling in Reverse, and Cal sets me back down carefully, like I might break. He puts some distance between us, blinking and shaking his head like he's waking up from a daze.

I'm not sure what to say, so I don't bother to open my mouth, waiting there as Callum yanks some sweatpants from his bag and chucks them at me. I slip into them and put my jacket and boots back on, tucking my leather pants and the shiny pink slippers into my backpack.

"Come dance with me again sometime," he says, and then he leads me to the door. I'm almost expecting him to kiss me when we part ways at the doorjamb, but he doesn't, and I don't know why I thought he would in the first place.

Or if I even wanted him to.

CHAPTER
THIRTY-ONE

For two weeks, we've been waiting for news of Principal Vaughn to hit the school, but starting Monday morning, Ms. Keating made an announcement that the principal was out sick and would be returning as soon as he was well.

By Friday, we get a whole new story.

"He's missing?" I repeat as we sit together in the cafeteria, surveying Billie, Kali, and their collection of assholes on the far end. The tension in this school is coming to a head, but I don't know when or where. It's just a feeling, this itchiness that travels across my skin and makes me nauseous.

"Apparently," Hael says, his mood dark and somber as fuck. He's still obsessing over Brittany. Fair enough. I'm also obsessing over Brittany. For whatever reason, I really, really don't want the baby to be his. *Because, you're a Havoc Girl, like you've always wanted, but you refuse to admit it yourself.* "Which is not good news for us considering we blew up his cabin."

"Why don't you yell that a little louder, just to make sure the whole school hears you?" Aaron snaps, ruffling up his brown hair.

"We're fine," Vic says, ever the pool of calm. Last Monday, I also found the rest of the morning-after pills we bought in my locker. Clearly, he broke in and left them there. But he hasn't once asked if I took them. I did, but he doesn't know that. "Whatever happened to Vaughn isn't our problem. He made his bed, he can fucking sleep in it. Hopefully a cougar mauled his ass. Oscar, any news on Brittany?"

I slide off the tabletop and onto the bench seat next to Callum. He eats constantly, but at lunch, I notice he usually goes for Pepsi and cigarettes. It's like he's too wound up to eat in this jungle we call a high school. Sitting this close to him, it's impossible not to think about our bodies moving in synchronous sensuality.

"Nothing unusual to report. She's been going to cheerleading practice, the gym, and her parents' house. She's barely attended any parties, and when she does, she doesn't drink. I'm almost positive she really is pregnant."

Hael makes a frustrated sound under his breath and stares out the window like he wishes he could climb in his Camaro, drive away, and never look back. He could, if he wanted to. But maybe he cares too much about the other Havoc boys to leave?

"And Kali and Co.?" Vic asks as Oscar pauses to adjust his glasses.

"They've been selling product, and not just weed either. Meth. Coke. Pills. You name it, they're hawking it. Clearly, they must be getting the drugs from somewhere."

"They're working with a bigger gang," Vic says, studying them like a predator on the savannah. The lion with his big, thick mane standing in the sun and staring at the gazelle, not at all concerned with letting them know they are, in fact, the prey. "Working for, I should say," he corrects, exhaling and leaning back. Vic's sitting on the other side of Callum. I've noticed he's been very careful not to sit next to me lately. It's driving me nuts. I figured at some point, he'd confront me, slam his palm into my locker, get in my face. But he hasn't.

Maybe Vic's waiting for me to come to him?

If he is, he'll wait forever. Fucking bastard.

I grit my teeth and suck on the straw I've jabbed into my chocolate milk.

"The only party anyone's talking about for Halloween night is the one at Stacey Langford's," Aaron adds, and I realize that all week, I've been left entirely alone. Nobody's given me a single order or direction to follow. Why is that? "I've already spoken with her about it. She knows to just let them in, and we'll deal with it after that."

"How are we planning on doing that?" I ask, and finally—*finally*—Vic deigns to look my direction.

"I haven't decided yet. You don't worry about it. Kali was your request, so we'll take care of her for you."

"But Billie and Kyler and Mitch," I add,

remembering how Oscar said they wouldn't bother with Nurse Yes-Scott because she wasn't part of the deal. "They're a Havoc problem, and I'm a part of Havoc, so —"

"Are you now?" Vic asks, cocking his head at me. "Because one minute, you seem determined to be our whore and that's it. The next, you're a part of the group. So, which is it?"

"Lay off, Vic," Aaron says as I bristle and dig the nails of my right hand into my thigh.

The two men share a long, studying look, and Vic finally stands up, but not like he's giving in, just like he's had enough.

He takes off for the doors of the cafeteria, and I follow after.

I'm not even really sure what my goal is, but as soon as I slip between the graffiti-covered doors, Vic is pushing me into the wall and penning me in with an arm on either side. Once, I wrote a scene like this for Mr. Darkwood's class to see if I could shock him with some racy teen sex, but all he did was cross out the word *penning* and replace it with *pinning*. I scribbled all over it and wrote *penning means to shut in, as if in a pen, not the same thing as pinning.* He responded with the comment: *writing for shock value, no substance*. I got an F. Pretty sure he was just being petty.

"Why are you in my face?" I ask, and Vic narrows his eyes on me, jaw clenching. I infuriate him like nobody else. I wonder if I melt some of his numbness away, like he does to me.

"Because you piss me off," he says, but he's leaning in way too close for somebody that's simply pissed off. He puts his face up alongside mine, and I have to close my eyes. Emotions arc through me like shooting stars, and I have to resist the urge to squirm. When Vic breathes across the side of my neck, I shiver and goose bumps spring up across the surface of my skin.

"The feeling's mutual," I manage to grind out as Vic puts his lips against the curve of my shoulder, and I find that I can't keep my hands to myself. My nails end up digging into his biceps as I cling to him. It's been a long two weeks, with him ignoring me the way he's been.

"All I can think about is your body wrapped around mine," he murmurs, slowly flicking his tongue against my skin. I'm aware we're standing in the hallway, but none of the other students will bother us. They know better than that. "I've watched that video of you and Hael every day this week and jacked off to it."

"Liar," I mumble, but then I open my eyes and Vic moves back to look at me.

"I came so hard every time I watched it," he grinds out, and my nails dig even deeper into his biceps. "And I imagined that I was coming inside of you again."

"We can't keep doing that," I say, and he pushes off the wall, grabbing one of my hands and pulling me down the hall.

"Like hell we can't," Vic says, storming over to the girls' bathroom and barging right in the door. "Okay, ladies, out." He hooks a thumb in the direction of the door, and all the students scatter, snatching up makeup and stumbling out of the stall doors.

Nobody wants to be left in here to face the rumbling thundercloud that is Victor Channing.

The room empties in a matter of seconds, and then Vic's yanking me into the stall on the far end. He closes and locks the door behind us as the scent of bleach wafts around me. *At least it looks like it was just cleaned in here,* I think as he turns back to face me.

"Turn around and put your palms on the wall," he commands, and I do it. *This is my deal with Havoc,* I think, but really, that's not why I'm here and we both know it. His hands skim the curve of my waist and come to rest on my hips. "You make me chase you, Bernadette, which is just fine by me." He wraps his fingers around the front of my neck and puts his hot lips up against my ear. "If that's what you want, I'll do it; I'm quite good at the chase."

"You're such a royal piece of shit," I snarl as he reaches down and unbuttons my leather pants, shoving them over the round curve of my ass. "I fucking hate you."

Victor chuckles, and I can feel his knuckles brush against my throbbing heat as he undoes his own jeans.

"We were both in the room that night, baby. Don't lie to me." Vic kisses the edge of my mouth and then mounts me with one, hard thrust, taking over my body with that way of his.

He fucks me into the wall, my fingers curling against the tile, my mind obliterated by his heat, his incessant need, his demand. I want more, even though I know I shouldn't. Part of me wonders if my obsession with Vic Channing is going to get me killed one day. But it's too late now, isn't it? I'm embroiled in Havoc's world.

We don't bother keeping quiet. Why should we? For a moment, I let that thought wash over me: Vic is king of the school, so that would make me queen in a way, right? We're engaged, after all, and everybody fucking knows it.

"I want to see that wedding dress of yours," he growls, like he can read my thoughts. "Oscar is lording it over me, and I don't like it." Vic yanks me harder against him, burying himself in my wet heat.

"Not until the wedding," I manage to grind out, even though I'm hot and achy all over, ready to have a full-on orgasmic meltdown in the girls' bathroom of Prescott High.

"I'm going to marry the shit of you, and then tear that dress off," he breathes, turning my head so that he can kiss me. My heart flutters in my chest, and a strange pang takes over me. *I'm falling for Victor. Shit, I fell for Victor years ago, and it's just now coming to bite me in the ass.* I'm like one of those idiot heroines in a bully romance who falls for her tormentors. And yet, even as I see my own folly, I can't avoid making it. "Our wedding night is going up in flames."

He moves his hand to my clit, slowing the motion of his hips to focus on my body, and he doesn't stop until I'm collapsing against the wall in a torrent of warm pleasure. As I'm shuddering and shaking, my body clamps down around his, milking his shaft until he's finishing inside of me in a hot, wet wave.

For several minutes, we just stand there, locked together.

"Get the fuck off of me," I grumble, and he laughs, stepping back to give me some space.

Vic doesn't leave the bathroom stall when I sit down to pee, so I just glare at him as he leans in the corner like a satisfied housecat.

"We are not at this level," I growl as he just smirks at me, crossing his arms over his chest. "This is, like, twenty years together married couple level."

"That'll be us someday," he says, leaning over to get in my face, just because he can. "I'm just jump-starting the process. Besides, I like to enjoy the aftershocks of sex, it's my favorite part, knowing there's a little part of me inside of you."

"Go to hell." I finish cleaning up—well, as best I can considering where we are—and then stuff some extra toilet paper in my underwear. I stand up and fix my pants as Vic opens the door and holds it for me like he thinks he can even *pretend* to be a gentleman after fucking me in the high school bathroom.

We both pause to wash our hands at the sinks, and I feel a hot flush creep into my cheeks.

Ugh. Gross. Blushing is most definitely *not* in my repertoire of tricks. I hate it. It implies a certain level of vulnerability, some physical acknowledgement of one's emotions.

After I dry my hands, Vic reaches out and takes my hand, running his thumb over my engagement ring. The whole school knows about us; I hear whispers in the hallway when I walk by.

"I'm taking you with me after school."

"I—" I start, but Vic cocks a brow and yanks me close.

"That's an official order," he says, and I grit my teeth. He finally lets go of me, and I head for the door before we can get caught up in each other again. Elbowing my way out, I find the halls empty ... and the rest of Havoc waiting for us.

"We were trying to give you time to finish up," Oscar says, his hands tucked into the pockets on his slacks. His gray eyes scan me with bored bemusement, but there's something else there, a glint or a spark or whatever. He blinks once and it disappears, but I know what I saw. "But we have a problem that needs our attention *now*."

"Yeah?" Vic says, lighting up a cigarette right there in the hallway. "What is it?"

"The Ensbrooks and the Charters are outside with Ivy Hightower," Aaron says, his voice low.

Panic shoots through me, but when I glance over at Victor, he's deadly calm.

"Where?" he asks, and the boys lead us outside toward the basketball courts.

Mitch and Logan Charter, Kyler, Danny, and Timmy Ensbrook, along with Kali and Billie, are all waiting outside. Mitch and Kyler are shooting hoops while the others sort of mill around nearby. It's not hard to see who the ringleader is here. I remember Mitch and Vic standing off outside the school that day.

But Mitch Charter is no match for Victor Channing.

"What the hell do you want?" Vic asks, the cigarette hanging out of his mouth as he makes his way over to stand on the opposite side of the court. "I don't like being interrupted when I'm fucking my girl, so make this quick."

My cheeks flush hot, but I'm not embarrassed, just irritated. *Fucking Vic.*

I move up to stand beside him anyway, with Aaron on his other side, and Hael, Oscar, and Callum spread out behind us.

"Ivy here had some interesting things to tell us about last weekend," Mitch says, tossing the basketball into the hoop and fist pumping when he makes the basket. He swaggers over to us like he thinks he's Hael Harbin or something, running his fingers through his dark hair. But he's nowhere near as handsome as any of the Havoc Boys really, or maybe I'm just biased.

"And I give a shit why?" Vic asks, studying the slightly smaller boy. When I look at Victor standing there with his purple-black hair and all that ink swirling down his arms, something strange happens inside my chest. It's that same damn pang I felt in the bathroom just now. *Affection.* My lip curls.

"Ivy says you killed Principal Vaughn," Mitch announces with a smirk. But it's a smirk that doesn't last long. A very dry, very real laugh escapes Vic's throat as he reaches up and plucks the smoke from his lips, flicking it in Mitch's direction.

"We're done here," he says, turning and heading back

for the back entrance of Prescott High.

"Don't you walk away from me," Mitch snarls, making the mistake of putting his hand on Victor's shoulder.

Holy.

Fucking.

Shit.

That man can move.

In an instant, Victor has Mitch screaming on the pavement, one arm twisted behind Mitch's back, his knee pressing down on Mitch's spine.

"Do not fucking touch me," Victor says, his voice ice-cold, his expression blank but edged with violence. "That's a mistake most people only make once. The only reason you're still breathing is because we're on school grounds. I don't kill people on campus."

"Help me, you pieces of shit!" Mitch screams at his friends, and surprisingly, they actually come forward to back him up. But as quick as Vic put Mitch on the ground, he releases him and backs up a few steps.

"Now, you listen here. We didn't kill Principal Vaughn, but ask yourselves this: even if we did, is that something you want to keep talking about?" The way Victor stares them down, it's not hard to see that he's making a very real threat.

"We'll call the fucking cops!" Mitch screams back, and only Kyler and Logan keep him from making the worst mistake of his life by rushing Vic.

"With twenty grand in product sitting your trailer?" Oscar asks, lifting up his iPad and showing off a photo

I've never seen before. There are bags full of white powder stacked near a table with a scale. It's not hard to figure out what that is. "I doubt it."

"But Ivy, that big mouth of yours," Vic says with another dry laugh, shaking his head and wagging a finger at her. "That shit is gonna get you in loads of trouble, sweetie."

"Screw you!" Ivy yells, stepping forward and wrapping her hands around Danny's arm. Great. So she's shacking up with one of the Ensbrook brothers now? "I know what I saw that night."

"You also know you've been spending Vaughn's cash and charging up his credit cards," Hael growls out, giving me a look and leaning in close to whisper. "Bet you regret being nice to that bitch now, huh?"

"No act of kindness goes unpunished," I reply, watching Ivy carefully. She's such a damn gossip. How did I ever think letting her go would lead to anything but this? In the past, it wouldn't have been a problem because she would've been too scared of Havoc to open that big mouth of hers. But now that she's got the Ensbrooks to hide behind?

"I've got class," Vic says, turning away again. "And I don't have time for this shit today. You want to play games with us, Charter, you come find us at Stacey's party."

"We'll fucking be there!" Kali screams out, dressed in a tight green dress with gold glitter on it. It's tacky as hell, but I'm not surprised. Pretty sure Kali's under the delusion that she looks nice.

"Should we be worried?" Aaron asks as we head inside, but Vic shakes his head.

"About Mitch and crew? You're joking, right?" Victor pauses as the double doors swing shut behind us, and then he turns to me, putting his big hands on either side of my face. When he kisses me, I'm too shocked to have much of a reaction. His tongue sweeps my lower lip and then dives in, consuming me, claiming me. And right there in front of all the Havoc Boys and …

"Ahem, Mr. Channing, Ms. Blackbird," Ms. Keating says, clearing her throat. Vic chuckles and releases me, glancing over at the vice principal in her black skirt suit. "Do we all have classes we should be attending?"

"Yes, ma'am," Vic says, sliding his inked fingers into the front pockets of his jeans. "I was just giving my girl a *see you later* kiss."

"Right," Ms. Keating says, giving me a sideways look. "Off you go, all of you."

We all scatter our separate ways, but as I'm reaching for the door to the gym, Ms. Keating stops me.

"Bernadette, do you have a moment?" she asks, and I shrug. I'd rather get an excused absence from P.E. than have to stand around and pretend like I give a fuck about volleyball. I follow the vice principal into her neat, tidy little office. The walls are covered with inspirational posters that say things like *Shoot for the Moon—If You Miss, You'll Land Among the Stars!*

Huh.

Starry-eyed millennial bullshit.

I'm a realist, through and through. That crap doesn't

work on me. The world is not an endless feast of exploration, discovery, and joy. Not for me it isn't.

"Well?" I ask, cocking a brow and leaning back in the chair. "You definitely didn't call me in here to discuss my stellar grades, and all the scholarship opportunities coming my way, so what's up?"

"Bernadette," Ms. Keating says with a sigh, folding her dark-skinned hands together, her nails painted a cheery yellow this week. Her brown eyes bore into me, but I just stare straight back at her. She's a good woman, but her cheery optimism and strong conviction would be better spent elsewhere, perhaps on younger kids who still have hope for the future. Those of us at Prescott ... well, it's just too late for us. Ms. Keating is wasting her time. "I've noticed you've started dating Victor Channing?"

It's cute that she phrases her statement as a question when we both know she just caught him grinding all over me in the hallway.

With a sharp smile, I lift up my left hand and flash the ring.

"We're engaged, haven't you heard? The gossip mill at Prescott usually runs pretty hot." I drop my hand again and shrug, just another blasé student the vice principal will have to deal with this week. I don't want her paying anymore attention to me than that. "Is that what you brought me in here to talk about?" I lean forward, tapping my dark nails on the surface of her desk. The color I've painted them is called *Lethal* by Urban Decay. Pretty sure they discontinued the shade, but I have two full bottles, so that should last me a while.

"I've heard from other students what happened here during your sophomore year," she says, and I feel my shoulders get tight. The expression on my face stays bored and uninterested. At least, I hope it does. "Those boys are bullies, Bernadette. In fact, I'd go so far as to say they're a gang."

I just stare back at her. She doesn't just *think* they're a gang, she knows, but she's trying to be gentle with me. Why, I can't possibly understand. "With Principal Vaughn missing, I've been asked to temporarily fill his position. Some of the things I found in his office were concerning ..."

My heart begins to pound, but it's too late. It's too late for some well-meaning teacher to step in and try to undo all the hurt and damage and hate. I went to the administration for help; I still believed in the system. Well, guess what? The system fucked me. It's over now. I've thrown the good girl towel in. What was it that Callum said? About surrendering to the dark? That it makes life easier?

"Whatever you found, it doesn't matter," I say, feeling the room shrink around me. It's suffocating in here. Maybe I rather would be in PE?

"Bernadette, you approached Principal Vaughn with allegations of bullying, and he did nothing but bury your report. I found your statement in a file box under his desk, along with other items indicating ... what do they call themselves?"

"Havoc," I whisper, putting my hands on the knees of my leather pants and picking at the slick fabric with my nails. "The Havoc Boys."

"Right, clever acronym. *Havoc.*" Ms. Keating sighs, and shakes her head for a moment, her colorful earrings swinging. "Well, the Havoc Boys are not, how should I put this, particularly savory characters. You can do so much better, Bernadette. You can *be* so much better."

I stand up suddenly, the chair skidding on the old carpet beneath my heels.

"Is this the part where you give me a trophy for trying my best?" I say, cocking a brow and knowing I'm essentially spitting in the face of someone who's been nothing but nice to me. But I've had people be 'nice' before, and then turn around and destroy my life, people like Principal Vaughn and Donald Asher, my foster brother, that social worker …

"Bernadette …" Ms. Keating starts as I begin to cough, hacking and choking and leaning on the edge of her desk in an Oscar-worthy performance. "Do you need some water?" she asks me, standing up and rubbing my back in a small circle with her hand. "I'll get you some water."

She grabs a plastic cup off a stack on the sideboard and pops into the hallway to fill it from the fountain. We hardly have anything as fancy as water bottles or coolers here at Prescott.

While Ms. Keating's in the hall, I move around the edge of her desk and grab the box. The window's open, and it's big enough for me to slip right out of.

Before she's even finished filling the cup, I'm sprinting down the length of the building and around the corner, heading toward the basketball courts and the hole in the fence. I manage to slip through unseen, but I don't stop running until I'm standing next to Hael's car.

Sitting down, I pull out one page after another in that box until I find my statement, scribbled in wavy pencil down a lined sheet of paper.

They're making my life a living hell. I'm scared to come to school. I'm scared to go home.

I stare at it for a moment, but it's too much, so I tuck it away and hit the rest of the box. I'm not the first student to have reported Havoc to the principal, but just like with my report, most of them have been filed away and forgotten. Prescott High's lacking in funds, so I bet these are the only copies of the reports. There's not going to be anything scanned into the computer system, or any complaints filed via an online system we don't have. Like I said, we may as well be nineties kids over here.

Flipping through page after page of incident reports and complaints from students, I know there's enough ammo in here for Ms. Keating to suspend or even expel one or all of the boys. There's maybe enough info in here to press charges on some of them.

Victor Channing punched me in the face between first and second period for saying Bernadette Blackbird was hot.

I check the date on the complaint and see that it's from ... sophomore year.

"What the hell?" I ask, seeing that the complainant is a student that no longer attends Prescott. Mostly because Havoc chased him off. But why would Vic stand up for me during sophomore year? That's the year they tortured me; it doesn't make any sense.

Licking my lower lip, I shove the paper back in the box and stare at it.

This is a lot of ammo.

This … is a ticking time bomb set to go off against the boys I hated more than anyone else, the only people I couldn't figure out a way to get revenge on. And here this box is, full of uncovered secrets. I bet Vaughn had the box in his office because he was getting ready to go after the boys again—Vic especially.

What would a Havoc Girl do though? I think, pushing the box away with my heel and trying to think. I could take this box, hold onto it and wait for the guys to finish my list up. Then I could nail them with it. At the very least, I might be able to get Vic kicked out of school, so he'd lose his inheritance—I don't really expect him to give me a cut anyway.

I could run, and pawn the ring, and …

But no.

Blood in and blood out, right?

"When you've been lied to by everyone around you, when you have nothing else, you realize the one currency you can carry is truth. So a single word does have meaning. A promise does hold importance. And a pact is worth carrying to the grave."

What would a Havoc Girl do?

She'd burn this shit to the ground.

CHAPTER
THIRTY-TWO

"You can thank me later," I say as the boys come around the corner and find me sitting on the ground next to Hael's car. I remember Vic telling me not to touch the damn thing without Hael's permission, but he doesn't seem bothered by me leaning against it.

"Thank you for what?" Vic says as he notices the still-smoking trash can sitting next to the dumpster.

"Ms. Keating found a box of everything Principal Vaughn had on you guys from over the years: reports of bullying, vandalism, violence. He had a freaking goldmine ready to nail your asses with. I'm guessing since he had it hidden under his desk, he was getting ready to use it."

"And how'd you end up with it?" Hael asks as Callum chuckles and leans in to examine the smoking remains. He glances up at me and winks one of those pretty blue eyes of his in my direction.

"She pulled me into her office for some sort of

ridiculous pep talk," I say, tucking my hands into my pockets and feeling my own report crinkle under my fingers. "I stole it and jumped out the window."

"Ooh, you're gonna be in so much fucking trouble on Monday," Callum says, grinning. Hael still looks distracted while Aaron stares at me like he's never seen me before. Oscar is studying me with a discerning eye, but at least Vic looks happy.

"What's in your pocket?" Oscar asks, blinking gray eyes at me. The question sounds casual, but there's so much menace in it. Nobody misses his tone.

"Empty your pockets," Vic says, frowning and giving Oscar a look. "If you're gonna accuse a member of Havoc, you carry it through. I don't like idle threats."

I do as Vic asked, my palms sweating as I pull out the crumpled piece of paper, my lighter, and two dollars in cash. Vic strides forward, sliding his hands up my side and checking inside my jacket for anything I might've missed. Or maybe he's just doing that on pretense, and is actually feeling me up instead?

Our eyes meet as he steps back and unfolds the single piece of paper.

Oscar's gaze darkens, like he expected as much, but then Vic turns and thrusts the stapled pages at his friend's chest.

"Don't doubt our girl," he warns as Oscar opens up the page and reads it, his eyes narrowing slightly before he passes it back to me, albeit reluctantly.

"I'm sorry, Bernadette," he says in that smooth, easy voice of his. "I was wrong, and I'm not often wrong."

"Wrong, how?" I ask, shoving the papers back in my

pocket as Oscar adjusts his glasses.

"I assumed you'd keep more than your own confession." He glances over at the smoking trash can. "That is, unless you stored the remaining pages elsewhere."

"Oscar, that's enough," Vic snaps, and even Aaron looks frustrated, raking his fingers through his wavy brown hair.

"You can doubt me all you want," I say, stepping up close to Oscar, my heels putting us more or less on the same level. "But I didn't have to steal that box. I could've just left it in Ms. Keating's office and let her drop the gavel on Havoc. Or I could've hidden it and you never would've known I had it." A smile curves my lips as I meet Oscar's eyes and stare him down. He's not an easy person to lock gazes with, I'll admit. But I refuse to back down. After all, I *did* beat his ass not too long ago. "Did it cross my mind to use that box against you? Yeah, it did." I step back and shake my head, reaching up to fluff my hair. "But I guess I'd rather let you guys get away with all the rotten shit you did than be a liar like everyone else I know."

Oscar smiles, this wicked sharp version of the expression, but I feel like I at least gained a point or two with him.

"No wonder Ms. Keating was running around in a huff," Aaron says, giving me an assessing sort of look, like he's wondering where good girl Bernadette went. I guess she died around the same time good boy Aaron did. Because, let's face it, nice guys really do finish last. "You'll get suspended, at the very least."

"Maybe," I say, well-aware of the risk. "But she also has this weird, savior complex thing going on. I might be able to get away with detention."

"Well-done, Bernadette," Vic says, pride clear in his rumbling voice. His eyes sparkle as he takes me in, rubbing at his chin. He's not going to let me forget that we fucked in the bathroom today. Without a condom. I grit my teeth. I know I'm being an idiot, but to be honest, it's hard to care. The only thing that matters is the here and now. The future is an intangible possibility that I may or may not be around to see. "Boys, let's load up and hit the Halloween store. We need fucking costumes— preferably with *masks*."

The Hellhole is a spooky little shop that's open year-round in Springfield, located in what used to be a seedy bar on Main Street. This time of year, it's overflowing with customers, but there are plenty of Prescott students who come here to buy (or steal) shit to wear to school. Case in point: the heels with the big silver skulls on them that I'm currently wearing.

Yep, got them at the Hellhole.

It's sort of like … the anti-Hot Topic. Like, Hot Topic is where you shop for goth shit if you go to Fuller High and live in a nice middle-class house in a nice middle-class neighborhood.

Hellhole is the place you shop when you eat middle-class kids for breakfast.

"It's claustrophobic as fuck in here," Aaron murmurs, looking through rubber masks on one of the walls. This place is not only packed to the gills with people, but there's so much product in here, the aisles are barely wide enough for a single person to squeeze down. Shit is hanging from the ceiling, the walls, the ten-foot racks in the middle of the room.

I notice the sweat on Aaron's brow, and I remember that he really is claustrophobic. On instinct, I reach out and brush some hair from his forehead. Then he freezes, and I remember that we've been broken up for years, and that I fucking hate his face.

"Buck up, Havoc Boy," I say, pulling a bloodied mask off the wall and slipping it over my head. "What do you think?"

"I think you're too pretty to wear a mask," he says, yanking it off my head and putting it on his own before I can think up a response. "Better?"

"You'll make Kara and Ashley cry," I say, turning away and moving from the masks section to the—for lack of a better word—slutty costume portion of the store. Look at that, I can be whatever I want to be—astronaut, firefighter, police officer—just so long as I'm selling sex while I'm doing it.

I notice Hael in the corner, tapping away at his phone, and I get this hot, angry flush all over my skin.

"Brittany?" I ask, and he lifts his head up, like he hadn't realized I was standing there. He shoots for one of his signature smirks, but it just doesn't stick.

"She wants to meet to talk," he says, shaking his head. "I don't know what to do. I just know that's not my fucking kid."

"Maybe she poked a hole in a condom?" I say, feeling annoyed that I even have to discuss Hael having sex with Brittany. I mean, I've had sex with a few guys I didn't really like, so it's not like we don't all make mistakes at some point in our lives. Still, I hate the idea of it anyway.

"Nope. I always provide my own condoms, always open them, always put them on." He lets out a long sigh, and reaches up to rub at his face, pausing as two freshmen giggle and apologize as they squeeze past him.

"What if you got drunk, got hot and heavy one night, and forgot a condom?" I suggest, but Hael just gives me a look.

"You don't forget unless you really like a girl," he says, glancing down at his phone again. He doesn't seem to notice the way my body tenses up. *Like how Vic always forgets? Or just doesn't seem to care …* "There's no way I'd ever forget with someone like Brittany. Having a kid with her would be my worst nightmare."

"Set up a time and place to meet her," Vic says, making me jump as he appears behind me, slipping out from the next aisle over, skeletons hanging over his head, and an animatronic Cerberus snarling behind him. "But make it after Halloween. Lie if you have to. We have enough shit to deal with this week."

"I'll fucking try," Hael says with another sigh, hitting the power button on his phone and turning the screen off. He slips it in his pocket and then grabs a mummy mask off the wall, looking down at it absently.

"Do you really think they're going to wait until Stacey's party to do something with the information they got from Ivy?" I ask, glancing over my shoulder at Vic. He looks down at me, and I feel that violent surge of ... *something* in my body. Feelings and emotions pour through me, half of them glittery and foreign, the other half gloomy and familiar. I frown. "Because I know I wouldn't. I wouldn't give us time to plan."

Vic smirks at me and then drags a lion mask over his head.

"No, I don't think they're going to wait. And neither will we."

He growls at me through the mask and then grabs a package from the wall, pushing it into my arms. My heart thunders as Vic turns and disappears into the maze of Halloween props and costumes, leaving me to stare down at a very sexy cheerleader costume.

Huh.

Well, Halloween is all about shedding one's skin and donning a new persona, right?

I'd be more likely to sprout red wings and a tail than become a cheerleader.

I'll take it.

We head to Vic's house after instead of Aaron's, but luckily, the place is empty.

As soon as I set foot inside, I can't stop my eyes from landing on the spot where Vic first fucked me against the wall. He notices me looking, slipping past and raising a brow in my direction. I return his gaze with a hard stare of my own.

"I'll make the girls a snack," Aaron murmurs, noticing my exchange with Vic and narrowing his eyes. My hand is clasped around Heather's. We picked her up on the way back from the Hellhole which is fine by me, but I'm not sure why we're here and not at Aaron's.

"It'd be easier for them to entertain themselves at your place," I say, following him into the narrow galley kitchen. Ashley and Kara don't seem bothered though, racing through the kitchen and letting themselves out the side door into the yard.

"Can I go?" Heather asks, yanking on my hand. Reluctantly, I let her go, but I watch out the window like a hawk, fully prepared for either Vic's dad or those awful men to show up.

"It is easier, but we're being followed, and I don't need the Charters or the Ensbrooks knowing where I live." Aaron opens the fridge and pulls out some apples and cheddar, sliding his pocketknife from his jeans before coring and cutting the green fruit like this is most definitely *not* his first time at the rodeo.

"We were being followed?" I ask, moving over to the living room area to stare out the front window. But it's pretty much impossible to see beyond the thick foliage at the edge of the yard.

"You have a lot to learn, Bernadette," Vic says, leaning in close to me and then standing up straight. "As soon as they back off a little, we'll drop the kids off with the sitter, and head out."

"And where exactly are we going?" I ask as Oscar turns away from the window to glance back at me and

Vic.

"We're crashing a Prescott party tonight," he says smoothly, the light from the window catching on the lenses of his glasses. "Victor, do you care to break the news?"

"News?" I echo as Hael looks up from his phone with his brows drawn together, a frown on his lips. "What news?"

"Listen, babe," Vic says, and my ears burn at that word. Babe. I'm not sure if I hate or … no, I hate it. I narrow my gaze on him as he studies me. Callum slumps into a seat at the table, that boneless fluidity of his a reminder of his past, of all the secrets he shared with me. "Kali is pregnant."

"What?" I ask, blinking through the words and feeling this sense of frustration and dread wash over me.

"And we don't beat up pregnant chicks," Callum explains in that hoarse voice of his, his blue hood pulled up over his blond hair.

"Good for you. Such outstanding citizens. I'll send you all some fucking metals." Victor steps forward as I snarl out the snarky insults and grabs both sides of my face, effectively cradling my head in his big, tattooed hands.

"We'll find a way to get her, Bern, I promise. But this changes our plans a little."

"So she gets knocked-up and she's suddenly exempt?" I snap, trying and failing to pull away from Victor.

"She's not exempt," he says, forcing me to look right into those dark eyes of his. "But we have to adjust our plans a bit. Don't worry, when we're finished with her, she'll be ruined." He looks down at me for a moment and finally releases me, but I can feel all the places he touched. I'm on fire on the inside.

"Right," I snap back, shaking so hard I feel like I might break if I don't punch something. "I get locked in a closet and chased through the woods and dropped off in the middle of nowhere, and she gets a free pass because she screwed some dude without a condom. Who's the dad anyway? Is it Mitch?"

"Doubtful," Oscar says as Hael leans against the living room wall, watching us. Oscar moves toward us in his ridiculous suit, the white shirt underneath unbuttoned just enough to show off his tattoos, and then he tosses his iPad down on the table next to me. "Unless she's been fucking Mitch for the past three months."

I look down and find a private text conversation between Kali and this other girl who goes to our school, Wendy something. I remember that first day I sat with Havoc at lunch, how Vic knocked Hael's tray over and Wendy scrambled to pick up all the garbage. Clearly, she owes Havoc for something. This must be part of her repayment plan.

Kali: *I haven't had my period in over three months.*
Wendy: *Have you taken a test? I could swipe a box or two from the pharmacy near my house.*
Kali: *Can you? I'll catch up with you after school. Mitch has shit to do today.*

Wendy sends her a thumbs up emoji, and then there's a gap in time before the messages start up again.

Kali: *They could be wrong, right?*

Wendy: *Girl, you took six. One could be wrong, six is pregnant, chica. Figure it out.*

I lift my attention from the screen to Oscar's face, those sharp gray eyes of his focused on me and not the iPad.

"Who was she sleeping with before Mitch?" I ask, trying to think if I saw Kali prancing around with anyone before the end of junior year. "She's two-timing him with some asswad from Oak Valley Prep, right? Is it that guy's baby?"

"No clue," Vic answers instead, but I'm having a hard time looking at him for some reason. When he talks, my pulse thunders. "Kali wasn't exactly on our radar until you gave us your list."

"You'd think it was fucking spring or something," Hael murmurs, his gaze faraway, jaw tense, neck tight. He's very clearly still focused on Brittany.

The back door opens and Aaron disappears outside to give the girls their snack, a paper plate covered in apple slices and cheddar squares. He smiles as the girls bounce up to him to grab some food, not looking at all put-out at having to take care of them. Like me, this is his sole purpose in life. This is his reason for living.

My chest gets tight, and I sit down heavily in the chair behind me.

"Just because she's pregnant," Callum muses, playing with that knife of his, the one I borrowed from his pocket and stabbed Kali with. Maybe I should feel bad about that, but it's hard to drum up sympathy for that girl. Or maybe my heart's just dead. Either way, I feel nothing. That is ... until Vic looks at me again, and then I feel everything. I clench my jaw. "That doesn't mean we can't mess with her face."

I raise my brows at the blatant threat of violence in his voice, at odds with the beautiful way he danced. Sure, he was angry, but he wasn't violent. But then I think about the baseball bat and the security guard, and the way he beat the ever-living crap out of Kyler.

"Scar her up a bit?" Vic says, bouncing Cal's idea back. "That would certainly mess with her future modeling career."

Aaron slips back in the door and comes over to join the rest of us, leaning back against the wall where Vic and I ...

"She's more than just a name on Bernadette's list. She's been openly and blatantly defying us. The whole school knows she started that shit in the bathroom with Billie. We have to make an example of her to the entire student body." Aaron kicks his boot up against the wall, crossing muscular arms over his chest as he scowls.

"Scarring her face up wouldn't do that?" Cal asks, glancing over his shoulder to where Aaron's standing. My ex shrugs his big shoulders and then gets out a cigarette, lighting up like he's been doing this forever. I know for a fact he never touched a cigarette until *after* his dad died and he joined Havoc. "Trust me: I know the cost of a good scar." Callum runs a finger along the scar that traces his jawline and sighs.

"I'm not saying that's not a valid idea, just that it's not enough." Aaron turns his green-gold eyes to the backyard, watching the girls giggle and scream as they swordfight with sticks. Ah, the resilience of children. I wonder when I lost that, the ability to let go and just have fun.

"Mm." Vic rubs his chin again, and then shrugs. "We always come up with something. For now, let's get dressed. Oscar, see if they've gone?"

"Get dressed for what?" I ask as Oscar heads for the front door and lets himself out.

"We've got a late-night class to attend," Vic says, his attention on the girls, too. He turns away and heads for his room, leaving me to either follow after him and demand answers or just wait and see.

I decide on the latter.

CHAPTER
THIRTY-THREE

We drop the girls off at Jennifer Lowell's place, this hideous upper middle-class McMansion with absolutely zero character. But it's nice, and it's a hell of a lot safer than my mom's place or Vic's place or even Aaron's place. There's a gate code to even get in here.

"Do I need to chip into the babysitting fund?" I ask, thinking about the two grand I buried in the backyard at home. I figured that way, even if I got kicked out or something, I could always sneak over the fence and find it.

"It's paid for out of the Havoc account," Oscar says, and I have to seriously wonder how much money is in that account if I get twenty-grand to plan my fake wedding with. My eyes flick over to the back of Vic's head as he sits in the front passenger seat of Aaron's minivan. It doesn't escape my notice that we use his van for gang activities. It's kinda funny if you think about it.

Aaron parks the van along the curb on Main Street, and we all climb out. I hear we're boosting a car tonight, and I guess this is how it's done.

The six of us walk four blocks down, toward the Washburne Historic district. The houses here used to be crumbling shitholes that pawned drugs like candy, but now they're all being restored, and the cars parked out front prove it.

"This the one?" Aaron asks, examining a shiny black SUV. "I've always wanted a Navigator."

"This is the one," Hael agrees, grinning as he pulls out a small white box from his bag. He presses the keyless entry button on the door's handle, and it beeps cheerily. "Hop in." It's an effort to keep my mouth from gaping open in shock as I climb into the unlocked vehicle and watch Hael press the *Start Engine* button. The SUV offers zero resistance as he releases the parking brake, and off we go. "No fun left in stealing new cars," Hael continues as we pull away from the quiet house with the cute carved pumpkins out front. According to the Havoc Boys, they try to steal the nicest cars around because the nicest cars usually have the nicest insurance. That's some messed-up moral code, but it makes a strange sort of sense.

I glance out the rear windshield to see if the owners have noticed, but nobody stirs from behind the curtained windows.

"Was it me, or was that just too damn easy?" I ask, and Hael chuckles, in a much better mood than he's been in all week.

"Key fobs produce a series of repeating codes, that's how they unlock the doors or start the cars on keyless systems. All you have to do is get one of these babies," Hael holds up the little white box, "and intercept the code when the owner unlocks their car. Wham, bam, thank you ma'am." He grins as he revs the engine, nodding in Cal's direction. "Start up some music, huh? And none of that prissy ballet shit."

"Go fuck your mom," Cal says, chuckling as he hooks his phone up to the Bluetooth system and starts *Bow Down* by I Prevail. Hael cranks the system, and the music comes pouring out like an assault.

I lean back in the leather seat and try not to let my nerves get the best of me. The plan tonight is to crash a Prescott party and show the entire school that Havoc *is* still a force to be reckoned with. Not sure what, exactly, we need the SUV for. Maybe Aaron just doesn't want his van involved in a confrontation?

There are three types of parties in Springfield: Fuller High parties, Prescott parties, and Oak Valley Prep parties. Prescott students wouldn't be caught dead at an Oak Valley Prep party; it's social suicide. Seeing fellow students kowtow to money just isn't our thing in the southside. But we will (and often do) crash Fuller High parties, if only to see the looks on those preppy faces. Security is lighter than at an Oak Valley party, and the Fuller kids don't look at us like some sort of social project or bad girl/bad boy trophy to tease their parents with. They just don't want us there which, of course, makes us want to be there more.

But there's nothing like a Prescott party, and everybody knows it. If an Oak Valley Prep student or a Fuller High student knows when and where a Prescott party is taking place, they will get there by any means necessary. As long as they don't act like they're better than us, we let them stay.

So tonight, the pre-Halloween bash that's being held in the old Prescott High building—the condemned one that's just ten blocks down from our actual school—is going to be *lit*.

The Charters and the Ensbrooks, including Billie and Kali, they'll all be there.

I see the cars start to line the curb several blocks away from our actual destination, and my heart leaps in my throat. This isn't like what we did to Principal Vaughn, out in the middle of nowhere with nobody to see. Here, everyone will see. Students from all three schools will be in attendance.

Hael slows the SUV down, and the boys all focus their attention out the window, like they're looking for something.

"That it?" Vic asks, pointing out the window at a blue car with white stripes down the hood.

"That's it," Hael says softly, his voice drenched in melancholy as he puts the Navigator into reverse. "A fully restored 1970 El Camino SS. This hurts my heart. You know that, right? You know that?"

"Shut the fuck up," Vic says with a sideways smirk. "Get out Bernadette."

"Okay …" I start, climbing out with Vic, Aaron,

Oscar, and Callum. Cal closes the door behind us and waves Hael off. He revs the Navigator's engine a few times, and then hits the gas. At the last second, he spins the wheel and smashes the big, black SUV into the much smaller El Camino. There's a screech of metal on metal as the smaller car flips over and skids across the pavement. Hael pushes it into the chain-link fence, and then backs up again, the smell of burnt rubber singeing the air.

"The '72 Datsun 240Z?" he calls out the window, and Oscar nods. "Fuck my life. I'm going to classic car hell for this." Hael puts the Navigator in drive again and rams a small brown car parked just two vehicles up from the El Camino, sending it flying into the side of an abandoned brick building. It crumples like a piece of aluminum foil, and I cringe.

"Mitch's car," Vic tells me, pointing at the El Camino. "Kyler's car." He nods in the direction of the Datsun, and then flips a middle finger at a hideous salmon-colored Ford down the block. "Kali's car."

It's a shitbox that's worth maybe a tenth of what the other cars were, but I get great pleasure from watching Hael destroy it with the stolen SUV. He hits it so hard that the windshield explodes, and my racing pulse rachets up a notch.

Anybody with a car has status at Prescott High; even a rolling trash heap like Kali's Thunderbird is coveted. That's it, by the way. The only three cars owned by their entire crew.

Hael climbs out of the Navigator, leaving it parked

where it is, the grill all up Kali's car's ass.

"Disconnected the Bluetooth," Hael tells Cal, tossing his phone over. "Let's go check out this party, shall we?"

His swagger is back as he turns around and we take off up the street. There are a couple students here and there, gaping at us, but they know better than to get involved. We pass through the open front gates of the old Prescott High. It's so packed with asbestos and lead paint, we'll probably get cancer just walking in the doors. But it's sort of a thing at Prescott not to care about shit that may or may not happen sometime in the future. We all sort of walk around hoping climate change takes us all out before we have to live with the consequences of our bad choices.

People whisper behind cupped hands, red Solo cups in their grips, as we move up the front walk in a group, kicking beer cans out of our way as we go.

"Are we here to party or all business?" Hael asks, turning around and making prayer hands at Vic. His brown eyes are glittering with the possibility of an actual night out.

"Have a little fun, but don't forget why we're here," Vic says, lighting up a cigarette as Hael's gaze passes over me for a moment. *I Love* by Joyner Lucas is blasting from several speakers set around the floor. They're all beat up, covered in stickers, Sharpie, and paint, but they do the job, even if the one on the right is a little tinny. People don't come to Prescott parties for the music.

They come for the drugs, alcohol, sex ... but mostly

the gossip.

Hael turns away and disappears into the crowd as I adjust the pink leather jacket I'm wearing. I stole it from the Goodwill that's down the block from my mom's place. It's old and beat-up, and there's a hole in the left elbow, but it looks badass anyway.

I've got on my best leather pants, a full face of makeup, and I've tamed my hair into a silken sheet that falls over my shoulders and halfway down my back. As people turn to stare at us, I feel it. *Havoc Girl.*

"I'll start searching the top floor," Aaron says, casting me a look before he slips past and heads up the decrepit looking stairs. I'm surprised they don't collapse under his weight, or the weight of the other students drinking, smoking, and making out along the steps.

"I'll take the first floor," Oscar says, moving off into the throbbing crowd and somehow finding a clear path between the packed, sweaty bodies of students. Cal stays with me and Vic as we navigate down the hall toward what used to be the classrooms. The music switches to *hot girl bummer* by blackbear, and I cringe. I fucking hate this song.

The crowd in the front room starts to sing in chorus, swaying together with their phones out.

Vic doesn't bother to knock, pushing open one door after another while Cal does the same on the opposite side of the hallway. The first room is full of students smoking weed and laughing at YouTube videos. The second still has desks in it, and there's a girl in a Fuller High cheerleading outfit getting nailed over one of them by Jim Dallon. Gross.

"Is that why you wanted me to get that costume?" I ask dryly, cocking a brow at Vic. He turns a grin over his shoulder and lets his eyes devour me from head to toe.

"Might've crossed my mind," he says with a smirk, continuing his search for the Charter crew. I roll my eyes, still completely unsure what the hell is happening here. I'm engaged to Vic. I'll be married to Vic. I'm bareback fucking Vic. And if I'm not careful, I'll end up like Kali with a cluster of positive pregnancy tests in my hand. No thank you.

We finish our search, but don't find any of the eight assholes we're looking for. Vic checks his phone for texts from Aaron and Oscar, and frowns.

"Nothing," he says, as we pause near the back door and wait for them to meet up with us. Hael is nowhere to be seen. "They must be out there somewhere." Vic gestures to the mass of people congregating in what used to be the rear courtyard of the school. The music back here is different, not quite as loud, and clearly not meant to dance to.

As soon as we get through the initial throng near the keg, we spot the Charter crew lounging on some old playground equipment. It must've been dumped here by the school district at some point, because this was always a high school. You don't often find yellow slides and swings past elementary school.

"Howdy boys," Vic says, tucking his hands in his pockets as the crowd clears away, leaving us in a bubble of empty space around the play equipment. "We've been looking for you. Seems there's a problem with your cars."

Mitch pushes Kali off his lap and rises to his feet, his pale face already tight with anger.

"You touched my fucking car?" he growls out, and Victor laughs.

"Touched? Nah, I wouldn't say that." He pauses dead center in the bubble of space, his dark eyes glittering with the thrill of the hunt. "We had a feeling you wouldn't wait until Halloween night to take us up on our offer, so we're intercepting you with a new challenge."

"We're not afraid of you, *Vic*," Mitch says, shaking, his nostrils flared as his boys stand up to join him. Billie, Kali, and Ivy stand in the back, tossing their hair and smirking. They won't be, not after they see the damage we did to their cars. They just aren't getting it yet. But as soon as they find themselves without a ride home, they will. "Havoc is old news. You built yourselves up on a rep you just can't maintain anymore." Mitch is smiling now as he strides forward, seemingly forgetting that earlier today, Vic incapacitated him in a split-second. "You thought you'd come here and what, beat the crap out of us?"

"That was the plan," Vic says with a shrug. "I mean, for starters. Have you checked your stash lately?"

"You think we didn't move our stash after you took that photo?" Mitch asks with a laugh, reaching up to rub at his buzz cut. He has tats all over his neck, but they don't blend into a seamless piece of art the way Oscar's do. No, they're too small and scattered, like stickers stuck to his thick neck.

"You think we don't know where you moved it?" Vic asks, cocking his head to one side and glancing back at Oscar. He pushes his glasses up his nose with a middle finger, and then makes a phone call.

"Blow it to kingdom come," Oscar says, and then hangs up. "I hope you have enough cash left to pay your supplier for all the coke we just blew to hell. I'm sure they'd do awful, awful things to you if you couldn't pay them back."

"They're bluffing," Kyler says, standing at Mitch's side with a smirk on his thin lips. His face is still recovering from that epic beatdown he got at Billie's trailer. The bruises are yellow now instead of purple, but I bet they still hurt.

I glance back as Hael makes his way toward us, his face tight and angry. He clearly did not enjoy his party time, whatever he did with it. I almost open my mouth to ask, but now is not the time and place.

"You haven't beat their asses yet?" Hael asks, coming up to stand between Aaron and Vic. "Let's get it done, so we can go the fuck home. I'm finished here. This party is lame as fuck."

My eyes meet Kali's across the cracked pavement, and I feel that same hurt and frustration that I did back in sophomore year, when she set out to destroy me. Why? Why did I deserve that? She knew all the shit that'd been heaped on me over the years, and yet, she chose to grind me further into the dirt.

"Hey, uh," Mitch starts, grinning as he takes another step closer to Vic. "You should say hi to our friends first. I mean, before we really get into it." He pauses and glances over to the right, nodding briefly in our direction.

The crowd parts, their phones raised to film the scene, as the entire Fuller High varsity football team appears.

"Fuck," Aaron murmurs, swiping his tattooed hand over his mouth.

"Unexpected development," Oscar agrees, watching as the group in front of us goes from eight ... to nineteen. And here we are, just the six of us. We are so screwed. I shake my jacket out and wonder if I should prep for an ass kicking. This was not supposed to happen when I hired Havoc, all of this nonsense. They're supposed to rule Prescott High, not be constantly fighting for their thrones.

I grit my teeth.

"Hey Prima," the leader says, his face dotted with three separate bandages from the coffee incident at the café. "Thanks to you, I had to sit out the game last week. Oh yeah, and my goddamn face is probably scarred for life." He sneers, eyes locked on Callum. "I'm going to enjoy beating your ballerina ass."

All eleven of those letterman jacket wearing assholes starts to come for us from the left while Mitch and his guys move forward from the front.

"Sorry, but that's not happening," Oscar says, pulling out his revolver and cocking the hammer. Most of the students gasp and recoil, some even take off running. "We don't let Fuller High football brats interfere in Prescott High matters. Take your friends and go before I get trigger happy."

"You wouldn't shoot me, in front of all these people," Quarterback Guy says, laughing.

"I wouldn't?" Oscar asks, and I lick my lower lip as déjà vu washes over me. Been here, done this before. "Move forward another six feet and see what happens. You can still play football with a burned face. Maybe not so much if I shoot you right in the balls?"

The Fuller High team looks undecided on what to do. That is, until Vic sighs and nods his chin at Callum. The 'Prima Ballerina' pulls out a weapon of his own, this black semi-auto that looks wicked as hell clutched in his hand. His blue eyes are dark as he levels the weapon in Mitch's direction.

"You can rush us, but how eager are you to get shot?" Vic asks, tucking his hands into his pockets. "Make your choice. Either way, Mitch, you should've just accepted your beating." He turns his attention from the quarterback to Mitch. "Prescott High isn't Fuller's bitch. Siccing a bunch of preppy football players on us doesn't make you look good, Mitch Charter." Vic shakes his head and steps back, nodding at the rest of us. "Let's go."

"Using guns because you're scared to take an ass kicking like a real man?!" Mitch shouts, and Vic pauses, snapping his fingers. A good dozen boys appear out of the crowd, ready to fight.

"Havoc is bigger than just the five letters in its name," Vic says, but Mitch goes for him anyway, drawing the rest of his buddies and the Fuller High guys with him. But before our group can clash with theirs, a sharp sound rings out, like a car backfiring.

Only ... I know a gunshot when I hear it. Pretty much everyone at Prescott does.

Blood explodes from Mitch's shoulder in a crimson spray, splattering Kali, Billie, and Ivy in red mist. His body collapses into a boneless heap on the pavement and for a minute there, I think he might be dead. Everything is silent but for the echoing ring of the gunshot, and I notice a boy in a black hoodie tuck a gun into his sweatshirt and disappear.

One of Havoc's lackeys, I suppose. Smart. It'd be damn near impossible to identify him, even with everyone using their phones to film the encounter.

That's when Mitch starts to scream and students scatter.

"Call the cops!" QB Dude is shouting, but the look Vic turns on him is pure, gleeful hell.

"Go for it. But remember: Prescott High doesn't like a snitch. Dial the police up, and you're digging your own grave. Peace." Victor waves his hand, turns, and heads for the back steps of the building.

Like the naughty little Havoc Girl I am, I follow after.

CHAPTER

Mitch might've thought he was being clever, but he just dug his crew's grave by inviting Fuller High to fight for him. Nobody at Prescott likes the Fuller High football team. In fact, Havoc has always acted like the school's anti-heroes, taking up turf wars on their own time and giving the underdogs some wins that none of us get elsewhere in life.

Their football team might clobber ours on the field, but the Havoc Boys make those spoiled brats *bleed*.

Still, I can't shake Kali's pregnancy ... or Brittany's.

Or the fact that I keep screwing Victor without condoms, like a total idiot. I've had sex ed; I know better than that. But really, it all comes back to not caring whether I live or die, if I have a future ... The only thing that matters is Heather, but the deeper I get involved with Havoc, the more I start to wonder if maybe I might have a life one day, too.

I'm standing in the bathroom where Billie stabbed me,

staring into a cracked mirror and reapplying my lipstick. Today's color is *Venom,* this glorious blood-red with a purple tint that makes me look just a little bit scary.

The entire school is buzzing with Friday's party news. Clearly, the entire event was a power play move by the Havoc Boys; shooting Mitch was not an accident. And now that Mitch's crew is tainted by their association with Fuller High? Well, the reverence is back in the gazes of the Prescott High students. Guess we did okay because we spent the rest of the weekend at Vic's and Aaron's, smoking weed, and working on schoolwork. It seems like the boys know how to take a break every now and again, at least.

The bathroom door swings open and there's Ms. Keating, staring at me with dark brown eyes, her mouth pressed into a flat line, just like I knew it would be.

"Am I expelled?" I ask, twisting the lipstick and watching the colored tip disappear into the tube. I glance her way as she sighs.

"No, Bernadette. I don't believe kicking students who need help out of school is a very productive way for a society to better its youth. Come with me, please." She steps out of the bathroom as I tuck the rest of my makeup away and head after her, turning the corner and moving into her office. She closes and locks the door behind me before taking a seat behind her desk. I notice the windows are also closed and locked today.

I sit down in the chair in front of her desk, and we spend several moments staring at each other.

"I know why you did what you did. Gang life can seem ... enticing, when you have nobody and nothing else. It gives you a sense of belonging, of purpose, of family. But none of it is real, Bernadette. No matter what you do for Havoc, you will never be anything but a tool for those boys to use."

"You sound like you're speaking from experience," I say, leaning back in the chair and staring her down. I think about Aaron, taking the blame for stabbing Kali. In all honesty, Ms. Keating is probably right ... about most people, about most gangs. But the Havoc Boys ...

"I am," she says, exhaling sharply and folding her hands on the top of her desk. Her hair is twisted up in a pretty chignon today, her makeup subtle but tasteful. I can hardly imagine her living the gangster lifestyle. "My high school career was less than stellar, and I ended up running with a very dangerous gang—"

"Havoc is different," I say, wondering why I'm bothering to defend them in the first place. I hate them. They ruined my sophomore year. They fucking tortured me. And yet ... Aaron with his girls, Hael's kindness at the pharmacy, and even Victor holding me in bed that night. They're not so bad really, are they? Ms. Keating's face softens, and she sighs again, like she feels sorry for me, like I'm brainwashed or something. "They could've done so much worse," I tell her, coming to a sudden realization. "They could've raped me. They could've beat me until I couldn't stand. But everything they did, it was calculated to inflict damage without leaving the worst sort of scars."

"Bernadette," Ms. Keating starts as I grip the arms of the chair, blinking through the idea that's just slid into my brain. *They didn't do those things because they didn't want to hurt me. They didn't want to hurt me. They didn't.*

Victor Channing punched me in the face between first and second period for saying Bernadette Blackbird was hot.

The words from that box come drifting back to me, and my heart begins to pound.

Havoc has done worse. They could've done worse. They *chose* not to.

Fuck, I need to talk to them.

"Can I go now?" I ask, feeling antsy, but Ms. Keating doesn't look like she's ready to let me off quite so easy.

"Bernadette, you stole a box of administrative files from my office. Do you understand how problematic that is?"

"I burned them," I blurt, squeezing the end of the chair arms, my nails digging into the wood. "I can't get them back."

"I wasn't going to ask you to bring them back," she says, "but I am going to ask you to write me a two-thousand-word paper on the implications of gang violence."

"Okay," I say, just wanting to get out of there as fast as I can. "I'll have it in tomorrow."

"Bernadette," Ms. Keating starts, but I'm already standing up out of the chair. "Just ... please, if you need someone to talk to, I'm on your side."

"Right," I say, but there's no part of me that believes her.

My list includes the principal, the foster brother, the social worker ... I've tried trusting people like her before, and it didn't work out for me. I'm not changing my ways now. Not a fucking chance.

I snatch the note she hands me and let myself out of the room, yanking my phone from my pocket and staring at our group text, wondering what the hell I'm supposed to say. Thanks for not kicking my ass too hard? I just now realized you could've killed me, and you didn't? I don't owe them a thank you for *not* being worse pieces of shit to me.

I put my back to the wall and take a few deep breaths, putting my phone away.

I must be losing my mind. I'm sitting here defending Havoc? Getting all excited about thanking them for … like, not raping me? This is insane.

I push up off the wall and head to my first period English class with Mr. Darkwood, flashing the note I got from Ms. Keating to excuse my tardiness. Kali doesn't even look at me when I walk in, but I know she's aware of my presence because her entire body goes taut. Wonder how she got to school today with no car? Or how she's doing now that her boyfriend's laid up in the hospital with a GSW in his shoulder?

Today's assignment is to write either a cinquain or another haiku. I seriously can't even understand how the cinquain works other than that it's five lines, so I go back to the haiku again.

> *You tormented me*
> *I thought you were all demons*
> *Were you always there?*

I frown and cross that out, scribbling down six more

versions that are all related to Havoc before I just rewrite the first one and turn it in. My mind is all over the place as I head down the hall to my second period class, and then float my way through to lunch.

The boys are sitting on the front steps with food from the cafeteria. Usually, I'm the first one to get food since my fourth period class is right next to the lunchroom, but this time, I took my sweet time in the bathroom before heading out here, just to collect myself.

When I see them sitting there, it's like they're bathed in a whole new light.

"You okay?" Vic asks, an edge of violence to his voice. I realize he's waiting for me to say I was bullied by Kali or something. I shake my head and sit down next to the boys in black, all of them but Oscar holding cigarettes and smoking blatantly in front of the security office.

"I'm fine," I say, leaning back on the sun-warmed brick steps. "Ms. Keating let me off with an essay assignment for stealing that box." I glance in the boys' direction and find all of them but Oscar staring at me. *Fucking asshole.*

"Remind me to make friends with Ms. Keating," Hael snorts, redirecting his attention back to his phone. *Probably fucking texting Brittany again,* I think, licking my lips in frustration. He runs his fingers through his bloodred hair as he types out a message.

"Ms. Keating hates you," Cal says with a chuckle. "Nothing you can do to change that now. Just accept that for the next seven and a half months, you're her bitch."

"I'm nobody's bitch," Hael snorts. Vic narrows his

eyes and reaches over, snatching the phone from his best friend's hand. "What the fuck, man?"

"You're nobody's bitch? Because it looks like you're Brittany's. Stop fucking kowtowing to her."

"Kowtowing? That's what you call it when she's threatening to sic her dad's anti-gang squad on us, and I'm doing damage control?" Hael says as Vic pockets his friend's phone, his purple-black hair shining in the sunlight.

"You wouldn't have to do damage control if you'd stayed the hell away from her," Vic says, and Oscar nods in agreement. The way Hael looks at his friend, I can sense a simmering anger that wasn't there before. I hope it doesn't have anything to do with what happened between the three of us, but maybe it does? "We will deal with Brittany after Halloween."

"Fuck, whatever you say, boss," Hael grumbles, looking back at me as Aaron pretends to be interested in a slice of pepperoni pizza. Has he noticed that I'm wearing his hoodie today? Or that I haven't washed it since I took it from him? I tell myself it's because I've been too lazy to do laundry, but that's not true at all.

It's because I like putting it on and being enveloped by his smell.

I pick up a chocolate milk off the tray between me and Vic, sticking a straw into it.

"Stay low this week, don't stir up trouble." Vic glances over at me, his obsidian eyes catching the light and taking my breath away. In the sun like this, they're not quite so dark. In fact, I can see shades of chocolate brown twisted with russet and auburn. "I'm sorry about

417

the slow progress on Kali. On your list, in general."

"I just said it had to be done before graduation," I say, wondering why I'm being so damn lenient. I hate them, right? This is torture, right? "I get it. Let's deal with Mitch and his merry band of assholes first."

Vic chuckles and shakes his head, running his fingers through his hair.

"Let's," he says, a strange emphasis on the word. He stares out at the street, like he's searching for something.

Whatever that something is, it never comes, the bell rings, and we all head inside.

The week passes by relatively quietly. There's no sign of Principal Vaughn, and no trouble from Mitch's buddies. Billie, Kali, and Ivy steer clear of me in the halls, and nobody mentions the trashed cars.

But instead of feeling relieved, I start to get nervous.

I've been with Havoc for two months now, and every goddamn day, it's something. Having things be so quiet makes me wary.

On Thursday, I ride with Aaron after school to pick up Kara, Ashley, and Heather. There's no after-school program today which is fine because our plan is to take the girls trick or treating at dusk, and then hit Stacey's party after.

Everyone knows the only good parties start after dark.

"What sort of costumes did you get the girls?" I ask, my voice loud in the quiet minivan. Aaron's hands tighten a bit on the wheel as he slides his green-gold gaze over to me, the brakes squeaking as we pause at a stop sign. Red, yellow, and brown leaves swirl against the windshield as a group of costumed children dart through the crosswalk.

"Last year, I tried to make their costumes, you know? Like I sat down and tried to sew shit."

"You tried to sew?" I ask, blinking in surprise and then clamping a hand over my lips to stop a surprised giggle. Aaron raises a brunette brow at me.

"You think that's so funny? Me sitting down to sew a princess costume?"

"I think it's hilarious," I reply, finally giving into the chuckle. "A seventeen-year-old inked-up asshole sitting down with a needle and thread? That's the punchline of a joke if I've ever heard one." He smirks at me and shakes his head, easing the van forward and heading toward Heather's school.

"Yeah, well, I wanted to give the girls something authentic or ... like, something I used to have ..." He trails off, and his eyes go dark, looking at something far, far away from here. The past, most likely. Until Aaron's mom left, she was the Suzy Homemaker type. She baked, sewed, decorated. His past and present are two completely different realities. "Anyway, the costumes fucking sucked, so this year, I gave in and just bought some bagged shit from the Hellhole."

He gestures to the plastic bag between our seats, and I reach down to peep inside. There's a pre-packaged fairy costume, some glittery wings made of wire and tulle, and various accessories. The second costume is a sassy little witch with striped tights.

"At least you went the extra mile and bought add-ons," I remark, noticing the carved wood broom beneath the bag, and the witch's hat peeking out from the back seat. "After Dad died, I didn't get costumes anymore. Well, I mean, there was that one year when I was eight and cried about it, so Mom cut holes in my sheets to make me a ghost ..."

"A pink ghost patterned with a gaudy Minnie Mouse print," Aaron adds, and I smile. It's not a nice smile though, more like a melancholy one. I'd almost forgotten that he knew all my stories. *We have history together,* I think, my fingers picking at the holey knees of my jeans. Silence reigns supreme for several moments before Aaron speaks up again. "But you're right: they'll remember I put in some effort, at least." He pauses again and wets his lower lip, like he's nervous. "Do you think you could help with their makeup? I fucking suck at it. No matter how many YouTube videos I watch ..."

I lift my head up to look at him, tucking some blond hair behind my ear. *He really is pretty, isn't he?* I think, shifting in my seat and trying not to let those old sour feelings of mine rush to the surface. We *have* to learn to get along. Blood in, blood out ...

"I'd be happy to," I say, unbuckling my seat belt, so I can climb out and grab Heather. As I reach for the door handle though, I feel Aaron's fingers on my arms. Adrenaline shoots through me as I glance back.

His face is resolute, determined, his jaw clenched.

"I know it can't possibly make up for everything that happened, but for what it's worth, Bernadette, I'm ... I'm sorry." My eyes widen, and I try to pull away, but Aaron won't let me go. His fingers dig into my skin, and my hands start to shake. "I've never stopped loving you; I just thought you should know that."

I tear my arm from his grip and slam the car door, putting my back to it and closing my eyes. I don't even care that Aaron can still see me standing there. *What the actual fuck?!* How dare he throw that shit in my face like that. How dare he. How fucking dare he ...

"Are you okay?" Heather asks as she approaches me cautiously, dressed in an orange and black Halloween sweater. Neither my little sister nor Aaron's girls were allowed to wear their costumes to either school. Makes me sad. I remember how everyone used to get dressed up, and we'd have Halloween cupcakes and candy during class. Guess times have changed a bit since I was in elementary school, huh?

"I'm fine," I say, pushing up off the van and signing the school monitor's little clipboard. I throw open the back door and hold her backpack while she climbs in. She, of course, is more than happy to see Aaron. The two of them start chatting about possible trick or treating routes—for years I've taken her to the rich people neighborhood in Oak River Heights—and I stare out the window, trying my best to process Aaron's words.

"I've never stopped loving you."

And that means what? That he still does love me?

I decide I can't deal with this revelation, not tonight.

We grab Kara and Ashley and then head back to Aaron's place where the rest of the Havoc crew is waiting for us.

"We have four hours until we need to leave for

Stacey's party," Oscar informs us, leaning over the counter in the half-bath near the front door. He's got a black makeup crayon in his hand, turning to face me with some ghastly dark circles around his eyes. I won't lie, I have to stop and do a bit of a double take.

"What are you supposed to be?" I ask, and a sharp smirk curves over Oscar's lips.

"You'll see," he warns, a dark note in his voice that makes me shiver. I shake the feeling off and roll my eyes, guiding the girls upstairs to help them into their costumes. Aaron hovers nearby, but finally gives up and heads outside to smoke a joint.

"Something happen between you two?" Vic asks me, cornering me as I herd the girls back downstairs for better lighting. He cuts me off at the staircase as the three little ones skip past. My skin feels suddenly too tight, and I have to resist the urge to squirm under that sharp gaze.

"If it did, would it be your business?" I ask, and he gives me this shit-eating grin.

"It would, yeah." Victor reaches out with that big hand of his, smoothing some of my hair back. Just that little touch makes me want him, and I hate that. I hate that I feel like a drug addict with a habit when he's around. "You're my girl, remember?"

"Since when?" Cal asks, appearing from the shadows of the spare bedroom. I've just barely peeked in there, but it's got one queen bed and a set of bunk beds on the opposite wall. Back in the day, when Aaron's parents lived here, it was his dad's office. Now, it functions as Cal, Hael, and Oscar's bedroom. Aaron obviously has his own room, and piece of shit Victor Channing gets the master all to himself. "You need to rein in that possessive streak of yours, boss."

Victor scowls at Callum, pushing up off the wall to give his much smaller teammate a look.

"Did you finish the props for tonight?" Vic asks as I notice the item clutched in Cal's hand. It's a black baseball bat with nails strategically hammered through the end, leaving the points sticking out precariously.

Callum grins and swings the weapon up to his shoulder, just barely missing stabbing himself with it.

"All ready," he says, and Vic nods. I don't know what they're all planning on as far as costumes go, and I haven't asked. I figure I'll see them later. For now, I use the lull in conversation to sneak down the stairs and finish up the girls' makeup. Well, Kara and Ashley's makeup anyway; Heather is once again going as Ryan Reynold's version of Deadpool, complete with full mask.

Once they're ready, Aaron and I herd the girls into the van, and I'm surprised to see that Callum joins us, grinning and winking at me as he straps himself into the back row.

"I'm your backup," he explains, "just in case."

I nod, but to be honest, I'm glad he's here. I have a feeling Callum could buy us whatever time we needed to get the girls out of a rough situation.

And the universe knows we'll probably be in at least one life or death scenario before the night is over …

Looking at myself in the mirror with my blond hair in a high, bouncy ponytail and my makeup done up like some MAC counter girl is surreal. I look like a different person, like the reflection of myself I might've been with a different upbringing, a different life.

The sort of life Brittany Burr and her friends have.

I reach out and touch my fingertips to the mirror, studying the reflection of my cheap cheerleading uniform and the way it shows off the ink on my midriff. This should be an interesting evening, dressed up like some preppy Fuller High asshole for the darkest night of the year.

Just a few more additions, and I'll be ready. I drag my makeup kit closer—pretty much all of my product is stolen, so I have a decent collection—and grab some of the fake blood and Halloween effects we purchased at the Hellhole.

Fifteen minutes later, and I'm done dirtying up my look.

I give myself a wry grin in the mirror and rise to my feet, flipping my hair and then rolling my eyes at my own reflection. Downstairs, I can hear the heavy bass of some hip-hip song from the early 2000s. My nose wrinkles as I open Aaron's door and realize the beat is *Ridin'* by Chamillionaire and Krayzie Bone.

When I get to the top of the staircase and look down, my heart freezes in my chest, and a cold, fearful chill chases down my spine.

All five Havoc Boys are waiting in the living room, dressed in identical Halloween costumes.

Their faces are fully painted, to the point that it's hard

to tell them apart from up here. Five gritty skeleton visages stare back at me, black around the eyes, teeth painted over lips. They all have their hair slicked back and sprayed black with one of those colored hairsprays that only lasts the night. And they're all decked out in matching black trench coats with black hoodies and black shirts underneath, black slacks, badass boots.

For a brief moment there, I feel like a helpless heroine in some scary teen Halloween slasher flick.

Shit.

I force my basic instincts to take a back seat. Sure, Havoc is dangerous, but … maybe not to me? At least not right now. *Good thing the girls are holed up in their room watching* Halloweentown *with the babysitter. This would scare the crap out of them.*

"Are you guys supposed to be Tate Langdon from *American Horror Story*?" I ask, swallowing hard as I hit the bottom step and find myself at the center of Havoc's attention. "Or Zombie Boy? The show makers based that look off of him, you know."

"We know," Oscar says, and my eyes flick back to find his gray gaze. For once, he's not wearing his glasses. I'm assuming contacts? But holy *fuck,* having his focus bared on me like that, without the lenses to protect me, it's intimidating.

I keep my head high and scan the group. Vic is obvious, based on size alone, same with Callum. Biggest and smallest. It takes me a minute with Aaron and Hael, but only until Hael grins and the music switches over to *Candy Shop* by 50 Cent and Olivia. Guess we're into the 2000s station for tonight.

"We're gonna fuck shit up," Hael says, tapping the end of his black baseball bat against the wood floor next to his boots as he moves over to stand beside me. He points out the red line across my throat and wrists, and all the fake blood I added. "Clever," he says, flicking the nametag on my uniform that reads *Brittany.* "Couldn't resist going as a *dead* cheerleader, huh?"

I give him a look and then bite down on the fake blood pouch between my teeth, letting red liquid dribble past my lips and stain the front of my uniform. Hael raises a painted brow at me.

"We're gonna fuck shit up," I agree, and his grin doubles in size as he reaches out to take my arm. I see Vic's eyes watching us, but he doesn't say anything as Aaron opens the door and Callum bounces out into the dark, opening his arms wide and sending his trench coat fluttering in the cool, night breeze.

"Gift for the newest member of Havoc," he says, turning and holding his arm out to indicate the black stretch limo gleaming against the curb. My eyes widen as Hael pulls me through the grass toward it.

"You got a limo?" I ask, a strange sense of déjà vu settling over me. Have I mentioned that the boys took me out to the middle of nowhere in a limo with Kali, tore my dress off and gave it to her to wear, and then kicked me out into the darkness to walk home in my underwear? Yeah, it was all sorts of messed-up.

My pulse begins to thunder and sweat drips down the back of my neck.

"We boosted a limo," Hael says, still grinning. "I'd open the door for you, but I know you're not into acts of chivalry or any of that shit."

"Fuck all the way off," I murmur, tearing my arm from his grip as Cal opens the door for me anyway.

"Your chariot awaits," he says, excitement emanating from him and Hael. They want to start shit; they want violence. I ... don't know what I want. My hands slide along the leather as I scoot down to the end, and the boys join me, eerie in their matching costumes. The door slams shut, and Hael leans over me to slam his fist against the window.

The limo pulls away from the curb as I raise an eyebrow.

"Who the hell's driving this thing?" I ask, and Vic offers up a tight smile.

"A friend," he says, and I know that he means a friend of Havoc's. Interesting. Wonder if it's the same guy that shot Mitch for us?

My fingers dig at the edge of the leather seat as I try to control my emotions and Hael dicks around with his phone, connecting it to the Bluetooth stereo. *The Violence* by Asking Alexandria comes on and he taps his fingers against the knee of his black leather pants with his painted fingers. The boys have taken their makeup down their necks and over their hands, coloring every bit of visible skin with the same somber black and white skeleton design. They've even gone so far as to paint right over their tattoos.

"Break out the booze," Vic commands, and Oscar kicks open one of the cabinets on the wall across from me, withdrawing a sleek bottle with a red logo that reads *Blavod* on the side.

"Black vodka," Oscar explains as he gathers up shot glasses from the same cabinet, pouring one for each of us and passing them around. There's a large carton of cigarettes as well that he grabs, opening it and holding it out so we can all snatch a few. I run the black length of the cigarette under my nose and smell cloves.

"Black vodka and clove cigarettes, now that's Halloween," Hael groans in pleasure as Callum breaks out several dark chocolate bars. We each take a square and then toast our shot glasses.

"To All Hallows' Eve," Vic says as we clink our glasses, down our shots, and enjoy the decadence of the chocolate. He glances over at me and smirks, the expression devilish buried under all that makeup. "To dark pasts, bright futures, and the power of Havoc."

"To Havoc," I say, and then I light up.

CHAPTER

Just because Stacey Langford is the queen bee of Prescott High, that doesn't mean she isn't dirt-ass poor like the rest of us. Tonight's Halloween party might be hosted by her, but it takes place in an abandoned old house at the edge of a cemetery. Total cliché, but apparently there's some abundance of radon in the ground beneath it or some shit, and the previous owner died of lung cancer. Nobody wants to live here now, but we're down to party in it.

We're just over an hour outside of town, in the middle of the woods, in the middle of the dark. When Callum lets me out of the limo and I look up, all I can see are stars.

"You can see them out here better than anywhere else," he whispers against my ear. I shiver, but I pretend it's because of the frosty autumn air and not his voice. Maybe we both know that's a lie?

The limo stands out in the weed-ridden gravel where

the rest of the partygoers' cars are parked, but it's definitely not the nicest car here. There are Lambos, Ferraris, and Maseratis, but then there are also Altimas, Mustangs, and Camrys next to the rusted-out shitboxes that belong to the kids at Prescott. Here and there I spot a vintage beauty that reminds of Hael's Camaro; it's sort of a thing at Prescott to fix up old cars.

"Everyone's here," I remark, studying the mixed bag of vehicles. "From Oak Valley Prep to Fuller High to good ol' Prescott."

"Everyone's here," Aaron confirms, but he doesn't sound near as excited as Hael or Callum or even Vic. He doesn't want a confrontation tonight. Pretty sure he's the only member of Havoc that doesn't though.

We head for the open front doors, the music booming out into the cold, dark night. Several students are gathered around outside, smoking joints or snorting coke. They watch us carefully, warily, like a pack of coyotes might study a pack of wolves. We're all predators, but they know if they make the wrong move, we'll tear them apart and spatter the frosty forest floor with their blood.

Inside, the old mansion is a crumbling mess. Doors are missing, wallpaper is peeling, and the floor is made up of chipped and broken tiles. Stacey and her girls have worked their magic though, filling the place with Halloween décor that they probably stole from Hobby Lobby or some shit. There are tall vases filled with fake black roses, black and purple streamers, and some animatronic ghoulies that are probably worth a fortune. Yep, definitely looking at a lot of stolen loot in here.

I blink through the green and white strobe lights, and

the sea of low-lying fog from the half-dozen fog machines in the corners.

Glancing over my shoulder, I see all five boys waiting behind me in a loose 'V' formation with—aptly enough—Victor at the head. They're all holding their black bats, trench coats fluttering in the breeze. Hael's bat is dragging on the floor as he throws back another mouthful of vodka and passes the bottle to Aaron. His bat is strapped to his back as he smokes with one hand and drinks with the other. Callum has his slung over his shoulder while Oscar clutches the base of the bat in one hand and balances the end in his palm. Victor puts the end of his on the floor directly in front of him and folds both hands together on the base.

The entire room takes a breath when we walk in, and even though it's hard as hell to see in here, I know everybody's looking.

"You like what you see?" Stacey asks, appearing on my left side in a sleek white dress, pointed black fingernails, and a ghostly gray wig. Her face is painted into the perfect mix of macabre and elegant, but I have no idea what she's supposed to be. She is, however, wearing a very pretty and very expensive tiara on her head. The Langford girls have been busy lately, I see. It takes a lot of work to pinch something that nice. "We've thrown the party in Havoc's honor."

"Smart," Vic says from behind me, his indomitable presence a sensation I can't ignore. "You know how to pick the winning side, don't you, Stacey?"

"Always," she says, her black painted lips curving into a smirk. "Can we offer you something to drink? Eat?

Smoke? Snort?"

"Nah, we're good," Vic says, lifting up the black vodka bottle and taking a swig. He passes it to me, so I can do the same, and then puts one big, skeleton-patterned hand on my shoulder. His breath teases my ear as he leans in. "Stay close tonight, babe."

I shrug his hand off. I can take care of myself, but I'm also not stupid. My eyes scan the room for any signs of Mitch's crew as I take a huge drink of the vodka. My head begins to swim with the kiss of alcohol as my gaze sweeps the grinding bodies of dancing students. The rest of the Havoc Boys clear paths through the crowd, looking for trouble.

The costumes tonight run the gamut, from the usual—vampires, serial killers, slutty nurses—to the unusual, like the girl in the red wig who's dressed up like Yona from a reverse harem anime I watched with Penelope once called *Yona of the Dawn*.

"Eclectic crowd tonight," I say, taking another drink of the vodka and passing it back to Vic. Without waiting for a response, I move into the thick of the crowd, the heat and the music enveloping me, drawing me in. The fog swirls around my ankles as I pause, examining the various rooms that lead branch off from the expansive foyer. It looks like the goddamn *Casper* house.

"They have a funhouse in here," Cal says, appearing out of the smoke, the black hood of his sweatshirt thrown up over his hair. "Mirrors and clown shit. Good place for an ambush. Pretty sure they stole all the stuff from the old party store warehouse. But it's also the only exit on the ground floor besides the front doors. Everything else

432

is boarded-up or blocked."

"I don't like that," Vic says, a muscle in his jaw working as he sighs. "Keep it clear and get some guys outside to watch it." His body is tense as his ebon eyes scan the room. Not seeing Mitch or Kali or the rest of those assholes could be taken as some sort of concession, like maybe they've actually decided to back down, but I'm not sure that I believe it. I don't think shooting Mitch is going to convince them to stop; I think it's pissed them off royally. But then, that's just my opinion. Havoc's been at this a lot longer than I have.

I lick my painted lips and think about my list. *No. 2. the best friend.*

Kali is up to something; I can feel it.

"Anything else of note?" Vic asks, and Callum shakes his head. "Good. Stay sharp, but have a little fun, okay?"

"Oh, I intend to," Cal says, reaching out and taking the vodka. He finishes the bottle off and tosses it aside, letting it shatter against the wall. He's not the only one throwing glass bottles; everybody's doing it. Intoxicated laughter poisons the air as he grabs my hand and pulls me into the crowd.

Vic looks decidedly pissed-off about it, but he doesn't interfere.

"Every drug under the sun is available in here, and you're more interested in dancing with me?" I ask as Cal wraps an arm around my waist and walks us back into the thick of the crowd. His smile is decidedly more wicked with those skeleton teeth painted across them, effectively doubling the size of his mouth.

"You're a special sort of drug, too, Bernadette," he

tells me, leaning forward to put his mouth near my ear. "I keep wondering if I should've kissed you in the dance studio." My skin prickles with goose bumps, but I don't respond, letting Cal guide our bodies in a synchronous rhythm with the throbbing beat of the music. I don't even recognize the song we're dancing to, but it doesn't matter. Callum knows what he's doing, and he takes me with him, manipulating my body the same way he did in the studio. "If I had, what would you have done?"

"Guess you'll have to run that experiment to find out?" I challenge, cocking a brow as my heart pounds. I'm not really sure what I'm doing here. What Vic means when he calls me *his* girl. What Aaron wants when he tells me he still loves me. What Callum intends by dancing with me in front of a mixed crowd from all three schools. Or what Hael thinks about when he's looking at me with those honey-brown eyes of his. Oscar ... clearly hates me, so there's not much to dissect there.

"Oh?" Cal asks, but then Hael is interrupting the entire party by climbing onto the dais where the DJ's set up. He requests a song, and there's a brief pause as the DJ scrambles to accommodate his request.

"Who's here to fuck shit up tonight?" he shouts, and the entire room goes nuts, lifting phones and bottles of liquor in solidarity. With a laugh, Hael lifts up a bottle of his own, swigs some liquid, and then raises a lighter in his right hand. He flicks the wheel and spits the alcohol out at the same time, creating a wave of flame that rushes over the heads of the crowd. Everybody just fucking loses it, and a mosh pit starts up in the middle of the room as Hael's chosen song comes screaming out of the speakers.

He's a pretty big fan of metalcore music, so that's what we get, this hardcore screaming that riles up the room into a frenzy.

Hael hops down from the dais, chucking his bottle and making his way straight toward me and Cal.

"May I?" he asks, gesturing at Cal to cut in.

"I don't know," I quip back, still holding onto the front of Cal's hoodie. "Will Brittany mind?"

"Oh, get fucked, Blackbird," Hael says, grabbing me and yanking me into his arms. It's pretty hard to dance to this song, so we end up just getting close and grinding together, pelvis to pelvis. My arms go around Hael's neck as I notice Brittany watching us from the edge of the room. *Speak of the devil ...* I think as her eyes glitter with a jealousy so intense it steals my breath away.

My eyes flick back to Hael's brown ones, surrounded by black makeup. Does he know she's watching us right now? I slide my fingers up the back of his neck, tickling his black-dyed red hair with my nails.

"Do you think Brittany likes my costume?" I inquire, nodding with my chin in her direction. Hael pauses, frowns, and glances over his shoulder, face tightening as he spots his ex on the fringes of the crowd. She's dressed up like Ariana Grande with a high pony and a cat-eared headband.

"Fuck my life," he grumbles as he turns back to me, keeping his hands firmly on the curves of my waist. "I don't give a shit what she thinks."

"You must've liked her at some point, to date her for so long," I press, my lips near Hael's chest. I wonder if he can even hear me above the wild thrum of the music.

He keeps me close and finishes up the song, but when I try to pull away, he holds me there.

"You get it though, right?" he asks, looking at me with his head cocked slightly to one side. "Dating someone who's not like you at all, just to see if there's something you're missing? I mean, you dated that douche Donald Asher."

My lips purse, but I have no comeback for that.

When I look for Brittany again, I see that she's disappeared into the party. Hael doesn't follow after her like I thought he might. Instead, he parks himself on a crumbling high-backed chair, kicking one leg over the arm and snatching up an abandoned bottle of whiskey. He doesn't seem concerned that he's drinking out of some random's bottle as he tilts it back.

I separate myself from the crowd, trying to have a good time but finding it impossible to shed that sharp-edged tension I've been nursing since moment one. *Something bad is going to happen tonight,* I think as I find a spot to rest next to Oscar.

He's standing near the curved edge of the staircase, watching the action from afar.

"This house is practically a playground," he says, glancing over at me. It's eerie, seeing him with all that makeup and no glasses. "Drugs, drinking, smoking, dancing, *fucking.*" He emphasizes that last word, make no mistake about it.

"So?" I ask, my head buzzing with alcohol and the thick cloud of cigarette and marijuana smoke.

"So, why are you over here with me?" Oscar asks, his bat leaning against the wall next to him. "You know I can't stand you; go bother somebody else."

My eyes narrow on him, but now that he's said that, I'm not fucking moving.

"What are you waiting for?" I ask, watching an Oak Valley Prep asshole with his hands all over Wendy's ass. Pathetic. My lip curls. These filthy rich boys think all the chicks at Prescott are playthings they can toy with, use, and then throw away like trash. An image of Donald rolling down the roof flashes in my mind, and I bite my lower lip.

"Trouble," Oscar says, pushing away from the wall and taking his bat with him. He leaves me there to blend into the shadows, my ears straining for gossip. Since the boys are all dressed in matching costumes, it isn't hard to pick them out of the crowd. As I do, I notice that Vic is watching me from across the room. I'm not sure I've ever left his sight.

"You heard what they did to Don, right?" this Oak Valley asshole asks, pausing at the table on my right to score some of the spiked punch with the plastic bones floating in it. I can tell he's from the prep school because he's wearing enough goddamn cologne that I can smell it through all the sweat and smoke. That, and I recognize the shoes he's wearing. My stepdad has a pair, and I know they cost mad money. Mom wouldn't stop talking about how she got them for free from a friend's husband because they didn't fit, and the guy couldn't be fucked returning them.

"I mean, he got the crap beat out of him, didn't he? I thought it was just a B&E sort of thing?" the other guy—who probably thinks he's clever, wearing a breathalyzer costume with a hole on the crotch that says *Place Mouth Here*—replies.

"That's the story, but it was fucking Havoc, man. They carved the word *Rapist* into his forehead. The wound was, like, deep enough that it dug into his skull. Don's gonna be in and out of laser treatments for years to get that shit removed." There's a long pause there where everything goes silent around me, my heart beating frantically in my chest. "They cut his balls off, too, man. They *castrated* him."

My throat goes completely dry and my eyes get wide.

"You okay?" Aaron asks, appearing beside me. I glance his way, but there are no words. I'm not sure if the gossip I just heard is true or yet more Havoc rumor and speculation, but ... Does the fact that I'm hoping it's true make me a bad person?

"Did you guys cut off Don's balls?" I ask as Aaron approaches me, and his face pales. Even beneath the layer of makeup he's wearing, I can see it. It's true. It's fucking true. "Jesus Christ."

"You didn't think we'd let him off easy, did you? Bernadette, I tried to warn you. We're messed-up. Havoc is fucking messed-up. You just—" He pauses, clenching his teeth to stop the flow of words, like he's just realized he's about to reveal something important to me.

"I just what?" I ask, turning and getting in his face. "I just never saw it? You guys were *fucked* to me, but ... you could've done worse. Why didn't you?" Aaron scowls at me and tries to turn away, but I'm not letting him go. I'm onto something here, I know it. "Aaron, talk to me, goddamn it. What did Kali have on you? Why didn't you guys fuck me up like you did Don?"

"Bernadette," Aaron starts, turning back to look at me, the skeleton makeup on his face turning his visage into a grim one. But then he pauses and looks up, eyes darkening. I follow his gaze and see that the crowd's parted to reveal a group of people standing near the front doors.

They're all wearing grinning clown masks, bandages on their right shoulders darkened with faux blood. I do a quick headcount and come up with almost two dozen people standing there. It's impossible to tell if they're male or female, with their masks and dark clothes.

"Jesus," Aaron grinds out as I feel my pulse start to pick up.

Shit.

This is what I was waiting for.

Havoc never gets a day off.

"Are those bandages supposed to be in support of Mitch or something?" I whisper as this EDM/dubstep rap comes on, blaring through the speakers as Vic moves forward to greet the new crew. Aaron clenches his jaw and looks down at me, like he's considering spiriting me out the back door or something.

"Well, well, what do we have here?" Vic asks, his voice booming out across the crowd. "Party crashers?"

"Havoc's rule at Prescott High is done," the leader of the gang says, his voice manipulated by a voice changer. "It's over, Victor."

"Is it?" Vic asks as several dozen people in the crowd remove plastic skeleton masks from inside their jackets, sweaters, and costumes, sliding them over their faces in solidarity. "If you want to rule that school, or this town, you'll have to fight for it."

"Gladly," the leader says, and then he pulls out a weapon from inside his jacket. People start to scream and scatter as Aaron grabs my hand.

"I'm getting you the hell out of here," he says, just before the first shot goes off, exploding one of the paper lanterns near the ceiling. Clown Dude—who I'm just sort of guessing is Mitch—has missed his shot. Instead of blowing Victor's head off, he's just been hit in the shoulder with Callum's nail-ridden bat.

A fight breaks out as the two sides rush each other, like soldiers going into war. Several more gunshots go off as the Havoc crew meets up with the newcomers.

"I'm not going anywhere," I grind out as Aaron tries to pull me toward the clown-covered archway that leads into the funhouse area. "I'm a part of Havoc, too." I try to tear my grip from his, but his hands are like steel. I'm not going anywhere.

The music continues to blare as the room empties out, the floors already spattered with blood as the two groups beat each other to pulps. A few of the clown-masked assholes are heading our way, but Aaron doesn't wait for them, yanking me into the funhouse.

The fog machines in here are insane. Paired with the red strobe lights and the myriad mirrors, it's impossible to see. But Aaron manages to drag me through anyway, putting some distance between us and the party. At first, I struggle, but pitting myself against one of Havoc's best fighters isn't going to win us any wars. So I follow after him, convinced that as soon as we get outside, I can break away from him and make my way around to the front.

Instead, we end up stumbling into a round room filled with cackling animatronic clowns. Plastic caution tape lines the walls, and as Aaron goes to try the door, he finds it locked from the outside. So much for those guys Vic sent around to watch the back. They must be getting their asses kicked right now.

"Goddamn it," Aaron growls out, using his bat to try to dislodge the heavy wood door. But it won't budge, and we're running out of time. Six of the clown-masked idiots stumble into the room, surrounding us. Aaron doesn't hesitate to hand me his bat, whipping a gun out from inside his trench coat. "Don't try me tonight, or I'll splatter your brains all over the walls."

"Really?" one of our attackers asks, and since her voice isn't being manipulated by a voice changer, I know right away that it's Billie I'm talking to. "Because we're here to meet you on your terms this time." One of the guys pulls out a pistol of his own and levels it on me. "You're going to choke on blood for what you did to my brother."

Aaron doesn't bother to respond to her threat. Instead, he just pulls the trigger and sends the guy stumbling back into the wall. He's shot him right in the shoulder, in the red spot where he'd applied the fake blood to his faux wound. Guess it's a real one now, huh? A nice match for Mitch.

But Clown-Guy isn't the only person in that room with a gun, and as Aaron moves his own weapon to take another shot, one is coming right at my chest. Without thinking, my ex steps right in front of me, taking the bullet meant for me.

It's all happening so fast, and it's so damn hard to see in here that I can't tell where Aaron's been hit. The thing is, he doesn't even drop. Instead, he lifts his own weapon up and fires again, shattering one of the mirrors. Everyone in the room scatters, including us, ducking behind the wood frames of the mirrors to hide.

Pretty sure I'm just saying *holy fuck* over and over again. My fingers search for blood as I probe Aaron's chest, and he slumps to the floor. He's shaking, but I don't see any red as I unzip his hoodie and find that he's actually wearing fucking Kevlar underneath. That is, I don't see any red until I grab his arm. Looks like in all the hubbub, he was shot twice, once in the chest and once in the left bicep.

"You guys don't fuck around, do you?" I whisper, quivering as Aaron forces a tight smile to his face.

"Not particularly," he says, pushing me aside and trying to sit up. Blood leaks from his left arm, smearing my fingers with crimson when I reach out to take a look. "No time." Aaron pulls away from me, stumbling a bit as he tries to stand. I don't know a lot about guns or Kevlar or any of that shit, but I do know that getting hit in a 'bulletproof' vest still hurts like a bitch and leaves one hell of a bruise.

I have a brief moment there where I wonder if all the guys are wearing Kevlar, and why I'm not. But there's not exactly a lull in the conversation for me to ask about that. Instead, two of the clown-masked dickheads break through the fog as Aaron lifts up his bat and takes a swing. I move back, out of range of the weapon, ready to jump in if I need to. *This is fucking insane,* I think, remembering how I agonized all summer about my choice to approach Havoc.

And this is where it's gotten me.

"Hey, bitch," Billie says, appearing behind me and lifting her mask up her face. She's got that knife of hers back in hand. My lips purse, but I'm not afraid of her. I've kicked her ass before, and I'll do it again. "Mitch thinks I should leave you alone, but I'm tired of seeing you strut around Prescott like you own the place."

"I do own it," I say, my voice cool and even, the air pulsing with music, fog drifting around my ankles. "Because I hold Havoc's leash." I shrug my shoulders, giving off the air of nonchalance, even if my heart is thundering, and I want nothing more than to glance back and check on Aaron. But no. I have to prove that I'm in control here. Fighting is one-part physical prowess and two-parts bravado. "If you hurt me, they'll kill you. You know that, right?"

"I'm not afraid of you," Billie says as a crash sounds from behind me, and I finally lose my own inner-fight and glance back to see Aaron struggling on the ground with a guy whose arms are the size of tree trunks. *Danny Ensbrook, Kyler's brother.* Speaking of …

My head whips around just in time to intercept Billie as she comes for me, swinging that knife of hers in an arc. It isn't hard for me to grab her wrist and drag her in close. It's much harder to use a blade in close contact like this. As soon as I've got Billie in range, I lift my knee up and slam it into her crotch as hard as I can. Not as effective as kneeing a dude in the balls, but it still hurts like hell. My next move cracks Billie across the wrist, knocking her blade loose and sending it sliding across the floor and into the fog.

Teeth gritted in anger, she comes at me like a whirlwind, fists flying, throwing herself at me with reckless abandon. And this is one of the reasons why she's so easy to beat. Not only is she thin and slight of frame, but she just goes into rages and stops thinking. I let her throw her entire weight into me and then duck low, slamming my shoulder into her stomach and tossing her over my back.

Billie hits the floor with a grunt, but as I'm turning to go for her, Kyler appears, his mask hanging around his neck. His yellow bruises flicker red in the dancing strobe lights as he sneers at me. There's no hesitation when he comes at me, and I have to at least give him credit for trying to defend his girlfriend.

His much larger form slams into mine, but I'm used to this. I've been fighting off grown men for years.

I let his weight throw me to the ground, turning the move into a roll that puts some space between us as he stumbles and does his best to recover his feet. As Callum mentioned earlier, one of the pluses of being smaller is being faster. I'm up before Kyler is, throwing my elbow down on the back of his neck as hard as I can.

With a growl, he shoves his shoulder into my stomach, sending me stumbling back into another one of the funhouse mirrors. Glass shatters, littering the floor beneath my feet. Thank fuck I'm wearing these stupid white tennis shoes with the ribbons instead of heels or I'd be on my ass in no time.

Kyler throws a hard punch at my face, but I duck low and he ends up hitting the wood frame of the mirror, knocking it to the floor and sending the fog fluttering around us. I can see Aaron from here, fighting desperately to get to me, but he's quite literally fending off three big dudes—including Danny Ensbrook—with another on the floor in front of him. Even with the face paint, I can see that he's pale, that he's hurting, and that he's running out of energy.

We don't have a lot of time here—especially if one of the Fuller High or Oak Valley idiots calls in the cops. Prescott kids know better, but those pretty, privileged assholes don't know how we handle things in Southside Springfield.

I duck under Kyler's next swing and dart past Billie as she comes at me, reaching up and grabbing onto the shoulders of one of Aaron's attackers. As luck would have it, I dig my fingers into the wound on the guy's shoulder and find my thumb bloodied as Mitch Charter screams in agony. Having his followers dress up with bandages on their shoulders was a smart idea, but he didn't bother to hide the hideous Nazi tattoo on the back of his neck. *Racist twat.*

Mitch stumbles back and slams me into the wall, trying to dislodge me, but as usual, he's underestimated my tenacity. My fight or fight harder instinct is going wild as I drop down and slide between his legs, twisting and falling onto my back so I can kick up and into his balls with my foot. There's a lot of power behind that move, and Mitch goes down screaming.

One of the other guys grabs me by the ponytail,

dragging me across the floor as Aaron struggles to break through the crowd and come to me. But he's severely outnumbered, injured, and shit out of luck.

"Calling out Havoc was the biggest mistake you ever made," Kyler snarls as Billie helps Mitch to his feet, and the three of them gang up on me. I can take Billie. I can take Kyler. I think I can even take Mitch. But all of them at the same time? That's a tall order. I'm a scrappy bitch, not some UFC champion.

"Bernadette!" I can hear Aaron calling to me through the pounding beat of the music, but I'm gritting my teeth too hard to respond. When I glance to my right, I can see him, on his knees, blood pooling on the floor. Danny and a few of the other clown-mask wearing guys are holding him down, forcing him to watch whatever the fuck Kyler, Mitch, and Billie have planned for me.

"Hold her down," Billie commands as she straddles me, and I flail beneath her. Mitch is stepping on my left arm, crushing my wrist into the ground as Kyler keeps his tight grip on my hair. My scalp and arm are a mess of pain, but I'm not done fighting yet. I spit in Billie's face as she accepts a pocketknife from Mitch.

She frowns at me and swipes her hand over those pretty features of hers, but she doesn't move.

"Shouldn't you be at home with your baby instead of out here causing trouble?" I snap. I'm not really into mom-shaming, but come on, Billie's a shitty mom if she'd rather incite gang violence than spend Halloween with her kid.

"Don't you even mention my goddamn kid," she says, flicking open the knife and then grinning at me. "What should we cut off first? Your hair? Your nose? Or maybe your tits? Considering what your boys did to Donald, I think all three of those things would be more than fair."

"What do you give a shit about Donald Asher?" I ask, but Billie just slams the tip of the knife into my arm, and a scream tears from my throat. Sharp, searing pain rackets up my arm and into my head, turning my skull into a mess of white-hot agony.

"I don't. But fair's fair. Clearly, Havoc has no boundaries, so why should we?" Billie pulls the knife from my arm and spins it around in her fingers. "And we're not letting you hurt Kali. There's not a soul at Prescott who doesn't know you're gunning for her." She traces the tip of the knife against my lower lip. All I can hear is the pounding beat of my heart, and the rush of blood in my ears. If she mutilates me, do I really care? I've honestly never wanted to be pretty.

"Are you enjoying this, Aaron?" Mitch snarls, fresh blood staining the bandage on his shoulder. "I hope so. Because when Billie's done, I'm going to let Logan and Danny have their way with your chick, right in front of you."

Aaron tears his arms from the grips of the guys holding him and manages to slam his elbow into the crotch of one of them before three more guys pile on, crushing him to the floor.

"Oh," Billie says, slicing a line from the corner of my eye to the edge of my mouth. Pain follows along in the wake of the blood, but I manage to keep myself stone-still, quiet, blank. I don't waste energy on protesting; I look for an out or an escape or at least a way to inflict some serious damage. I figure if I go down, at least they hurt with me. "Aaron doesn't like the idea of sharing. Funny that, considering you whore yourself out to all five Havoc Boys."

"Doesn't bother Mitch that Kali's cheating on him with some douche from Oak Valley Prep, so I don't see why you give a crap," I blurt back, and Billie hits me as hard as she can in the face. I see stars, but all I have to do is keep them busy for a few. The other boys will be here; they'll come. I fucking *know* it.

"We're running out of time," Kyler says, glancing over his shoulder, like he can feel the same energy that I feel. Havoc doesn't play games. They don't lose. They used to be my tormentors, but now they're my dark angels. I turn my head and make eye contact with Aaron. He's gone completely still, building up energy as he pants and bleeds, waiting for one last chance to break free.

His green-gold eyes meet mine, and I can see a million different truths just waiting there to be revealed. He didn't want me in Havoc because he knew that, eventually, something like this would happen. In his own way, Aaron was trying to protect me.

"We should take these assholes with us and go," Mitch adds, and Billie scowls.

"Why? Take them where? We're in the middle of the fucking woods. And you said you had enough guys to deal with Havoc. Let's bring the other four in here and they can all watch as you take turns on their girl."

"That's not a bad idea," Danny says, laughing. His eyes rake over me before he splits off from the group and disappears momentarily. Meanwhile, Billie continues playing with her knife, cutting open the front of my cheerleading costume with a laugh, exposing a large portion of my breasts.

"I have a bad feeling about this," Mitch says, swiping at the sweat on his face. "Let's just kick the shit out of these two and call it a win. I don't want to stick around here any longer than necessary."

"Don't be such a pussy," Billie snaps as Danny comes back into the room and kicks one of the fog machines against the wall, shattering it into black plastic bits. "Well?" she asks, looking up at her boyfriend's brother.

"There are a few people passed out in the foyer, but that's it. Looks like our guys chased theirs into the woods." Danny checks his phone, scrolling through messages. "Nate says they've lost most of them in the trees, and they're heading back this way now."

"Good," Mitch says, pushing down a little harder on my arm. "What about Vic?"

"Dunno," Danny says, tapping out a text message. He pauses a moment and then shakes his head. "We can't find any of the Havoc Boys." He glances over at Aaron and then grins. "Except for this one."

"Get fucked," Aaron growls out, and gets a right hook to the face from Timmy for the trouble.

"I still say we take them with us and get out of here while we have the upper-hand," Mitch continues, just before the sound of breaking glass gives us all pause.

"What upper-hand?" Vic asks, appearing from the fog with his bat in hand. He swings it hard and hits Mitch in the thigh, drawing a scream from one of the Charter brothers while the other—Logan—launches himself at

Victor. The two of them end up in a fight while I use the moment of surprise to throw a punch at Billie's face.

She howls with pain as Oscar appears and grabs Kyler around the neck, putting him in a chokehold and yanking him back. There's a momentary burst of pain before Kyler loses his grip on my hair, and I sit up, shoving Billie off of me. She sprawls to the floor as I crawl over her, hitting her in the face. Once, twice, three times. As she groans and tries to crawl away from me, I stand up and turn to help Aaron.

But Callum's already there with his own baseball bat, hitting Danny in the shoulder before he goes for Timmy next. Hael is on the other side, taking care of two more of the clown-masked wearing idiots.

I stand there stone-still in the middle of the brawl, breathing hard, watching as the boys systematically take down their rivals—skeletons versus clowns. It's a ghastly sight, the fog swirling around our feet, clown faces leering at us from the ceiling. I have to say, Stacey Langford is one crazy bitch to have set all of this up.

Aaron finally finds his feet, panting and covered in blood. Our eyes meet, and his go wide.

"Bernadette!" he shouts, and I turn just in time to see Danny Ensbrook lift a revolver up and point it at my face. His finger clenches on the trigger, and my heart stops in my chest.

Callum's bat hits him hard in the side of the neck, knocking him over and sending the shot wide. Danny stumbles, falling hard to the ground, the nails from the bat raking through the side of his throat. And then there's blood, so much fucking blood.

The fight doesn't stop though, the remaining members of Mitch's gang throwing themselves at Havoc in one, last frenzied attack. Even Billie gets back to her feet, coming at me again. You'd think she'd have enough sense to get the hell out of there, but she must really want to prove herself. She throws her body into me again, knife point forward, but I knock the thrust aside and then hit her right in the throat.

She stumbles back as several more skeletons appear from the fog, tying up the loose ends and quieting the last of the dissenters. A few of the clowns take off when they realize this is over, that they've lost, abandoning their comrades in a way that Havoc never would.

"Everybody out," Oscar says, nodding at Mitch Charter, groaning and passed out on the floor by Vic's feet. "And take everyone but Danny with you."

The unnamed Havoc Boys scramble to follow Oscar's orders, leaving us alone with Danny Ensbrook. It takes me a minute to figure out why he'd be the exception to the rule. But then I look down and notice that my sneakers are standing in a pool of ruby red.

"Shit, shit, shit," Cal says, kneeling down and putting his hands on the side of Danny's neck. "He's bleeding everywhere; I think I hit an artery."

"Femoral artery, more like," Vic says as Oscar drops down next to Danny's body.

"And Cal," Oscar says, pulling his friend's hand away from Danny's neck. "He's not bleeding anymore; the nails tore right through his neck." Oscar looks at up at the leader of the Havoc Boys with an expression that says it's already too late for Danny. "He's dead," Oscar confirms coolly, rising to his feet and giving Vic another look.

"Are you serious?" Hael asks, cursing under his breath as he moves over to stand beside the … body. I have to admit, my mind's gone completely blank at that word. Dead. Danny is dead? Despite the guns and the bravado tonight, I don't think anyone was supposed to die. If they were, Victor would've put a hole in Mitch Charter's head.

"Unfortunately," Oscar says on the end of a long sigh, staring down at Danny's slumped form.

Callum stands up and stumbles against the wall, hands over his face. There's fucking blood everywhere. The metallic smell of it is making me sick; I feel like I might throw up.

"I've screwed myself, haven't I?" he whispers, shaking all over. But all I can think is *you did it to save me*. I move over to Callum and put my hand on his arm. He stiffens up, but he doesn't push me away.

"It was self-defense," I say, and then pause. "Well, defense of me anyway. He was going to shoot me, and I don't think he cared where that bullet hit. It didn't look like a warning shot to me."

"We should've made her wear the fucking Kevlar," Aaron grinds out, giving Vic a look.

"A vest wouldn't have protected her head," Vic replies calmly, sighing and swiping a hand over his face. "Okay, we can deal with this. Aaron," he says, and my ex raises his head a bit, looking like death warmed-up. "Take Bernadette back to your place." Aaron manages a nod as Hael helps him to his feet. I cling to Cal's arm, shaking from the rush of adrenaline, marveling at the fact that I almost died here tonight.

I've been waiting for death for a long time, almost praying for it. But now that I've gotten a glimpse, I'm not so sure I like what I see.

Before I get a chance to delve too far into the darkness of my thoughts, Vic is grabbing me and putting his arms around me, hugging me so close that I can smell the musk and amber scent of him, even through the sharp copper smell of blood.

"It'll be okay," he tells me, and maybe he even believes it. I want to have faith in Havoc, but holy shit. This is so much more than turf wars between rival high schools. This is some real-life shit with real-life consequences. "Go home, clean up, and we'll meet you there later."

"What are you going to do?" I ask, but Vic just purses his lips.

"Later," he tells me, gesturing in the direction of the cold draft from the now open back door. His makeup is smeared, giving it an even ghastlier sort of look. "Now get the hell out of here and drive fast."

Aaron doesn't speak as he drives us back into town, taking the dark roads at an almost alarming speed, and then slowing down when we hit the edge of Springfield. Getting pulled over right now would not go well for us. That is, if we couldn't convince the cops that all of this blood was fake.

We left the limo behind, grabbing an SUV out back

that the boys had planted there as a getaway car. When they did that, I'm not sure, but it's quite clear that they had a lot of things planned for tonight.

I just don't think they intended for Danny Ensbrook to die.

"Are you okay?" Aaron asks me when we hit the quiet suburban streets near his house. "I mean, obviously not, but …"

"I'm fine," I say, because I know what he means. Am I broken? Am I shattered? Am I scared? But I'm none of those things because those things were stripped out of me a long time ago. I'm amped up on adrenaline and nerves, and I'm worried about Cal, but that's about it. What happened to Danny Ensbrook … that shit was *deserved.*

Still, I don't want the boys to get in trouble, to go to prison.

I swipe both hands down my face and then drop them into my lap. Aaron's driving one-handed, his left arm resting in his own lap. I'm tempted to reach out and take his hand, but then what would I say? There are no words.

I turn back to face the windshield as we turn the corner.

The first thing I notice is that there's a second car parked in Aaron's driveway, next to the minivan. The second thing I notice is that the car is a police cruiser.

The third thing …

My throat closes up, and I feel the very first edges of panic rolling through me.

"What the fuck?" Aaron snaps, raking his fingers through his hair. He makes a split-second decision and pulls the SUV over, calling up Jennifer Lowell's number and waiting for her to answer. When she doesn't, he curses and sends a text, waiting several minutes before shoving his phone into his pocket. That's when he notices the look on my face. "What?" he asks, his voice laced with panic. The girls are in there—*our* girls are in there. "You look like you've seen a ghost."

"Worse," I choke out, fisting my fingers in the bloodied skirts of my cheerleading uniform. I'd recognize that police cruiser anywhere. "My stepdad."

Aaron whips his head back around and then guns it, parking next to Vic's motorcycle on the curb and climbing out. We should probably clean up before we go in there, but all I can think about is Heather, Kara, and Ashley in the same room as that pedophile fuck.

We burst through the front door and find the Thing sitting on the couch with a girl by his side.

But not one of our girls.

No, it's the infamous Kali Rose-Kennedy that stares back at me.

And standing in front of the fireplace, bags under his eyes and hair disheveled, is none other than Principal Vaughn.

"Hello, Bernadette," the Thing says, dark eyes sparkling. "Take a seat, and let's talk."

T O   B E   C O N T I N U E D . . .

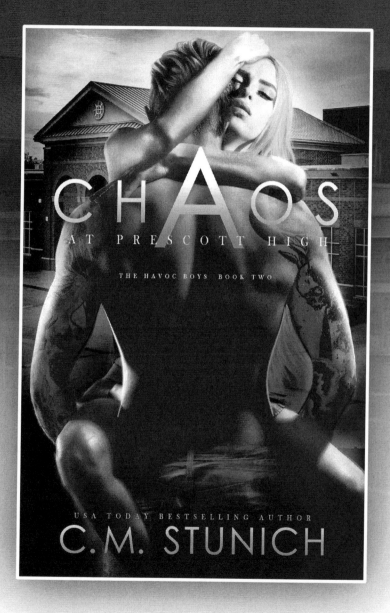

CHAOS

AT PRESCOTT HIGH

THE HAVOC BOYS BOOK TWO

USA TODAY BESTSELLING AUTHOR

C.M. STUNICH

THE HAVOC BOYS #2
JANUARY 2020

FILTHY RICH BOYS

RICH BOYS OF BURBERRY PREP, YEAR ONE

FILTHY RICH BOYS

ALL BETS ARE ON ...

USA TODAY BESTSELLING AUTHOR
C.M. STUNICH

ADAMSON ALL-BOYS
BOOK ONE
ACADEMY

The
Secret
Girl

*If they only
knew my secret ...*

USA TODAY BESTSELLING AUTHOR
C. M. STUNICH

I WAS BORN RUINED

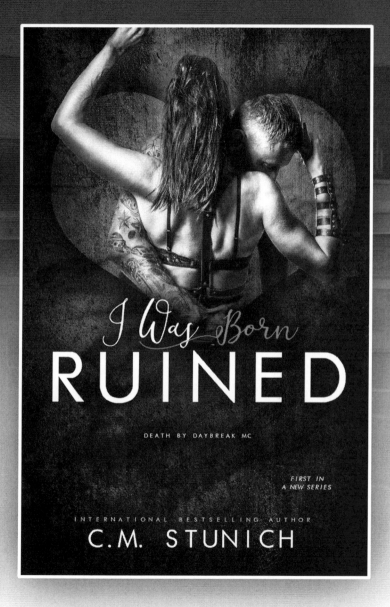

I Was Born
RUINED

DEATH BY DAYBREAK MC

FIRST IN
A NEW SERIES

INTERNATIONAL BESTSELLING AUTHOR
C.M. STUNICH

DEATH BY DAYBREAK MOTORCYCLE CLUB #1

JOIN THE
C.M. STUNICH

DISCUSSION

GROUP

Want to discuss what you've just read?
Get exclusive teasers or meet special guest authors?
Join CM.'s online book clubs on Facebook!

www.facebook.com/groups/thebookishbatcave

STALKING

LINKS

JOIN THE C.M. STUNICH NEWSLETTER – Get three free books just for signing up
http://eepurl.com/DEsEf

TWEET ME ON TWITTER, BABE – Come sing the social media song with me
https://twitter.com/CMStunich

SNAPCHAT WITH ME – Get exclusive behind the scenes looks at covers, blurbs, book signings
and more http://www.snapchat.com/add/cmstunich

LISTEN TO MY BOOK PLAYLISTS – Share your fave music with me and I'll give you my
playlists (I'm super active on here!) https://open.spotify.com/user/12101321503

FRIEND ME ON FACEBOOK – Okay, I'm actually at the 5,000 friend limit, but if you click the
"follow" button on my profile page, you'll see way more of my killer posts
https://facebook.com/cmstunich

LIKE ME ON FACEBOOK – Pretty please? I'll love you forever if you do! ;)
https://facebook.com/cmstunichauthor & https://facebook.com/violetblazeauthor

CHECK OUT THE NEW SITE – (under construction) but it looks kick-a$$ so far, right? You
can order signed books here! http://www.cmstunich.com

READ VIOLET BLAZE – Read the books from my hot as hellfire pen name, Violet Blaze
http://www.violetblazebooks.com

SUBSCRIBE TO MY RSS FEED – Press that little orange button in the corner and copy that
RSS feed so you can get all the latest updates http://www.cmstunich.com/blog

AMAZON, BABY – If you click the follow button here, you'll get an email each time I put out a
new book. Pretty sweet, huh? http://amazon.com/author/cmstunich
http://amazon.com/author/violetblaze

PINTEREST – Lots of hot half-naked men. Oh, and half-naked men. Plus, tattooed guys holding
babies (who are half-naked) http://pinterest.com/cmstunich

INSTAGRAM – Cute cat pictures. And half-naked guys. Yep, that again.
http://instagram.com/cmstunich

ABOUT THE AUTHOR

C.M. Stunich is a self-admitted bibliophile with a love for exotic teas and a whole host of characters who live full time inside the strange, swirling vortex of her thoughts. Some folks might call this crazy, but Caitlin Morgan doesn't mind – especially considering she has to write biographies in the third person. Oh, and half the host of characters in her head are searing hot bad boys with dirty mouths and skillful hands (among other things). If being crazy means hanging out with them everyday, C.M. has decided to have herself committed.

She hates tapioca pudding, loves to binge on cheesy horror movies, and is a slave to many cats. When she's not vacuuming fur off of her couch, C.M. can be found with her nose buried in a book or her eyes glued to a computer screen. She's the author of over thirty novels – romance, new adult, fantasy, and young adult included. Please, come and join her inside her crazy. There's a heck of a lot to do there.

Oh, and Caitlin loves to chat (incessantly), so feel free to e-mail her, send her a Facebook message, or put up smoke signals. She's already looking forward to it.

Printed in Great Britain
by Amazon